Also by Alicia Gaspar de Alba

Novels
Desert Blood: The Juárez Murders
Sor Juana's Second Dream

Poetry and Prose
La Llorona on the Longfellow Bridge: poetry y otras móvidas, 1985–2001
"Beggar on the Córdoba Bridge" (in *Three Times a Woman: Chicana Poetry*)
The Mystery of Survival and Other Stories

Nonfiction
Velvet Barrios: Popular Culture and Chicana/o Sexualities (ed.)
*Chicano Art Inside/Outside the Master's House: Cultural Politics
and the CARA Exhibition*

Calligraphy

—OF THE—

Witch

Calligraphy

— OF THE —

Witch

Alicia Gaspar de Alba

ST. MARTIN'S PRESS NEW YORK

For my goddaughters,
Bianca Fernanda and Yazmín Sylvia,
and for my moonchild,
Luzía Etienne

Detail from a map of Boston with its environs, 1806. Courtesy of Historic New England. (Negative # 11376-B.)

www.stmartins.com

Design by William Ruoto

LIBRARY OF CONGRESS CATALOGING-IN-PUBLICATION DATA

Gaspar de Alba, Alicia, 1958 –
    Calligraphy of the witch / Alicia Gaspar de Alba. — 1st ed.
        p. cm.
    ISBN-13: 978-0-312-36641-4
    ISBN-10: 0-312-36641-8
    1. Mothers and daughters—Fiction. 2. Witches—Fiction. 3. Slaves—Fiction.
4. Massachusetts—History—Colonial period, ca. 1600–1775—Fiction. I. Title.

PS3557.A8449C35   2007
813'.54—dc22
2007021964

First Edition: October 2007

10 9 8 7 6 5 4 3 2 1

Contents

How the night changes from one country to another.

—Maryse Condé, I, *Tituba: Black Witch of Salem*

I have ridden in your cart, driver,
waved my nude arms at villages going by,
learning the last bright routes, survivor
where your flames still bite my thigh
and my ribs crack where your wheels wind.
A woman like that is not ashamed to die.
I have been her kind.

—Anne Sexton, "Her Kind"

I am my own hangman
I am my own prison
The punishment and the punisher
Are one and the same thing.

—Sor Juana Inés de la Cruz, *Romance 48*

PROLOGUE

The Pledge

Hanna Jeremiah

(ROXBURY, 1704)

How do I tell my children that I am the daughter of a pirate and a papist? Is that a necessary thing for them to know? I doubt it. Just as I doubt the wisdom of visiting Grandpa Tobias's decrepit little house in Roxbury, looking for some ill-begotten truth that Mama Becca made me promise, on her deathbed, to find. And yet, here I am, honoring my pledge to the only woman I ever wanted as a mother.

"The commandments, Hanna!" Mama Becca gripped my arm with an uncanny strength for one too weak to raise her head for a sip of water. "I am taking two broken commandments to my grave. Don't let me die a liar, as well."

"You've broken no commandments. You're the saintliest woman I know."

"She keeps appearing to me in my dreams, reminding me of what I promised her. Please, Hanna. Do what I ask."

"I don't even remember Thankful Seagraves," I lied, stroking Mama Becca's clammy forehead. "Why should she matter so much to you now?"

"I swore upon your life that I would tell you the truth. That I would give you the letters that Thankful Seagraves left for you to read. After . . . after she disappeared, we found a trunk in Grandpa's house. It was locked, but it was the only thing left. Maybe she left the letters in there. I don't know if anybody's taken it, or if it's survived after all these years, but promise me you'll go and find out. Promise me you'll go and find the truth."

"I know the truth, Mama. I was not born of your flesh. The woman who gave birth to me was a papist slave that Papa purchased from the pirate's ship. I know you raised me and she left me. That's all I need to know. The rest of it doesn't matter. What's done is done. Don't vex yourself so much."

"You must help me keep my vow, Hanna," Mama Becca muttered, pulling me so close to her face I could smell the sour milk on her breath. "The key to the cottage is in a hollow in the witch hazel tree by the well. You will find what Thankful Seagraves left for you there. I gave my word on it and you shall have your truth or my soul will not rest for all the wrongs I committed against your mother."

It was the only time Mama Becca ever admitted to any wrongs against Thankful Seagraves. And one of the few times she ever referred to her as my mother. I think the illness was distracting Mama Becca's mind, but she seemed so certain that she would be judged a liar on Judgment Day that I had to promise her to come to Roxbury and look for this so-called truth. I did not want to leave her bedside, knowing how weak and close to the end she was, but the desperation in her eyes and her relentless pleading were too much for me to bear. I denied Caleb's request to come with me, and I will not bring the twins into this, either. They know nothing about Thankful Seagraves. Their grandmother was Rebecca Greenwood, a merchant's wife, a Visible Saint in the Massachusetts Bay Colony, not some mixed-breed, forked-tongued, Catholic woman transported from an ungodly country on a pirate's ship.

The pirate that sired me was not English but Dutch or French, light haired and dark skinned, with eyes like mine, I was told, the color of fresh tree sap. Those who feared this man, my unknown pirate father, said he was more awful than Henry Morgan or William Kidd. Papa called him a buccaneer or a privateer, never a pirate, as it would not look well for the chosen children of God to be doing business with pirates, and nothing but Captain Seagraves to his face, though his real name was something else, something foreign that Papa could never remember.

Thankful Seagraves, the woman who delivered me into the world, hated this man, said little else about him save that, after pillaging her body and seeding a child inside her, the pirate had sold her like a household slave to the English merchant who is now, thank God, my papa.

"A mestiza can never be a slave!" Thankful Seagraves used to say to me, incensed at an injustice that I could never understand. Even when I was old enough to tell the difference between a slave and an indentured servant, between a blackamoor and an Indian, I didn't understand or care what a mestiza was. She had a Spanish father and a mother who was a mix of Indian, Spanish, and some Oriental race, but all it meant to me was that Thankful Seagraves was a mongrel. She had eyes of different colors—one brown, one green—and skin like cinnamon bark and an accent so thick it made English sound like a foreign tongue. When she spoke, I cringed as though she were spewing spiders from her mouth. The truth is, I was afraid of Thankful Seagraves. I was afraid I would catch the way she spoke or that one of my eyes would change colors and look like hers. I did not want Thankful Seagraves to be my mother. She was a papist and a mixed breed and a foreigner. Who would want to be born of a mother like that? We had different family names, so it was easy for me to pretend we weren't related. It was Mama Becca I always wanted.

Sometimes when she slept, names tumbled from Thankful Seagraves's lips. For as long as I knew her, she denied that Thankful Seagraves was her name. "That is a falsehood," she would tell me in her weird English.

"Everything here is false, except you, my reason for living." When I'd ask her who she really was, what her true name was, she would only shake her head. "That one drowned," she would say. "This husk of a body is all she left." Mine—or at least the names she gave me, not the ones I was christened with—she said most often, *Juana Jerónima,* pronounced in that raspy way of hers, in that foreign accent which turned the first letter of each name to a hiss. If it hadn't been for Mama Becca insisting that Thankful Seagraves give me a proper Christian name, I would have gone through life sounding like a papist. Thank God for Mama Becca, who made her christen me Hanna Jeremiah. It is a fitting namesake: Jeremiah, full of woe, full of strife and dissension. I have been conflicted as far back as I can remember. All of my life I have opposed and rebelled, and the object of this rebellion has been my own self, a hidden part of myself that I have tried to forget but that now presents its shadowy form.

There was a time when I feared the sign of Thankful Seagraves would show itself in the faces of my children, that they would be born red skinned like her or, worse, with two-colored eyes. Perhaps the odd mixture of bloods that produced that variance in Thankful Seagraves has alchemized into a purer strain now that Caleb's good English blood has joined the Dutch or French in my own veins. Still, the girls bear one telltale mark of the mixed breed: Clara's skin has the color of honey, Joanna's is like a light maple syrup, and yet Clara's eyes are round green filberts, while Joanna's are chestnuts, light brown and with the slightest downward slant. Oddly, both have full heads of curly auburn hair, where Caleb's is flaxen and mine a hazel brown. Thankful Seagraves's hair, I remember, was Indian straight and black. That curly hair must be a trait the girls inherited from the pirate.

I still do not know why Mama Becca was so prejudiced against my using those names for the twins—Clara and Joanna. And I know not why, when I held them for the first time, one in the crook of each arm, I was so certain those had to be the girls' names. Caleb had no say in it. I just remember Mama Becca's disappointment, the way she shook her head and muttered, "It must be in the blood." I can only surmise that those names must have had something to do with Thankful Seagraves, but that is a secret that Mama Becca took with her.

The twins know nothing of their heritage, for they are still too young to understand such things, but even when they are older, I will not tell them. I have never felt the obligation or the desire to share the dark intimacies of my childhood with anybody. Even Caleb, who was there much of the time, does not know everything. I could have put it all behind me and lived the rest of my life a contented woman, but now I am forced to return to Grandpa Tobias's house in Roxbury and face this specter named Thankful Seagraves.

BOOK I

The Neptune

(JUNE 1683)

CHAPTER 1

Laaaand fall!"

Captain Laurens de Graaf opened his spyglass and looked out. Yes, there it was, the dreary, foggy New England coast. The Puritan merchants had commissioned him in January to bring sugar, molasses, and slaves to the Bay Colony. Back then, the Captain had not been rich as he was now. At the time he had signed the agreement with the Puritan merchants, the siege of Vera Cruz was only a dare that Captain Van Horn had thrown in de Graaf's face during a night of Christmas feasting in Port Royale.

If the Captain had known in January that Van Horn's outlandish plan would work so well, that they would pull off the siege of Vera Cruz with the Spanish colors flying from the masts of their own buccaneer ships, while the Spanish Fleet sat like hens in the harbor, he would never have agreed to do business with the Puritans. This foggy, gloomy wilderness, which the Puritans referred to as the city built upon a hill for the chosen children of God, always gave Captain de Graaf nightmares. More and more he had come to despise his annual visit to the Boston port. Having to return twice in one year was enough to depress him until Christmas.

"Reyes!" the Captain called to his Spanish manservant. "Lay out my wig and greatcoat, and don't forget the wool stockings. We'll be putting into harbor soon." Even in early summer, the coast of New England chilled his blood. "Tell Cook to get the grog ready. I want it hot." He turned and yelled for the quartermaster in French, ordering him to set up the auction table.

Though born of a *mulata* woman in the Netherlands and weaned on the odd dialect of the slaves, the Captain had been apprenticed at an early age to a cousin of his Dutch father's who was a quartermaster in the Spanish navy, there to remain until his own induction as a sailor for the Spanish Crown. Thus, he managed Castilian more fluently than his own native Dutch and could be counted on to interpret the mixed argot of the slaves he carried across the Atlantic. He knew French as well, having picked it up from the corsairs who, ten years earlier, had captured his Spanish vessel and then invited him to join their company. Not one to bite the hand of Opportunity, Captain de Graaf had become a buccaneer and now commanded two ships, his favorite of which was the *Neptune*. Though he had some French sailors on board, his crew on the *Neptune* was mostly from the British Isles, and so Captain de Graaf had had to learn English, too. A lifetime on the high seas had darkened the Captain's skin like a vanilla bean, and the loose curls on his head, like his brows and his beard and even the lashes of his hazel eyes, had been bleached by sun and sea wind to the color of new beer.

The only Spaniard among them was Reyes, a sailmaker from the Captain's Spanish navy days, who served as the Captain's groom and, when necessary, bedmate. Reyes went below deck, and the Captain watched the crew scrambling on the poop, taking in the sails, uncoiling the anchor ropes, loading the guns to announce their arrival, shouting and slapping one another on the back in anticipation of going ashore. The Captain yelled for the quartermaster again and told him to inform the crew that nobody would be leaving the ship. They would send out the longboat to bring the merchants aboard, dispose of the cargo, and sail the same day for Virginia. It was early enough still, and a good wind would find them once they left the cold shadow of the Boston port. The New England coast reminded him too much of the English dungeon where he'd been imprisoned at the beginning of his buccaneer fame.

The cannon went off, and he blessed himself with the triple sign of the cross. Though a Lutheran, Captain de Graaf was a superstitious man, and he had picked up many of the habits of the Spanish.

"That little bitch *hija de puta* made a mess in your cabin again, *mi capitán*," Reyes said when he returned to the poop.

"¡Joder, hombre! For fuck's sake!" the Captain swore at Reyes. "I told you to keep an eye on the wench. What now? Another fire?"

"Looks like she got into your logbook this time, sir. There's chicken scratch all over the pages."

"I curse her whore of a mother!" said the Captain, snapping his spyglass shut. "Why did we let her loose again, Reyes?"

His lips pursed tightly, Reyes followed the Captain down the ladder, wanting to say, You've been craving bitch meat ever since she came on board, but *el capitán* de Graaf, the infamous Lorencillo, scourge of the Spanish Main, took to insolence the way he took to the pox. "You wanted her last night, *mi capitán*."

Reyes tried to keep the edge of jealousy out of his voice. "You know she always pays you back in some way."

"Damn her to Hell! I should've left her in Campeche. What am I doing with that crazy wench aboard?"

Mexican half-breed bitch, Reyes wanted to correct him, but again he kept his mouth shut. In his cabin, the Captain threw his arms up in anger. The wench had spilled the inkhorn on the floor and smeared ink all over the bedclothes. The written pages of his log were torn in half, the other pages . . . The Captain dragged the lamp across the desk to see his logbook better. "By your life," he said under his breath. "This is no chicken scratch, you imbecile! This is the calligraphy of a trained scribe."

On one page the wench had written the name *Jerónima* over and over, on the other pages a long verse, in a penmanship so elegant and curlicued it confirmed his suspicion that the half-breed he'd been sporting with for the past five weeks had been educated in a monastery. How she'd gotten mixed in with the Negroes he didn't know. It wasn't common buccaneer practice to take Indians or half-breeds for slaves, but the girl was attached to one of the Negro girls in his share of the plunder they'd captured in Vera Cruz and had pleaded with him to take her along, had actually knelt at his feet and kissed his groin, promising to do whatever he wanted in exchange for coming on the *Neptune*. Captain de Graaf had a weakness for brave women. Besides, he had never bedded a wench who had eyes of different colors: one dark as Jamaican rum, the other green as French chartreuse.

At first, the girl was dutiful and obedient, though she was a virgin and wept each time he took her. Then the Negro girl, who was her friend, caught the pox from some of the slaves they'd picked up in Havana. His quartermaster had ordered them all thrown overboard to keep the rest of the cargo from getting infected. Ever since then, the half-breed wandered through the decks, calling for her friend, wailing like a madwoman.

At midday, when the slaves were brought up to the deck to eat and exercise, the coffle of men to the starboard side, the women to the larboard, the girl served their food, chanting the Latin Ave Maria with such sorrow that the slaves and some of the Irish sailors broke into sobbing. Cook said that when the girl helped him in the galley she talked to a black figure that she carried in a wee purse hanging from her neck. She could stand for hours in the stern, staring at the water, ignoring storms or squalls or even the sailors' pinching and fondling, holding an invisible rosary between her hands, her lips moving in silent prayer.

When the Captain brought her to his bed, she stared at him with crazed, terrified eyes, shouting a rhymed verse to him—something about stubborn men and the flesh of the Devil—until he finished.

One evening she had almost castrated Cook.

Dozing in his hammock, Cook had told the Captain, he did not feel the hand on his groin, untying his breeches, until the fingers raised his member. He could smell that it was the half-breed touching him and kept his eyes closed, expecting something else, swelling quickly. The tip of the blade cutting into his flesh startled him awake. In the glow of the lantern, the half-breed's eyes burned like a lunatic's. Cook wrenched the bone of her wrist, and she thrust the blade into his testicles. He released her. She ran out of the galley shrieking curses, Cook was certain, in her heathen tongue.

"The wench about gelded me, Captain."

"Did she damage you, Cook?"

"Hard to tell, Sir, but I don't think so. Just a bit of bleeding, I hope."

"Then you are not to damage her. Understood?"

"Aye, Sir."

"Warn the others. A murdered wench would bring us evil winds. She is to be left alone. She should never have been touched in the first place."

"All due respect, Captain, but she's a danger to the crew, is what I think. The way she can sneak up on a fellow. And there's that black doll she be forever whispering to, that voodoo thing she carries around her neck."

"The men can take care of themselves, Cook. If I were you, I'd sport with someone else. The wench doesn't take well to our kind of sporting. As to that figure she's always talking to, that's not a voodoo doll. I've seen it. It's just a game piece."

"Funny games she plays, Captain."

"Well, you never know the ways of women."

"Aye, that's God's truth, Sir."

The Captain thought the girl had lost her wits completely, but this writing on the page showed him that he was wrong, that there was still hope of getting rid of her at a good price. The Captain scanned the stanzas of the verse, chuckling to himself at the sweet prize that Lady Fortune had just bestowed on him. This was no simple wench. Whoever wanted her would have to pay her price in coin.

"Reyes! Go find her, quick! I need to talk to her before the merchants arrive."

When Reyes had gone, the Captain sat down at his desk and drew up a bill of sale, dipping the pen into the thick puddle of ink soaking into the floor.

I, Captain Laurens-Cornille de Graaf, commander of the buccaneer frigate the Neptune, hereby sell this half-breed wench, captured in war on the coast of New Spain and subject to servitude. Her name is Jerónima. She is approximately twenty years old. Has all her teeth. Is immune to the pox. For her sturdy health and her knowledge of letters, her price is 50 sterling pounds. 21 June 1683

The Captain signed the bill, sprinkled sand over the ink, and poured a generous shot of Spanish brandy into his polished silver goblet to celebrate his good luck. If there was one friendly thing he could say about the Puritans, it was that they knew how to appreciate good penmanship, even in a wench. He heard the guns go off in the harbor and knew that the New England merchants were on their way.

CHAPTER 2

She could not remember how long the voyage had taken. After Aléndula's disappearance, she stopped counting the days since the pirate's ship had left the port of Vera Cruz. She stopped listening to the wailing of the slaves and to the strange sounds of the pirates' language. She heard only water, the flapping of sails, the night wind howling through the portholes.

In the mornings, when she mashed the horse beans for the slaves' only meal of the day, the stench of it brought her momentarily out of the numbness that had grown around her like a silkworm's case. In that slit of time, she would notice where she was and remember what had happened to Aléndula. She would see the slimy planks of the galley floor that she scrubbed every night, where once the cook, reeking of onions and rum, had taken her like a dog, entering a part of her body that she did not know could be entered, which felt like being skewered on a hot spit. She would hear the clank of chains on the ladders and know that the slaves were being prodded to the upper deck for their pitiful ration of horse beans, weevil-ridden hard tack, and rank cider. After they ate, one of the pirates would pound stupidly on a drum, and the other pirates would prod or whip the slaves to dance to the drumbeats, their chains rattling, their moans making a perverse harmony.

It was this, more than being shackled to the lower deck, breathing the fumes of excrement and listening to the constant keening of the other slaves, it was this denigrating dance in the open air that had most poisoned Aléndula's soul, until finally she could not stand up any longer and could not climb the ladder out of the hatch and had to be left below. The little water she drank convulsed her body.

She remembered saying, "You're making this more difficult for us, Aléndula. You have to eat. You have to get up. Look at you! You'll die down here without any air. Please try to get up!"

"I know my *papi*'s ashamed of me, locked up in this convent for three years. I have to get out of here. I have to be free. You can get me out, Concepción; I know you can. Even if you free just one person you'll be a *cimarrona*. Then you can go with me to San Lorenzo and we'll both be free."

"Does this look like freedom to you? We're not in the convent anymore, Aléndula. I did get you out, don't you remember? We escaped from the convent and walked all the way to Vera Cruz and ended up getting captured by pirates. Please, Aléndula! Tell me you remember!"

"My mother's a free woman. Tell them that, Concepción! If my mother's free, I'm free. Don't they know that? I'm not a slave. They can't make me a slave! I'm from San Lorenzo! I'm the daughter of a free woman and Timón de Antillas, the king of the *cimarrones* of New Spain. I'm the goddaughter of Eleguá."

From lack of water and air, Aléndula had become delirious, her mind still traveling to the village of San Lorenzo de los Negros, where there was no such thing as a slave, she said, where old women smoked cinnamon bark to see the future and sacrificed roosters to talk to the dead, the village where Aléndula was born and to which she would have returned before the foiled insurrection in Mexico City and the ambush and the hanging.

"I told him my dream about the parrot. He knew what it meant. He knew they would be caught, and still he went forward with the plan. Why didn't they hang me, too, *chica*? I was their scout. They caught me, first. I should have died next to my papi."

Concepción had seen the execution of Timón de Antillas and his band of refugee slaves in the Plaza Mayor. She still remembered the way the prisoners had been gutted, like fish, the cloying stench and the dogs snarling over the spilled entrails.

"But he didn't bleed. Not a drop of blood, took all of his *aché* with him to Olorun. It's the worst thing for my people, you know, to let them spill any of your blood."

One morning Aléndula refused to dance with the others on the top deck and the pirate beating the drum came up and kicked her in the belly. Aléndula's eyes rolled back in her head, and she started screaming, "¡Eleguá! ¡Eleguá!" her voice like the cry of a rabid cat. The pirate kicked Aléndula again and again until she stopped screaming, blood and the gray foam of bean mash dribbling from her mouth.

Concepción had watched Aléndula's beating with a hatred so pure it felt like a blessing, like a bath in holy water that purified her spirit. Her mission was clear. She had to kill somebody. She had to kill the Captain. The next time he takes me to his bed, she told herself, the next time he rams himself inside me, I will wait until he falls asleep, and then I'll slice his throat open with his own sword. But that night, after the Captain had used her, he was called to the top deck and left her alone in his cabin. She would have to do something else. Break everything in the room. Or better still, set the cabin on fire. She took the lamp and smashed it on the floor, watched the oily puddle grow blue, then explode into flames, felt the smoke in her eyes as the flames tunneled into the Captain's chair and caught on the camel hair. Somehow the Spanish pirate, the one who spit at her whenever he took her to the Captain's chambers, stopped the fire, and the Captain thrashed her with a wet rope in front of the other pirates and locked her up in the bilge.

With no pirates defiling her, no Aléndula to cradle and sing to and fight with, nothing but the stinking bilge water and the continual rocking of the ship to distract her, she was able to sleep and forget her floating purgatory. At first the memories that came to her in dreams had been only contrapuntal sounds: the high voices of nuns chanting in a choir and the peal of ribald laughter in a tavern, footsteps echoing on the flagstones of a church and the clatter of horses' hooves on a cobbled street, the gentle chords of a mandolin at a recital or the flourish of trumpets announcing an execution. Gradually the sounds collected weight. Like magnets, they drew pieces of images to their core, became shadows and then figures that moved like puppets on a makeshift stage.

In her dreams, she was back in the convent, living in Madre's two-story cell, sharing a bed with Madre's *mulatta* slave, Jane, though she, herself, was not a slave but an indentured servant. She saw a great house with many rooms, and many mysteries within the rooms, and many bells, so many bells. A courtyard crowded with women in white and black veils. Cats basking around a fountain. Bright arches of bougainvillea. Fields of sunflowers and calla lilies and roses. And a shed in the fields where Aléndula lived in chains.

She heard voices. An angry old woman telling her: "In here I am not your father's mother. Never call me Grandmother. Never forget your place. You are here only because I am the Mother Superior of this cloister and because my son felt pity for you and didn't want to put you into the street."

And a younger woman, her mistress, protesting. "Stop calling me Madre, Concepción. I will never be anyone's mother. I am neither mother nor woman, as only by serving a man and bearing his children can one become a woman. I am a nun, a sister, not a mother."

And then a song, the saddest song she'd ever heard, about a woman named

Señora Santa Ana whose child wept for a lost apple. "Señora Santa Ana, porqué llora la niña? Por una manzana que se la ha perdido. . . ."

When she emerged from these dreams, the sobs tore at her belly. What was the name of this convent? Who were these voices, these women who were neither mother nor grandmother, whose child wept for a lost apple? She recognized that sad voice but could not place it; nor could she remember to whom the other voices belonged. She would hold her breath trying to remember, trying to force their names or faces from the dark water of her memory, but only ended up fainting from the strain. Once, it came to her, the face that used to sing that child's lament. She saw it clearly, the soft dimpled cheeks, the black tumble of curls on each side of the face, the light brown eyes wet with tears. She tried to name it, but her heart felt as if it was going to explode and her ears popped like hot oil in a wet skillet. She felt the back of her head hit against the planking.

"Hungry, bitch? Here, bitch! Can you smell it? Come and get it! You don't know what you're missing!" The Spaniard lured her out of confinement with a piece of roasted turtle meat dangling from a stick. The smell of the meat turned her mouth into a pool of saliva, but she knew that right behind him was the cook with his net. They had played this game before. They would not catch her again. She let them think they had baited her. Just as the net swooped down, Concepción kicked her way out of the Spaniard's grasp and scrambled up the hatchway to the slave deck.

The reek of excrement was stronger than ever. Nearly half the slaves had died already on the journey. The ones who remained did not attempt to speak to one another anymore. Chained sideways by the neck and ankles, they whimpered and moaned and waited for their destiny. Concepción found Aléndula feverish and covered in a slimy vomit. She had lost some of her teeth and her gums bled. The ash-gray skin of Aléndula's arm bunched like cloth under Concepción's grasp.

"Aléndula! Are you awake? ¿Qué te pasa?"

The crust around Aléndula's eyes cracked open. "Concepción? Where have you been, *chica*? That mistress of yours never lets you visit me anymore."

"We're on a pirate's ship, Aléndula. We left the convent weeks ago."

"Take me back," said Aléndula. "You've got to make them take me back."

"Back where? I'm losing my memory. I can't remember how we got to Vera Cruz. I can't remember the name of the convent we came from, or even the name of my mistress in the convent."

"I had the alligator vision again," Aléndula said, her breath smelling of sewage. "It's him, my *papi,* el Caimán, remember? I told you the story of el Caimán."

"I'm telling you, I can't remember things, Aléndula."

"He's calling me, Concepción. My *papi* wants me to join him in the water. He's come to rescue me, finally."

Concepción realized Aléndula's mind was trapped in the past. She had no sense of the voyage, no notion of what was happening to her on the passage between New Spain and wherever they were going. In opposite ways, both of them were losing their wits on this ship of nightmares.

"I'm happy, Concepción. I know the way now."

"You're burning up," said Concepción, feeling her friend's forehead with the palm of her hand. "I have to go get you something for this fever, Aléndula."

"It was a long dream, Concepción, I was walking with my *papi* to the swamp, and it was very bright and windy, the time of the northerlies. My *papi*'s voice kept getting lost in the wind, but I know that he was telling me to call Eleguá, that Eleguá would meet me at the crossroads if I made my head burn. I can free my *aché* in the water, Concepción."

She paused to lick the cracked leather of her lips.

"Stop it. You know I don't understand this *aché* business. This Eleguá thing. It scares me. Just stop it!"

"At the edge of the swamp under the ceiba tree," Aléndula continued, "my *papi* danced Yemayá's dance and then he rolled on the ground and his body changed into an alligator and he swam away into the swamp. He wants me to follow him. Don't you see? My *papi* wants to free me; I'll be free in the water. Yemayá will take me to Eleguá."

Concepción shook the bones of Aléndula's shoulders. "Please stop all this babbling, Aléndula. You're scaring me."

Aléndula raised her manacled hands and stroked the side of Concepción's face with a rough finger. "Don't be afraid. It's the only way, *chica.*"

"Listen to me, Aléndula. I'm going to go to the Captain's cabin and get some tobacco leaves for you to chew. They'll be bitter, but they will bring your fever down, and you'll feel better, I promise."

"No. I have to make my head burn, *chica.* I'll be free in the water."

"You'll be dead in the water," Concepción said.

Aléndula paused to swallow. "There's always an escape for a *cimarrona.*"

Concepción started to sob. "*Cimarrona?* Is that what you are? Can't you see? We're both slaves now. We didn't escape anything!"

The slaves had started to wail again, and she saw in the pearl-gray light slicing in through the portholes that Aléndula's eyes darted back and forth in her heated face. The acrid smell of Aléndula's body made her want to retch.

"I'll be back," she said. She crawled through the open spaces between the bodies of the slaves and climbed out of the hatch. It was a calm twilight, the sea still as a pool of quicksilver, and she could hear the pirates gathered in the stern singing their drunken sea ballads to the fiddler's music. No one would see her scrambling up the rigging to the crow's nest. She needed to get the tobacco from the Captain's cabin, but first she wanted to be as far as possible from the stench of the lower decks, to wash herself in the spray of seawater and night air.

She stayed up there, watching the rise of a fat copper-colored moon, trying to remember the name of the woman who sang about the sad child and the lost apple, until the pirate who served as the lookout climbed back to his post and found her. The man made signs at her, gesturing that he was going to throw her overboard. She scuttled down the rigging, right into the Spaniard's net.

"I'd break your neck," he told her, "but the Captain wants your dirty hole again."

The next morning, Aléndula's shackles were empty and those of several others next to her as well. The Spaniard would not tell her where Aléndula was. He sat on the foredeck patching a sail, grinning like a fool under his wide-brimmed hat. She asked him again and again until he stopped grinning.

"Enough, ¡*hija de puta*!" he said. "Your nigger friend caught the pestilence of the Havana slaves. We threw them all to the sharks last night while the Captain was having his way with you."

Chapter 3

They were puking all night, the black blood," one of the men told her when Concepción scrambled down the ladder to the slave deck. "They were dead by the time the pirates dragged them out of here. Get away from me. I saw you talking to her. If you catch it, you'll give it to me."

Concepción felt her teeth cutting into her bottom lip. Like a cat, she leapt up the rungs of the hatchway and ran to and fro across the decks, peering left and right of the stern, seeing nothing but the waves slapping against the hull of the ship. She searched in the head, the galley, the crew's quarters, the hold, even the Captain's cabin. At last, she stopped running. She knew now that Aléndula had been making herself weak on purpose. Whoever Eleguá was, Aléndula had wanted him to come and claim her.

Suddenly she hated Aléndula. For hours she stood at the bow of the ship, behind the head, and did nothing but hate Aléndula, hated her so much she hoped with all her strength that Aléndula would be torn apart by every creature in the deep. It was Aléndula's fault that she was here, alone, violated by pirates, trapped in a floating prison heading God knows where on the rocking nightmare of the open sea. She had lost everything, and for that she cursed Aléndula to eternal bleeding at the bottom of the ocean.

May the ocean turn red with your blood. May you never stop bleeding. May your blood feed all the fishes and all the monsters and all the spirits of the sea.

Finally, she was empty. She remembered nothing except Aléndula, her ghost twitching from the rigging of the ship, flapping on the sails, howling with the wind. Her own name shriveled on her tongue and vanished. And then the singing started. The words ululated through her vocal cords in a language that was not her own, Sancta Maria, Mater Dei, salve mater, misericordia, mea culpa, mea culpa, Ave Maria, Alleluia, mea culpa.

For the rest of the voyage, she stood at the railing night and day, splashed by rain and salt water, skin scorched to a tawny red, her tongue swelling and her flesh wrinkling from thirst and a self-imposed starvation. Only the ocean held her interest, and she stood mesmerized by the way that the light folded itself across the water, waiting for Aléndula's ghost to rise with the moon, to appear in the crow's nest or against the main mast, and the Latin canticle would flow out of her like blood. The thought that her own blood had not flowed fretted her for a moment and then receded. Above her, the ship's sails would become women in white tunics and black veils bending down to bless her.

At times, with the Captain on top of her, she would see the woman who did not want to be called Madre in the background, sitting at the Captain's desk behind a pile of books, dipping the quill into the ink, writing, dipping, writing, and in the doorway the shadow of a cloaked man holding a long, hooked staff. Mashing yams or scouring pots in the galley, she would suddenly remember the figure she kept inside a pouch around her neck. Carved of onyx, the figure wore the crown and robes of a queen. She would hold the figure in her palm and stroke her face, knowing she had a name and a function, a saint perhaps, but not remembering what it could be.

One morning just before dawn, standing at her vigil for Aléndula with the onyx figure clenched in her fist, she noticed a sharper briskness in the air and white birds perched on the rigging. She saw something stirring in the water, something dark and heavy nearly rubbing up against the ship. It arched out of the water, sleek and gray and huge, and then plunged in again, soaking her in the heavy splash of its forked tail. She had seen other ocean creatures on the journey, but none had amazed her as this one; none had showed her how profoundly alone she really was. The creature jumped again, and Concepción's memory rushed back with the force of the splashing tail.

"It's the black queen!" she said aloud, kissing the figure. Madre had given her a pouch of coins for the journey and the black queen from her own chessboard, and she had named the queen Jerónima, in honor of the house of women and bells where she had lived as Madre's scribe, the house of San Jerónimo. "Take this chess piece to remember me by," Madre had said, "and all the good work we did together. Don't forget you have an education." Madre . . . Madre . . . this was all she had called her mistress, and she could not recall her full name. Madre had trained her to take dictation and copy manuscripts, to read Latin and play chess. She had insisted that Concepción learn calligraphy. "Anybody can copy a piece of writing, Concepción. You must learn how to embellish the text like a Benedictine monk."

She rushed down to the Captain's cabin and wrote the black queen's name down on the only parchment she could find. *Jerónima,* over and over so that she would not forget it again. Halfway through the page, something happened to her writing. She found her hand turning the quill on its edge and stroking the letters individually, flourishing the arm of the *J* and the tail of the *r,* adding a curve to the eye of the *e,* dotting the *i* with a tiny star, and placing a sharp diamond over the *o* for the accent. The quill fitted easily in her hand, brown ink bleeding over her fingers. The horn inkpot on the Captain's table reminded her that she, too, had owned an inkwell, blue porcelain, with the name *Concepción Benavídez* painted in tiny white script along its base. It was the inkwell she had received from her mother on her fifteenth birthday.

My name is Concepción Benavídez, daughter of María Clara Benavídez.

"Maria Clara Benavídez," she whispered, and the name brought such longing to her that it stung her eyes. That was the name of that beautiful face that used to sing to her. Her mother's name. It was María Clara who had indentured Concepción to the house of San Jerónimo to protect her from the typical fate of a tavern worker. "Girls with your talent for embroidery should not be serving drunks," her mother had said, "especially not when they have a *criolla* grandmother who is the abbess of a convent." Concepción's father was a *gente de razón,* or person of reason, as the Spaniards were called in New Spain, and María Clara was his mistress and the keeper of his *pulquería.* Concepción had shown him a sample of her embroidery and he had taken her to the cloister of Santa Paula, of the order of San Jerónimo where his own mother ruled as abbess, and indentured her there for a period of fifteen years. Refusing to acknowledge the girl as a relation, the abbess had given her to another nun, and so Concepción had become . . . what was that word that Madre liked to call her . . . the nun's amanuensis, just a fancy word for a scribe.

As she continued to write the name *Jerónima* over and over in different strokes, an image flitted through her mind, brief but vivid as a butterfly. The Captain's cabin became a large room fitted with bookshelves and desks. She saw an astrolabe and a telescope and hundreds of books, books of all sizes, crammed into the shelves, piled on tables and chairs, papers strewn all over the black-and-white-checkered floor. She saw Madre standing behind her in a white tunic and a long black veil, a huge rosary pinned to her shoulder, an escutcheon the size of a small shield on her chest, ink-stained fingers.

She saw a stack of pages scribbled in Madre's almost illegible hand. A magnifying glass appeared, and through the glass she could discern that the writing formed a long poem that she had to copy on gilt-edged parchment. Concepción turned to a fresh page, inked the pen again, and began to write.

> Stubborn men who accuse
> Women for no reason,
> Not seeing yourselves as the occasion
> For the very wrongs you accuse.

It was a philosophical satire about the hypocritical ways of men who wanted women to be both chaste and wanton, as befitted the master's pleasure. Concepción had laughed at the boldness of the verse, written by a cloistered nun, but Madre said it was not meant to be funny, but to warn women that no matter how they behaved or what they did, they would always be judged as errant in the eyes of men.

> With either favor or disdain
> Men have equal displeasure,
> If a woman mistreats they complain
> But if she loves too well they censure.

"Has this happened to you, Madre?" she remembered asking. "Have you loved a man too well and been censured?"

"You know better than that, Concepción," Madre had answered sharply. "I would never give my love to any man, though the love I have felt is one I myself must censure."

She continued writing, "Quién es más de culpar," wearing down the nib of the quill with her embellishments, exaggerating her capitals, adding swirls to the tail of the *Q* and shadows to the spine of the *s,* scattering flourishes on the ears of all the *g*s.

> Who is more to blame,
> Although both be guilty of transgression:
> She who sins for a commission,
> Or he who for sin will pay?

The lamp smoked and flickered over the parchment, making her eyes burn as they used to in the convent after hours and hours of copying.

Hence with much logic do I unravel
That men's arrogance wins the battle
For in ways direct or subtle
Men are the sum of world and flesh and devil.

Men are the sum of world and flesh and devil, she mouthed the words to the last line, trying to imagine it written as an equation. World plus flesh plus devil equals men. Vaguely, she was aware of the pen sitting in the inkwell, of the poem finished on the page in a calligraphy that did not even feel of her own making.

The cannon boom startled her. She smelled sulfur. The ship had slowed down. Feet pounding the upper deck. The squeak of rigging and masts. The weight of the anchors dragging the ship to a heavy stop. She climbed on the Captain's chart table and through the porthole saw dark green islets hung with a thick fog and, in the distance, just beyond the ship-cluttered harbor, rows and rows of stone and timber buildings sitting almost on top of one another, their sooty brick chimneys poking into a low, gray sky, no light save for a pallid haze from the bank of clouds overhead. This was a land she had never seen. The white birds she had spied earlier circled in and out of the fog, screeching like birds of doom. The pirates had arrived at their destination. The Captain would be looking for her, she knew. He would be leaving her here in this bleakness.

She ran out of the cabin and down to the lowest deck to hide in between the turtles in the hold. But the Spaniard found her, punched her hard in the belly, and dragged her kicking and howling back to the Captain's quarters. She bit him, and he backhanded her, cursing the bitch of a mother that bore her and the holy host of the Church.

"Me cago en la hostia y en la puta que te parió," he hissed at her.

In the galley, the pirates lined up in two rows, laughing at her as she passed, spitting on her face one by one, except for Cook, who turned his back to her, lowered his breeches, and farted.

"Fair winds to you, lassie," he said, and the rest of them followed suit.

CHAPTER 4

Reyes knocked on the Captain's door and came in, dragging the half-breed. Her face and hands streaked with ink and soot, a wild look in her eye, the girl could pass for a savage. She was clutching the black game piece between her hands and mumbling into her fingers like an idiot. Maybe he was wrong about her.

"Did you do this?" asked the Captain, pointing to the written pages.

The girl glanced at the logbook and shook her head.

"¿Soís Jerónima?"

Taken aback by the sound of the name, the girl pressed her sooty hands to her ears and started to whimper.

"¿Soís Jerónima?" the Captain repeated in a louder voice.

The girl shook her head again. "Concepción," she mumbled. "Me llamo Concepción Benavídez—"

"¿Concepción?" the Captain interrupted. "Ese nombre es demasiado difícil. The people here will find that name too difficult to say, and they'll christen you any way they wish. You've written Jerónima all over my book. That name will be easier for these English tongues. I've called you Jerónima on this bill of sale."

The girl's eyes turned to water, murky ponds of green and brown. "Bill of sale?" she asked. "Like a slave?"

"What did you think?" the Captain said. "I'm a man of business. I didn't bring you all the way to New England to let you off without paying for your trip."

The girl had pressed her eyes shut, and the tears streaked the grime on her gaunt, brown cheeks. "Mestiza," she muttered against the game piece. "I'm a mestiza, not a slave."

The Captain realized that in the six weeks of the journey he had never heard the girl speak. He perceived a very clear Castilian lisp to her speech. "What is that you're holding?" the Captain asked. "Let me see it." He tried to take the thing away from her, but she quickly slipped it back into the leather pouch she wore around her neck.

The girl's eyes reddened, the pupils dilating in the glare of his lamp. "My father," she said hoarsely, clutching his arm. "He is a Spaniard. My mother—"

The Captain pulled the girl by the elbow toward his chart table. "Your parentage matters not in this part of the world," he said, unfurling a map. "We have arrived here, in Nova Anglia." He pointed to the New England coast. "A land that belongs to the English. This place we've docked in is called Boston. Can you say 'Boston'?"

"Bastón?" she repeated.

"No, not *bastón*. Not cane. Boston. Look. We've sailed frome here—" He moved his finger south along the Virginia coastline toward the Bahaman islands and Cuba, and then west across the Gulf of Mexico to the port of San Juan de Ulluóa. "And you came aboard here"—he tapped the map—"in Vera Cruz. All of this land belongs to Spain. Do you see the difference? Do you see the distance between these two places, where you come from, Nova Hispania, and where you are now, Nova Anglia? Much distance, you see? Muy lejos."

The girl placed a dirty finger on the map and moved it over the words "Nova Hispania," and then traced the words "Golfo de Mexico." "Muy lejos?" she echoed, looking up at him, frowning like a confused child.

"Hear me carefully, Jerónima," the Captain found himself explaining. "These people are English. They are enemies of the Spanish. Because you come from New Spain, they will think of you as an enemy. They do not know your language, so you must—are you listening, girl? If you want to survive among them, you must learn their language right away. They will not tolerate you speaking in a tongue they do not understand. Especially the Romish tongue. They are Protestants, they hate Roman Catholics, and any language spoken by Roman Catholics is a Romish, or a popish, tongue. These people consider the Pope himself an emissary of the Devil."

"The Devil? Yes. Madre said, 'Man is world and flesh and devil.' "

The Captain sighed, annoyed with her crazy babbling. "Most importantly— are you listening?—you must never pray or chant or let your wits go out of control as you've done on the *Neptune*. Do you understand what I'm saying, Jerónima?"

The girl had not stopped staring at him. "Neptune?" she said. "Neptuno alégorico?"

"No, not the allegorical Neptune. My ship, the *Neptune*." The Captain held

the girl's gaze. He could definitely see the learning in her eyes, a clear space under the dark layer of madness. But it wasn't madness, after all. The girl, he realized, was full of rage, a rage so bitter it had changed her face, made her seem
wild as the Arawak boy who had stowed away on his ship many years ago. To
think he had actually slept in her presence, especially after the incident with
Cook! The wench could have slit his throat or pumped him full of powder. The
thought made his groin jump, and he wanted to take her one last time, slide
between her puerile thighs and tame her wildness.

"I don't want to stay here; I want to return to New Spain," the girl said.

"No, Jerónima. You begged me to bring you aboard the *Neptune,* remember
that. I would have left you in Vera Cruz. Now, you must forget New Spain. You
will live here from now on. In New England."

The Captain tore the pages of the girl's writing out of his logbook and
stitched them to the tattered embroidery of her blouse. He opened a chest and
pulled out a striped shawl from his stash of silk plunder and draped it over her
thin shoulders.

"It's a cold country," he said. The girl fingered the fine green and black
fringe on the shawl and looked at him again with watery eyes.

"The English don't like women walking around with their naked heads
showing," he said, lifting the shawl over the girl's shorn head. He looked down
at what was left of the girl's sandals. "They don't like the feet or ankles to show,
either, but we can't do anything about that. Reyes! Bring a wet towel and clean
Jerónima 's face!"

The girl did not take her eyes off the charred wick of the lamp as Reyes
scrubbed her face with the wet rag, mumbling insults to her under his breath.
The Captain looked at his reflection in the silver goblet and liked what he saw.
The jeweled hilt of his cutlass, the velvet epaulets of his greatcoat. He donned
a plumed hat over the flowing tresses of his black wig and blessed himself with
a sign of the cross. On the way out, he instructed Reyes to take the girl to the
poop deck and stand her away from the Negroes. This one would not be auc-
tioned. This one had a *precio fijo.* A fixed price.

CHAPTER 5

The auction table had been fitted with inkhorn, pen and paper, hourglass, punch bowl, and cups. The quartermaster was ladling Cook's famous rum and wormwood grog for the English merchants. Samuel Parris, the merchant who had commissioned the Captain last January, stood there looking pompous in his white wig. Next to him fidgeted his partner, Nathaniel Greenwood, a troubled-looking man with a perpetual rash on his sunken cheeks.

"And what is this, Captain?" said Merchant Parris. "Have you taken a wife?"

"I have brought something quite unique, Mr. Parris," said the Captain. "This half-breed wanted to escape the papists of New Spain and begged me to bring her along. She's a diligent maid, good at laundering and making victuals, but her real skill is with the needle, and she's also an accomplished scribe, as you can see for yourself. That's her penmanship there on those pages. No doubt the girl's been educated in a monastery."

The Captain handed the bill of sale to Merchant Greenwood.

"You can't be serious about this price, Sir," said Greenwood in disbelief. "Fifty pounds for a pirate's wench? That's twice as much as an indentured man from England."

"Fifty pounds for a *cursed* wench, I'd say," Parris corrected his partner.

"Why say you she is cursed, Mr. Parris?" asked the Captain. "Surely one who is cursed could not manufacture such godly penmanship."

"She has the two-colored eyes of a devil, Captain," said Parris sharply. "And her fine penmanship is curled around popish trash. I would not take her even if she were free. No telling what manner of evil she's brought to harbor. Now, about the sugar, Captain."

"You know how it is in the Spanish colonies," said the Captain. "The races mix, unlike here. She is not a devil, sir. She is a half-breed."

"Tell me, Captain Seagraves, is there a difference?" said Parris.

Captain de Graaf always shuddered at the nickname he'd been given by the Boston merchants. "I've told you before, Sir, that *de Graaf* does not mean 'Seagraves.'"

The merchant waved off the comment and turned to his partner. "Nathaniel, I know there's a shortage of servants in Massachusetts, but you're not seriously contemplating the purchase of this heathen wench, are you?"

"I doubt she's any more of a heathen than your two Indians," Greenwood said.

"Those Indians have been catechized, Sir," Parris rejoined, but his partner was tearing off the pages that the Captain had sewn to the girl's blouse.

"Rebecca's father's gone lame. His chicken farm is in serious neglect," Greenwood explained, scrutinizing the girl's writing through a pair of silver-rimmed spectacles. "The Old Goat can't abide the way Negroes smell, and he doesn't trust indentured servants. My wife wants us to take him in, but I'd rather get him this overpriced wench than have him and his chickens move in with us. I'll give you thirty pounds, Captain."

"Yet you'd pay twenty for a simpleminded slave." The Captain shook his head. "She's part white, Sir, as you can see. Her price is fixed. If you don't want her, I'm sure some gentleman in Virginia will appreciate her unique qualities and skills."

"Captain? You did bring the sugar, I trust?" asked Parris, glancing around the deck again. "I don't see the goods."

"Can she count?" asked Greenwood.

"Surely one with such impeccable writing wasn't spared the knowledge of numbers, Mr. Greenwood." To Parris the Captain said, "We've brought you thirty-two barrels of raw sugar and eighteen hogshead of molasses. We'll bring up the rest of the cargo as soon as we take care of the slaves."

"Captain Seagraves, our agreement stated—"

From the corner of his eye, the Captain was watching Greenwood as he examined the girl's teeth, using the ivory end of his knife handle to hold down the girl's tongue. With his other hand, he pinched his nostrils against the smell of rot on the girl's breath.

"Yes, Mr. Parris, our agreement stated that we would provide you with fifty barrels of sugar and twenty-five hogshead of molasses, but you see, Sir, it's been a dry season in the West Indies, and there aren't enough buccaneers doing business in sugar anymore. They've all gone to the slave market these days."

"You forget, Captain, that I have experience in the West Indies. There's no such thing as a dry season in Barbados."

Now Greenwood was prodding the girl's sandals with the toe of his buckled shoe. The girl's eyes were like smoldering coal under the sparse line of her brows. Her gaze fixed on the iron-colored sea.

"The Spanish Main isn't what it used to be when you lived in Barbados, Mr. Parris," the Captain said. "It's easier to procure silver than sugar these days. We're lucky we liberated this much. We did, however, bring you double the slaves you asked for. Of course, the pox and the fever always take their toll on the passage. Nothing we can do about that. Even so, there's twice the amount you requested."

Greenwood straightened up and flicked the girl's shawl off her head with the back of his knuckles. "You didn't say she was bald, Captain!"

"Six weeks among slaves," the Captain implied, but seeing that neither of them understood, he added, "Lice. We had to shear the head and wash her down with turpentine. But she's clean, now, I can vouch for that, clean all over." He arched his eyebrows and nodded, but again, they didn't catch his drift.

"Will you be touring this way before winter, Captain Seagraves," asked Parris, "to deliver the goods you owe us, or shall I discount it from today's compensation?"

"This will be my last tour to New England, Sir. You may deduct the difference between the sugar and molasses I owe you and the profit from the extra slaves. According to my own calculations, the difference is not more than fifty ducats."

"Perhaps the difference is the cost of this wench," said Greenwood.

"The wench is my own property, Mr. Greenwood. She stays if you pay her price. Her sale has nothing to do with our agreement. Besides, fifty ducats does not equal fifty pounds, now, does it? I didn't get where I am by not knowing the difference between ducats and pounds, Sir."

Greenwood read and reread the bill of sale, then took a blank bill of exchange from inside his jacket and set it on the table to write in the girl's price and sign his name.

"No paper on this one," said the Captain. "Ready money or nothing."

"What? And give you the only currency I have left?" The splotches in Greenwood's cheeks reddened further. "All I have are ten doubloons and a few guineas, Captain. You know we don't see that much coin in New England."

The man glared at him for a moment and the Captain could tell he was about to change his mind. "Of course if you've got forty pounds in coin, you can give me the rest of it in paper," the Captain said. He could always exchange the bill in Virginia for good tobacco.

Samuel Parris pulled out his timepiece and checked it. "Pay the man, Nathaniel. We've got more important business to take care of, and I'd like to get back to my warehouse sometime today."

Greenwood filled in the note for ten pounds, then took a heavy leather purse from the satchel he was carrying and counted out ten large silver coins. The Captain counted them into his own palm, then quickly stuffed the doubloons and the note into his pocket.

"A redskin papist wench!" muttered Samuel Parris. "That's all we need in the Bay Colony! Just don't say I didn't warn you, Nathaniel."

But Greenwood's eyes were on the girl, and the Captain saw the rise in the man's britches. "You ought to be thankful," Greenwood said to the girl, "that the Captain brought you here among God's chosen in the new Zion. We shall name you Thankful Seagraves, in honor of the Captain." He set the bill of sale on the table, took the pen out of the inkhorn, and scratched out *Jerónima*.

"Thankful Seagraves," he said aloud as he wrote in the girl's new name. In a flash of movement, the girl bolted across the deck, her shawl fluttering to the boards.

"What does she think she's doing?" shouted Greenwood.

The Captain yelled to the crew to stop her, but she was over the railing before any of the men could reach her. The Captain rushed to the side of the ship, followed by the merchants.

Behind him, he heard Parris laugh. "Fifty pounds for a drowned wench! Fitting name you gave her, Nathaniel. Seagraves, indeed!"

The Captain ordered the second mate to jump in after her. He was the only one of the crew who knew how to swim.

"But I got the ague and the water be like ice, Sir. I'll catch me death, Captain," the puny man protested. Captain de Graaf dragged him by the tail of his hair and shoved him overboard.

"She better be alive, you swine shit!" the Captain bellowed after him, making a mental note for the quartermaster to whip the insubordinate knave as soon as he surfaced with the crazy half-breed.

CHAPTER 6

Fixed price.

"I'll be free in the water," Aléndula had said. "There's always an escape for a *cimarrona*."

She felt her legs running. The rebozo slid off her shoulders. She heard shouting and gunshots behind her. Felt the hard thump of her knees hitting the side of the ship. Her hands gripped the rigging overhead. The muscles wrenched in her shoulders, and her body swung out past the rail, suspended for an instant, and then she was falling, falling fast and heavy to join Aléndula at the bottom of the sea.

The water, like thousands of icy needles, pierced her bones. She had never known so much cold. Her veins grew numb. She opened her eyes and they stung from the salt. She saw her arms floating above her in the gray water, nothing but inky depths below. Her sandals slipped off. The pouch that held the black queen drifted away. Her skirt clung to her like a shroud. A current of joy heaved through her chest. She was free. She had escaped the destiny of that bill of sale.

In a gush of memory, it all came back to her then, everything that had brought her to this vortex between life and death: their escape from the convent, the journey through the mountains, the pirate siege in Vera Cruz.

She saw herself fumbling in the darkness of the shed, trying to find the keyhole in the manacles that bound Aléndula's ankles and wrists. Her head pounding as though she had woodpeckers trapped in her skull, Concepción felt a cry swelling in her throat. Her fingers were moving too slowly. Help me, Virgencita, she prayed to the Virgin of Guadalupe in silence. The key clicked into place and she felt the shackles release. She crossed herself quickly.

"They're off," cried Aléndula, kicking off the fetters. "Let's go!"

But the door hinges squeaked. Aléndula's hand clamped around Concepción's arm. The cry in Concepción's throat leaked out. They'd been caught. Sor

Agustina would whip them both within an inch of their lives with her hook-tipped scourge.

But no. La Virgen was with them. Concepción felt something soft brush against her foot. It was only the convent cats, meowing gently. She reached down her hands to them and spoke in a calm voice, bidding them all good-bye.

"¡Vamonos, Concepción!" Aléndula said again. Holding hands, they inched out the door. Startled birds flapped out of the hedge of jasmine bushes that surrounded the toolshed. By the time they reached the mulberry grove at the back of the orchard, near the lay sisters' graveyard, the sky had turned from black to indigo. The clear, high voices of the nuns at matins rose from the open windows of the church.

They could not leave until the night gendarmes went away at daybreak, and they waited up in a mulberry tree, barefoot and huddled together, trembling with fear and cold, until the bells of all the convents and monasteries of the city announced the first Mass of the day. Only then did they let themselves drop to the cobbled street. Concepción wore the pouch of coins Madre had given her for the journey on a strap around her neck, hidden under her clothes. The black queen from the chessboard that Madre had insisted she take with her fitted snugly into the pouch. At the *mercado,* Concepción bought a homespun shirt and breeches for Aléndula and a plain cotton skirt and blouse for herself to hide the silk *enaguas* and embroidered *huipiles* she wore underneath. Straw hats, huaraches, and striped sarapes completed their campesino disguise.

Down by the canal Aléndula stripped off the stinky sackcloth that had been her only garment for three years and scrubbed herself with the bracken growing wild at the water's edge. The rough fronds freed her skin of vermin; the roots loosened the grime and mud caked in her hair. Still wet, she stepped into her new clothes. Concepción was amazed at her friend's transformation. Except for the kink of her hair, she could have passed for an Indian boy, with a gaunt face and a body more bony than lean.

They tried not to run to the causeway south of the Plaza Mayor, which at that early hour was crowded with mule trains and merchants from the outlying villages pushing their heavy carts past the ramparts. Bands of Gypsies and Indians were lugging the wares they were going to sell in their stalls in the Plaza, and teams of mounted soldiers patrolled the lake of bodies moving into and out of the city.

They had left the convent at the beginning of April, during a dark moon. The moon had grown full and returned to dark and was waxing again by the time they came in sight of Vera Cruz. It had taken them more than six weeks to cross the mountains and reach the coast. The only way to reach San Lorenzo was by taking a boat from Vera Cruz, because the jungle was too swampy to cross on foot. From the foothills, they could see the big ships anchored by the fort, the Spanish colors waving in the hot wind. Aléndula said it was the Flota, the Spanish Fleet that came twice a year to the port of San Juan de Ulluóa, bringing cargo and passengers from across the sea. Concepción was tired of traveling, tired of sleeping in the open air and foraging for food. She still had one gold peso of the money that Madre had given her, and she wanted a real meal sitting at a table, she said, and a full night's sleep in a real bed before they headed out to San Lorenzo. They each needed a new pair of sandals, too. All those weeks on the trail had worn down the soles of the huaraches she'd bought at the *mercado* in Mexico, and the blisters on their feet matched the holes that had formed in the shoe leather. She imagined a bazaar of colored silks and leather goods, tables piled high with tropical fruits and fragrant heaps of exotic spices, baskets filled with olives gold to green. Instead of a bazaar they walked into a pirate siege. Instead of seasick *españoles* and watery-legged priests coming to ply their trade in New Spain, Vera Cruz was occupied by earringed men with red and black rags tied to their heads, wielding swords and curses. The flyblown air burned with the screams of women being forced, of men being tortured, of blacks and mulattoes falling to the blade and the musket. Within moments, Aléndula had been caught in a clanking coffle of slaves.

Concepción had stopped sinking. The air was no longer bubbling from her mouth and she felt herself suspended in currents of warm and icy water. Something popped inside her head, a deep pain shooting from her ears to her throat. She shook her head and saw blood oozing from her nose, congealing into ribbons in the water. A creature glided past her face. Something pale and phosphorescent swirling in the water, coiling and uncoiling like a snake. Was this Eleguá, god of Aléndula's people, here to save her? Or was it the Devil sent to punish her for taking her own life? Hail Mary, full of grace, the Light is with you, she prayed in silence, deliver me from evil.

The creature opened its mouth and she saw two rows of luminous fangs come toward her. She gasped and her stomach bloated with salt water and the salt water churned through her belly and loosened her bowels and suddenly she was drowning in her own filth.

In the wild kicking of her heart she knew she needed air. She wanted air.

She needed to cough, to breathe. Repent for her sin. Mea culpa, mea culpa. Her arms and legs pumped like windmills in the soiled water, but her body continued to sink. Sancta María, Mater Dei. She was sobbing, now, choking on the humors of the sea, fighting the currents like a netted fish, *salve mater, misericordia,* until at last she felt something wrenching at her hair. She reached up and dug her nails into two human wrists and felt herself pulled straight up out of that icy hell. Then her head broke through the surface and her face came up and she swallowed air.

BOOK II

Thankful
Seagraves

(1683–1688)

CHAPTER 7

There'll not be any woman living under my roof 'tweren't my wife or daughter. This one'll be my wife or nothing at all," said Tobias Webb behind his dog-eared *Almanac*. Nathaniel cursed the Old Goat in silence.

"But Father, she's a foreigner," said Nathaniel's wife, Rebecca. "You can't marry a foreigner, and a papist, to boot. She can't even speak English. Nathaniel purchased her to be your maid, to help out with the farm. See this?" She held out a weathered piece of parchment, which Tobias pretended not to notice. "She writes with a good hand, Father. She's smart." Rebecca placed the parchment and the bill of sale on the old man's lap.

"Find me a manservant, then," said Tobias. "I want no slaves or smart women on my property."

"Her main purpose, if you please, Tobias," interjected Nathaniel, "is to run your poultry farm. It is your intention to rescue the farm, is it not, Sir?"

"What concern is that of yours, Mr. Merchant?" said Tobias, slamming his *Almanac* on the trestle table. "'Tis my farm, and they be my chickens. Leave me be, both of you, and take this bald strumpet with you."

"Your farm is not paying its taxes, Tobias. I am, or was until today," said Nathaniel. "I have bought you some help, and I expect to be repaid her price."

Tobias threw his trencher of vegetables at Nathaniel, followed by his cane. "Get thee gone, you merchant, you thief! And you, too, you merchant's whore!"

Nathaniel and his wife stood on the doorstone outside the old man's cottage, pulling peas and corn kernels out of their hair and throwing them to the chickens milling about in the yard. From within, Tobias was still yelling at them to take the foul creature out of his sight.

"What are we supposed to do now, may I ask?" said Rebecca, her cheeks flushed. "I told you Father wouldn't like this idea."

"Leave the wench here. I'll not have another mouth to feed. Let the Old Goat choke on her."

"Don't be disrespectful to my father, Nathaniel. It's not his fault that he's crippled. He can't fend for himself anymore. Can't you be kind to him?"

"I'm doing the best I can, Rebecca. And what do I get in return? Vegetables flung in my face! Do you call that respect? Do you call that kindness?"

"I could use the girl at home for a spell. Now that Mercy's gone back to Salem, the house is too large for Sara Moor and me to take care of. I could teach her English. Maybe then Father will accept her. He's just afraid of her foreignness."

"You heard him. He wants a wife, the old gander."

"He's not that old, Nathaniel; he's only sixty-two."

"Are you saying he should marry her, then?"

"Don't be ridiculous! All I'm saying is she reminds him of . . . you know . . . the attack. The way she looks, Nathaniel. She could pass for an Indian."

"I told you, Rebecca, she's a half-breed. He's not blind. He can see the difference in her eyes, can't he? The wench stays here. Let him do whatever he wants with her. He can throttle her for all I care anymore."

"Fine, then. But the girl needs to learn how to speak, Nathaniel. She can't run the farm or serve my father if she has no language. I won't be like Mrs. Lowell or Mrs. Thatcher, speaking to their Indian servants in signs."

"Teach her what you will, Rebecca. This is your business, and he's your father. All I want is my fifty pounds back."

Rebecca poked her head through the open shutters that framed the only window of the cottage. "I'll be back later with your supper, Father. Don't vex yourself. And do try to show some charity to this poor creature. She almost drowned in the sea."

Tobias heard the carriage pull out of the barnyard. "Damn them both," he said aloud. "Now I've got a bald wench to look at. Charity, my arse!"

The girl hunkered down in the corner of the hearth had not taken her strange gaze off him, with that catty green eye staring straight at him and that slanty dark one looking off at something just above his head. She had her long bony arms wrapped around her knees, her muddy toes gripping at the straw on the floor. He glanced at one of the papers Rebecca had given him, lines and lines of papist words written in a fancy script.

" 'D'you write this?" he asked the wench, holding up the document. Even in the dim light of the cottage, he could make out the wild flourishes of the Platt-hand capitals, the long, thin strokes of the Italian cursive known as Fiorenza.

These were some of the very hands he used to teach, though he had never seen them executed quite like this. "This your writing?"

The girl puckered her eyes, trying to figure out what he was saying. She moved her mouth to mimic him.

"You a papist?" he asked.

"Papa?" she repeated.

"Not Papa, you fool. Papist. You are a papist."

"Papa," she said again.

"Damn fool," he muttered, and turned his attention to the bill of sale. Half-breed . . . New Spain . . . Twenty years old . . . Knowledge of letters . . . Fifty pounds.

"Fifty pounds?" he shouted, and started to cough. "That tightfisted husband of hers paid that much for a papist?" He cackled. "No wonder he's so anxious to get his money's worth. I'll pay him back!" Tobias lifted one buttock from his chair and farted hard. "There's one pound right there, Mr. Mealy Merchant!"

He looked up and saw that the girl was helping herself to the dregs of his morning porridge, scooping it out of the kettle with her fingers and stuffing her wall-eyed face. She was strange but comely enough, he figured, once her hair grew out, and if you could forget the fact that she looked part Pequod, with that tawny skin and ugly nose of hers. Her limbs looked strong, scrawny as they were, and she had a neck thin and long as an Englishwoman's. He supposed he could try her out. Somebody had to clean this pigsty of a cottage since his own daughter wouldn't lift a finger other than to bring him his meals. That's what he got for having fostered her with the mighty Mathers.

"Hey!" he bellowed. The girl stopped eating and turned to look at him, both cheeks bulging, porridge smeared on her chin.

"Says here your name is Thankful Seagraves." He pointed at her. "Thankful Sea-graves," he repeated. "That's you."

She shook her head so hard it looked like it was coming unhinged from that skinny neck, then went back to feeding herself, mumbling between bites a slew of foreign words that sounded just like ducks quacking.

He took a long draw of beer and closed his eyes, silently cursing this crippled fate that God had seen fit to give him. Once, he had been a writing master of some renown at the Latin School in Boston and had tutored the likes of Samuel Sewall and Joseph Dudley and even the snotty Cotton Mather in their letters. How could he have ended up like this? For a moment he was awash with melancholy, remembering that afternoon in Lancaster eleven years earlier. Alice's kinsfolk lived in Lancaster. The grandmother had been ailing all winter and Alice had wanted to see her before she passed, get her blessing for the children. Their late-born second son, six-year-old Robert, was playing with bowling pins in front of the hearth. Suddenly that savage had appeared out of nowhere, stabbing the grandmother, scalping both goodwife and son while two other savages shot Tobias's leg full of gunpowder. Rebecca and Robin had been sent to fetch firewood from the cellar when the attackers came.

Tobias had survived by the grace of God and the charity of the parishioners at the First Church, but his life was spoiled ever since. His leg went putrid from the knee down, and he lost the bottom half of the limb. Unable to walk or fend for himself, he'd forfeited his post to an upstart from Harvard College, surrendered his daughter to a merchant, and, two years later, his firstborn son to the sea. Rarely did Tobias Webb give any of these memories free rein, except when he wanted to feel sorry for himself. When he opened his eyes, he was startled to find the girl crouching right beside him, ogling his mug like a thirsty dog.

"What! Get back! I don't want you close to me, wench! What're you looking at? You can't have any of my beer."

But with a strength he wouldn't have expected from one so frail, the girl grabbed the tankard with her porridge-slimed hands and bent her head over it, sticking her tongue inside to lap up the beer.

"What!" He boxed her ears, but she didn't let go, just kept right on slurping and pulling until she made him loosen his grip, and then she brought the tankard up and guzzled the rest of the beer in one long draught.

"Damn greedy wench!" he said, and spit at her face. He wrenched the mug out of her hands. "Don't you ever do that again! I don't share my beer. You find something else to drink! Understand?" He pointed at the mug and then at his chest. "My beer!"

The girl belched in his face, wiping his spittle off her cheek.

CHAPTER 8

Lying in the trundle bed across from the hearth, the girl moaned again. Her teeth chattered, though she had the quilt pulled up to her ears.

"The Devil's taken the wench, I tell you. When she's not stuffing her face, she's sleeping and thrashing about. Thrashing and croaking all day and all night. Sounds like a damn toad. Make her stop, Rebecca, or I shall clobber her with my cane."

"She's not croaking; she's ill, Father. Lower your voice."

"Never knew someone ill could eat so much. I told her to stop being such a glutton. Eats all the food you bring me and then brings it right back up. And she stinks worse than a blackamoor, too."

"Goody Simpson says she picked up some disease from the slaves on board the ship, but I think she caught a cold humor when she fell into the sea."

"Well, do something, woman! All that croaking and coughing is a nuisance. I've not had a decent night's sleep since you two forced her down my throat."

"Goody Simpson's done everything she can, Father. She's tried every medical recipe you can think of, wormwood and cow dung and plaster of spiders, but the fever's set in her bones, so even the lancet can't get it out. Goody Simpson says they don't usually last this long when the fever gets this bad."

"Is the wench dying, is that it?"

"I don't know, Father. Something's keeping her going."

"Some help you brought me!"

"That's what Nathaniel says. For once you agree on something."

"Damn merchant and his big ideas!"

"I wish you would stop being so bitter, Father. Nathaniel's my husband and the father of your only grandchild. I know you don't care for him, but he really is trying to do good by you."

"Whole colony's gone to seed with all these merchants," snarled the old man. "There she goes again with her croaking."

"The poor thing. She's skin and bones. I don't know how she's holding on. Nathaniel wants to turn her out. Send her back where she came from, he says."

"She's not going anywhere! She's mine, isn't she?"

"Not until you pay him back, Father."

"And what should I pay him with, my head on a platter?"

"Hush, Father. That's a blasphemy."

The old man settled back against the pillows, mumbling to himself behind the vermilion curtains that surrounded the posters of his bed.

Rebecca lifted the girl's head and spooned some medicine into her mouth. Goody Simpson had given her some horehound and lungwort to boil with wine, some oil of fennel to drop into the girl's navel three times a day, and poultices of boiled mint leaves and juniper needles to place on the girl's chest and back. It was Rebecca's idea to place hot rags over the poultices, and it seemed to ease the girl's cough, at least until the rags cooled down and Rebecca had to heat them again with a hot stone from the hearth.

Nathaniel was right to question her devotion to this girl, but she couldn't tell him that it wasn't the girl she was caring for. It was the seed that had sprouted inside the girl's frail body she wanted to protect. She'd suspected as much from the beginning when Father told her about the girl's incessant hunger and her morning bouts of retching. But Rebecca had kept her mouth shut, not wanting to alarm either Father or Nathaniel. Now Goody Simpson had confirmed her hunch. The girl was carrying a pirate's child, no doubt, and didn't even know about it, delirious as she was with this fever.

Rebecca stroked the damp hair off the girl's forehead. She decided not to break the news to Nathaniel until the girl's womb swelled enough to tell. Rebecca was afraid he'd live up to his threat and send the girl back to the Indies, and then Rebecca would lose her only chance to have another child. The girl's child was hers by right, or her husband's at least, but she knew Nathaniel would never understand this, even though he, too, longed for siblings for six-year-old Caleb. He wouldn't want to bring up a slave's child as his own, especially not one who was born of a papist half-breed and a pirate.

Rebecca had her father's will, and one way or another, the girl's child would be hers, if she lived. And she would live. Rebecca would come three times a day and feed her and clean her and read aloud to calm her sleep. She would air out the cottage and bring sweet hay to scatter on the floor and change the bedding regularly and make her father relieve himself out in the privy instead of using the chamber pot under his chair. She would tie bundles of lavender and chamomile over the trundle bed to keep the odor and smoke of her father's pipe away from the girl's sore lungs, borage to cheer her senses, and plenty of sage to stay miscarriage.

And always, in Rebecca's mind, she would talk to the child, tell her to be strong and survive the sickness. Rebecca placed her hand on the girl's tight belly and rubbed in circles. Grow, she said silently. Be mine, child. You're my child, letting the thought flow down into her hand as she rubbed the growing child in the foreign girl's feverish womb.

CHAPTER 9

The little room that served as Nathaniel's office at the back of the warehouse had grown too warm to work. He was finding it difficult to balance the accounts, and twice already he had perspired over the ledgers, blurring numbers and names. At any rate, it was time for dinner. He'd walk over to the Red Lion, where he could catch a bit of a sea breeze with his food. In this heat, he couldn't stomach a full meal; just some ale and an eel pie would do. The noon bells tolled, and he hurried to the front door. Standing on the threshold, he mopped up the sweat under his collar, watching merchants and customers alike rush to home or tavern for the midday meal. He took out his bundle of keys and was about to lock up when he saw William Reed trudging down Merchants Row, lugging his sack full of fresh crabs.

No sense in closing up now, Nathaniel told himself. For a second, he contemplated just paying the man's fee and getting it over with. It was Nathaniel's habit to weigh the crabs individually and record each weight in his ledger, and then there was the business of haggling over the price of the load. He didn't haggle with his other fishmongers, they either took his price or left it, but then none of them fished the icy waters of Marblehead that produced such fine crabs. By the time he finished, it would be time to reopen the warehouse. He'd just have to send his errand boy over to the Red Lion to collect his food.

"G'day, Master Greenwood."

"William."

"Got some beauties this week, Sir. Mammy cooked up crab cakes last night and they was sweeter than mincemeat pie. Thick, juicy legs on all of 'em."

"Come on in, William. I'll get my book."

Out of the corner of his eye he watched William Reed removing the crabs from the sack, talking to them as though they were his pets. When Nathaniel returned from his office the crabs had been piled on the platform next to the balance, the hard-shelled red ones on the bottom, blue ones on top, too dazed by the heat to open their pinchers but a little.

"No kings yet?"

"Early fall, Sir. King crab don't like the summer. Got some good blue crab, though. Those on top got soft new shells, just perfect for frying."

"My wife sure likes that soft-shelled crab. Pick out two or three of the best blue for her, William."

"Gladly, Sir. How does the mistress?"

"Hardly see her, nowadays. She's off to Roxbury every day, tending to her father's sick slave."

"Tending to a slave, Sir? That don't seem right. And she's a foreigner, to boot, I hear. Just don't seem right."

"Taking wifely charity a bit to the extreme is what I say, William. Women are strange, you know. The wench acts like a lunatic, just mumbling and shrieking in her papist tongue."

"Foul tongue it is, Sir. My father used to speak it when he flogged us."

"Did he, now?"

"Said we had the Devil in us when we disobeyed, said we acted like papists."

"Was that the French or the Spanish tongue he spoke, William?"

"Must've been Spanish, Sir, since he learned it as a sailor back in the Old Country, said he'd sailed as a boy with Sir Francis Drake on the Spanish Main."

"Did he, now? And did you understand what he said, William, when he spoke his papist words to you?"

"Not much to understand, Sir, other'n that me and me brothers was full of devilry and needed to have it flogged out of us."

"So you didn't really know what he was saying?"

"Not to save my life, Sir. But there be one in Boston that might know."

"Pray tell the man's name, William."

"'Tis not a man, Sir. 'Tis Merchant Parris's slave, the Indian woman, Tituba."

"You don't say."

"The wench speaks all manner of vile tongues, I hear."

William Reed placed the last few crabs into the tank of seawater that stood near the door while Nathaniel tallied the numbers. He owed the man for thirty pounds of crab. If he bought it for one and a half shillings each pound, he could sell it for two and a half and make a quid and a half profit, but Reed knew the quality of his goods and Nathaniel might not get the load for less than two and a half quid. He settled on one and three-quarter shillings a pound. He'd sell it for two and a half and still make upward of one quid profit.

"Here you go, William," he said, finding William's account in his ledger book. "It says here you have a balance of one quid, two shillings, for some canvas material and turpentine you took last time you were here. I owe you two quid, six shillings, for your load of crab here. If I subtract what you owe me from what I owe you . . ." He wrote the numbers into the ledger book. ". . . that'll leave us a difference of one quid, four shillings, that I have to pay you. Do you follow?"

He took a guinea and two shillings out of his cash box and placed them in William's palm, red and crusty as the crabs. The man stared at the three coins.

"I'm giving you one and three-quarter shillings per pound, times thirty pounds, equals two quid, six shillings."

"What about these three, Sir, you had me put aside for the goodwife? Them's over two pounds right there."

Damnation, he had forgotten about the blue crabs and not factored them into the profit margin. "I'll trade you those two shillings for this piece of eight, then," said Nathaniel, testing the man to see if he'd notice he was shortchanging him by sixpence, not to mention the shilling he'd already filched earlier.

"Two little coins for a whole night's work," said William. "Hardly seems like enough, Sir."

"When it comes to money, William, it's never enough."

"Was counting on a few pence more, Sir, for the trip and all, Sir."

"I don't finance your way from Marblehead, William."

"I know, Sir, but Mammy's been under the weather, you see, and she be needing her herbals."

"Come, now, William. You and I, and everyone from Marblehead to Boston, know that Wilmot Reed makes her own herbals. Could be an apothecary if she weren't tippling all day. No call for lying to your best client. It'll have to be two and a half quid for today, William, or I suppose you could take your load over to Shrimpton's."

"Mr. Shrimpton and me never seen eye to eye. Never pays with coin the way you, do, Sir. This'll do, then." The man's fist closed over the coins.

"I'll need you to place your mark in my ledger here, to show we're all square on the account."

William took the quill that Nathaniel had already inked and made an elaborate squiggle on the page. "There you go, Sir. And, Sir?"

"Yes, William?"

"If the wench be sickly, I could see if Mammy wanted to look in on her. I'm sure she wouldn't charge ye more than a shilling or two, Sir, for her service."

"Don't bother with it, William. The wench is bedridden, mayhap even on her deathbed. I doubt Rebecca'd let anyone see her at this point."

"Deathbed, Sir? She that sick?"

"Sick and rambling on like a lunatic."

William Reed stroked the graying stubble on his chin. "Of course, it be none of my business, Sir, but 'twould be good to know what she be saying, don't you think? Wouldn't want her cursing you and the goodwife in Romish on her deathbed."

"You've got a point there, William."

"For a small fee, Sir, I'd be willing to go to Roxbury and listen to the wench myself, see if I can figure out what she's rambling on about."

Nathaniel eyed the man up and down. If they left right now, he could probably have dinner at the farm and wouldn't need to spend money on food today. "How about a nice plump game hen from the Old Man's farm for your trouble, William? Your mammy'd like that, wouldn't she?"

The man beamed a black-toothed smile at him. "Reckon she would, Sir."

"Let's get going, then. Day's not getting any younger."

Just before locking up the warehouse, Nathaniel spotted Sara Moor's brother playing at spillikins across the street. "Get over here, boy, and watch this door!" Nathaniel yelled, climbing into his rig beside William Reed.

CHAPTER 10

The smell of spoiled fish on William Reed turned Rebecca's stomach, but his manner seemed honest enough. If he could help them decipher what the girl was saying, it was worth a few minutes of Rebecca's time.

"Who's that?" called the Old Man, peering through the drapes around his bed.

"It's William Reed, Father," Rebecca replied. "He's here to see if he can interpret what Thankful Seagraves is saying in that ungodly tongue of hers."

"Stinks like a fishmonger!" growled Tobias.

"He *is* a fishmonger, Tobias," said Nathaniel, shaking his head at William Reed.

William's gaze adjusted to the shadows of the cottage. The coals glowed red under the kettle hanging in the hearth pit. He heard the sizzle of steam under the lid. Smelled something rich and spicy cooking in the kettle. Saw the trundle bed and could tell that there was a body moving around under the bed-clothes.

"Where's my dinner?" cried the Old Man.

"The pudding's not ready, yet, Father. You know black pudding takes its time. Now be quiet. Mr. Reed won't be able to hear the girl with all your shouting."

Still muttering, the Old Man let the drapes close.

"Well, then, I've got a business to run," said Nathaniel. "Might as well get to it, William." Nathaniel helped himself to a hefty wedge of cheese from the cheese wheel on the table. "Looks like I'll be having a light dinner, today."

"If I'd known you were coming to Roxbury at this hour, Husband, I would have hurried with the pudding," Rebecca explained, "but it's washing day, and Sara Moor and I have been scrubbing linens all morning. Father's been relieving himself on the sheets with no one to lift him out of bed."

"It's of no consequence," said Nathaniel. "The cheese is fine."

"The fever's made her completely delirious," said Rebecca, stepping behind the table to remove herself from the man's smell. "I'm afraid she may make no sense at all, Mr. Reed."

"Figures," mumbled Nathaniel, wiping the sweat off his neck. "William, pull up a stool. I'll just take my cheese and wait outside. It's too close in here for all of us."

"There's beer in the cellar," Rebecca called after her husband. "And there might be an apple or two ready to pick."

William Reed approached the trundle bed and knelt beside it. Under the bedclothes, the girl's arms and legs squirmed like netted fish. In the red glow of the hearth, he could see the sweat running off her dark brow, though her teeth chattered loudly. The mistress hovered at his back.

"Dios te salve María, llena eres de gracia," the girl uttered.

"There she goes. What is she saying, Mr. Reed?"

"It's too fast, Mistress. Can't make rhyme or reason of it, yet."

He placed one hand over the girl's heaving chest and with the other supported the back of her sweat-drenched head, her neck fragile as a ewe's.

"Mr. Reed, I don't think any touching is necessary."

William ignored her and leaned his ear close to the girl's mouth. Her hot breath made his buttocks tighten.

". . . bendita eres entre todas las mujeres y bendito el sagrado fruto de tu vientre . . ."

"Well, Mr. Reed?"

"Sounds like gibberish to me, Mistress," he said, lowering his head and placing his ear on the girl's breast. "Or maybe a papist prayer of some sort."

"Mr. Reed, I doubt you need to get that close to the girl to understand what she's saying. I really must object."

William Reed let the girl's head drop back on the pillow and got to his feet. "Beggin' your pardon, Mistress," he said. "I'll go, now, if you like."

"But you haven't deciphered what she's saying."

"It be hard to hear her and answer your questions at the same time, Mistress."

"Yes, I see. I suppose I could go outside and wait with Nathaniel. Caleb's here, after all. I suppose it's not too improper. I'll step outside, then."

"Very good, Mistress."

"Keep an eye on Mr. Reed, Caleb. I'll be just outside the door, Father," she said over her shoulder, but William could hear the snoring of the Old Man.

When the door closed behind Mistress Greenwood, William knelt down again, the blood pounding in his ears. He had never seen a naked woman be-fore, never been this close to a woman who wasn't his own mammy. Gingerly, he pulled the coverlets down and gathered up the girl's sweaty gown, raising it over her legs. At first, he was disappointed. Knees as bony as a boy's. He raised the gown farther and saw that, even though her ribs poked through as sharp as her hip bones, she was a woman, after all, with a black patch of hair between her legs and large plum-colored tits on her brown breasts. With one hand he held the gown over the girl's face; with the other he pinched her tits.

The girl stopped squirming and nearly sat up in the bed, shrieking in protest, but William kept her down with his elbows, crooning to her to quiet her down. Rocking his hips, he pressed his hard member against the side of the bed. If he hurried he could get his relief in his pants. He ground his hips against the bedding, digging his hand into the black patch, and imagined himself taking the girl, doing to her what he did to the ewes in his mammy's barnyard, but then he heard something scraping behind him. He turned his head and saw the mer-chant's boy crouched under the table, eyes agape and hands clapped over his mouth. Immediately William lowered the girl's gown, raised the coverlets, and rushed outside, his face on fire, cap held down in front of his bulging crotch.

"No luck, Sir. Beggin' your pardon, Mistress. Couldn't make out a thing beyond that prayer she's rambling."

"Prayer?" said Nathaniel. "All we need is for Increase Mather to hear there's a papist prayer being uttered aloud in my father-in-law's house."

"He won't be hearing it from me, Sir," said William.

Rebecca narrowed her eyes at his flushed ears and face. "I would hope not," said Rebecca. "That's not even your parish."

"Here's that game hen I promised you, William," said Nathaniel, holding a scrawny white hen by the legs.

"Mammy'll like that, Sir. We ain't tasted poultry for months, now."

"We'll be on our way, then," Nathaniel said to his wife, touching her shoulder. "I'll be home for an early supper. There's a meeting at the Town House this evening."

"Oh?"

He lowered his voice so that William wouldn't hear. "Reverend Mather's heard rumors of the King revoking our charter."

"No!"

"Mum's the word, Rebecca."

"I'll make you a fine supper to make up for today," Rebecca said softly. She wanted to feel his lips on hers but knew that even here a pair of eyes might be upon them, and they'd be reported for indecency and put in the stocks.

"Send Sara Moor over to Samuel Parris's house," Nathaniel said to Rebecca. "William says his maid might speak the girl's tongue."

"The Indian woman?" Rebecca looked startled.

Nathaniel shrugged. "It's worth a try. She is catechized, Rebecca."

"Perhaps it would be best to wait till the girl's more coherent."

"It's your decision, Goodwife. Off we go, then, William."

"Afternoon, Mistress," William said, genuflecting like a papist before he climbed into the rig.

"My regards to your mother, Mr. Reed."

Rebecca watched them leave with an odd feeling in her belly. She found Caleb inside standing over Thankful Seagraves, tears running down his cheeks.

"Caleb? What's the matter, Son?"

"He didn't know I was here, Mama. I watched him."

"What do you mean, Caleb?"

"He uncovered her."

"What? Are you sure?"

The boy nodded.

"He didn't . . . do anything to her, did he? Didn't lay on top of her or anything?"

Caleb shook his head, now tucking the blankets in around the delirious girl. "There's something black, like a big spider, right here," he said, pointing to his own groin. "Do you think he was trying to take it off? He was pulling on it real hard."

Rebecca ran out to the barnyard to slap the fellow's face and make him apologize in front of Nathaniel, but the rig had already trundled off into the road. That filthy fishmonger, thought Rebecca. That's all he came for, to get his jollies and a game hen for his trouble. She was going to have to speak to Nathaniel about this. She should have trusted her instinct about the fellow, him and his fishy smell and devious eyes roaming all over the room. Couldn't keep his hands to himself. He had left his stench in the room, and no doubt the girl needed washing if he'd had his filthy hands on her private parts.

Angrily Rebecca took a bucket to the well and lugged it back into the cottage. Thank God her father had had the foresight to buy his farmland near a well. She poured the water into a kettle over the fire and asked Caleb to climb up the ladder and fetch a tub of soap from the loft.

"That was bad, what he did, wasn't it, Mama?" said the boy.

"I hope you never disrespect a woman like that, Caleb."

"Even a papist?"

"Even a papist. A woman is a woman, Caleb. Now do as I say."

Rebecca leaned over the trundle bed. For the first time in months, the girl's eyes were open, and her gaze was fixed and full of wrath.

"It wasn't me," Rebecca uttered. She reached out, but the girl winced before she even laid a hand on her. "Shh," Rebecca soothed, stroking the girl's hot forehead. Rebecca lifted the girl's gown and saw where the fishmonger's filthy hands had left scratch marks on the insides of her thighs.

CHAPTER 11

A sharp pain needled her temples. She couldn't open her eyes. Her stomach was queasy, like the first days on board the ship. She felt queasy and seasick and thirsty, so thirsty. Where was she? All she could remember was jumping into the sea.

It seemed that she'd been underwater for years. At times the water felt so cold it numbed her bones and made her teeth chatter so hard her head pounded like a drum, the sacs of her lungs nearly bursting with her held breath. Other times the water boiled her skin and she felt like she was sweating underwater, panting from the heat, lungs racking with a hot cough, suffocating under waves of wool, the smell of lanolin and menthol thick in her nostrils.

She could hear people talking at the edges of the water, their voices rippling and rising like tiny bubbles in her ears. The voices grew louder, more distinct, drowning out the swish and slap of the water. She could not understand what they said, but she recognized the woman's voice and the gravelly voice of an old man. She recognized the woman's hands kneading her chest, feeding her salty broths and sweet gruel, washing her body with a rough sponge. There was another set of hands that touched her, firm, cool hands that smelled of herbs feeling her forehead and her belly, inspecting between her legs.

She refused to open her eyes, even when the hunger shook her and the saliva dribbled down the side of her face. She dreamt food all the time, mostly the cool fruit she had not tasted since before the voyage. Tangerines, pineapples, papayas, bananas, and mameyes. When her body burned, she yearned for hibiscus or tamarind water. When the chills took her, only the frothy, cinnamony sweetness of hot chocolate could fill her longing.

Sometimes she could hear women chanting in her dreams, the Hail Mary rising and falling in plaintive repetition:

Ave Maria, gratia plena,
Dominus tecum, benedicta tu in mulieribus,
et benedictus fructus ventris tui.

The needling pain increased. She heard the women chanting about the blessèd fruit in the womb again, and out of their Latin canticle arose a deep, soft voice she recognized, singing in Spanish: "Señora Sant Ana, ¿porqué llora la niña? Por una manzana que se la ha perdido . . ." It was her mother's voice singing that ballad that she remembered from her childhood. But what did this song have to do with the womb of the Virgin Mary? Perhaps the apple was the fruit of the womb and the fact that it was lost and the child was weeping meant that someone was losing the fruit of her womb. Who was Señora Santa Ana? Her mother's name was María Clara Benavídez. "Señora María Clara," she heard herself singing in the dream, changing the words, "why does your child weep? . . ." She could not understand the song. If she was the daughter of María Clara, then why was she weeping for a lost apple? Was the lost apple a lost child? Her own child? She didn't have a child. Herself? She didn't have that, either. She was the windfall apple tossed on a pirate's ship and sold like a slave in a foreign land. Even her name, she remembered, had been taken away.

These thoughts were making her dizzy, the queasiness stronger now, the nausea gripping her gut and making her heave. She turned sideways to reach the bucket, but there was something in the way, something under her or inside her, poking her in the stomach, not letting her move. Get out of the way, she wanted to shout, but the gruel she'd been fed earlier came up in bitter spurts.

Thankful Seagraves . . . Thankful Seagraves . . . Thankful Seagraves.

All those voices, all those women smelling of yeast and sweat—so many of them they didn't fit in the one-room cottage, a line of greasy bonnets and stained aprons spilling out into the yard. Laughing and pointing, the women spoke words to her that she didn't understand. Some of them pulled the hair out of her head. Others jabbed their fingers into her face or pulled her ears. A pair of older women kept fondling the embroidery on the tattered sleeves and hem of her *huipíl,* mumbling and nodding to each other and asking her questions she couldn't answer.

Sitting in a big, lion-pawed chair in front of the hearth, the Old Man was filling his pipe from a tin of tobacco that was being passed around to all the men at the table. They all had mugs of beer and slices of a meat-filled pastry on pewter plates in front of them. The cottage was dark from the smoke of the chimney and the smoke of all their pipes. At first she thought the men were the pirates sitting at the galley table waiting to spank and pinch her as she came around to serve them. But when the Old Man, seeing her awake, called out, "Papist," pointing his pipe at her, she remembered what had happened. She remembered how the pirate captain had led her to the poop deck, where two men waited, watching the hourglass, their faces white as death under their black hats, each with eyes like glass shards. Though she had not understood what they were saying, she knew the men were haggling with the pirate over her price. After that she had jumped into the sea, understanding, finally, why Aléndula had let the pestilence take her.

Poor, poor Aléndula—waiting three years for Concepción to free her from a life of sackcloth and shackles in the convent, only to wind up being captured by pirates and then thrown to the monsters of the deep. Forgive me, Aléndula, for having cursed you to eternal bleeding at the bottom of the ocean, she thought, making the triple sign of the cross over her forehead, mouth, and chest. She opened her eyes when she heard them gasp, all those strangers, watching her bless herself and gasping as though they'd seen the Devil.

"Papist!" the Old Man cried out, flinging the tobacco tin at her.

CHAPTER 12

The Visible Saints were restless today. Increase wanted to believe it was just the Indian summer heat streaming in through the long windows of the North Meeting House, worse on the women's side than the men's at this hour of the day, but more likely it was the sermon making everyone fidget.

"None but the Father, who sees in secret, knows the heartbreaking exercises wherewith I have composed what is now going to be exposed, lest I should in any one thing miss of doing my designed service for his Glory, and for his People; but I am now somewhat comfortably assured of his favorable acceptance; and, *I will not fear; what can a Satan do unto me!*"

Increase had invited his son Cotton to speak to the congregation this morning, wanting to give Cotton an audience for a discourse he was writing on the wily ways of the Evil One, but he was on his second turn of the hourglass and the lecture gave no sign of waning. At least the boy had deposed himself of the annoying stutter that had plagued his speech up until his fifteenth birthday, when he'd graduated from Harvard. Not hearing the stilted footprint of that stutter was a debt Increase owed to the painstaking discipline of Tobias Webb, though not even Tobias could remove the hyperbole and histrionics that now punctuated Cotton's language, a style his son had been perfecting since he had preached his first sermon at North Church, three years ago.

"I have indeed set myself to countermine the whole *plot* of the Devil against New England, in every branch of it, as far as one of my darkness can comprehend such a Work of Darkness," Cotton expounded emphatically, going so far as to point a finger at the clump of Negro slaves in the gallery. Samuel Parris's servant, the Indian woman, Tituba, cowered under the intensity of Cotton's speech.

The boy is overzealous, thought Increase, not dwelling on the obvious similarities between his son's speech and the text of the new essay Increase had just delivered to the printer's on the subject of Satan and the possession of one Elizabeth

Knapp," which he had titled "An Essay for the Recording of Illustrious Providences." Certainly, God was sending recordable signs of his displeasure to the Bay colonists, evidence in the form of smallpox and Indian raids that New England was nearing the brink of perdition if they did not rein in their penchant for commerce and individual gain and turn again to the laws of Scripture. It was as if Elizabeth Knapp, the epitome of moral decline that had served to illustrate Increase's argument, was a symbol for the ugly turn of affairs in New England, possessed of demons and running about shrieking, "Money, money!"

Increase surveyed the faces of the congregation. Someone was missing on the women's side whom he couldn't place. There in the front pews with their India fans working furiously and their daughters dressed in overbright tones beside them sat the upper crust of the ladies: Mrs. Thatcher, Mrs. Dempsey, Mrs. Shrimpton, the Widow Cole, Mrs. Richards, Mrs. Belcher, and of course, his own dear wife, Maria. Behind them were the more common goodwives, each with her brood all around her: Williams with four, Johnson with three, Hibble with eight, Griggs with five and one on the way, Stokes with three, and Collins with seven. At the back stood the indentured girls whose mistresses aspired them to saintliness by dragging them to church each Sunday, and in the gallery the slaves and the beggars.

Increase looked over to the men's side to find each woman's corresponding gentleman, goodman, brother, or son. His inventory revealed the culprit. The two widowers, Captain Clarke and Deacon Oliver, of course, had no helpmeets, but neither did Merchants Parris and Greenwood. Parris's wife, Elizabeth, had remained feeble after a difficult birthing last winter, and so, with Increase's permission, she came to Meeting very sparingly. It was Greenwood's Rebecca who never missed, and it was her face that was absent among the women. It shocked Increase to think that one he had fostered like his own daughter could be so remiss. He would have to speak to Greenwood about this and charge him an extra tithe for the transgression.

Everyone in Boston knew that Greenwood had purchased an Indian woman off a buccaneer ship back in the summer, and Increase had heard from Samuel Parris and others of his congregation that Rebecca spent an inordinate amount of time training the girl in the ways of the English. Increase had no disagreement with this, though he doubted trafficking with buccaneers was a godly thing, but he had much disagreement with Rebecca Greenwood's absence from Meeting. If he recalled correctly, she had been absent from last Thursday's Lecture as well. This behavior could not be tolerated. She was a merchant's wife, of the upper echelons of Boston society only through God's grace. What flagrant ingratitude was she displaying—let alone setting a bad example to the girls and goodwives and leaving her soul open for the Devil's advances—missing the Sabbath? Clearly, he would have to do more than charge a tithe. He would have to say something about it now, as soon as Cotton finished his long-winded sermon.

"We are still so happy, that I suppose there is no Land in the Universe more free from the debauching, and the debasing Vices of Ungodliness. The Body of the People are hitherto so disposed . . ." Cotton's voice rose to a high pitch and a ruddy color flushed his face. ". . . that *Swearing, Sabbath-breaking, Whoring, Drunkenness*, and the like, do not make a Gentleman, but a Monster or a Goblin, in the vulgar Estimation."

Just as suddenly, Cotton's pallor changed, and he measured his words again, so that his next utterances were hardly audible, save for those in the very front pews and Increase, sitting behind him.

"All this notwithstanding, we must humbly confess to our God, that we are miserably degenerated from the first Love of our Predecessors . . ."

I have trained the boy too well, thought Increase, though Cotton's twenty-first birthday was but three months away. Increase watched the sand pass through the glass. Even Deacon Oliver and Major Richards, perhaps the most upstanding citizens of the entire colony, save for Increase himself, were nodding off. Increase surrendered to the realization that he would not be getting a turn at the podium this morning. His admonishment of Rebecca Greenwood would have to wait till the second exercise after dinner.

CHAPTER 13

Concepción had climbed up to the eaves above the Old Man's bed to get away from all the strangers who wanted to gawk at her, their poking fingers and inquisitive eyes, their English tongues calling her that name over and over, a name she would never own. The trundle bed was too heavy for her to move, so she had dragged her bedding up to the loft, including the pillow and the feather mattress and the quilt, and she had taken one of the Old Man's books, a pair of candles, a tin lamp, and a tinderbox she had found in one of the drawers of the blue-lacquered cabinet where the dishes and linens were stored. To keep anybody from following her, she would pull the ladder up behind her. A pain shot down to her tailbone each time she hefted the ladder, but at least she could be alone up there and they couldn't get to her.

She would lower the ladder only when all the strangers left and the Old Man was snoring in his bed. Only then did she climb down and devour whatever food was left on the plates scattered all over the table or in the kettle hanging from a pole inside the chimney: a crust of pastry with some bits of chicken and carrot still attached, a hunk of brown bread spread thick with butter, a piece of cheese, the remnants of a badly spiced stew.

She was eating so much that her belly was growing round, her breasts getting hard and full like wineskins stretched to their limit. Her body had stopped its monthly bleeding on the ship, and she was glad of it, not having to worry about where to find what she needed or how to hide it from the Old Man. She knew, of course, what this meant, that the pirate's seed had taken root inside her and that the hunger was not her own but came from the creature growing in her womb. Conceived against her will, it was no more than a pest to her, a parasite feeding off her flesh, bringing memories that tormented her.

There were two women who came each day to feed and care for the Old Man. One was the red-haired woman with blue eyes whom the Old Man called Becca, the other a black woman whom Becca called Seramur. Concepción watched them from the eaves. Together, they would move the Old Man from his bed to his armchair, which was fitted with iron wheels under the legs and allowed them to push rather than carry him to and fro. There he would sit in a clean gown with his beer and his book while Becca kneaded the dough that she would roll out into pastry crusts and fill with meat and vegetables, while Seramur changed the linen on the Old Man's bed. Through a knothole in the garret, Concepción could see Seramur, in a sea of chickens in the yard, washing the soiled sheets and pillowcases in an iron tub and hanging them to dry on a line of rope stretched between the apple tree and the barn. Then she would clean the Old Man's chamber pot, using leaves and twigs first and then dipping it into the laundry tub, where, at the end of the day, she would wash the plates and mugs.

"Thankful Seagraves?" Becca would call up to her. Concepción would peer over the platform of the loft and see the woman standing down there with one hand on her hip, the other wagging a wooden spoon at her, blue eyes blazing as she uttered a barrage of English impossible to understand.

"Thankful Seagraves!" Seramur would cry out, stamping her foot and yammering angrily, shaking the clean chamber pot or the sack of chicken feed so that Concepción could see that she wanted her to do some of the work.

"I can't understand you," she would say in Spanish. "Leave me alone."

Each of them used another word that was becoming familiar to her: "help." They would point up at her, say that ugly name they had given her, point down, and say, "Help." She had not the palest idea what it could mean.

"Concepción Benavídez!" she would call down. "Me llamo Concepción Benavídez!"

She wouldn't pay attention to them afterward. She would light the candle in the lamp, lean against the whitewashed stones of the wall, and read the Old Man's book. She could not really read the book, but at least this language used the same alphabet as her own and she could try to learn the language phonetically and maybe memorize the way the letters looked on the page. The slits on the sides of the lamp cast glowing crescents on the walls. It was not good reading light and made her sleepy and dizzy sometimes, but she forced herself to memorize ten words a day, beginning with the title: *A Narrative of the Captivity, Sufferings and Removes of Mrs. Mary Rowlandson, Who was taken Prisoner by the Indians with several others, and treated in the most barbarous and cruel Manner, by those vile Savages: With many other remarkable Events during her Travels.* Words like "who," "those," "the," "with," "Mrs.," and "other" she could not figure out how to pronounce, but a few were almost identical to Spanish—"narrative"/*narrativa,* "removes"/*remover,* "prisoner"/*prisionero,* "Indians"/*indios,* "barbarous"/*bárbaro,* "cruel"/*cruel.* She took it to be a story about cruel and barbarous Indians taking away a prisoner. Like me, she thought. I was taken prisoner by cruel and barbarous pirates. It was a story she wanted to be able to read.

Becca and Seramur would leave after the midday meal, once the Old Man had eaten and been put back into his bed, the clean linen folded up into the cabinet again, the dishes washed except for the kettle that was always left hanging from a crane in the chimney with food. But there was never enough food. And she longed for *agua fresca,* made of the pulp of watermelon and cucumber, and fresh sweet cream made with cows' milk, not the sour goats' milk they drank here, and for the inimitable flavor of a quesadilla, the melted cheese and squash blossoms cooking into the cornmeal shell.

Once, stirring the coals of the chimney with a pair of long iron tongs, she found in the ashes two eggs wrapped in blackened leaves. She broke the shells and found the eggs gray and solid. She wanted to take her time savoring each one with a pinch of salt, but before she knew it, she'd stuffed both of them in her mouth, their dry olive-colored yolks nearly choking her. As she was still hungry, it occurred to her that there were chickens outside and roosters that crowed in the evenings instead of the mornings. She lifted the beam from the door and stepped outside, surprised at how cold it was. She hurried back inside, took the Old Man's lap blanket from the armchair, and wrapped herself up in it. If she could just catch one of those chickens, wring its neck the way her mother used to do, pluck the feathers, and singe the skin, she could boil it in the kettle and make a *caldo de pollo,* a light simple broth with chicken and vegetables.

She glanced around the yard, looking for a well, saw nothing but fowl—white, red, and speckled chickens and yellow chicks—darting back and forth between the barn and the coop. Hens roosted in the apple tree and in the dried vegetable beds along the back of the house. A cold gust buffeted her face and her skin prickled. Her ears felt chilled. She pulled the blanket tighter around her neck. There had to be a well somewhere, because Seramur boiled water in the tub to do the washing. Maybe it was behind the barn, but no, she found nothing back there but a fallow little corn patch mulched with corn husks and dead leaves, and a long water trough sagging off the rails of the fence.

She looked out over the fence and saw that the road ended in a copse of trees and realized that the barn stood only a stone's throw from the forest. She remembered walking with Aléndula through forests of cypress and piñon, but the woods here looked different, darker and more foreboding, huge evergreens and other trees she had never seen with leaves of different colors and a dense growth underneath that gave off an emerald light. The wind had picked up and her ears felt numb, the sky moving toward a darker shade of gray. If she didn't hurry, she wouldn't get her soup made before dark.

She followed the length of the fence toward the front of the cottage and finally saw the well across the road, a small stone structure crowned with a weather vane, nearly hidden in a tangled clump of dead branches. Behind the well sprawled a large pasture, and she could smell salt water in the air, as though they were close to the ocean. She pushed the gate open, turned back to look at the house, and took her first steps in the outside world. She didn't get very far, but the act of walking across the road, narrow and muddy though it was, gave her a sense of freedom and purpose. At the well, she saw the rope looped around the crank and realized she had not brought a container to carry the water back to the cottage. How silly could she be? Come to think of it, and she wasn't thinking very clearly at all, what vegetables was she going to use in this soup of hers? There was nothing growing in the vegetable beds but a thatch of weeds.

She sat and sulked on the edge of the well. A white cat with a freckled face ambled across the road and came toward her. She reached down to pet the cat and one of the straggly branches of the bush caught in her hair. "My hair's growing back," she said aloud, jumping to her feet and happily kneading her fingers into the short, thick mat on her head. "Do you see that, kitty? My hair's growing back!" Why it gave her so much pleasure she didn't know. The cat purred loudly, rubbing against her leg, then scrambled over to the bush and dug her nails in the bark. Concepción noticed, then, that the bush wasn't dead at all. The bark was green where the cat had scratched, and the branches were covered with tiny green buds. What season was this? she wondered, remembering only that it had been summer when they'd left Vera Cruz. How long have I been here? For a second she felt like she had gone backward in time to the spring, and then she panicked at the thought that maybe she'd gone forward by nearly a year and couldn't remember it. Had she been so ill she'd slept through the cold seasons? Was she going crazy? A shudder ran down her spine.

"Maybe it's this place that's crazy," she said, hunching over to pet the cat again. Black freckles covered her face like a mask, and she had one small black spot over her nose like a mustache and a row of black and brown freckles down her back. "Pecas," Concepción said, scratching between the cat's ears. "I'm going to call you Pecas because of all your freckles." The cat blinked at her and butted her head against Concepción's hand.

She returned to the barn to look for a pail, followed by the cat. The stench of the chicken dung reminded Concepción of being in the bilge of the pirate's ship, made her gag, and she ran out. At the back of the cottage she spotted a short flight of stone stairs that led under the house. She remembered one of her hiding places in the hold of the ship, surrounded by barrels of biscuit and yams, bottles of oil and wine, thick salted hams covered in burlap hanging off the beams. Her mouth watered. She knew there had to be food stored under the house. At the bottom of the stairs she found a little door that opened into a dark cellar. She looked up and noticed the sky, the color of ashes now, and couldn't remember the last time she'd seen the sun. Must have been on the ship, she thought, and remembered standing on the top deck, gazing at the horizon of water and the sun shimmering like ruddy gold as it slipped into the dark sea. She needed light. She tiptoed back into the cottage and took the oil lamp from the Old Man's bedside table.

In the cellar she found a cask of beer so bitter it turned her stomach and a bushel of old mildewed corncobs, half-eaten by rats. There were straw-lined bushels of carrots and apples, long, thin tubers that smelled of onions, a sack of dried peas, cold and hard as wooden beads, and half a barrel of chicken feed.

"Since I can't make *caldo de pollo,* how about a pea soup with carrots and onions?" she asked the cat. The cat licked her paw, agreeing with Concepción. Pea soup would be good, especially in the cold. And she wouldn't have to kill the chicken or take time plucking and singeing it. She would have to go up to the house again and get a kettle to bring back the water. It would be heavy, but it was all she could find.

When she stepped into the cottage, something sharp struck her in the head. The Old Man had thrown his cane at her. She felt herself falling back, hitting her shoulder on the doorjamb, her cheek landing flat on the doorstone. The last thing she saw was the cat staring down at her, her green eyes widening as she leaned over to sniff Concepción's face.

CHAPTER 14

Goodwife Mehitable Thorn was nervous about her neighbor Tobias Webb. No telling what that papist creature they'd brought to live with him might do. Goody Thorn knew the creature was evil, soon as she laid eyes on her, didn't have to witness any sundry acts of wickedness to know that for a fact. But witness it she had. First, Goody Thorn, and everyone else in Roxbury who had trooped over to Tobias's house for a Town Meeting, had seen the creature making signs over her face and kissing her thumb and such, right out in the open, natural as licking her fingers after a meal. Reverend Lowe had stepped out of the room with Merchant Greenwood and himself had not seen the offensive gestures, but even Tobias had remonstrated to the creature in a shrill voice. Goody Thorn was willing to let it go as flagrant papacy. More obstinate than a Quaker and just as ignorant as a savage, the creature didn't know any better, didn't realize she'd come to live among God's chosen, where papacy had no root. But now, this thing with the cat proved her wrong not to worry. It wasn't just papacy that the creature were bringing to her neighbor's house. It's outright witchery, if you ask me, she thought to herself. There was no doubt in Goody Thorn's mind that Tobias was in danger.

"Hurry up, Polly," she called over her shoulder to her indentured girl.

"Did you see that, Mistress?"

"See what? Hurry up, now. Those people at the market ain't gonna wait all day for us to show up, even if we do make the best cheese in the Bay Colony."

"But, Mistress, didn't you see the white cat? Why was it licking her face like that, Mistress? Did she die or faint or something? Should we go and find out?"

"Whatever it is, Polly, I'm sure it's none of your business. Now keep moving, girl, and stop being such a busybody!"

But Goody Thorn had seen the whole thing. The creature falling down in the doorway of the cottage for no good reason, as though she'd been struck down by God or the Devil himself. The white cat sitting by the doorstone, staring into the creature's face like she were inquiring after her health, licking her chin and all, like her familiar. Wait till I tell Mary Penfield, Goody Thorn thought. Though she seemed quiet as a mouse, Cotton Mather's maid worked more quickly than the town crier.

"Not a word, Polly, do you hear me? Not a word if you don't want to find yourself looking for a new situation."

CHAPTER 15

Up in the loft Concepción had found two trunks covered by a dusty tapestry. The smaller trunk was too heavy to move, and the lock was fastened tight. She had looked for the key in all the drawers in the linen cabinet downstairs, tried to pry the lock open with the flat ends of different spoons and with the two pewter forks she found, as there were no knives anywhere in the cottage, but had succeeded only in bending the tines. For now, the trunk served as a bedside table. In the larger trunk lined in cedar-wood, she had found piles of men's clothing, carefully folded: dark green breeches with wooden buttons at the knees and a brown woolen vest, a yellow brocade jacket, two wide-sleeved linen shirts stained at the collar and under the arms, two pairs of cotton drawers, a nightgown, a red cap, three pairs of thick red hose, a blue woolen cloak with blue satin lining under the hood, hair ribbons, an ivory comb, a worn leather satchel, three leather gloves, and a pair of black buckled shoes that were twice as large as her feet.

Becca had laughed when she saw Concepción climb down the ladder from the loft wearing the green breeches and the linen shirt and the brocade jacket, but the Old Man had yelled and yelled at her, gnashing his purple gums until a foam gathered in the corners of his mouth and his face turned bright pink. She had never seen him so angry, not even when the man in the ruffled collar they called Natanio sat at the table writing in an account book and counting coins.

"Son, son, son"—the Old Man kept yelling. "They are. They are. They are." *¿Qué* son? Concepción wanted to ask. What are they? Becca pointed up to the ladder and gestured for her to get out of the clothes, shaking her head at her and saying, "No, Thankful Seagraves," followed by something else that ended with the word "son."

Because he left her alone most of the time, except when he wanted her to fetch him more beer from the cellar or help him move from the bed to his reading chair by the fire, Concepción trusted the Old Man, though she slapped at his hand every time he wanted to pet her like a dog or fondle her breasts. He didn't seem to mind that she spoke to him in Spanish or that she ate most of everything that his daughter cooked for him. Usually, his anger was reserved for Becca or Natanio, but seeing Concepción in those clothes made him furious. She sat on the dirt floor and cried under the Old Man's relentless barrage of meaningless words that spelled his displeasure.

The next day, Becca brought her some women's clothing, luring her down from the loft by showing her and naming each garment as she held it up: "shift," "stockings," "garters," "petticoats," "waistcoat," "apron," "coif," "pocket," "shoes." Three of the garment were called petticoat, the first and longest one a dark-gray cotton, the second one a thin red wool, the third and shortest one a heavier brown wool trimmed with black. The apron looked threadbare, but the stockings seemed hardly worn and the shoes looked new and soft as slippers with a hard sole, though Concepción had a hard time distinguishing the right foot from the left. Her favorite piece was the long pouch tied around her waist that the woman called pocket. Becca wore a sheathed knife tied to the strap of her own pocket, but she did not give Concepción one of these. Concepción pointed to the knife and then to herself.

"No, Thankful Seagraves," said Becca, "no knife for you."

"Nye," said Concepción, poking the knife with her finger.

"Chicken," said Becca, picking up a dead hen from the table and holding it out to Concepción. "Pluck. You—" She pointed at Concepción. "Pluck the chicken. Help." Becca pulled a handful of feathers out to show her what to do, casting the feathers into the fire.

The smell of the burning feathers turned Concepción's stomach, and she almost retched. Becca poured her a cup of milk from a pitcher she had brought for the Old Man.

"Drink. It will settle your stomach," said Becca.

"Leche," said Concepción.

"No popish talk," said Becca. "You speak English, now. Say 'milk.'"

"Meel," Concepción mimicked, grimacing at the taste of the goats' milk. "Nye."

"No knife for Thankful Seagraves."

Concepción took her time plucking the scrawny chicken, one feather at a time.

They were startled by the cries of the Old Man calling out to them from the privy. Becca ran outside, leaving her knife on the table next to the sweet potatoes she had been peeling. Without hesitation, Concepción took the knife and scurried up the ladder. Sitting on her heels, she pried at the lock on the trunk, but it refused to give.

"Thankful Seagraves?" she heard Becca calling her from downstairs. "Thankful Seagraves . . ." Whatever else she said drifted into the chicken cackle of the afternoon.

Turning the knife on its side, Concepción slipped the blade under the lid and pushed hard against the lock, the sweat gathering under her coif now, not even hearing Rebecca as she climbed the ladder.

"Thankful Seagraves . . . ," Becca said, her face and shoulders clearing the top of the loft. She motioned for Concepción to come down, gesturing with one hand that she wanted her knife. Concepción shook her head.

"Pocket," said Concepción, showing how she wanted to wear the knife next to her pocket like Becca did.

"No," said Becca, pointing to herself. "My knife. Rebecca's knife."

"My nye, Rebecca," said Concepción, tapping her chest with the tip of the blade. She wanted the sheath, too, she said in Spanish, but Becca did not understand. "Nye pocket," Concepción said, holding out her hand, eyes level with Becca's.

Even in the smoky light of the loft, Concepción could see that Becca's face was flushed, that her eyes blazed like blue fireworks.

"You have taken enough," said Becca. "Enough, Thankful Seagraves."

"*Y* no, Becca."

She watched Becca descend the ladder and return to her work. She tossed the peeled and the unpeeled tubers together into the boiling water in the kettle and threw the lid on with a clang. Concepción knew she had angered Becca, but at least she had a knife, now. Returning to the trunk, she managed to force the lock open. What she found inside made her cry out. The trunk was filled with leather-bound books, all of them inscribed on their front leaves with the name *Robin Webb.* The titles to most of them had the letters arranged in an order that made no sense, but they were beautiful books with gilded pages and different-colored covers. She separated one in each color and piled them on top of Mary Rowlandson's book, which she had still not returned to the Old Man: green, *An Apology for Poetry,* Sir Philip Sydney, 1595; red, *Day of Doom; or, A Poetical Description of the Great and Last Judgment,* Reverend Michael Wigglesworth, 1662; blue, *A Narrative of the Trouble with the Indians,* William Hubbard, 1677; brown, *The Tragicall History of the Life and Death of Doctor*

Faustus, Christopher Marlowe, 1616; and black, *The Tenth Muse Lately Sprung Up in America,* Anne Bradstreet, 1650.

Another black one made her weep, the memories of her life in the convent washing over her like a cold wave. *Moriae Encomium* by Desiderius Erasmus, 1509, in Latin. She could read Latin very slowly, but it was the image on the frontispiece that made her weep. A man in the robes of a scholar sitting by an open window in a castle, bent over a book with a quill in his hand. Instead of the man she saw Madre in a long scapular and veil, the same posture, the same quill in hand, sitting by the open window of her cell, snow-topped volcanoes, Popocateptl and Ixtaccihuatl, in the distance.

At the very bottom of the trunk, she found a wooden box with a hinged, sloping lid. Under the lid, she found a red ribbon embossed with an image of a she-wolf being suckled by two children, the words *"Schola Latina Bostoniensis"* under the wolf's feet. She also found paper, seventeen sheets of vellum paper with the word "Harvard" inscribed at the top.

"Arvard," she heard herself say, tracing her finger over the gold lettering. Was that his name, she wondered, the man who had worn these clothes? She found a chunk of ink cake and two pens, a white goose quill, moth-eaten and with a frayed nub of a point, and a sturdier brown turkey quill, almost intact, its square point crusty with old ink.

She picked up the quills in one hand, brought the ink cake to her nose with the other, and inhaled that scent, that memory of writing. Hours and hours of pushing the quill over the page, penmanship exercises, calligraphy exercises, rows and rows of different-sized loops and strokes and flourishes, and her hand moving clockwise, then counterclockwise over the page. In the background she could hear Madre's voice instructing her, dictating to her while she wrote, the candlesticks fastened to the table with pools of wax.

The smell of sweet potatoes cooking in molasses and butter brought her out of it. She could hear Becca muttering angrily to the Old Man and the Old Man raising his voice at her.

"They're my chickens," the Old Man bellowed. "Even if I'm bedridden, they're still my chickens and this is still my farm. It's all I've got left, Rebecca."

"Father, you agreed to let Nathaniel and me manage the farm, remember? We're not trying to take anything away from you. Quite the contrary. That's why we got you a servant. Once we get the girl accustomed to our ways and our language, Nathaniel's going to train her to work with the chickens, and the farm is going to double its worth. You'll catch up on your arrears, and eventually we'll breed turkeys, too. It's a good business, Father. Nathaniel has invested a fortune in it already."

"That husband of yours comes from a line of thieves," the Old Man told her. "He's picking up where his father left off. It wasn't enough to rob me of my fields, my cows and goats, to take the very foundation that you and your brothers were raised on. Your husband killed my son, turned my daughter into a merchant's consort. Now he steals my chickens!"

"You had to sell your property to pay off Robin's debts, Father. Nathaniel's father was simply collecting the money you owed him for Robin's tuition. And it wasn't Nathaniel's fault that Robin took the skiff out that day. His mates told us he'd been drinking immoderately because he hadn't passed his exams and he couldn't face you. You must stop blaming Nathaniel for my brother's foolhardiness, Father."

"Begone, woman!" the Old Man hissed. "Your wits are tainted by Greenwood's lies. I know what I know."

They would be fighting until Rebecca left for the day. Concepción realized she had understood the gist of their argument, but she didn't care about their anger, and she wasn't afraid anymore. She had a mission now. This evening, after feeding and cleaning the Old Man and closing the curtains around his bed, after washing the dishes and banking the embers in the fireplace, she would sit at the table and clean and sharpen the quills. She would dissolve the ink cake in vinegar and add lampblack to reset the quality of the ink. And she would take a sheet of paper and write on it in her own tongue. She would need an inkwell and a sand caster and eventually more paper when the seventeen sheets were used up, but for now, she had everything she needed. She did not know what she would write, and it hardly mattered. Even if she just made loops on the page, she would be happy. What an odd thing, she thought, to find joy in a quill and paper. To be able to speak in her own tongue, even if only on a mute page. Mute page. Madre had used that very expression. "How lucky you are, Concepción, to have your own tutor. All I had when I was your age was an inkwell and a mute page."

Chapter 16

To you, the creature growing inside me,

I know that you're there because you kick and move, but I don't believe it. I don't believe you will really be born. It's not that I fear you will die. I hardly believe you're alive, or that you will come from within me, a tiny living being who will grow into a person with your own name and your own life. I wonder if my mother felt this way when I was in her womb?

I'm not sure if you will ever read this letter or if I should just burn it in the fireplace as soon as I'm finished, the way Madre used to burn the letters she used to write to a friend of hers who died, but I would like to tell you about my mother, your grandmother, whom you will never meet. Her name was María Clara Benavídey, and she was said to be the shrewdest tavern keeper in New Spain, a mixed-race beauty of the caste known as china poblana. She was tall, broad hipped and olive skinned, with Philippine eyes in a light brown color, and thick African hair that hung down her back in black ringlets. Always impeccably dressed in vividly embroidered huipiles, gold filigreed hoops dangling from her earlobes, beads of lapis and jade and coral adorning her neck, silver bracelets up to each elbow, she ran a clean and decent pulqueria, though she was a quick-tempered woman who once maimed a drunken soldier for pawing at me when I served his table. Of my Spanish father I know little, save that he took my mother away and his family had a coat of arms.

I come from another part of the world, a place called Mexico, many weeks' distance from this cold country of Massachusetts. I was brought here on a pirate's ship, and sold into slavery by the pirate captain who sired you. I wasn't a slave in Mexico. I was a scribe in a convent and the nun whom I assisted was a woman of great learning with a profound passion for books and letters. I wish I remembered her name, but to me, she was always Madre, though she disliked being called that as much as I dislike being called by the English name I was given, something foreign that I cannot spell or pronounce. I pray to the Virgen de Guadalupe that you will never know what it means to be captured and pillaged and bartered by pirates. To be bought with coin like a cow or a piece of furniture.

I live in a dark little house with an Old Man who has a mean temper and half a leg missing, the upper half shriveled and pocked with scars. The house is but four stone walls and a thatched roof, but it looks bigger than it is from the outside because there's a loft over the Old Man's bed, which is where I sleep now that the illness has passed and I can climb the ladder without fainting. But the living space inside is all crowded into one room. The Old Man's four-poster bed occupies nearly a full half of the space, and across from it the kitchen hearth is so large you can walk in it. In the middle of the room, there's a trestle table with a long bench on one side and a small settle on the other, a big blue-lacquered cabinet under the window, and a wheeled armchair near the hearth where the Old Man likes to sit and read and smoke his pipe all day. The floor is nothing but hard dirt covered with hay.

Outside there's a little barn with a broken door, an empty chicken coop, and a yard tapestried with chicken feathers. There are chickens everywhere! I've seen only two roosters, a blond one that struts around like a court jester and a smaller speckled one that is constantly mounting the hens. Once when I was scattering the chicken feed, a wild turkey flew into the yard, but the roosters quickly attacked it and chased it out. Not even the white cat that lives in the cellar tangles with the roosters, although once in a while I do find a dead chick on the doorstone. I scold the cat sternly and she slinks away, taking the dead offering with her.

I think I was brought here to be the Old Man's maid, though his daughter, Becca, and her slave, Seramur, do most of the cooking and the cleaning. The house sits at the corner of three dirt roads, so close to the forest I sometimes hear drumming, and I see shadows of people moving under the trees. I believe there must be Indians here, wild Indians that live in the woods, not the broken Indians of Mexico. Twice I have seen what looks like an Indian woman with long black hair standing in the road, and I imagine that she is calling me to follow her into the forest. I don't know what I'm so afraid of; it isn't like this life is something I want to hold on to, so I guess it is you I am protecting.

I have not ventured out past the gate except to the well. It must be the only well around here, because I see neighbors from one direction and the other stopping by to fill up their jugs and buckets. Some come on foot, some on wagons; others push carts like the one that sits in the barn covered in chicken droppings. If they see me sitting on the doorstone, they stare, but they don't speak, and I have taken to ignoring them when they pass. I don't know how far this place is from the sea, though I can smell the salty air on those mornings when the air is nothing but a cold, thick mist that blocks my view of the trees.

I hear bells tolling in the distance. There must be a church nearby, and I imagine they must have curfew bells here like we had in Mexico. It is time to put out the lamp. I'm nearly at the bottom of the second side of the page anyway. I should be frugal with this paper, limited as it is, and I should cut a finer point to the nib of the quill to make my writing smaller. My belly gurgles. Is it you who are hungry, or is it me? I imagine you tiny and blind as a newborn chick opening and closing your beak. There's no more food, little one. Go to sleep.

Until the next letter, receive good night wishes from . . .

> Your mother,
> Concepción Benavídez (not Danfu Sigray)

CHAPTER 17

Every Thursday after meeting, they tucked Caleb between them under lap blankets in the carriage and traveled the three miles to Roxbury to have supper with Rebecca's father. It was a ritual that Nathaniel despised more than closing his warehouse and sitting at the meetinghouse all day. The Old Man was always on his worst behavior, instigating belching contests with Caleb or smoking his pipe through the meal. The Old Goat was completely indifferent to Nathaniel's concerns about the farm and would listen only to Rebecca recount the themes of the day's lectures. Now, after the first snowfall, Nathaniel could not even go out for his walk to Goodman Thorn's place, else risk exposure to the icy winds blowing in from the bay. Nathaniel had taken to bringing his ledgers along and balancing the warehouse accounts so that he had something to do while he waited for the bloody ritual with the Old Goat to be over. The only part Nathaniel enjoyed was the ride, and even that could be miserable in the snow. Rain, snow, sleet, or shine—nothing short of a blizzard could keep Rebecca away from Roxbury on Thursdays.

"She stole your blade?" Nathaniel pulled on the reins and slowed the horses as they approached the snowbanked peninsula of the Neck that connected Boston to Roxbury and the rest of the mainland.

"She didn't actually steal it, Nathaniel. She took it. She needed it, I guess. Anyway, she didn't return it. She sees Sara Moor and me wearing knives."

"And you left her there alone with the Old . . . with your father? With a knife in her possession?"

"Are you suggesting she's going to stab my father, Nathaniel? Honestly! What an unchristian thought!"

"I don't see why not. Who's to stop her? She is part Indian, after all, and could go on a rampage at any minute, Rebecca. Have you forgotten what happened in Lancaster? She could be cutting your father's throat as we speak. For all you know, she could be terrorizing all of Roxbury by now."

"What if she scalps Grandpa?" asked Caleb, his gray eyes dark with fear.

"Oh, stop it, Caleb! Really, Nathaniel, you have no charity toward the girl. She's not a lunatic. Just because she's a foreigner doesn't mean she's going to kill everybody."

"Do you expect me to believe that you're not the least bit alarmed about this half-breed keeping a knife?"

"I bet she did scalp somebody," said Caleb.

"The only one she really hates is you, Nathaniel. I don't think any of the rest of us are in danger."

"Very funny, Rebecca. And tomorrow, when you discover your father's head floating in the well, I'll be the one laughing at you."

"Oh, Caleb, dearest, don't look so frightened. Your father's exaggerating, as always. Please, Nathaniel, stop scaring him. Anyway, she's had the knife since October. If she were going to decapitate anybody—"

"Three months? Do you mean to tell me, Mrs. Greenwood, that she's been in possession of your knife for three months? Is that why you had to purchase another one? Don't think Parris didn't tell me you were in his warehouse perusing his knives."

"Yes, Mr. Greenwood, you've found me out, and as you can see, I am deeply chagrined. Now, let's get on with your lesson, Caleb. You were reciting your catechism for us." The boy obediently sang out the new psalms he had learned in school.

"Perfect," said Rebecca. "No mistakes, this time. Now, Mr. Greenwood," she lowered her voice and spoke over the boy's head, "do you want to hear the real news?"

"Let me guess. The girl's got the dysentery again. No? Oh, I know. After six months of giving her English lessons, you've discovered that she's deaf and dumb."

"I didn't say it was necessarily bad news, Nathaniel. And your wit is starting to tire me. Do you think you can talk without making a witty remark every other word?"

"And do you think I'm trying to be witty, given what I have had to put up with since I brought that wench ashore? In half a year she's had the dysentery, the whooping cough, and the ague, she refuses to speak our language and is, therefore, completely useless to the farm, and she now has possession of your knife. Now why would I be expecting bad news, Rebecca?"

"The girl is with child, Nathaniel."

"What's that?" said Caleb.

"Good God! Are you certain?"

"Eight months into it, says Goody Simpson."

"Mama, what's that?"

"That lousy thieving buccaneer bastard! He sold me a pregnant wench, carrying a corsair's child! No wonder she looks like a sow!"

"That's probably why she's been so ill."

"Mama!"

"We're going to have a baby in the family, Caleb."

"We most certainly are not! Couldn't you tell, Rebecca? Aren't there signs of some kind, women's ways to determine this sort of thing?"

"She were on her deathbed for five months, Nathaniel. It was all I could do just to keep her alive, and since then, it weren't just English I've been teaching her. Men don't realize how much work it is to run a house, even a small house, and with having to move my father to and fro, and her learning the difference between a pullet and a cockerel, who has time to be noticing signs, Husband?"

"I don't believe you, Rebecca. It must have shown that the wench were in a family way."

"Are you calling me a liar, then, right here in front of our son?"

"I will make atonement for that; forgive me. Caleb, I did not mean to insult your mother. But I am going to put that slattern on the first ship out of port. Parris was right. She's been nothing but trouble since I signed that bill of sale. Good riddance!"

Rebecca touched his arm. "What about your fifty pounds?"

"Fifty? With Goody Simpson's bills, the extra food you're buying, all the candles she's using—I've never seen anyone go through so many candles; how much light does a body need to have?—not to mention that the poultry business is all but aborted, that bloody slave has cost me a bloody fortune."

"So why get rid of her, Husband? Why let someone else benefit from all your expense? She's fully healed now. She understands almost everything I say, even if she is still a bit shy about speaking. She's got an excellent ear for dictation, accomplished calligraphy, and her needlepoint, Nathaniel, her needlepoint is unbelievably beautiful, perhaps even more beautiful than her writing. Besides, the babe could be useful. Eventually, I mean."

Finally, Nathaniel saw the equation in his mind. "It's the babe you want, isn't it, Rebecca? You don't really care about the wench."

"I wouldn't mind a babe in the family, of course, but you're wrong; I do care about the girl. I've grown fond of that curious face of hers. She's quite smart, you know."

"Is she smart enough to know what's going on?"

"Hard not to know when you have someone kicking inside you, and that little one has a strong pair of legs, truth be told. The poor girl nearly leapt out of her skin the first time it happened."

"Strong pair of legs, eh?"

"Quite strong. Goody Simpson said feed her plenty of cornmeal and cheese to develop the bones, and good hot chowder and lots of bread—"

"I meant, Rebecca, is the girl smart enough to know what you're doing?"

Rebecca dug her nails into his sleeve. "Maybe it'll help me, Nathaniel. Having a babe nearby might awaken my womb again. Caleb needs brothers and sisters, don't you, dear? It's been nearly seven years."

"I don't want brothers and sisters, Mama."

"And if it doesn't help you conceive, Rebecca, if all it does is make you sour and angry and envious, what will you do then? Or were you simply planning to keep the girl's babe?"

Rebecca turned her face and stared out at the fog coming in over the river.

"That's it, isn't it, Rebecca? You know you'll not conceive again."

"The wench belongs to us, doesn't she?" said Rebecca in a low voice, her face still turned away from him. "The babe is ours anyway!"

Chapter 18

End of the year?

Little Heart,

I felt your heart beating in my navel late last night. I was dreaming about being back in the convent, taking dictation at my little desk with Madre standing behind me as she usually did, but she was angry with me because I had stained my blouse with ink. I knew in the dream that it was the satire about stubborn men and their hypocritical views of women that she was dictating, the poem I was copying the night Aléndula and I escaped from San Jerónimo, but for some reason I kept making mistakes and crossing out the lines, and she was getting more and more annoyed with me about the waste of ink and paper. Then the dream changed and we were no longer in Madre's study, but in the locutory where she was entertaining a group of guests by reciting the poem backward:

"Culpáis que mismo lo de
Ocasión la sois que ver sin
Razón sin mujer la a
Acusáis que necios hombres."

"You're such a clown, Juana," a woman called out, laughing.

That's when I felt your heartbeat strong in my belly and I awoke with the memory of her name. Juana. Sor Juana, not Madre Juana.

Sister, not Mother, Juana. Such a simple name.
How could I have forgotten it?

It's gotten much colder now, and in the
mornings there's a crust of ice on the water in
the chicken trough. When I open the window to
air out the smoke and let some watery light into
the house, the Old Man's jaw and knees start to
quiver and he yells at me to keep the shutters
closed. I left the door ajar the other day while
I went to the well, and when I returned the
whole cottage was full of chickens, leaving their
muck all over the floor. One of the hens was even
trying to lay an egg on the Old Man's pillow. I
thought he would strike me with his cane for
that, but he laughed so hard he wet the bed.

The only beauty that I find in this bleak
place is the way the leaves change on the trees,
as the climate gets colder. I have never seen
leaves turn crimson or coral or gold mottled with
violet. The leaves on the apple tree changed from
green to pink overnight, and the ivy growing on
the crude fence around the cottage has turned
dark purple. Strangely, the rangy bush by the
well is in full bloom. The flowers opened bright
yellow, like sunflowers, but the petals look more
like tufts of yarn sprouting from a reddish-brown
shell. I think it is a nut-bearing bush, because
there's a thick layer of shells all around the
well.

Nobody seems to take much notice of the
leaves, and so I imagine it is common for them
to change and for the yarn-tree to flower in the
cold. I have gathered a variety of leaves, placing
them between the pages of the Erasmus book to
keep them bright and flat, so that I can copy
them into an embroidery I want to make for you,
a pattern of five kinds of leaves with a border of

blue-spotted butterflies like those I've seen in the
woods. Since I have no cloth, I will use one of
the pillowcases and stuff it with chicken feathers; it will make a nice warm blanket for you.
I found a sewing basket in the cabinet, well
stocked with scissors, needles, buttons, thimbles,
spools of every color of thread, and a pincushion
in the shape of a heart. I wonder if it belonged
to the Old Man's wife? Becca brings her own
sewing basket when she visits, so I have taken
this one for myself.

I let the cat, Pecas, into the house when
the Old Man goes to sleep. She keeps me company
while I make the Old Man's apple compote for
the morning, while I peel and pare the apples,
grind the cinnamon, rub the slices with butter,
and set them to boil in a mixture of water, molasses, and salt. She's so stunning with that
mask of black and brown freckles. She follows me
around, rubbing against my petticoats, blinking
her green eyes at me, and wanting me to feed
her. After she eats whatever scrap I give her, a
rind of cheese or the dried crust of a pie, she
likes to curl up by the hearth and sleep. She
does not like for me to pick her up in my arms,
but when I am sitting on the settle trying to
read the Old Man's Almanac she climbs into my
lap and stares up at me. You have probably felt
her purring on my belly. That's when I like to
sing my mother's song about the lost apple—
"Señora Santa Ana, ¿porqué llora la niña? Por
una manyana, que se le ha perdido"—for I
imagine that between the purring and the
singing and the smell of the apples stewing in
the hearth, you are lulled into peaceful dreams.

The logs in the hearth are turning to cinders
now and I feel suddenly very chilled. The Old

Man is moaning in his sleep. I pray that he doesn't waken. I am too tired to lift him out of bed and sit him on his chamber pot. I must let the cat out quickly, in case he does awaken and yells to high heaven about the creature being inside. Good night, little heart. I think you stirred at the name Juana in my dream because you are going to be my Juana in this life. Perhaps you will be as intelligent as Madre and as headstrong as my mother. I pray you're a girl.

CHAPTER 19

The day Concepción had met her father for the first time was the same day her mother had nearly chopped off a soldier's hand in the *pulquería,* the tavern she used to run in Mexico where night and day she served a fermented cactus juice to men of every caste, from muleteers and soldiers to students and priests. Seeing the soldier pawing at her daughter, María Clara Benavídez was not one to mince words. She simply grabbed her machete from behind the bar and threatened to turn him into a gelding if he didn't get his sorry excuse for a prick out of her tavern immediately. To prove she was serious she swung the machete and brought it down on his hand, chopping off the first digit of his little finger. Too stunned to retaliate, the man wailed in pain, blood spurting from the severed finger like a little red fountain. The tavern cleared out in a hurry, all the drunks milling out into the street and María Clara yelling at their backs: "Bestias humanas! Degenerados! Hijos de puta!" She called them every foul name she could think of: degenerate human beasts and sons of bitches.

She ordered Concepción to slide the post over the door and close the shutters while she washed the slime off the floors.

"It's my fault, *cariño,*" she kept saying in a trembly voice, "for bringing you up in this squalor. You're part *criolla;* you deserve a better life than this."

It wasn't long before they heard horses outside and a man's voice demanding that they open the door in the name of King Philip. María Clara obeyed, and a tall, very thin man with blond hair and a brocade coat stepped into the gloom of the tavern. He was so beautiful, he seemed almost godlike to Concepción.

"What's going on here, María Clara?" the man asked. "It has been reported to me that you crippled and nearly castrated a soldier—"

"Lies!" she interrupted. "Does a man's finger equal his prick?"

"Such a foul mouth, woman! Why have you closed the *pulquería*? What is the meaning of this insolence? I have not given you permission to close early."

"Would you rather have those beasts who come here think they can do whatever they please with your own daughter?"

Concepción did not know until that moment that this was her father, Don Federico de Alcalá. Overcome with embarrassment, she hid behind her mother.

"That is your own affair, María Clara. The only daughters who concern me are not the bastards of a *china poblana.* This is a place of business, not a nursery."

"Concepción?" her mother said. "Be respectful. Kiss your father's hand."

"I shall have no daughter of a whore soiling my hand, thank you," said Don Federico.

Concepción felt her blood boil at his words. "My mother is not a whore, Señor. Maybe you are referring to your own person?"

Don Federico raised his hand to slap her, but María Clara stepped between them, clutching her machete.

"Go ahead," she taunted him. "Dare to strike her and you'll lose a lot more than your finger."

The man's face colored and he backed down. "Do you see the kind of manners you have bred in this whelp after all the money I've paid for her education at the orphanage, as you requested?" he said.

"What do you expect if she grows up in a *pulquería* surrounded by drunks and lechers?"

"Where else do you want her to grow up? You're not suggesting I take her home with me, I hope?"

"And turn her into your wife's kitchen maid? I don't think so. Come, Concepción. Tell your darling father what you want to do."

"My mother thinks I should work in a nunnery, Sir, where I can make good use of my needlepoint skills. I can embroider. I can make lace."

"Mestizas do not embroider in convents," he said. "That is the work of the novices, the *criollas,* the nuns. Mestizas scrub floors and slop chamber pots."

"Isn't your widowed mother a prioress at one of the convents, Federico?"

"That doesn't mean she can alter the natural order of things, María Clara. A *criolla* is a *criolla;* a mestiza is a mestiza. Everyone has her place."

"*Hija,* bring the sampler of your work to show your father," her mother nudged. Concepción ran behind the bar, took her sampler from its lacquered box, and ceremoniously presented it to Don Federico. He unfurled the cloth and stepped out onto the narrow sidewalk where he could examine the needlework in the light.

"It's quality work," he said, reentering the tavern and returning the sampler.

"But what's wrong with the orphanage, María Clara? She can ply her skill there, can't she? Indeed, she could apprentice herself to any tailor in the city. I would pay for that."

"She can't board at the orphanage," María Clara reminded him, "and I certainly wouldn't trust her in the hands of any tailor. She'll be safe in a nunnery. She's your bastard, Federico, and if you won't place her in that convent, Señor, I won't run your tavern anymore."

"What nonsense are you spouting, woman? You owe me your life."

"I owe you nothing. Bring your lady wife to run the tavern, why don't you? Or find another *china poblana* you can defile. Better still, run it yourself! Spend your days and nights inhaling the vile odors of that slime they love to swallow. Walk in the urine that runs underfoot, staining your shoes." She drew a large key ring out of her apron pocket. "Here are the keys to your tavern, Don Federico. Concepción? We're leaving!"

"Who do you think you are!" said Don Federico, grasping her mother's arm and yanking her back to face him. He stared at her for a moment, and Concepción could read, even in that penumbra, his need for her as clear as his jade-colored eyes.

María Clara had always said that she was the only woman Don Federico truly loved, that he would do anything for her as long as she let him believe she would never leave him. "He detests that imbecile he's married to," María Clara had told Concepción once, "but he's an hidalgo; he's not going to leave his pure little *criolla* for a mixed-race *china poblana,* no matter how much he loves me."

"The only possible thing I can do," Don Federico decided, glancing at Concepción, "is indenture her services to the nunnery. Are you willing to do that, María Clara? To indenture your daughter's life? The minimum period of service is fifteen years. Can you live with your daughter being holed up in that convent for fifteen years?"

"If it spares her innocence, if it saves her from this pigsty and gives her a better life, I can live with it."

"I don't want to live in a convent," Concepción interjected. Nobody was asking her what she wanted.

"Don't be ridiculous," her mother scolded. "You're part *criolla.* You deserve more than I can give you. We'll accept your father's offer as long as he promises that you won't be scouring chamber pots in the convent."

"I can promise no such thing, María Clara!"

"And I cannot promise to be faithful to you, either."

CHAPTER 20

Epifania
Little chick,

According to the Old Man's Almanac, it's the sixth of January, and today is a feast day in New Spain, called Epiphany, the feast of the Three Kings. On Epiphany in New Spain, mothers give three gifts to their children, in honor of the gifts of the three wise men to the baby Jesus. Since I have nothing but promises to give you, here are my three gifts to you:

1. In the place of myrrh, I promise to learn this English better.
2. In the place of frankincense, I will school you in the skills of the scribe and teach you to write in Spanish.
3. In the place of gold, I will make you a tiny scapular and teach you about my faith in la Virgen de Guadalupe.

But this is not a Catholic country and none of the Catholic feast days or saints' days are celebrated here. There are no posadas at Christmas, no gifts for Epiphany, probably no Ash Wednesday or Good Friday or Corpus Christi or day of the Immaculate Conception, my namesake. The pirate told me that in this country Catholics are hated. They have many names for us here. They sound like "papistas" and "popiches," in reference to the Pope, I think, and "romiches," having to do with the Romans, as in "Roman Catholics," I imagine. So many different ways to name what they hate.

It occurs to me that you will grow up hearing these words and hating Catholics as much as the English do. The thought of it fills me with fury! I will have to observe these feast days on my own for now, and then you and I will celebrate them together, in secret.

Becca has taken a liking to the leaves I embroidered on the baby blanket and has asked me to embroider something on her neck cloth. Instead of the leaves, I think I will copy the yellow flowers I took from the tree by the well. I asked Rebecca the name of the tree, and she called it something I have never heard. When I asked her to write it for me in the Almanac, she wrote: Witch Hazel. I tried to copy her pronunciation of the words, pouting my lips for the first word and smiling broadly for the second, and ended up making her laugh. I have run out of yellow thread, though, and had to borrow some from Becca's needlepoint basket.

After the first snowfall, I expected the bush to lose all its foliage, but it's still in bloom. I love looking out at that splash of yellow across the road. That and the perpetual green of the forest are the only colors I see outdoors these days. All the other trees stand naked and rimmed with frost.

Why do you kick so much? My ribs ache from your kicking, and there's something hard as horn pressing against the bottom of my back. I can barely move now that you've gotten so heavy. When will you come out? I'm tired of carrying you, tired of being kicked and stretched to accommodate your stubborn, growing bones. You don't feel like a little chick anymore, but like a heavy stone lodged against my tailbone.

Becca, or "Mistress Rebecca," as she now wants me to call her, keeps smiling at me, wants to rub my belly all the time. She actually speaks to you in a gibberish I don't bother to understand. Her son, Caleb, eyes you, or rather my belly, since you're not here yet, jealously. I have taken to helping him with his letters since his handwriting is worse than a three-year-old's. He pretends not to like it when I sit next to him and place my hand over his to help him with his penmanship loops, but occasionally I catch him sneaking glances at me, and then he blushes and throws himself against me, giggling. As soon as he feels you kicking, he jumps up and runs to his grandfather. He is a sweet child and will be a friend to you, I hope.

I'm beginning to worry about your sex and your name. I remember Jane telling me that when a pregnant woman has a round belly, it means the baby will be a girl, and a long belly means a boy. My belly is round and thick as one of those pumpkins Rebecca has baking in the oven to make pies. I know you must be a girl (at least I pray to la Virgen that you are), and that I'm going to name you Juana, but I've been wondering about a middle name: Juana Concepción, Juana Aléndula, Juana María ("Juana Clara" sounds silly), but I think I've decided to give you a name that is yours alone, but also a name that is connected to my life in Mexico, and so I've decided to call you Juana Jerónima. And if you turn out male, I'll name you Federico after my father, only because I had a father and at least I knew his name.

Becca has given me her son's baby gowns and caps, and I'm embroidering them with tiny poinsettias and sunflowers and calla lilies—flowers that I remember from the convent. Strange how some memories can be so exact and yet I cannot remember being brought to this cottage from the pirate's ship, or when it was that I first started to love you.

Now I've made myself cold again. It doesn't help much to rub my hands together to stir the blood back into my fingers. Despite the breeches and the flannel nightshirt I wear under this waistcoat and gown and the two extra pairs of stockings, the cold still bites right through my skin, like the fangs of the wolf I see sometimes sniffing around the snowy barnyard at twilight.

The snow is another beautiful thing about this country, even though the cold it brings can freeze a chicken solid. We did have winter in Mexico, but it was not a comparable cold. Bellowing the coals in the brazier could dispel that cold. This is ice in the well and frost on the eyelashes and toes that grow blue and stiff between the cottage and the outhouse. This is the kind of cold that chafes your face like a razor and makes your ears fall off if they're not covered. And the silence. I never knew such silence was possible, where the loudest thing you hear all day, other than an Old Man's snoring and farting, is the constant clucking of the cooped-up chickens. There you go again! It hurts so much and the pain makes me so tired. I just want to burrow into the feather bed and sleep for days. Buenas noches and happy Epiphany.

Your mother,
Concepción

CHAPTER 21

She awoke, sweating and startled, unable at first to place where she was.
She could hear people talking down below. Irritated voices speaking a foreign tongue. I know those voices, she thought, recognizing the language, and then she realized where she was, and the vestiges of the dream evaporated.

"I'm the only foreigner here," she muttered. She hauled herself out of the tangled blankets on the feather bed and rolled to her knees, feeling the child kicking again in her womb, harder than ever, wanting to be freed, to be fed. She needed the chamber pot badly; the pressure in her bladder was excruciating. Despite the pain, her mouth watered at the smell of something baking. It must be Thursday, she remembered, when Rebecca and her family came to supper with the Old Man. Her eyes adjusted to the shadows, and she saw that the loft ladder had been lowered, though she could not recall climbing the ladder today. Had she been ill again? What had she been doing other than spinning melancholic dreams? She saw the writing box lying open beside the mattress, all the written pages scattered over the boards. She had no more paper left, and the dregs of the ink cake smeared the sides and bottom of the porringer.

"Thankful Seagraves?" called Rebecca from the hearth. "Are you awake? You need to come down here and help me with supper."

"Come down this minute, Thankful Seagraves. We have a chicken farm to discuss." It was Ruffled Collar's voice, and as usual he sounded angry.

"I hear you!" she called down, gripping both sides of the huge watermelon that her belly had become, squeezing her thighs tight as the kicking resumed and a trickle of water escaped down her leg. Stand still, she told herself. Stand very still and wait for the pain to pass. Instead of passing, the pain extended the length of her spine, coiling tightly at the nape of her neck and shooting back down to the small of her back. She closed her eyes and imagined the child tearing at her from the inside, pushing its hard little heels against her rib cage and forcing her womb to open. Her knees wobbled, and she felt as though she were going to fall from the loft.

"Mistress, help me!" she cried out.

"What is it, girl? Is it the babe? Nathaniel, the babe is coming! Get up there! We have to get her home, quickly."

"Home? Are you saying we're taking her to Boston? Have you lost your mind?"

"I can't care for her here, Nathaniel. Hurry!"

"She better not give birth in the carriage, Rebecca."

"It'll be your fault for dillydallying if she does. Hold on, Thankful Seagraves. Hold on!"

But Concepción couldn't hold it anymore, and the water gushed down her legs with the force of a cascade.

CHAPTER 22

¿Aléndula? ¿Eres tu? Is it really you? Don't go. Don't leave me again, Aléndula."

"What is that name she keeps saying? Ellen Dula? Is that it?"

"I don't know, Mistress. She been callin' me that since she came to. And she won't let go of my hand. Look at how she squeezes it!"

"For goodness' sake, Sara Moor. You can't just sit here all afternoon holding hands with her. You haven't even started dinner."

"I'm telling you, Mistress, every time I try to get up she grabs on to my arm and won't let go. Look, I'll show you."

"¡Por favor, Aléndula! Don't go! Stay with me!"

"See what I mean? She's under a spell or something."

"Well, we've got to break her out of it. The babe needs to be fed, poor soul, don't you, little one? Hasn't eaten right for two days, poor crippled little girl."

"Put the child down, Mistress. Maybe if she felt the babe, she'd let go of me. That child be fussing loud enough to wake the dead, she's so hungry."

"Maybe you're right. Here, Sara, lay her down. Careful. You don't want to smother her. That's it."

"Mistress, look! She's passed out again, and the babe wants to suckle."

"Open the gown, then, Sara Moor; don't just stand there. Hurry up and unlace it, girl!"

"She can't suckle no babe if she's in a trance, Mistress."

"She's not in a trance, you fool; she's simply weak from the strain of the birth. This is absurd. Run down and fetch the smelling salts out of the livery cupboard, Sara Moor. The child needs her nourishment."

Rebecca could not resist picking up the newborn again, so tiny and soft, so beautiful she was except for that poor little crippled foot. Goody Simpson said the foot had probably gotten lodged in the mother's rib cage because of the fevers and had failed to develop properly, growing thin and curved as a toy scythe with five perfect little toes at the end of it. She unwrapped the little foot and kissed it. Startled by the cold touch of her hands, the tiny toes splayed and the babe began howling again.

"There, there," crooned Rebecca, nestling the babe's face against her breast. If only I had milk to give you, little angel, she said silently, I could be your wet nurse, and maybe you could stir the life back into my womb. The child gnawed at the wool of Rebecca's gown. What harm could it do, anyway, to give her breast to the child and calm her? Quickly Rebecca unlaced her bodice and her white breast spilled out for the child to take. The tiny lips fastened around Rebecca's pale teat and pulled hard.

"Gentle, gentle, little girl; I've not done this in a few years." But the child paid no heed. Her little face reddened, and her fists shook from the exertion of drawing out the milk that wasn't there. The pain of it drew tears to Rebecca's eyes, but it was a sweet pain, and she blinked fast until her vision cleared. Sara Moor scurried back into the room swinging the bag of smelling salts.

"Mistress! Are you trying to suckle that child?"

"Mind your business. Open the bag and place it right under her nose. Not that close! You don't want her to inhale too much of the stuff! She'll faint again."

"It's working, Mistress; she's coming to. Thankful Seagraves? Wake up, now. Got to feed your baby. Wake up."

"Slap her a bit, Sara; see if that helps. Ow!" The babe's gums felt suddenly sharp as razors. Rebecca pulled the little mouth away from her breast just as the girl opened her eyes and focused on her swaddled child in Rebecca's arms.

"It's a girl, Thankful Seagraves," said Rebecca, keeping the babe close to her breast. "You've a beautiful little daughter."

"Juana Jerónima," she said, holding out her arms to take the child from Rebecca, but Rebecca held on.

"This is what you have to do, Thankful," she said, tucking the babe against her belly again and grasping her breast with her free hand to guide the nipple into the waiting little mouth. "See how hungry she is? But you've got to hold your breast up like this so you won't suffocate her."

Concepción raised herself on an elbow, eyes blazing suddenly, and pulled at the blanket. "My!" she said.

"Give her the child, Mistress!"

"Shut your mouth, Sara Moor. I'm just showing her what to do." Rebecca felt her face coloring. Embarrassed by her exposed bosom, she thrust the baby at Thankful Seagraves. "Here, then! Take the brat! What do I care if you smother her?" She laced up her bodice quickly and tightened the shawl around her shoulders, mumbling, "Ingrate! Here I went and brought you to my house to make sure you were comfortable, and this is how you thank me."

Concepción was not listening to her. She was staring down at that little face, tracing the pale outline of the eyebrows, the wet eyelashes, the tiny flared nostrils, and the heart-shaped lips. "Juana Jerónima," she whispered to the child, who had gone completely quiet and stared back at her, as if she recognized her voice.

"That doesn't sound like an English name, Thankful Seagraves," said Rebecca.

"She not English, she mine," said Concepción.

"If she's born in an English colony, she's English. Doesn't matter what you are, you know. She's one of us."

"One of you?"

"Yes, she's English, like us."

"Tell her about the foot, Mistress," said Sara Moor on the other side of the bed.

Concepción turned and looked at Sara Moor, her eyes widening for a moment. Aléndula, she almost said, but realized it was just the color of Sara's skin that resembled Aléndula's.

"Don't be looking at me that way; I'm no friend of yours," snapped Sara Moor. "Best be lookin' at your babe's foot."

Concepción glanced anxiously at Rebecca, and Rebecca nodded. "She won't be able to walk, I'm afraid. Her left foot's damaged."

Concepción sat up in the bed, wincing from the pain between her legs. "Damage?"

"Hurt," said Rebecca, demonstrating with her hand how the little foot curved inward.

Concepción undid the swaddling and quickly inspected her daughter's body before removing the knitted boots. "Holy Virgin!" she exclaimed in Spanish, holding the bad foot with two fingers. "You've got a crooked foot. What happened to you, *bebita*?"

"Now listen here, Thankful Seagraves, I don't know what you're saying, but that sounds like the Romish tongue to me. You know you can't speak that profane language around here. You have to learn how to speak like a Christian woman."

"Spanish language, Mistress. Not profane."

"It's a heathen language, I tell you, and that child is not going to grow up speaking impiously among the chosen children of God."

"What 'heathen' means, Mistress?"

"Never mind that now. Cover her up; don't you see how blue she's getting from the cold."

Rebecca tried to fit the socks back on the child, but Concepción pushed her hand aside. "'Way!" she said. "I look hurt foot." She inspected the joints of each toe, the firm little anklebone, the tiny half-formed heel that curved into a slender, useless flap. But the toes were good and so was the ankle. All she needed was a cast to shape the foot. The bones were soft enough yet and could still be molded. "I fix it with starch," she said, but the babe had waited long enough for her mother's milk and began wailing again.

"Feed her, first, Thankful Seagraves. And don't get your hopes up. The midwife, Goody Simpson, doesn't think we can do anything for her."

The child wriggled and pulled at the dark brown teat, but nothing happened.

"Looks like she's having some trouble pulling the milk," said Rebecca. "Are you cold, Thankful Seagraves?" She felt the girl's face with the back of her hand and found it icy. "Sara, there's a warming pan under my bed. Go fill it with coals and bring it here. She needs the heat to get her milk flowing."

"I ain't getting no warming pan ready for no Romish, Mistress!"

"You're to go straight down and do as I say, and don't you dare be impudent with me again!" Rebecca boxed Sara Moor's ears to remind her of her place.

The infant took a deep breath and started wailing again, so hard her face turned a dark pink and her little body shook with ire.

Thankful Seagraves rocked the child and started to sing in her Romish tongue. The child opened her teary eyes and quieted, staring up at her mother. Rebecca left the room. She could not bear to hear that heathen tongue, but she would allow it this one time. Somehow the song soothed the child, and it was best for her not to vex her baby heart so much so soon after her birth.

CHAPTER 23

"Señora Santa Ana, why does your baby cry? Because of an apple that she's lost."

Concepción sang the sad ballad softly, gazing at her daughter in amazement: the little hands, so white they looked pale blue against Concepción's brown breast, the long blond eyelashes and tiny tufts of blond fuzz on the baby's earlobes that matched the color of her thin hair. Concepción's own hair was black, like her mother's, but her father's, Don Federico de Alcalá's, hair, she remembered, had been the color of corn silk, and the pirate's had looked almost white against his dark skin. She wet a corner of the bedsheet with her saliva and cleaned the dried crust off the baby's cheeks and chin. Ran her fingers lightly over the perfect little half shells of the baby's ears. Gently tapped the tip of the baby's nose and the tiny peak of her heart-shaped lips. Juana Jerónima, mi hija, she thought.

"Por favor, Virgencita," she whispered a prayer to the Virgin of Guadalupe, "protector of the humble and Empress of Heaven, help me make her foot right; don't let her be a cripple. And please, Holy Mother, don't let her have eyes like mine. Let her eyes be normal. I don't care what color they are as long as they're the same. Grant me these wishes, Santisima, and I promise to make a scapular with your image embroidered on both sides, and to wear it under my clothes every day of my life. I promise to pay homage to you with food and flowers on your feast day and to bring up my daughter to serve you as I do."

As if she had heard, the child opened the opaque seeds of her eyes and looked at Concepciòn. It was difficult to know this early what the color would be, but she was certain that la Virgen had heard her plea, and she made the triple sign of the cross over herself and then over the child's forehead, mouth, and heart.

Cuddling the baby, Concepción leaned back against the pillows. The child turned toward her mother's breast and fed at last. "I'll make you well, Juana Jerónima," Concepción whispered, "and I'll teach you to speak Spanish, and nobody but you and I will know what we're saying." The child stopped suckling for an instant, listening, then continued, pulling hard, her little eyes sliding back and forth under the pale blue lids.

Concepción noticed for the first time that she was not in the Old Man's dark, smelly cottage but in a tiny bedroom with a sloping roof and an arched window fitted with real glass. At the foot of the narrow bed stood a small chest draped with a sheepskin and to the side a washstand and a small green-lacquered desk pushed up under the window. A leather-bound Primer and a child's slate tablet with the alphabet inscribed atop were on the desk. This must be Caleb's room, she thought, feeling a pinch of envy followed by gratitude toward Rebecca for having taken her from that pigpen of the Old Man's.

She could smell something cooking and allowed herself to imagine that she was back in the convent, helping Sor Juana in her study upstairs while Jane filled the downstairs with the delicious scents of her cooking. On a cold day like today, it would be tamales filled with pork and red chile, served with black beans and squash stew, and hot cornmeal *champurrado* to drink.

Another song came to her while the baby fed: "Sancta María, grátia plena." A song of gratitude for the Virgin's blessing. In Latin.

Concepción held the child under her breast and wept. Even in the midst of all of this strangeness, she felt overwhelmed with a happiness she had never known.

CHAPTER 24

Y ou can't call her by that papist name and that's final," said Rebecca, watching as the child took her mother's milk in deep, thirsty swallows.

"Her name Juana Jerónima. That her name, Mistress."

"The minister will not christen her unless she has an English name, a Christian name. This is our custom, Thankful Seagraves. You have to change her name to fit our custom, just as my husband changed your name. You want her christened, don't you?"

"I hate 'Thankful Seagraves.'"

"Well, you shouldn't hate it; it's a fine name. Now we can make the name you want an English name or we can choose a new one for her. What do you want?"

"I want 'Juana Jerónima Benavídez.'"

"That's too many names, Thankful Seagraves. Just two names." She held up two fingers. "Thankful Seagraves. Rebecca Greenwood. See? Two names."

"Juana."

"Hanna."

"Jerónima."

"Hu— What? Say that again."

"Jerónima."

Rebecca took the tablet off Caleb's desk and handed it to Thankful Seagraves. "I don't understand you, so I can't think of an English equivalent. Write it out so that I can see what it looks like."

The girl stared at the slate, picked up the chalk dangling from the short length of rope fitted to the frame, wiped the slate with her other hand.

"Go on, then, Thankful Seagraves," said Rebecca. "Your master purchased you because you could write, so let's see it. Write out the name you just said."

"Write?"

"Like this," said Rebecca, yanking the chalk from the girl's hand. Rebecca printed her name in capital letters across the top of the slate. Then, pointing to each letter, she said aloud, "*R-e-b-e-c-c-a*. Rebecca." She tapped her chest. "My name is Rebecca."

The girl nodded and took the chalk. *C-O-N-C-E-P-C-I-O-N,* she wrote under *REBECCA.* "My name is Concepción," she said.

"No, no, no!" Rebecca scolded her. She pointed to the baby. "The baby's name. Write the baby's name."

"Ah," said the girl, nodding in comprehension. "Yes, yes. I know." She wrote out *J-U-A-N-A J-E-R-O-N-I-M-A.*

"Jerónima?" said Rebecca. "That sounds like a slave's name. You don't want such a beautiful baby to have a slave's name, do you?"

"What is slave?"

"Slave, you know," said Rebecca, feeling her ears grow warm. "Like you. Like Sara Moor." She crossed her arms at the wrists and pretended they were shackled together. "Slaves."

The girl frowned, and Rebecca could not tell whether she had gotten her meaning or not. "Never mind," Rebecca said. "Here. I have an idea." She took the tablet and wrote out the girl's English name underneath the Popish one.

J-U-A-N-A J-E-R-O-N-I-M-A
H-A-N-N-A J-E-R-E-M-I-A-H

"There. That's a Christian name. See?"

She handed the tablet back to Thankful Seagraves. The girl traced the outline of the letters with her index finger, silently mouthing out the name.

"Hanna Jeremiah," said Rebecca. "It's a beautiful English name. Just beautiful."

She took the tablet out of Concepción's hands, pretending not to notice the tears that had suddenly welled up in the girl's eerie two-colored eyes.

"Reverend Mather's going to be very pleased."

"Benavídez."

"Sorry," said Rebecca, "no more names. Just Hanna Jeremiah."

"Jerónima," said the girl behind her. "I call her Jerónima."

"Call her whatever you wish, then," said Rebecca, tired of dealing with the stubborn creature. "But she will be christened with a good Christian name, and it would be best not to confuse the child and make her think she's somebody else. And you, by the way, are never to refer to yourself by that other name. Your name is Thankful Seagraves, and that's final." She scribbled *T-H-A-N-K-F-U-L S-E-A-G-R-A-V-E-S* at the bottom of the slate.

Concepción spit at the slate and wiped the name off.

CHAPTER 25

If she ain't fussin' with the baby all day, she be playin' with that needle and thread, Mistress," said Sara Moor. "But she ain't mendin'; she be making pretty thread pictures on the baby's clothes. She ain't helpin' me at all."

"It's called embroidery, Sara Moor," said Rebecca, testing the bathwater with her elbow before slipping the baby into the tub, "and very fine embroidery, at that, with all manner of intricate stitches I've never seen before, though I hate to wonder where she might have learned that skill."

"What you mean, Mistress?"

"A nunnery, I would venture," said Rebecca.

"Ain't that a place for trollops, Mistress?"

"Well, that's what we call it, Sara Moor, but it's actually a place where women live together as wives of Christ or some such blasphemy. They still have them in Ireland, and of course all of Spain and France are papist countries, full of nunneries. Young girls are left there—many against their will, mind you—to take vows and live in a cloister for the rest of their lives. It's the nunneries that make the most expensive lace and, judging from this one's embroidery, the finest needlework, too. That and the Spanish dollar are all the good that comes from the papists, I'm afraid."

"If she be papist, Mistress, and papist be evil, then anything she make with papist hands be evil, right, Mistress? Beautiful or not, that baby blanket she be embroiderin' be wicked."

"Hush your mouth. That's precisely the kind of talk that can get a body into trouble with the ministers. Didn't you see that new book of Reverend Mather's that everyone's talking about, Sara Moor?"

"You know I can't read, Mistress."

"Increase Mather believes we lost our charter because of some supernatural powers that have taken hold of the Bay Colony. He's blaming all our travails, including our Indian wars, on supernatural powers, of all things! Coming from the pen of a minister as influential as Increase Mather, you can be sure everybody's going to be fretting about uncanny things. So you keep your mouth shut about this girl being evil, Sara Moor, or I'll be visiting you with my switch. She's not evil; she's just foreign. That's why we have to teach her to speak correctly posthaste."

"She can't cipher a word I say," grumbled Sara Moor.

"She can cipher well enough," said Rebecca. "She's just being stubborn. Giving birth can turn a woman into a mule. I just wish I could make her understand how important it is that she stop speaking that heathen tongue of hers and speak only English. How do we get that through to her, Sara Moor?"

Sara Moor shrugged. "Beat her, I suppose, Mistress. Every time she says something Romish, give her a good flogging. That'll teach her. You beat me whenever I do something wrong."

"How can I beat her with a babe at her breast? Christ's wounds, Sara Moor, that's a beastly idea. We need help. There's got to be somebody in the Bay Colony who can speak her language. What do you know of this maid of Merchant Parris's? Nathaniel mentioned her to me some months ago."

"She be from the West Indies is what I heard, Mistress."

"But what is she? Indian? African? Do you know her, Sara? Is she civilized? She's not going to take our scalps off, is she?"

"I know she goes to the meetinghouse on Sundays."

"Nathaniel did say she'd been catechized. Being from that part of the world, there's a chance she might be able to decipher Thankful Seagraves. I hear there's all manner of papists in the West Indies. I suppose I should at least try her out."

"I can fetch her if you want."

"What are you waiting for? Fetch her at once! Tell Mistress Parris I would have come myself, but there's this babe that needs tending to. Take one of those pies for her."

"Mistress Parris has a babe, too, Mistress. Sickly thing. Both of them."

"What a gossip you are, Sara Moor. I certainly hope you're not sharing information about what goes on in my house with any of your acquaintances."

"Not a word, Mistress. What would I be sayin'?" Sara Moor was bundling herself up in an old cloak of Rebecca's.

"Take care not to let Nathaniel see you in town."

"Didn't you say it was his idea, Mistress?"

"Stop asking me so many questions and just go on and do as I say."

"What shall I tell Goody Parris, then?"

"Tell her Mrs. Greenwood has need of her maid for a few hours. We need to see if she can help us make Thankful Seagraves understand what we're saying."

"The Parrises live all the way over to Copp's Hill, Mistress. Take me a long time to walk there with all the slush in the streets."

"Well, then, you'll have to use the shank's mare, won't you? And no dilly-dallying with your friends at the inn, Sara Moor. I want you back before Nathaniel and Caleb come home for dinner."

When Sara Moor had gone, Rebecca rolled up her sleeves and bent over the cradle. "Now then," she said, scooping the child out of her swaddling. "It's time for your first bath. Can't go to your christening on Sunday smelling as you do now."

The child stared into her eyes and squealed in her hands. Rebecca expected her to cry when she felt the water, but instead she paddled her tiny feet and splashed the water with her hands, her eyes dancing in the firelight.

"You like that, don't you?" said Rebecca, rubbing the bar of greasy soap over the child's delicate skin. Caleb, she remembered, had never liked baths, always burst out into offended cries the instant his foot felt water. She kept her hands firmly around the thin little body—so sweet and soft and slippery with the soap—and washed her quickly. Luckily, the babe's eyes got sleepy before the water lost its warmth. Rebecca scooped her out and dried her quickly in front of the fire and bundled her up, first in her swaddling, then in her baby gown and bonnet, and finally in the soft fleece blanket that had belonged to Caleb. Soon it would be time to take her up to Caleb's closet and tuck her into bed with Thankful Seagraves for nursing, but for now, Rebecca held the child to her bosom, clean and warm and smelling of sweet baby skin. The child fell fast asleep.

"If only I had milk to give you, little Hanna," she whispered to the child, but that was the one thing Rebecca couldn't do for her, much as she tried when no one was looking, swiftly untying her bodice and pulling her breasts out for the child to taste. When she wasn't hungry, she would suckle the dry nipple that Rebecca offered her and be comforted just with the motion of her little mouth working on the pink teat. If she felt hunger and found nothing for her labor, the child would open her eyes as if startled and take a deep breath like one insulted and let out a howl loud enough to wake the horses in the barn. At the sound Thankful Seagraves would sit up in the bed and angrily demand that Rebecca give her back her child.

"My!" she would say, and yank the little bundle out of Rebecca's arms and place her under her own dark breast, so full of mother's milk it leaked out the sides of the child's mouth.

At first, Rebecca had been embarrassed when Thankful Seagraves found her trying to suckle the hungry child, and she would stomp out of the room before the tears welled up and spilled all over her face in front of the foreigner. Now it had become a way with them. Rebecca would lace up her bodice and stay in the room until the child had finished suckling on both breasts. This, Rebecca had discovered, made her own body more suppliant when Nathaniel wanted to have his way with her, more responsive to his eternally insistent need. Each time she would close her eyes and imagine that her womb was being quickened and that the seed he was leaving there would find fertile ground once again. It was a vain hope, but something she clung to when the babe was not in her arms to fill the emptiness she felt.

Rebecca kissed the child's forehead, inhaling the clean scent of her again, and then took her up to Thankful Seagraves.

"There's a visitor coming," Rebecca said, placing the sleeping child in the girl's lap. "Someone who knows your language, I hope. You've lived among us nine months, now, Thankful Seagraves. It's high time you learned to speak."

Rebecca turned on her heel and hurried back down to the keeping room. With Sara Moor gone, it would have to be she who cooked the midday meal. Soon Caleb and his father would return from the warehouse. Nathaniel had taken the boy that morning to help him with the inventory. They'd be hungry and cold, so she set about making potato and corn chowder. With slices of cheese and mincemeat pie for dessert it would be a fine meal. She would make enough to feed the visitor; it was the least she could do for the woman's trouble. Even if she was an Indian woman.

CHAPTER 26

Carrying the baby again, so sated with mother's milk there were drops leaking out of the corners of her tiny mouth, Rebecca was startled to see what looked like a heathen woman in an English bonnet coming up the narrow stairwell behind Sara Moor.

"This be Merchant Parris's maid, Mistress," said Sara Moor. "Tituba Indian."

"Tituba?" said Rebecca, trying to hide the fear she felt at having a live Indian in her house. "What an unusual name." The Indian woman smiled at her and dropped into a curtsy, and Rebecca loosened her grip on the babe. At least she's got nice manners, she thought.

"At your service, Ma'am," said Tituba in perfect English, only the slightest trace of an accent in her speech. Her voice was husky as a man's.

"So you're from the West Indies, Tituba."

"I were brought from Barbados, Ma'am, but I were not born there. My people come from the coast of New Granada."

"Is that, by any chance, in New Spain, Tituba?"

"It be closer to the colony of Venezuela than to Mexico, Ma'am, but it all be under the Spanish flag."

"But your English is nearly impeccable."

"Barbados be mostly English and Dutch, Ma'am. All of my masters in Bridgetown were English."

"Have you lost your Spanish tongue, Tituba?"

"My native tongue be Arawak, Ma'am, but I also heard much Spanish growing up, though I have lost practice with it since I were speaking English since I were fourteen years old and taken to Bridgetown."

Rebecca couldn't help marvel at the woman's speech, the complex sentences she could make in English. Who would ever think that an Indian could sound so much like a civilized Christian woman? "Has Sara Moor told you that we need your help interpreting for us with this stubborn girl who seems incapable of learning English? Do you think you'll be able to understand her, Tituba?"

"I be happy to help out, Ma'am, if I can."

"You're a godsend, Tituba," Rebecca exhaled. "You have no idea how long I've been trying to make this girl understand me. She was brought from New Spain, but clearly she comes from a less civilized part of that ungodly country that had no contact with English and is, therefore, dumb as a doornail."

"She cannot speak, Ma'am?"

"She jabbering all day long," piped in Sara Moor.

"If she cannot speak English, Sara Moor, she might as well be dumb," said Rebecca. "She's some sort of half-breed, part Indian and part Spaniard, I suppose, and apparently she's had a good education in letters, which is why my husband paid the outlandish price the pirate, I mean the buccaneer, wanted. But the creature is either terribly willful or terribly dense, and in any case, she's quite useless, isn't she, Sara Moor? I'm feeling quite a bit annoyed by her, I have to admit. Can you please try to communicate with her, Tituba? At least let her know my husband plans to put her on the auction block if she doesn't start earning her keep."

Tituba trained her gaze on Thankful Seagraves, and Rebecca felt her flesh crawl at the look of recognition that crossed their faces.

Tituba spoke first, and Thankful Seagraves's eyes filled with tears. They exchanged words back and forth.

"Can you understand her, then?" Rebecca interrupted. "Does she make sense?"

"She says she isn't a slave, Ma'am. She's from a religious house in New Spain."

"I knew it! See, Sara Moor, I told you so. Was she a nun?" The very idea of it curdled Rebecca's blood.

"No, Ma'am. She were a scribe and used to work for one of the sisters there."

"Good. Then she does know how to read and write. Tell her, Tituba, if you please, that she must stop speaking the Romish tongue and forget about her life in New Spain. She has to learn English immediately. Tell her my husband is at the end of his rope waiting for her to recover. Tell her she has much work to do on my father's farm."

Tituba translated. Thankful Seagraves held out her hands for the babe and said something in a nasty tone.

"What now?"

"She says she wants her baby back, Ma'am."

"I'm putting her to bed, Thankful Seagraves," said Rebecca, drawing the child closer against her. "And you best be thinking about your work if you don't want my husband to sell you back to some buccaneers."

Another exchange, and Rebecca heard Thankful Seagraves say her Spanish name.

"None of that!" snapped Rebecca, shaking her finger.

Suddenly Thankful Seagraves started to weep, a long string of words punctuating her tears.

"What's she blubbering about, now, Tituba?" asked Rebecca.

"Better not be cursing us in her Romish tongue," said Sara Moor.

"She were not cursing anybody," said Tituba.

The Indian woman looked from Rebecca to Thankful Seagraves and back again. Another slew of words poured out of the stubborn half-breed.

"Well?" prompted Rebecca, beginning to regret the pie she had sent to Mistress Parris in exchange for Tituba's time. She could already hear Nathaniel chastising her: You brought her a mate, not a translator, Rebecca. And it cost you a good mince pie, too.

"She says she apologizes for being ill, Ma'am," Tituba spoke at last, "and that she will do her best to improve soon so that she can take care of her child and stop being a burden to you."

"Is that what she said? That's very thoughtful, tell her, but the babe is the least of her problems. The first thing is learning English."

Tituba translated Rebecca's words. Again, Thankful Seagraves burst into tears.

"Why does she keep crying, Tituba? She'll spoil her milk with all that crying."

"Maybe she's got that cryin' illness, Mistress," offered Sara Moor.

Thankful Seagraves said something to the Indian woman. "She says that with my help she will learn the English faster, Ma'am."

"We can't impose on Merchant Parris," Rebecca said to Thankful Seagraves. "We've already interrupted Tituba's day. D'you think her master would be willing to part with her on a daily basis just to come and tutor you?"

"My master would not be contrary to the idea, Ma'am. His shipping business does not fare well and he has extra expenses now with the ailing baby, so he rents out me and John Indian by the day when our mistress can spare us."

"I really don't think I need to know all that, Tituba," said Rebecca, though she was looking forward to telling Nathaniel that Samuel Parris was in financial trouble. Rebecca's eyes shifted quickly from side to side as she evaluated the situation. She saw no way around it. It was the girl's last chance. Nathaniel's patience had run thin. "Very well, then, I'll talk to my husband. If he agrees, you'll have your tutor, Thankful Seagraves. But do tell her, Tituba, she'll have only the twenty days left of her lying-in to do her learning. She needs to go back to Roxbury posthaste. My father and the chickens require her service."

Tituba explained what Rebecca had said, and Thankful Seagraves's eyes turned bleary again. She spoke for a solid minute.

"What's her problem now, Tituba?" The baby was getting fussy in Rebecca's arms. She lifted her up and patted her little back to get the wind out of her.

"She says she is grateful for all your help, Ma'am, and she hopes to be worthy of your service so that she and the child will always have a home with you."

"She's an effusive one, isn't she?" said Rebecca. The child belched. "Tell her that she and little Hanna will always be welcome here, but that she was bought for the express purpose of running a poultry farm and caring for my father."

"If you like, I can stay and give her the first lesson, Ma'am."

"We'd better wait till my husband has had a chance to talk to your master, Tituba. I don't want you working behind his back."

"He will not be the wiser, Ma'am. Master Parris stays in his store nearly to curfew. I would be home, by then."

"And your mistress? Isn't she indisposed or something?" Rebecca flushed, embarrassed at revealing that she'd heard the gossip about Goody Parris's sickly condition.

"She were with her sewing circle until past teatime today, Ma'am."

"Well, if you're sure it won't be any trouble, I suppose one small lesson wouldn't hurt," said Rebecca. "Just till she's finished nursing. And you'll stay for dinner with us, and my husband will take you back when he returns to the warehouse."

Tituba grinned at Thankful Seagraves, a wide, gap-toothed grin that sent a shudder down Rebecca's spine.

"Mistress, the babe shit right through the blanket," said Sara Moor.

Rebecca didn't feel right leaving the Indian woman in the room with Thankful Seagraves, but it wasn't good to dawdle, either. She had to go change the baby again lest she get another rash.

"Come with me, Sara Moor," Rebecca said, pulling the girl out of the room by the ear. "How many times have I told you not to use vulgar language in my presence?"

CHAPTER 27

¿Quien sois? Who are you?"

"Me dicen Tituba. That is the name they gave me when they took me from my people."

"¿Eres de la Nueva España? Are you from New Spain, like me?"

"From Guiana, in Nueva Granada. The Spaniards landed there, too."

"What am I doing here, Tituba?"

"She's not going to let you speak Spanish. I'm here to help you learn English."

"They've turned me into a slave. My name is Concepción Benavídez. I'm a mestiza, daughter of a *china poblana* and a *criollo*. My caste is not a slave caste. I was a scribe trained in a convent by a very educated nun."

"For the English, all of us who are not white are slaves. And all of us have to learn to speak like they do."

"I want her to give me back my child. She is always taking her away from me."

"You speak like the Spaniards, but you're as brown as I am."

"And you speak like the English."

"But I'm a foreigner, just like you."

"What did she say, Tituba?"

"That you were brought here to care for her old father and run a chicken farm."

"A chicken farm? I'm a scribe, Tituba. I don't know anything about farming chickens."

"She wants you to learn English in the twenty days you have left to recover from the birth. Then they'll send you back to work in her father's house."

"I can't go back there. The house is barely big enough for the Old Man. And it's freezing there. How can I raise a child in that cold?"

"It's better for you to say yes to everything, Concepción. You have to stop crying. She's getting impatient with you."

"What are you telling her, then? Are you translating what I'm saying?"

"I'm telling her what she wants to hear. That way you get what you want."

"What I want is to escape from here and return to New Spain."

"And your baby? She would die "I'm telling her what she wants to hear. Thaton such a journey. Babies don't live long on the open sea."

"What are you telling me, Tituba?"

"At least wait until she grows older. She might withstand the journey when she's six or seven, if she lives that long."

"Six or seven? ¡Ay, Tituba! How will I survive all those years?"

"The same way I have. You learn what you need to learn day by day, and you try not to forget where you come from. But be careful with your child, Concepción. She will grow up here among the English, and she will become English. I have seen it happen."

"Never, Tituba. I would not allow that."

"Then you will have a double battle, with the English and with your own child."

CHAPTER 28

With nobody to talk to but herself most of the time, Concepción had not needed much English on the farm and could get by on the few words that Rebecca required she memorize and those she taught herself with the help of the books she had found in the Old Man's cottage. Here in Rebecca's house, once Concepción had recovered fully from her delivery, she had been going out into the town with Tituba and Sara Moor, surrounded by people who were constantly chattering to her, asking her questions, expecting her to understand. As a consequence, Concepción had learned more of the English in the four weeks she had lived in Boston than in the eight months she had lived with the Old Man.

Rebecca taught her the words associated with needlework and child rearing: "embroidery," "thimble," "needle," "knitting," "yarn," "thread," "mittens," "cradle," "hood," "milk," "croup," "rickets," "fits," "colic," "vomit," "soil," "christening blanket," "clout," "pilch." In exchange, Concepción showed Rebecca some of the more difficult stitches she admired in Concepción's needlework, but always Concepción was careful not to name the stitches in Spanish or else risk being scolded by Rebecca, who had grown more and more intolerant of what she called the Romish tongue. She guarded Concepción closely lest she use the forbidden language with the child. Even at night, sometimes, she could hear Rebecca shuffling just outside the door of Caleb's little room, listening for a transgression, and so Concepción had gotten into the habit of whispering her evening prayers in the babe's ear as she made the triple sign of the cross over her little forehead, mouth, and heart: "Con la Virgen te acuestas; con la Virgen te levantas, con tu ángel de la guarda, y con el espíritu santo." With the Virgin you slumber; with the Virgin you waken, with your Guardian Angel and the Holy Spirit.

Mornings after Jerónima had been fed and changed by the fire and was put down for her first long nap of the day, Rebecca insisted Concepción spend time with Sara Moor, who schooled her in the language of servants. Sara Moor taught her the names of platters and porringers, tankards and beakers, mortars and pestles, trenchers and kettles, and candlesticks and firedogs. Keeping room. Outhouse. Laundry. Sara showed Concepción how to tuck her apron and petticoats into her waistband before getting near the fire, warning her to lower her sleeves and skirts and get "decent"/*decente* before leaving the kitchen, how to churn butter and make soap. How to press apples, steam puddings, and pickle pork and beef in brine. Sara introduced her to fish and seafood she had never seen, like eel and smelts, oyster and crab, and patiently named the vegetables stored in the cellar: onion, carrot, sweet potato, turnip, beet, pumpkin. Sara taught her the difference between cider and vinegar and how the second was made of the first when the cider went rancid or flat. "Sugar," "hickory," "pot roast"—so many words that tripped up Concepción's tongue. The ones she learned most easily were those for which she had a Spanish equivalent: "biscuit"/*bizcocho*, "pudding"/*pudín,* "salt"/*sal,* "money"/*moneda*, "chocolate," "coffee," "maize." When they went out to do the marketing, Sara Moor showed her how to haggle with the cheese monger and the miller, how to trade with the other maids. To her friends, Sara Moor introduced her as the "foreigner, Thankful Seagraves, the pirate's wench, who can read and write," acting as though it elevated her status to be seen with Concepción.

Caleb tutored her in reading aloud, correcting each mistake in stern imitation of the teacher who stopped by the house each afternoon to tutor him in his penmanship. "No, Thankful Seagraves. You don't pronounce two *l*'s like a *y*. Try it again and get it right, or I shall have to flog the dickens out of you."

From Caleb, she learned to distinguish between "snow" and "ice," between "sleet" and "rain," "wind" and "squall," "slushy" and "slippery," "gloom" and "fog," "sled" and "skate." When they exchanged places and it was her turn to help him with his letters, she made him bring her sheets of paper from her father's desk, and while Caleb practiced his exercises in his blank book she made sentences with the new words in as fine a calligraphy as she could muster with the boy's old crow quill.

In the evenings after Caleb had been tucked into the trundle bed in his parents' room, Natanio sat with Concepción in the keeping room and taught her the business of running a poultry farm and keeping books. It took nearly a fortnight for her to understand what he was talking about, how laying birds were worth more than meat birds but not as much as roosters, how cockerels could be turned into capons for a steeper price, how the paying customers would pay less for their eggs than those who bought on credit. All of it, he said, would get recorded in the accompt-book, a ledger of rows and columns, every egg and pullet sold, charged, or bartered written down in the book next to the name of the buyer. Any expenses like the cost of feed and mash and scratch she would need to record in a separate column. The difference between one column and the other would give her either a profit or a loss. Profits were good; he feigned applause next to the word. Losses were bad; he lowered his thumb and shook his head. "The way to keep your losses down, Thankful Seagraves, is to sell more on *credit*. See?" Credit, not trade, not cash, was the way to make a profit. You can charge more for credit.

She would stare back and forth between the account book and all the words and drawings he'd made to explain his concepts and shake her head. Finally, one night, he hit upon the idea of an example. He showed her a page in one of his ledgers that had the name *Thankful Seagraves* written across the top; in the column on the left he had listed her room and board for four weeks with the cost of each week tallied on the right, including sundry expenses such as the midwife's services, the time he paid for Tituba to help her with the English, the piece of Holland linen for Jerónima's christening blanket, the special shoes from the cobbler Concepción had begged Rebecca to have made for the child, the cradle and hood, the cost of Rebecca's knife that she had taken months before, the writing paper Caleb had taken from his desk and that she thought she was getting away with, the clothes on her back, the candles and soap she used, and now the brushes and lye to clean the farmhouse. It totaled to nineteen pounds, twelve shillings.

She understood that there was a balance under her name. Whatever the amount meant, she couldn't pay it. "No money," she told Nathaniel.

" 'Credit,' " he said, writing out the word next to her name and underlining it twice. "Very important word for business. You owe me this amount, and I will give you credit for it. Each time you sell a chicken or an egg from the Old Goat's farm, I will deduct the price from your bill until you finish paying it off."

"You profit from my credit?"

"No, no, no, Thankful Seagraves. You're not getting this at all. How could I profit from you, with all the losses I've accumulated since I purchased you from that pirate? All of these expenses you see here in this book, and the countless others that my wife hasn't recorded, these are all losses. You would need to sell chickens for the rest of your life before I could make a profit from you."

"The Old Man say they be his chickens."

"Yes, but you're in charge of feeding the chickens and collecting the eggs and selling the poultry here on market days. You'll be in charge of writing everything down in the accompt-book. I'll take care of the rest. Do you understand?"

"I cannot," she said.

"What do you mean you cannot? That's what you were bought for, Thankful Seagraves! You've lived amongst us nearly a year, and we've nothing to show for it save this bill, here, and your bloody bill of sale. And now you've given us another mouth to feed. It's high time you started paying your keep, woman. Otherwise I'll put you on the auction block myself."

"Master, I cannot," she repeated, trying to find the words to explain herself. "I need—" She held up the inkwell and the ledger. "I need ink and book. I need more the English."

"Well, of course you need writing materials! D'you think I'm daft? I don't expect you to memorize the accounts. And I won't even add it to your bill, either, since that's part of the business expense and not your own, like everything else." He turned to another page in the ledger that had the name *Roxbury* on it and wrote in his cramped penmanship: *two pens, inkpot, and ledger.* "I'll bring these from the warehouse and take them to the farm once you're ready. As to needing more English, you'll need to practice more, that's all. And be quick about it. By springtime you should be fluent enough. Until then, we'll get you to caring for the flock, growing the broods in the barn, candling the eggs. That should take care of things for a spell."

"What means 'candling eggs'?"

He frowned at her question. "Hasn't Rebecca taught you anything about the business? It's a way of making sure the yolks don't have chicks inside the egg. Can't be selling bad eggs, now can you?"

"Selling where?"

"Once you're ready and the weather clears, you'll be coming into town twice a week. Market days are Tuesdays and Saturdays."

"Here to Boston, Master?"

"I'll get the cart in the barn repaired and bring you a few cages for the meat birds. And I'll make sure you get some paying customers . . ."

He kept talking, but all she could think about, all that mattered, was that she would be coming into Boston twice a week and on those days she would be able to see Tituba, and this was reason enough to learn the chicken business.

Once the curfew bells tolled, the fire had to be put out in the hearth and the coals gathered into covered pans to heat the beds. Sara Moor slept on the settle in the keeping room, which was the warmest part of the house, as the hearth embers usually lasted through the night. Concepción lay in Caleb's bed with Jerónima tucked under her arm and the blankets tented over her head to ward off drafts and would go over the lessons of the day. She would fall asleep imagining herself peddling chickens in Boston, pushing a cart around the town like the women she would see when she went with Sara Moor to do the marketing. Mostly the women were loud and brash, *verduleras,* they were called in Spanish, hawking fish or vegetables door-to-door. ¡Ay, Madre! She would sigh, thinking, I have gone from a scribe to a chicken peddler. Cockerels, capons, roosters, credit.

On the day of their last English lesson, Tituba was agitated. The time of Concepción's lying-in had ended, and Rebecca and her husband were going to take her back to Roxbury at the end of the week.

"I will miss you, Concepción. You're like my family, now."

"But we can see each other twice a week when I start coming to Boston to sell the chickens."

"I don't think so, Concepción. The mistress hardly ever takes little Betty with her to her sewing circle these days, and I have to look after her now, and the master has got it in his head that he wants me to marry John Indian. The minister has complained that we are living together in sin, so I'll be too busy to get away and to see you. And besides, how will I even know that you're in town?"

"Ruffled Collar said I would be coming on Tuesdays and Saturdays."

"Mondays is better, Concepción. My master's got me helping out at George's Tavern on Mondays; it's on the Neck close to Roxbury. I could come see you in the morning, and we could go to the woods together. I'll show you things in the woods. There is much wisdom in the woods."

"What kinds of things, Tituba?"

"Things to pick, things to eat, things that will protect you against your mistress."

"Protect me against what?"

"You have to take special care with her, Concepción," Tituba said. "She means to take your child away; I can see it."

"Where can you see it, Tituba?"

"In the way she acts, but also, in the water."

"In the water?"

"You can see things sometimes in a bowl of water that you crack an egg into. The yolk forms an image that shows the future. I've seen your daughter.

She be about Caleb's age and she be hiding behind your mistress as if she is afraid of you, Concepción. She denies you."

"That is a falsehood, Tituba. I do not believe visions in water tell the truth. How can an egg yolk make all those images?"

"I can draw the cards for you, if you prefer, Concepción. Maybe you will believe the cards."

Concepción did not realize Tituba was experienced at divination. A shudder went through her, but all she did was shake her head.

"I will raise this child with so much love she will never deny me." And yet she perceived a flutter of fear in her belly.

CHAPTER 29

24 March 1684

Mi niña,

Before you were born, I was dying from a
fever that settled deep in my bones after I was
brought from the pirate's ship. Rebecca says the
midwife could neither bleed it nor purge it
away. The only thing that broke the fever was
your birth. One of my earliest memories in this
country is your life charging through me like a
young bull let loose in the arena. Your little
head, hard as horn, battering at the small doorway of life until you broke it open and squeezed
into the icy gray-blue light of a February morning in the land called Massachusetts.

I remember that your skin was the same color
as the sky is right now, a bruised blue-gray.
Rebecca says that you kicked wildly at the midwife's hands as she tied the cord. Each of your
eyes was a dark seed, clenched tight in your
tiny, wrinkled face; your blue lips stretched
wide, lungs and throat quivering with your cries.

"Juana Jerónima," I said. The first words I
remember uttering in this country were your
name.

I held out my arms and took you from Rebecca's hands. At the sound of my voice you went
quiet for an instant, as if you had recognized a
familiar sound in the cold strangeness to which I
delivered you. I could tell that you were listen-

ing, waiting for me to say more, but someone
spoke before me, and you started howling again.

I can find no trace of Indian in you, and
very little African, though both of them run in
my veins. The pirate must have been half-white,
despite that his skin looked darker than mine.
When he bought me from the pirate's ship,
Becca's husband called me a half-breed because
of the two colors of my eyes. Becca says he
named me Thankful because he wanted me to be
thankful that I was brought to live among the
chosen children of God in this city upon a hill,
but I do not see a city, such as the great city
that I was born to in New Spain, with its
royal palace and its great cathedral, its playas
and causeways, its hospitals and theaters and
university, its throngs of people of many castes
and colors.

The city where you were born, Jerónima, is
called Boston, and I find it cramped with narrow, gabled houses set close together, with crooked
cow lanes that pretend to be streets. I think
this whole city would fit inside our Playa
Mayor in Mexico. There's a market square surrounded by a few crude shops, docks, and piers
and warehouses, but everything is muddy. In the
thickest places, the mud is like a swamp and
one's shoes can stick in the mud and never come
out. This is the only similarity I find with
Mexico, the way the rain floods the ground and
turns the streets, even the cobbled ones, into a
cesspool. You will find more trees than houses
here, with huge canopies of colored leaves, except
that they are all bare right now and look like
gibbets. Only the great pines of the forest aren't
dead.

Seramur, who is a slave like me, talks all day

long. At first, she ignored me or spoke crossly when the mistress made her do things like bring up my supper tray or help me down to the outhouse. Once the wound of your birth started to heal between my legs and I could stand and walk without support, I started helping her in the kitchen. Light work like peeling potatoes and shucking corn was all I could do at first, but slowly I have built up my strength so that I now do most of the cooking. They seem to like the food I make, especially my quesadillas, which they call "cheese pasties," and my hot chocolate with its high crown of froth. I cannot yet haul water or carry wood, but Seramur insists that I scrub the pots and wash the dishes; otherwise she will not take me with her when she goes to market.

Despite the cold and the mud, I enjoy going to the market, walking in a crowd of people, even though they all stare at me as though I were a jester on the Plaza Mayor, seeing shops and taverns and horses and carriages. The Widow Cole's place is my favorite of the shops. She sells "sundries," which means a little of everything, and I love gazing on the many-colored ribbons and yarns and threads. She sells fabric, too, all manner of fabric, and I find myself imagining the matching clothes I would make for you and me if I could afford it. That blue linen would make a nice petticoat. That rose damask a good coat. That green silk a pretty shawl that I could embroider with parrots and palm trees. Seramur always pulls me away and tells me to stop dreaming.

After we finish the marketing, Seramur visits a friend of hers who works at one of the inns near the docks. The first time she took me there, when I saw all those ships sitting in the bay, I remembered Vera Cruz and the pirates, and I started to shake uncontrollably. Her friend at the Blue Cat Inn made me a hot toddy and the fear passed. Her name is Mary Black. She's a mulatta from a place called Jamaica, and she can read fortunes in our palms. When she speaks she has an accent that reminds me of the Creole sailors aboard the pirate's ship. I am amazed that it doesn't seem to offend anyone the way my accent offends Rebecca. She told me I would soon be married to a foreigner, but that he would die and leave me a wealthy woman. Seramur got a good laugh out of that. At least it is a merrier vision than the one Tituba says she saw in her bowl of water.

The other day an Indian woman walked into the inn wearing a wolf pelt draped over a leather dress covered with beads. Bells tinkled as she walked. She bought an iron pot from the innkeeper and paid him with strings of shells, which Seramur called wampum. On her way out the Indian woman stared at me as if wanting to say something, and I realized she's the same woman who sometimes stands in the road that leads to the forest by the Old Man's farm.

There are many things I don't understand about this country. I looked everywhere for a church; I wanted to light a candle to la Virgen to protect you, but all I find are two-story wooden buildings with spires and tiny belfries, no cathedrals, chapels, or basilicas. I have also not seen any priests, though there are men in white collars that Seramur says are called "ministers" or "teachers." They stare at me as though I were the very Devil standing in front of them. I have a feeling their faith is as foreign as their language.

I have seen no one else like me. It is as if castes do not exist here. There are blacks like Seramur, and Indians like the ones who appear suddenly out of nowhere, walking in a straight line through the town, scaring people out of their wits, or the captured Indian women who get dragged to the auction block down by the docks. Mostly, everyone looks like Rebecca and Ruffled Collar, their skin like milk, eyes like blue glass. I see no mestizos, moriscos, mulatos, chinos, albinos, yambaigos, coyotes, hang-in-the-airs, jump-backwards, or any of the other castes, or racial mixes, that we have in New Spain, nothing other than white or black or Indian.

How can I explain about castes so that you understand why I am an aberration in New England, though in Mexico, which has many racial mixes, I am as common as salt? The mestizo is the offspring of a Spaniard and an Indian woman, and as there are more Spaniards and more Indian women than anything else, they produce the most offspring. But even among the mestizos there are many varieties. If a mestizo mixes with an Indian woman, it results in a coyote, but if a coyote woman mixes with an Indian man, it produces a chamizo. There are also Africans who were brought by the Spaniards, and produced a different caste: mulatos, if the African women mix with Spaniards, moriscos, if the Spaniards mix with the mulata women. Castes that don't improve, that is, whiten, their status are called tente-en-el-aire, or hang-in-the-air; castes that go darker rather than lighter are salta atrás, or jump-backwards. An Indian man mixing with an African woman, for example, is a jump-backwards, making a lobo, which means "wolf" in Spanish, and which is what my mother's father, your great-grandfather, was. If a lobo mixes with an African or a Philippine woman (your great-grandmother), going further backward, they create a chino. This is the caste that pertains to my mother, your grandmother, María Clara Benavídez. The women with Philippine blood are known as chinas poblanas, not because they are from the city of Puebla but because theirs is a mixture of three races, with no Spanish blood, and so they are considered part of the pueblo, that is, the dark people. Perhaps, to make up for their lack of whiteness, las chinas wear the most colorful and extravagant clothing, beaded huipiles, embroidered shawls, lace aprons, and as much jewelry as they can afford. Las negras and mulatas like pearls and bright turbans that match their aprons, but none are as resplendent as the chinas poblanas. Since my father was a criollo, that is, a Spaniard born in New Spain, my caste is much higher than my mother's, and I am considered a quarter china, with one part Indian, one part African, and two parts Spanish. It is why my eyes are different colors. My mistress in the convent called me castiza but I prefer simply mestiza.

The pirate had amber eyes, yellow hair, and European features, but his skin looked as African as Aléndula's, so I believe he was probably of mixed race, too, at the very least a quarter mulatto. If you had been born in Mexico instead of Boston, a product of a mestiza and whatever the pirate was, your caste would have been higher than mine. With your coloring and your features, and your predominance of white blood, you would be considered limpia, or clean, though the seed of the Indian and the African reside in your blood.

What would my mother say, I wonder, if she

were to behold you, her first grandchild? I can almost imagine her delight. No doubt she would smother you with kisses, and she would want to dress you up in the lively raiment of a china poblana baby and paint a little beauty mark on your dimpled chin. My mother would die of shame if she saw what has become of the daughter she raised. I saw myself the other day, for the first time since I was brought here. We were in the Widow Cole's shop and Seramur was admiring the shoes and hats and I was lingering over the writing desks, lifting the lids to all of them to see what they held inside. One of them had a looking glass fastened to the inside of the lid, wide enough for me to see myself from the waist up. At first I gasped, and then I laughed out loud when I saw my reflection. Seramur came over to see what was so funny.

"That cannot be me," I said. "I look like a boy in a skirt."

"It were worse when you was bald, Thankful Seagraves. Bald and with a big melon under your apron."

I was too overtaken by my appearance to be offended. My hair is no longer than my ears and sticks out in all directions, like a hill of windmills. The bones in my face form a hexagon, sharp at the forehead and the cheekbones and square at the chin. My lashes and eyebrows have grown thicker, making my eyes look larger and emphasizing the difference in the color of each iris. I rolled up my sleeves and saw the long, thin sinews of my arms, the acute angles of my elbows, which are rough and gray. Though my breasts weigh on me like udders, they hardly show under this waistcoat and bodice and shift. Even my skin seems to have changed to a paler shade of its normal color. There is no sign of the china poblana's daughter I used to be.

I am different, and this is a different world, Jerónima, and it will be, for now, the only world you will ever see. I am beginning to understand why Tituba says that I should just make my peace with staying here, as it looks very unlikely that we will ever be able to cross the sea and return to New Spain.

Rebecca says you will be English, like they are, and I don't argue. I know la Virgen is everywhere, even here if we call to her, and you will grow up speaking Spanish with me, and learning about la Virgen: her Immaculate Conception, her virgin birth, her sacrifice. You are my daughter, and no matter what language you speak or what name they baptize you with, you carry New Spain in your blood. I will not let you forget that.

Tomorrow evening we are to leave Rebecca's house and return to the Old Man's farm. The midwife says I'm strong enough to go back to work, and even though I know the mistress doesn't want me to take you away, she's gotten so attached to you, she must obey her husband and send me back to Roxbury.

You awaken, at last, hungry as usual, and bawling out of the injustice of having to wait. I don't care anymore that you were placed here by a pirate's violation. You are now my reason for living, my reason for remembering, and I will do whatever they want me to do to give you a decent life, a life not marked by a bill of sale, and that means, first of all, learning to speak this English tongue.

Always,
tu madre, Concepción

CHAPTER 30

What is that you're making, Thankful Seagraves?" asked Rebecca, coming into the keeping room still wearing her cloak and beaver hat, cheeks flushed from the cold. "Sara Moor says you've been at it since we left for Lecture this morning. Look at this mess."

"This be food from Mexico," Concepción said, smearing the last of the cornmeal into the final corn husk. She had found a sack full of dried husks in the cellar, and the idea of making tamales had taken possession of her, though she could remember having made tamales only once in the convent with Jane.

Rebecca draped her cloak on the sideboard and lifted the hat over her blond ringlets and set it on the carmine wool of the cloak. "It's terribly close in here, don't you think? How's little Hanna doing?" She bent over the wicker cradle that Concepción had placed on the settle to keep the baby close to her while she cooked.

"The baby sleeping, Mistress."

Rebecca picked up the child anyway and walked over to the hearth to look into the pot hanging off the lug pole. "What in Heaven's name have you boiled here, Thankful Seagraves? It looks like some kind of witch's brew."

Here was another expression that Concepción had never heard, "witch's brew."

"Is that like the witch hazel, Mistress?"

"Did you boil toads in here, too?" said Rebecca, poking into the pot with the end of the paddle. She saw naught but the chicken feet and the gizzards and the garlic.

"It just be stock, Mistress." She had boiled the chicken in tarragon and thyme. She would have preferred oregano and bay leaf, but she could find neither herb anywhere, and she had to make do with these blander flavors. She'd saved the broth to add to the dry cornmeal, kneading the meal and the broth until she had the sticky texture of masa that she needed to smear into the softened corn husks. Not having any pork and red chile to fill the tamales, she had decided to make do with the shredded chicken and some dried cranberries to liven the flavor of the meat, adding a sage leaf to each *tamal* before rolling it up. The maize was ground thicker than it should be and produced a grainy masa that would take longer to cook and would give a heavier texture to the tamales, but at least it was food from her own country. She wrapped up the last tamal in its husk, folded over the bottom end, and pressed the top end together, using the wet cornmeal as a seal, to make a tight bundle.

Rebecca stood next to her, surveying her work with a curious frown. She turned around and peered into the kettle where Concepción was stacking the tamales over the flat basket used for winnowing wheat flour. The basket itself was balanced on a pewter tankard inside the kettle.

"This is an interesting contraption you've rigged up here, Thankful Seagraves."

"For steaming, Mistress. The steam cook the cornmeal."

Concepción poured another cup of broth over the tamales, making sure not to let the liquid reach the basket. She placed a layer of wet corn husks on top of the heap of tamales, then set the heavy lid on the kettle and swung it on its hook into the flames.

"What do you call this dish, then, Thankful Seagraves?"

"Tamales be the name."

"I beg your pardon. What are you speaking?"

"Only the name, Mistress."

"I've told you time and time again, Thankful Seagraves, that you cannot use your ungodly tongue here, nor are you to speak it to this child. She has an English name, she lives among English people, and you must speak to her, and to all of us, in English. If you expect anybody to eat this food, and I sincerely hope you haven't wasted good cornmeal or my husband is sure to put it on your bill and box your ears for good measure, you'd better have a Christian name for what you've just made. Look, you've gone and upset the babe. Now she'll just fuss the rest of the day."

Concepción held out her hands to take the baby from Rebecca, but the other woman stepped back and shook her head. "You've got quite a bit of cleaning up to do before dinner, from the looks of it, or were you just planning to sit in the rocking chair with the babe at your breast and watch me clean?"

"Mistress, I clean and feed the babe. Tamales take much time to cook. Be ready when you be home from Lecture tonight."

"And what are we supposed to eat for dinner, now that you've gone and taken up the hearth with these, these, well, these *cakes* or whatever they are?"

"Cake, yes, Mistress, cake of corn. Good name?"

"Well, no, it's not corn cakes; that's something different altogether." She picked up a soggy corn husk and looked at it for a spell. "It's more of a dumpling, actually, that cooks inside a corn husk. See? This is a corn husk. Corn-husk dumpling, that's what we'll call them, Thankful Seagraves. Can you say that?"

"Corn-husk *dumplín'.*"

"See how easy it is to be civilized? Good, we've invented a new dish. Shall we serve it with the salt pork or the salt fish, do you think?"

Concepción had imagined a different accompaniment for the tamales. Something tart and fresh like *nopalitos,* a salad of tomatoes and tender slices of boiled nopal cactus, spiced with lime juice, cilantro, and chile, a nice dry cheese crumbled over the top. Of course, there was not a cactus to be found in New England. The closest things to *nopalitos* were string beans, and it was much too late in the year for anything fresh. "Not good, Mistress. Tamales have chicken inside. Not good with pork or fish. Serve with green vegetables."

"It's snowing outside, in case you hadn't noticed, Thankful Seagraves. The only green vegetables we have are dried peas."

"Peas good, Mistress. I make pea soup."

"Pea soup? For supper? Absolutely not. Salt pork and corn-husk dumplings is what we'll serve tonight. I want you to mull some cider to go with it. We'll make it a festive occasion. I might even invite the Mathers to join us. Would there be enough for two more, Thankful Seagraves?"

"Plenty tamal—I mean, dumplin' for seven or eight people, Mistress."

"Lovely. We'll have guests for supper. And I want you to set out the china, too, and our good candles, make the table look bright and merry. But you'll have to work alone, mind you. Sara Moor has tubs of washing to do, and won't be able to help. We'll show Nathaniel just how good of a maid I've taught you to be."

"Mistress? Jerónima hungry."

Rebecca looked down at the squirming child. "Yes, well," she said, thrusting the babe to Thankful Seagraves, "aren't we all? You'll need to work as you feed, no time for sitting down, is that clear? Master Greenwood wants to take you to Roxbury immediately after supper."

Concepción waited for Rebecca to leave her alone before she unbuttoned her waistcoat and unlaced the bodice of her dress. Already there was a wet stain on her shift. Jerónima squealed with impatience as Concepción knotted the ends of her shawl behind her neck to make a sling that kept the babe close to her breast while she cleaned up. She gathered the dirty bowls and paddles and took them out to the lean-to, and scrubbed while Jerónima suckled.

"Take your fill, *hija de mi alma*," Concepción whispered, using one of the epithets her own mother had used with her—daughter of my soul. Out in the garden, she could hear Sara Moor complaining to Rebecca.

"I ain't washing anything of hers, Mistress."

"You do as I say, Sara Moor. I want that babe's swaddling white as milk. God knows it'll be the last time she'll ever be this clean."

Concepción dreaded returning to the Old Man's farm, but Tituba was right. She had no choice than to go along with it, just as she'd had no choice than to learn English, if only for her daughter's sake. She would be growing up here among the English, and it would be necessary to know what they were saying to the child. Concepción would miss living in this large, clean house, having her own little room with a glass window and a real bed, but there was nothing to be done about it. The only choice she had was to take charge of the Old Man's house and make it a decent place to raise a child.

She would sweep out the cottage, scour the walls, boil all the cooking implements until every bit of grease caked in the grooves dissolved, wash every stitch of the Old Man's clothing, and put the Old Man outside every day to air out the smell of tobacco and urine in his skin. Just a few minutes in the cold air wouldn't kill him. In the spring, she would plant a kitchen garden like Rebecca's. She would sow corn in the little plot behind the barn. She would learn the business of peddling chickens and come to town on Tuesdays and Saturdays and visit with Tituba on Mondays and learn the wisdom of the woods. It was a completely different kind of life from what she'd had in the convent with Sor Juana, but then, that girl she had been, who ran away with Aléndula, who imagined the world was a safe place in which to wander—that girl died in the sea. Now she had a new name, a new land to inhabit, and a new life to protect.

Chapter 31

Between Concepción's attending to the needs of the baby and the Old Man and the chickens, life in Roxbury passed quickly. With the excuse of spurring Concepción's vocabulary in English, Rebecca came every other day to check on the baby. Nathaniel came once a week to check on the chickens. Caleb came along with both of them and played at tops and cat's cradle with the Old Man. Concepción was glad for their company (with the exception of Natanio), for Caleb's entertainment of the Old Man, and especially for Rebecca's help with the baby while she worked with the chickens.

Every three weeks, like clockwork, a new clutch of chicks hatched, and Concepción set about the task of separating the pullets from the cockerels. The cockerels she kept in the coop, to be fattened with acorn scratch into meat birds. Some of these would become capons, which drew twice the amount of a regular bird, and Nathaniel would clip their tiny testicles himself, slaughtering a few in the process. Any bantam cocks she was to let loose in the yard, to learn from the roosters how to behave with the hens. Bantams brought an even higher price than capons. The rest of the chickens were kept on a lean diet of corn, oats, rice, and kelp. She had taken to mixing a mash of herbs and seeds into the feed once a week, the mustard seed deepening the color of the egg yolks to an almost orange yellow.

Every morning she gathered eggs, finding them not just in the nest box in the barn but wherever else the hens had decided to roost the night before: in the apple tree, in the corn patch, in the vegetable beds. Once, she discovered a run of chicks teetering along the roof of the cottage and knew that some biddy had flown up there and made herself a little nest in the thatch. Concepción would candle the eggs in the dark cellar, separate the fertile from the infertile yolks, throwing out only the ones that had blood inside the shell. She would return the fertile eggs to the nest box and keep the infertile ones for cooking or selling. It was the large eggs that sold the best, and these she would store in a contraption she had rigged using straw-lined baskets inside a covered barrel. In the spring and autumn, the eggs would keep fresh for a week in the cellar. Summers they lasted only two days, and in the winter she had to store the eggs in the house to keep them from freezing.

She learned myriad ways to cook chicken. The Old Man's favorite was gizzard and oyster pie. They had eggs every day for breakfast or dinner: fried eggs and omelets of a dozen varieties, with cheese and herbs and mushrooms and vegetables from the garden. She made *tortilla española*, or potato and onion pie as Rebecca called it. When Rebecca taught her to make custard, she modified the recipe, adding nutmeg and cinnamon and a crust of burnt sugar to transform it into flan. When Jerónima came down with a cold or a stomachache, Concepción fed her nothing but the broth of a hearty *caldo de pollo* until she recovered. When Concepción's own longing for Mexico brought her to tears, she would gorge herself on chicken tamales or one of her mother's favorite recipes: *arroz con pollo,* chicken and rice.

Concepción had no time to write or read, other than the ledgers. She couldn't remember when Jerónima grew her first tooth or when the child spoke her first word: "Becca." Concepción remembered the merriment each feat had caused in the Old Man. The rewards Rebecca would shower upon the child so that even Caleb got jealous. The way Rebecca bickered less with her father and more with Concepción. Mostly, what she remembered of those first four years in Roxbury, apart from the chickens, was the Indian woman, the woods, and Tituba.

When Concepción first returned from Rebecca's house, while she hoed the mulchy ground of the corn patch behind the barn or laundered clothes in the barnyard with baby Jerónima asleep in her cradle on the doorstone, the Indian woman would stand in the road just outside the fence and gesture for Concepción to approach her. Afraid that the Indian woman wanted to steal her baby and carry her off into the woods, like the story of Mary Rowlandson, Concepción would take the baby inside and not come out again until the Indian woman had gone. One morning, Concepción found a stiff leather purse hanging from the hook high on the barn door. Painted with green and yellow arrows and fringed in soft leather, the purse was filled with corn kernels, speckled beans, and what looked like melon or squash seeds. Concepción knew it was the Indian woman who had left the purse there, but she didn't touch the seeds or plant them. The next day, while Concepción rutted rows into the corn patch using the cart from the barn, she noticed tracks in the dirt that were too large and deep for Pecas, the cat, to have made. Concepción was thinking it had to be a wolf or one of those masked creatures she had seen in the woods at twilight that looked like a cross between a dog and a cat skulking around the barn at night. As she squatted over the tracks, it wasn't until she heard a tinkling sound that she realized the Indian woman had approached the fence.

"Are you Wabanaki or Narraganset?" the woman asked in English.

Startled, Concepción looked up. Her belly lurched as she straightened up. In the bright morning sun, the woman's long black hair shone like silk. She wore a beaded leather dress and beaded moccasins.

"Leave me alone," Concepción said. "What do you want?" She looked over her shoulder in the direction of the doorstone, where the baby's cradle sat.

"Fear not, Odey," said the Indian woman. "I just asked you who are your people."

"My people are not from here," Concepción said. "My home is far away. A place called Mexico."

"You came from across the water? Like the Africans?"

Concepción nodded, turning to look at the doorstone again.

"I have seen eyes like yours among our people. Have you been banished?"

"I was taken captive by pirates and brought here on a pirate's ship."

"What do they call you?"

"Thankful Seagraves."

"Thankful Seagraves?" the woman repeated. "It is an odd name, like all of theirs. My name is Makwa, which means 'bear' in my language, but I am of the Wolf clan of the Mohawk nation. We are the Dream People."

"The Dream People? Am I dreaming you, then?"

"No, it means that we are guided by our dreams. And it means you will only see us if we have something to say to you."

"But I have seen you here before, and in Boston, too."

"Yes, I have been trying to speak to you for some time."

"I have seen the English capture the Indian women. Why do they not take you?"

The Indian woman smiled, and Concepción was taken aback by the whiteness of her teeth that lent an unreal radiance to her brown face.

"We are known as the praying Indians. There was a white man who lived with my people at the beginning of the Dark Time. He made a school to teach us how to read his holy book. We have been passing his language on to our children ever since. It keeps us from getting captured."

They stared at each other and neither one said anything. Concepción kept worrying about the baby, looking over her shoulder to make sure some Indian warrior didn't sneak up and snatch Jerónima out of her cradle while her mother stood there talking to the Indian woman.

"Why are you always calling to me, Makwa?"

"We can help each other. We can make a trade."

"You can't have my daughter."

The Indian woman frowned. "I don't want your daughter. I want half of what grows in your little cornfield."

"Nothing grows in my cornfield yet."

"That is why I gave you the Three Sisters. You must plant the beans and the pumpkin seeds together with the corn and the three will grow together and protect each other, like sisters. The thorny vines of the pumpkin plant will keep animals away from the field, and the beans will climb the cornstalks and keep the corn nourished and strong. In exchange, we'll bring you firewood."

One of the costlier items on Greenwood's inventory of expenses for the farm was cordwood. Even the bit Concepción managed to trade for with the neighbors cost her a tub of soap or a laying bird.

"How much firewood?" Concepción asked.

"One cord for each harvest. If you agree, we will never speak again. But know that we are there, should you need our help for anything, Odey."

"What did you call me?"

"Odey. It is the word in my language for 'heart.' For we have seen in our dreams that your heart is pure like water, but heavy like ice. Do we have a trade?"

How could she not agree?

She planted the Three Sisters, as Makwa had told her, and in late spring she found a cord of wood, split and stacked behind the barn, and half of the green corn taken, the other half tasseled. Midsummer it was the beans, and late summer the fully ripe cornstalks that were halfway harvested, and each time another cord of wood neatly piled behind the barn. Finally, in the autumn, it was the perfectly round gourds of the pumpkins, colored a deep orange and a creamy yellow, larger than anything sold at the Market Place, and wood piled upon wood behind the barn.

She did not see Makwa again, not even when she went into the woods on Thursdays to burn the letters she wrote to Aléndula. No longer afraid that her baby was in danger, she would take Jéronima with her, wrapped in a sling tied behind her neck until the child learned to walk. The woods mesmerized Concepción. Walking in the woods was like being inside a cathedral made of trees. Instead of granite *bóvedas* and marble pillars, canopies of leaves and fragrant evergreens stretched high above her. In the clearings there were beds of wildflowers as vivid as stained-glass windows. Bright orange and yellow butterflies flickered like candles in the heavy shade of the trees, and berry bushes dragging with fruit slaked thirst or hunger, like the bread and wine of Holy Communion. There were alcoves that looked like chapels and fallen trunks that could have been church benches and tree stumps as big as altars. Once she even found a tree hollow wide enough for her to crawl inside and kneel as though in a confessional. It was there that she prayed to la Virgen. And it was on the soft bank of the creek that she built her little pyre of twigs and kindling and burned her letters to Aléndula, moving the smoke toward the water to be carried to her friend's bones at the bottom of the sea. In the autumn, Concepción's favorite season, she and Jerónima would roll in the soft mounds of freshly fallen leaves, watching as flocks of angels in scarlet and golden wings descended over them. The silver light of the first snowfall that stumbled upon them in the woods made Concepción weep, the large white flakes melting like icy tears on her face, and for the first time since she'd been brought to New England she felt a kind of peace settle over her like the snow.

It was only in the woods that Concepción felt free and lighthearted. The rest of the time, she worked, and the work was not about sitting at a desk copying manuscripts or delivering missives to the palace or running errands at the market, as had been her tasks in the convent, privileged as she'd been in the service of Sor Juana. This was the labor of servants and slaves, though the goodwives who were her neighbors engaged in the same kind of labor, the labor that Madre had told her did not apply to those with an education. This was the labor of making everything from scratch, of carting wood and water into the house from morning to night, of scrubbing dishes and scouring pots in the open air, whether the air was warm or wet or frigid. This was the labor of growing most of what one ate, of tending to field and garden, barn and chicken coop, and of an old man needing to be fed and washed and moved from his bed to his chair and back again throughout the day. This was the labor of squinting over needlework in the bad light that came from the hearth, of boiling and baking and brining, of mucking and shucking and trucking, of pushing a cart laden with cages of chickens and barrels of eggs and a child who had to be strapped down to keep her from bouncing over the sides while Concepción trudged three miles across the Neck, over a road that was either rocky or muddy or flooded over, to peddle her poultry.

On market days, Concepción would cage the meat birds and the capons ready for sale, bring up the egg baskets, and load everything into the cart. She would leave the Old Man layered with lap blankets in his armchair with the chamber pot underneath, his pipe and his beer and his chicken pie dinner on the table. After settling Jerónima into the cart with an apple or a cheese pasty, a pair of corn-husk poppets to keep the toddler entertained, Concepción would pack the ledger and the writing set and her piecework into a canvas satchel she had made and push the cart from Roxbury all the way to Boston's North End and back again. At first her whole body would ache as though she'd carried the cart on her shoulders, but eventually her back grew strong, her arms and legs sinewy.

After the marketing was done and the accounts settled at Greenwood's warehouse, she would meet Tituba at the Widow Cole's shop, where Concepción liked to teach Jerónima the names of things in a whispered Spanish. *"Pluma,"* she said, letting the child hold one of the goose quills. *"Papel,"* showing her a page of deckle-edged paper. *"Tinta,"* opening the inkpot and dipping the tip of the girl's little finger into the black ink.

"Together, they make a *libro,*" she would say, opening one of the books, running her finger under the words. "Palabras. Escritura. Libro."

"Pluma, papel, tinta, libro," the girl repeated in a high voice.

"Shhh! Quedito, mi hijita. Lower your voice."

"Why?'

"Because the lady who owns this place doesn't like Spanish."

"Why not?"

"Because she doesn't understand it. Can you be very quiet?"

"Pluma, papel, tinta," the girl whispered.

"Yes, that's good, *mi hijita.* It's good that you can speak Spanish."

"One day this is going to get you into trouble, Concepción," said Tituba.

"Why must you always make such gloomy predictions, Tituba?"

Later they would go to the Blue Cat Inn and share a shepherd's pie and a pint of beer that the owner of the inn gave to them in exchange for some washing that Tituba did for him on the side. On Saturdays, Tituba would bring her mistress's child, Betty, to play with Jerónima and the girls played on the bench with the poppets, while Concepción and Tituba visited with Mary Black at the inn. Sometimes Sara Moor would join them and they would all huddle together around Mary Black's little fortune-telling table in the back, watching her tell the fortunes of sailors. Mary Black's specialty was palms. She was learning to read the cards, and sometimes she would say outlandish things that Tituba was at odds with, and they would argue over the meaning of one card or another while Concepción worked on her commissions.

Of her own free will, the one they thought they'd taken away from her with that bill of sale, Concepción had started a piecework business, embroidering aprons and coifs and handkerchiefs and neck cloths for a small fee that could be paid in coin or country pay. She had struck a bargain with the Widow Cole to trade her embroidery for writing materials: a set of pillowcases bought her a good pen, a dozen dinner napkins, a glass inkpot, a tablecloth, a ream of parchment. Now she had her eye on a blank book, not the expensive leather-covered kind with gilt-edged pages that came from Italy or Portugal and that Widow Cole ordered special for the ministers and the magistrates and other worthies, but the regular cloth-bound blank books used as copybooks and diaries.

Except for the smell of rum rather than pulque, the sound of English instead of Spanish all around her, Concepción found it very familiar to squint over a piece of embroidery in a dark tavern. She had done that in her childhood, before her mother indentured her to the convent.

In clear weather, Tituba visited her on Mondays, right after sunrise, and Concepción would make breakfast for them—buttered eggs and corn bread and sweet coffee—and they would sit together on the settle and speak in low voices while they ate, not wanting to wake Jerónima or the Old Man from their slumber. There were times when the innkeeper at the George would send Tituba home early on Mondays, and these grew more and more common as other taverns opened on the Neck closer to Boston near the town windmill and the saltworks. Then Tituba would come back to Roxbury and help Concepción with the soap making or the cider pressing or the berry conserving or whatever other tasks around the farm required four hands instead of two.

In the early spring, with the ground still frosty in the vegetable beds that Concepción had weeded when she'd returned to Roxbury after Jerónima's birth, they planted green beans, asparagus, and sweet peas; late spring they laid down carrots, parsnips, onions, and strawberries and a separate herb bed of savory, sage, pennyroyal, tarragon, and chamomile; late summer they planted winter squash and cabbage. Tituba missed persimmons and plantains, Concepción mangos and chirimoyas. Fruit was limited to cherries, grapes, apples, and a tart crop called rhubarb that wasn't a fruit at all but a kind of red celery that was used in dessert pies. What they had in abundance was nuts (acorns, filberts, chestnuts, hickory nuts) and berries (blueberries, blackberries, cranberries, raspberries), all of which grew wild and plentiful in the woods.

Tituba knew much about the woods. She was a secret follower of Saint George, the Catholic saint who jousted with dragons and liked offerings of nuts and berries, which she would leave for him in bundles tied from the branches of a crooked pine tree. It was Tituba who told her Saint George would carry her prayers to their source if she burned them in the woods, with an offering and a prayer. It was Tituba who taught her how to make ink.

"You know how to make ink?" This amazed Concepción. Ink, to Sor Juana, had been almost sacred, like oil or perfume. You didn't waste ink; you didn't let your quill sit in the pot and absorb all the ink. You didn't let the ink blot your clothes or your page.

"I know how to make ink *and* paper. Master Parris had me working at a bookbindery when we first arrived. They instructed me how to make books, too."

This was more than Concepción could believe.

"I'll teach you. We'll make ink, first, and you'll see I'm not lying."

They spent hours in the woods looking for the black shaggy-capped mushrooms that produced a good dark ink and that grew among the slender, brown-tipped stinkhorns, called such because of their stench of putrid meat. Tituba taught her that these liked the mulch at the feet of the oldest cedars in the densest part of the forest. Their season was short, from the heaviest of the fall rains to just before the first frost, six weeks at most. It took upward of twenty mushrooms to make one pot of ink. They could not go out to the woods when the storms raged, but if they collected forty or fifty mushrooms each time they went, Concepción could make enough ink to last through the spring, as long as she was frugal and extended the life of the ink with vinegar. She left some of the ink liquid, but the smell of spoilage was so strong, she blended egg white and honey into it to form a paste, as Tituba had taught her, and the paste hardened during the winter, forming a hard black cake that did not freeze and kept the quality of the ink strong for the whole year.

Making paper was harder. It required rags and lye and days of waiting for the lye to break the rags down into pulp. The pulp smelled sharp and the water burned her hands when she dipped the screens to collect a layer of pulp that would dry into paper, after she soaked out all of the water through the bottom of each screen. It was a slow and laborious process, and Concepción said she preferred that nice gold-leafed parchment or simple sheets of cotton bond that the Widow Cole sold to these stiff, handmade sheets that absorbed too much ink. The first and only time they made paper, Tituba made seven perfectly smooth sheets in the time it took Concepción to make one bumpy one. Tituba sewed the pages together with hemp thread and made a little book. Concepción gave it to Jerónima as her Epiphany gift; a commonplace book, Rebecca called it, but there would be nothing commonplace about it. Concepción intended using it to write the Spanish prayers she was teaching the girl. Her hands stayed raw from the lye for weeks, no matter how much butter she salved them with, and Rebecca forbid her ever to make paper again.

"Who on earth gave you permission to make paper? The nerve of you taking things on behind our backs!"

If only you knew, Concepción said to herself, thinking about the set of Holland napkins stitched with biblical passages that she had in the satchel for the Widow Cole. Concepción was going to trade them for a large piece of light-gray bird's-eye silk, stout but very soft, the newest fabric from London, on which she was planning on embroidering a special sampler for Jerónima. She did not recall the full text of Madre's poem about stubborn men—it had several stanzas, she remembered, organized in rhyming quatrains—but she could embroider the first eight lines and the last four and a few of the ones in between. She would write the words on the cloth with her quill first, in a courtly elegant font with decorated capitals and flourishes on a few of the tails and cross-arms of some of the letters. It would take her at least a year to embroider the lettering, maybe longer, if she added gold shading to the incipit of every stanza and a border of gold fleurs-de-lis to the text to strengthen the eye motif of the cloth. It would be next year's Epiphany gift, and by then the girl would be nearly five years old and, with her mother's diligence, able to read the poem herself, perhaps even recite it by heart.

Chapter 32

The cat watched them from her perch on the mantelpiece. The girl trudged in behind Concepción, carrying her little bundle of kindling. She'd grown an entire foot since the summer and was now up to Concepción's waist. A mantilla of fresh snow covered her bare head. Again, the girl had gone out without a bonnet and without a coat. Concepción felt the cold like icy blades in her joints.

"I wish you'd at least wear your coat when we go outside, *bebita*. I don't want you to get sick."

"I'm not cold."

Just in the few minutes it had taken them to go down to the cellar to get wood, Concepción's ears had gone numb beneath the flaps of the wool cap she wore.

"Can you finish the story, now?"

"Who's letting in all that cold air?" the Old Man grumbled behind his bed hangings.

"Grandpa, wake up! Thankful Seagraves is going to tell the part about where she escaped with her friend, Lindula."

"Aléndula," Concepción corrected, touching her index finger to her lips to shush the girl. "You know today is baking day. There's no time for more storytelling." Directing herself toward the Old Man's bed, Concepción added, "Go back to sleep, Old Man. I'll wake you when the bread is ready."

"But you said—" The girl narrowed her eyes at Concepción.

"I said we have baking to do." She lowered her voice. "And I have to tell you the story in Spanish. I can't tell it in English."

"Why not?"

"Because I don't have all the words I need in English. I'll tell you about the escape while we're turning the dough. It's going to take another hour before the oven is ready, anyway."

"But we already turned the dough, Thankful Seagraves."

"It takes more than one time, else the bread will be harder than the Old Man's caca."

Jerónima giggled.

"Hand me those two logs," said Concepción.

She stoked the fire in the oven and then rinsed her hands in the wash bucket. She rolled up her sleeves, shivering as a cold draft from the chimney startled her bare arms. It was time for the second kneading, to make the dough rise soft and pliable. The bread baking was Rebecca's job, but with all the storms that had befallen since early November, they were housebound. There was no coming or going between Roxbury and Boston. Concepción's main job was keeping the chickens warm, the roosters and cockerels in the coop, the hens and pullets in the barn, letting a rooster into the barn once a day to keep the broods growing through the winter. With nothing else to do but tend to the Old Man and her daughter—no marketing, no gardening, no laundering, no walking in the woods, no visitors to serve, no Rebecca or Ruffled Collar to argue with—Concepción had plenty of daylight time to learn to bake bread. Her first few loaves were hard and tasteless and could not be eaten unless they were soaked in syrup or milk, which the Old Man actually loved, though it constipated him for days. Eventually she learned the right measure of salt and yeast, and she'd use some of the sage or tarragon she dried over the sideboard to season the dough. This she would serve to the Old Man with gobs of butter and a pennyroyal tea that tasted just like *hierba buena.*

"Go get your copybook; I have some new words for you," Concepción said to the girl. The long days without her usual work also gave her time to teach Jerónima the rudiments of writing. With the help of the stories she was telling the girl about her life in Mexico, Concepción was showing her the relationship between the letters of the alphabet, which she had already learned in the summer, and specific words, which Concepción had her write over and over in her copybook.

The girl scurried up the ladder, and the cat followed her. "Get away from me, you ugly cat!" she scolded. "Ow, don't bite me. She's biting my ankles. Come here, silly cat; you'll see what's good for you. Bad cat! Ugly cat!"

For all of her scolding, Concepción knew that the girl was up there bundling with poor Pecas, who mewed to get free of the girl's grasp.

"Hurry up, Jerónima. The story's waiting.

"After Aléndula and I escaped from the convent, I had to buy new clothes for us at the market that would hide who we were, but we still had to get away from the Plaza Mayor as quickly as possible. I used two *reales* . . . write that down, *bebita;* it means coins, pieces of eight." She spelled the word slowly, watching the girl align each letter meticulously. "I used two reales to bribe a fruit vendor to give us a ride on his canoe from the Jamaica Canal all the way to the town of Chalco in the foothills. From there we walked. Days and days of walking. So much walking it wore holes in the hide soles of our huaraches." She stopped to spell that word, too, explaining that it meant open shoes made of cords of hemp sewn to a leather sole. "In the afternoons, the heat shimmering off the limestone road burned our feet, and we had to rest under cottonwoods and weeping willows until sundown, nothing to do but count the dried carcasses of cicadas clinging to the tree trunks, vultures circling overhead."

"What's a cicada, Thankful Seagraves?"

"It's like a cricket, only bigger and prettier. We survived on prickly pears and pomegranates and figs . . ." She stopped to spell the name of each fruit— *tunas, granadas, higos.* ". . . until we came to a small village and I used more pieces of eight to purchase provisions—dried meat, pecans, and hard cones of molasses known as *piloncillo.* At night we slept in the broad limbs of a cypress or a mulberry tree. Lulled by the constant buzz of the cicadas, Aléndula slumbered immediately. I stayed awake, shivering under my sarape, listening to the sounds of the night—coyotes howling, owls hooting, creatures scurrying in the branches—afraid to sleep and fall out of the tree, prey to mountain lions or rattlesnakes.

"Aléndula assured me she knew the way to her village of refugee slaves; San Lorenzo de los Negros, it was called. She said she knew the paths from the mountains to the coast like the lines in her hand, but we got lost for days, returning over and over to the same village plaza until finally I paid a muleteer we had passed at least twice on the road to take us to the next town. For five reales the man offered to take us all the way to Tepeaca, just on the other side of the *volcánes.* He let us ride behind him on two blind mules, their hooves clattering over rocks and shale on the steep, winding road that climbed between *Popocateptl* and *Ixtaccihuatl.*"

The girl frowned as she took down the letters that Concepción was dictating. Each name took up an entire line in her copybook. Cocking her head to one side, she studied the letters and tried to pronounce them, then looked up, frowning. "I can't."

"It's not Spanish. It's the Indian language spoken by the Aztecas, the natives of my country before the conquistadores arrived. Those are the names of the volcanoes that you can see from anywhere in the entire valley of Mexico."

"What's a volcano, Thankful Seagraves?"

"It's a huge hill, much taller than a tree, that has fire inside it and smoke comes out of the top."

"Are there any hills like that around here?"

"I don't think so, *bebita.* Shall I continue? The snowy crests of the volcanoes looked luminous in the turquoise twilight—"

"Wait! How can they have snow on top and fire inside, Thankful Seagraves?"

"I don't know, *bebita.* That was one of the mysterious things about them. They were named after a legend about an *Aztec . . .* capitalize the *A;* it's the name of a tribe—"

"A tribe of Indians?"

"If you don't stop interrupting me, Jerónima, the Old Man is going to wake up and I won't be able to finish telling you the story. Yes, I told you, the Aztecs were the Indians who lived in Mexico before the Spaniards arrived. And the legend about the volcanoes said that Popocateptl was an Indian warrior and Ixtaccihuatl was his murdered princess, frozen forever. You see, the name Ixtaccihuatl means 'Sleeping Lady,' and Popocateptl was said to guard over her, still alive, sending out a plume of smoke now and then, sometimes a hot belch from his entrails, just to remind people that he was still there."

"That's scary, Thankful Seagraves."

"Don't be silly. It's just a story. Far below us, the torches of Mexico, the city of my birth and of my mother's birth, glowed like fireflies in the dark valley I was leaving behind *para siempre,* forever.

"After Tepeaca, the landscape changed. The road climbed through woods that were cool and sharp with the scent of pine, the mulchy ground branched with streams. We bathed in waterfalls so cold the water looked like ice crystals pouring between the rocks. We slept in caves to which swarms of bats returned at sunrise to claim their darkness. We spotted deer and puma and once a heron fishing in the stream. We saw mountain hamlets surrounded by cornfields and clouds. At twilight, we would knock on the doors of little *ranchitos,* and people would let us pass the night in their barns and feed us hearty breakfasts of chorizo and potato and coffee.

"Days later the landscape turned warm again. Cypress trees gave way to coconut palms, and a new heat came out of the ground, hotter than a greenhouse, so heavy and wet it was as if the day itself were sweating. We ate *plátanos,* bananas, and *piñas,* pineapples, right off the branches. Orchids grew wild from the trunks of the magical ceiba trees, where flocks of parrots—scarlet and turquoise and lime green—made their nests. I could smell the briny air of the sea. From a hilltop, we saw a fleet of ships at bay. Aléndula said that at last we were in sight of Vera Cruz. The end of our long journey was near. I fell to my knees and thanked the Virgin of Guadalupe for having allowed us safe passage out of the convent, out of the city, out of the hills and mountains and jungle. For having delivered us, finally, to our *destino*."

"Why are you crying, Thankful Seagraves?"

CHAPTER 33

"This'll be the last time I ask you, Thankful Seagraves. Will ye or will ye
not marry me?"

"How many times do I have to tell you no, William Reed? You've
asked me since my daughter were in the cradle, and I've given you the same answer for four years. Are you hoping I'll change my mind, or are you just simple
in the head and can't get the meaning of 'no' in your skull?"

"High time this little lass had herself a decent family, wouldn't you say,
lass? Wouldn't you like a real father?"

Jerónima wrinkled her nose at him. "You smell bad, Mr. Reed."

"I see the girl inherited your cruel streak, Thankful Seagraves."

"Leave us alone, now, won't you, William?" Concepción pushed on the
metal-studded door of Greenwood's warehouse and found it locked. "Where is
he?" she asked the young boy who watched the shop. "Why is the warehouse
locked?"

"Everyone be off to the meetinghouse," said the boy. "There be a witch in
Boston."

"Aye, and her name be Thankful Seagraves," said William. "Looks like
Master Greenwood don't want me lobsters today. If ye see him, tell him I went
on to Shrimpton's. And don't think I'll be extending myself to you again, ye
old thornback."

"That'll be one blessing, at least."

"What's a thornback?" asked Jerónima.

"Don't pay any attention to William Reed, *bebita*. He's just a mean, old
canker sore. Let's go see if we can find Tituba."

She wheeled the cart around and headed in the direction of Dock Square.
Tituba was waiting for her on the stoop of the Widow Coles's shop, but the
shop was closed. The market square looked deserted. Even Goody Thorn's
cart wasn't around, and only a blizzard could keep Goody Thorn away from
market day.

"What's going on, Tituba? It's a Saturday, isn't it? Where is everybody? Even Greenwood's shop was closed."

"Didn't you see the horde of people in front of South Church, Concepción? Didn't you read the bulletins posted on every tree? There's a trial today."

"What's a trial?" said Jerónima, popping up from the cart where she had been feigning a nap.

"I've been making deliveries on the North End, Tituba. And being harangued by another proposal from William Reed. I don't have time to read bulletins." Concepción mopped the sweat from her face with her apron.

"Where's Betty?" said Jerónima. "I wanted to play with Betty today."

"Do you remember that girl with Sara Moor at the May Fair, Concepción?"

"The Irish girl?"

"Yes. Tessa Glover. She were the washerwoman for the Godwin family, and one of the children accused her of stealing linens. She were dismissed, but her mother, the Widow Glover, marched into the Godwin house and cursed them for calling her daughter a thief. Now the Godwin kids be acting possessed, falling into fits and such. It's Mary Glover on trial today at South Church."

"Do you believe in witches, Tituba?" asked Concepción.

"That's not the point. This Mary Glover is Irish Catholic. She's foreign, she's Catholic, and she speaks no English to boot. Only Gaelic. They're bringing interpreters. Does that sound like witchcraft to you, Concepción?"

"Tituba, guess what?" said Jerónima, standing up in the cart between them, "William Reed called Thankful Seagraves a thornback."

"Siéntate," Concepción told the girl to sit down. "And be quiet."

"It's useless to stay here," said Tituba. "You won't be getting any customers today. I told Sara Moor to save us some room."

"I can't go with you, Tituba. Where would I leave Jerónima?"

"You'll have to bring her along. Don't you want to see what's going to happen to that poor woman?"

"I want to go with Tituba," said the girl.

"We have to hurry, Concepción. The trial may have already started. They may not even let us in."

"Greenwood's going to choke."

"Let him choke. Himself is probably in the front pew, along with all the other good men and women of Boston, there to gloat at someone else's misfortune."

"And what do I do with the cart, Tituba? I can't just park it outside the church. People will help themselves and Greenwood will have my hide."

"We can leave it at the King's Chapel cemetery," Tituba suggested. "No one will take anything if it's on hallowed ground."

Concepción and Tituba pushed the cart away from the market square. The street that led down to South Church was too crowded to get the cart through. They cut across Brattle Street to Tremont and reached the King's Chapel burial ground from behind. Concepción pushed the cart all the way into the cemetery, hiding it behind one of the taller graves, hoping nothing would be amiss or Greenwood would be sure to add it to her column of losses. The chickens clucked loudly.

"Someone's going to hear you. Be quiet!" Concepción scolded the birds.

"Be quiet, you silly chickens!" Jerónima called out.

"Hold on to me, Concepción, and you, child, hold on to your mother. Whatever you do, don't let go of me, do what I do, and keep pushing forward. Ready?"

Concepción picked up her daughter with one arm and locked elbows with Tituba with the other.

"Put me down, Thankful Seagraves," ordered Jerónima, fidgeting. "I can walk."

"Do you want to get trampled like horse dung?" Tituba snapped. "Now hold on, both of you!" At first it felt like being swallowed in a moving mass of bodies. Slowly and expertly, Tituba elbowed her way through the crowd, braving insults and jabs in the ribs. Concepción mimicked her movements. They were like twins joined at the elbow, cutting through the horde of spectators, tripping on hems and stumbling on feet, until at last they reached the top step of the church, panting and soaked in sweat. The door was open against the heat but guarded by sentinels. They could hear the thunderous voice of Cotton Mather all the way outside.

"An Army of *Devils* is horribly broke in upon the place which is the *Center,* and after a sort, the *First-born* of our *English* Settlements; and the Houses of the Good People there are fill'd with the doleful Shrieks of their Children and Servants, Tormented by Invisible Hands, with Tortures altogether preternatural."

"There's Sara Moor!" shrieked Jerónima, waving frantically at an open window in the gallery. "Sara! Sara Moor! Wait for us!"

Sara Moor was leaning out of the window, shading her eyes against the sun. She gestured for them to wait. They watched her duck inside, disappear into a blur of heads and shadows, and emerge minutes later at the front door, looking very much bedraggled. She spoke to one of the sentinels, who at first ignored her, until she whispered something in his ear, and then he nodded and gestured for the others to let them through.

"What did you say to him, Sara Moor?" Concepción asked.

"Never mind. Let's hurry. I don't want to miss this. Poor Tessa is beside herself."

They wriggled upstairs to the gallery, where Tessa Glover, pale and red eyed, tried to reserve a space for them behind her. As the daughter of the accused, Tessa was allowed a front-row space in the gallery to watch the proceedings.

Cotton Mather was still expounding at the lectern.

"When is he going to shut up?" someone said.

"He never shuts up," said Sara Moor.

"Why are all these blackamoors in front of us?" groused a woman behind them, shoving her way to the banister with a boy in tow. Tituba leaned over and whispered in Concepción's ear.

"That's Hoped For Ruggles. I used to clean her house until I learned she likes to beat her servants with a wet switch."

"Since when do you black things get the best view in the house?"

". . . we're friends of Tessa Glover, Goody Ruggles," said Sara Moor.

The boy crossed his eyes and stuck his tongue out at Jerónima.

"Bring out the witch!" someone else cried out.

"She's innocent." Tessa Glover wheeled about, crying. "She did nothing to harm those children. Nothing, I tell you. Since when were it a crime to keep poppets?"

Sara Moor placed her hand on Tessa Glover's shoulder.

"Poppets?" said Jerónima, looking up wide-eyed at Concepción.

"Babies made of rags and straw," Tessa Glover continued, her chin trembling violently. "That's all they are. They're not bewitched. My mother's not a witch. She's just a widow."

"Calm yourself, Tessa," said Tituba.

"Here she comes," said Sara Moor.

Concepción watched the old woman hobbling to the bench, her hair sticking out in wooly gray mats. Her coif and apron sooty, her gown soiled, she moved like one walking in her sleep. Her dirty feet shuffled against the floor. A man sat to each side of her on the bench.

"Look at what they've done to her," Tessa said, sobbing against her hand.

"Behold, Mary Glover!" Cotton Mather exploded, startling everyone in the meetinghouse. "This widowed Irishwoman that you see before you, magistrates, this recalcitrant papist that was by her own deceased husband named a witch before he joined the congregation of the dead, has in recent days bestowed a hex upon the children of John Godwin of South Boston, and they have become visited with strange fits beyond those that attend an epilepsy or a catalepsy. These unnatural tortures I have observed with my own eyes. It would break a heart of stone to see their agonies, gentlemen."

He directed himself to Mary Glover. "What do you think is to become of your soul, woman?"

The old woman blinked her eyes at him. One of the men sitting beside her translated what he'd said into Gaelic, and the other spoke her response in English to Cotton Mather: "You ask me a very solemn question, Sir, and I cannot well tell what to say to it."

"Do you deny that you have bewitched the Godwin children? Do you deny that you cannot recite the Lord's Prayer without making a mockery of it with your Gaelic depravations, though you own yourself a Roman Catholic and can recite your Pater Noster in Latin? Do you deny that you torment the objects of your malice by using puppets such as those that were discovered upon searching your house?"

The translators were finding it difficult to keep up.

Cotton Mather walked to the bar and produced two corn-husk dolls, holding them up for all and sundry to see. A loud gasp washed over the church. Jerónima glanced up at Concepción again, her little hands tightening on the banister. Concepción reached down to soothe the girl, but the girl pulled away.

Mather faced the magistrates again. "This hag has not the power to deny her interest in the enchantment of the Godwin children. Upon our finding these vile objects, the hag acknowledged that her way to torment the children was by wetting her Finger with her Spittle, and streaking these Images. Need we hear more of a confession, magistrates? Indeed, need we even perform this examination in light of such a confession?"

"Sir, may it please the court," one of the interpreters interrupted.

"Speak, man. What is she saying?"

Jerónima pulled on Sara Moor's sleeve. "Why does that man keep speaking for her, Sara Moor? Can't she speak for herself?"

"She be speaking the Irish," Sara Moor told the girl in a low voice, cutting her eyes at Concepción, "another Romish tongue, like your mother's."

Jerónima looked up and scowled at Concepción.

"The accused believes, Sir," the interpreter continued, "that she is visited by spirits or angels. It is they who tell her to clean the faces of her poppets. She says she means no harm by it."

"Will Dr. Thomas Oakes please step up to the bar?" called one of the magistrates.

A balding man with a lace cravat approached the magistrates' table.

"Please tell the court what you have concluded about these distempers of the Godwin children, Dr. Oakes."

"Sirs, nothing but an hellish witchcraft could be the origin of these maladies."

"And do you concur, Dr. Oakes," Mather intervened, "with the other physicians who were appointed by the court to examine the accused very strictly, and see whether she were not craz'd in her Intellectuals, that Mary Glover is compos mentis, that she has not procured to herself by Folly and Madness the Reputation of a Witch?"

"She is not a madwoman, Sir. She is a witch."

"Mary Glover!" called Cotton Mather as though the woman were in another room. "I set before thee the necessity and the equity of breaking your covenant with Hell, and giving yourself to the Lord Jesus Christ, by an everlasting Covenant."

"She says you speak a very reasonable thing, Minister, but she cannot do it."

Again everyone gasped. Jerónima slipped her hand into Sara Moor's and stood closer.

"She's going to go to Hell, isn't she?" said the girl.

Concepción wanted to press the girl's head against her apron, but she didn't; her daughter was clearly favoring Sara Moor.

"Would you consent or desire to be prayed for here in God's house, then, Mary Glover?" Mather continued.

"She says, Sir, that if prayer would do her any good, she could pray for herself."

"Are you rejecting Our Lord Jesus Christ, then, Widow Glover? Will you not pray with me to redeem your wicked soul from this diabolical confederacy?"

"Sir, she says she cannot pray with you unless her saints give her leave."

One of the magistrates pounded the gavel to quiet the room.

"It is the determination of this court that the sentence of death be passed upon Mary Glover for the crime of witchcraft against the Godwin family," pronounced the other magistrate. "We see fit to commit you to the jailer's custody until such time as you shall be hanged by the neck in the Common."

The translators looked back and forth at each other, neither one wanting to break the news to the old woman. They both spoke at once, repeating in Gaelic the pronouncement of the court. Mary Glover remained impassive, as though it were someone else being condemned.

Tessa fainted where she stood and would have fallen over the handrail if not for Sara Moor catching her by her apron strings. Someone started to wail, and Concepción realized it was Jerónima wailing from the shock. The Ruggles boy reached out and elbowed her in the stomach, and just as quickly Concepción cuffed his ears.

"How dare you strike my son, you black thing!" the Ruggles woman admonished, slapping Concepción's face. Jerónima flinched.

Concepción slapped the woman back.

"How dare you raise a hand to a white woman!" The woman gawked, her face shading to a strawberry color. She clawed a handful of Concepción's hair at the nape of the neck and held her fast.

"Go get the constable, boy," the woman said to her son. "Tell him this black thing dared raise her filthy hand to your ma." To Concepción she said, "You'll be spending the rest of the day in the stocks, I warrant."

Jerónima cowered behind Sara Moor.

"Please release her, Mistress." Tituba tried to appease the Ruggles woman. "It were a big mistake. She were just protecting her little girl."

"You'll be keeping your friend company in the stocks if you don't mind your own business, Tituba Indian. Off with you. Off with all you black things. They shouldn't even let your kind into the meetinghouse."

"Take Jerónima with you, Sara Moor," Concepción cried out, but the Ruggles woman yanked another handful of Concepción's hair around her fist to keep her quiet.

Jerónima cringed against Sara Moor. "I want Mama Becca," the girl cried.

The constable dragged Concepción to the pillory outside the Town House, forced her head and arms into the stocks, and charged her a tithe for public disturbance. By the time Rebecca appeared with Jerónima trailing behind her, the sand in the hourglass was halfway gone.

"What in heaven's name did you do now, Thankful Seagraves? Do you realize what Nathaniel's going to do to you when you get out?"

"That Ruggles woman's son hit Jerónima, Mistress, for no reason."

"Hit who?"

The swollen wood of the pillory chafed Concepción's neck. "My daughter. I was defending my daughter."

"To begin with, I can't believe you took this child into that meetinghouse and allowed her to witness such a sordid affair, Thankful Seagraves. What's the matter with you? If that Widow Glover really did have supernatural powers, any child could be afflicted."

"That lady had poppets like mine, Mama Becca," said the girl. "Are my poppets evil, too?"

"Do you see what I mean, Thankful Seagraves? Because of what she saw, she now has this idea in her head, and no doubt it'll be giving her nightmares. I'm taking her home. She needs a few days away from you, don't you, Hanna?"

"No, Mistress. She's going back to Roxbury with me as soon as I'm released."

"I want to go with Mama Becca."

"You're going home with me, and that's final."

"And will you have the child just sit here and wait until you've served your punishment? Have you completely lost your senses, Thankful Seagraves?"

"You can wait with her if you want, Rebecca. She's not going with you."

Exasperated, Rebeccca turned to face the girl. "Do you see what I mean, Hanna? Your mother's pigheadedness will be the death of you, yet."

CHAPTER 34

The pastures on either side of the Neck looked parched. No rain had fallen since early spring, and the river was so low, she could see the rocky bottom of the riverbed, clumps of minnows gathered in the few pockets of water that collected between the rocks. Jerónima had not said a word to her since they left Boston. She sat at the front of the cart, her back to Concepción, staring straight ahead of her without moving. Concepción half-expected the child to jump out of the cart and run back to Rebecca, whom they had left behind at the King's Chapel cemetery, stewing in her own ire next to her irate husband.

Greenwood had slapped Concepción when he learned she'd left the cart at the cemetery. "What? You left the merchandise unattended? If anything's missing, it's coming out of your pelt, Thankful Seagraves," he had said. Only one egg had suffered, broken by a squirrel or a chipmunk, no doubt, and not one chicken was missing, but he still had to make his point. Rebecca was still angry about Concepción refusing to allow Jerónima to go home with her. And now Jerónima was cross at her, too.

"*Bebita*, I'm sorry. I couldn't leave you there. There's too much superstition in Boston right now."

The girl didn't respond. She reached beside her and took hold of her poppets, and for a moment Concepción thought the girl was going to take some solace in the dolls. But no, she had her eyes on the road, waiting for the right moment. They approached a mound of fresh horse manure and the girl dropped both dolls into the dung.

"What are you doing, *bebita*?"

"I hate poppets," the girl said. "They're evil."

When they reached the farm, Jerónima climbed up to the loft and threw down her two other dolls. One of them struck the Old Man on the head, upsetting his pipe right out of his mouth.

"What the bloody hell is going on with that miscreant?" the Old Man said, craning his neck around to look up at the loft.

Concepción had made a doll for each of the girl's birthdays, stuffed with chicken feathers, with braided yellow yarn for hair and tiny little aprons that she embroidered with the girl's name and a special motif, like stars or butterflies, the number of which corresponded to her age. It was painstaking work because the stitches had to be minuscule, and she could only do the work outside in the natural light.

Concepción picked up the dolls and handed the Old Man back his pipe, telling him about the trial and about the poor Widow Glover being sentenced to hang for bewitching children with poppets. "And now Her Highness up there fears poppets."

"It's the damn merchants. They be the ones dreaming up these diabolical distractions to steer our attention away from their own crimes. First it's King Philip's War; then it's the loss of our charter; now it's poppets and witches. Next thing you know they'll be levying a tax of some kind for weeding out witches. Did they hang the woman right away?"

"No, they took her back to the prison."

"It's a ploy, I tell you! They'll likely leave the woman in jail for weeks to run up her jail fees before they take the noose to her. That's not a sentence; it's a money trap."

Concepción didn't want to admit her real worry to him: that Mary Glover was punished for being Irish and Catholic and not knowing the English tongue. Except that she is Irish and I am Mexican, we have much in common, she said to herself.

Jerónima had started to bawl up in the loft.

"She's spooked, I think," said Concepción.

"A good whipping is what she needs," said the Old Man.

"Are you coming down to supper?" Concepción called out to the girl.

"Leave me alone, Thankful Seagraves."

"She's angry at me because I didn't let her go to Rebecca's."

"Give her a thimbleful of my cranberry wine. She'll stop her bellyaching soon enough."

Concepción made a pennyroyal tea with a piece of honeycomb and a drop of the cranberry wine and took it up to the child, who was still crying into her pillow.

"You can stay at Rebecca's on Saturday. Now, sit up and drink this, Jerónima."

"Mama Becca says my name is Hanna."

"Do as I say."

The girl sat up and drank the tea in tiny sips from her spoon.

"I don't want any more poppets," she said.

"And what would you like me to do with them, *bebita*? Give them away?"

The girl shrugged. "They have to go live with the chickens."

"Am I to have no supper, either?" called the Old Man down below.

"I'll make you the milk and rice dish as soon as she goes to sleep, Old Man."

Tituba had brought her fresh cinnamon the last time she'd visited, and with the milk and prunes she'd traded a dozen eggs for she could make a big pot of *arroz con leche* that would keep for breakfast. She could hear the Old Man grumbling about merchants and witches. Halfway through the cup of tea, Jerónima's eyes started to droop, and Concepción undressed her and tucked her into the feather bed. The Old Man was snoring in his chair when Concepción came back down. She tucked a pillow under his head and let him sleep. My two children, she thought. She still had the chickens to unload from their cages and the rice to boil for the evening's meal, but for now, she would use this quiet time to write a quick letter to Aléndula. She had to tell someone about her fears.

13 June 1688
Dear Aléndula,

An old Irishwoman was accused and condemned of witchcraft today. Although we did not witness the actual execution, her being sentenced to hang reminded me of the time I saw your father dangle from the gallows in the Plaza Mayor. I remember how they quartered him, and how the pack of dogs in the playa ate his entrails. It was after that you came to live at the convent. I still thank la Virgen that you escaped your father's fate on the gallows, even though you used to pray for deliverance from the toolshed where the nuns had you imprisoned. That mean Sor

Agustina! I can still see the wounds she would leave on your back with her hook-tipped whip, the raw welts from the lice-infested hair shirt she made you wear when you worked in the flower fields. How can people be so cruel to other people, Aléndula? Whether they're Catholics or not, they will punish those who are different from them to the death. It terrifies me. Now that poor woman, Mary Glover, whose only crime seems to be that she makes poppets (like I do) and doesn't speak English (like I couldn't), will hang from the neck until dead. I suppose I should be grateful to Rebecca for insisting that I learn to speak her language. But that doesn't change the way I look or the fact that I speak an accented English that makes even my daughter cringe with embarrassment.

How do I keep Jerónima innocent? How do I keep from losing her to these English ways? And now she's got it in her head that the poppets I've made for her are evil. She wants me to take them outside to live with the chickens, she says, but I'll just hide them at the bottom of Robin's trunk. Perhaps this fear of hers will pass and she will want to play with them again. They seem pitiable to me right now, their splendid little aprons and corn-husk shapes, the tightly braided strands of yellow yarn sewn to the tops of their heads. Such painstaking work to be so reviled.

CHAPTER 35

"The news in Boston is that Samuel Parris sold his house and his shop and took a post as minister of Salem Village," Rebecca announced as soon as she walked in the door. "Smells good in here."

Concepción was ladling meat and squash stew into pewter bowls. The scent of the mint she used to flavor the broth rose in a steam from the kettle.

Concepción dropped the ladle into the pot, splashing her apron. "He what?" Her voice was shrill. "When?"

"Just like that, Father. From one week to the next. Nathaniel didn't even know Parris had been ordained."

"From merchant to minister!" the Old Man spit at Rebecca's news. "It weren't enough to rob people of their money; now that crafty Parris'll be robbing them of their souls, to boot. Poor sods in Salem!"

"And Tituba?" asked Concepción.

"You don't suppose he left his servants, do you? Didn't Tituba say anything to you, Thankful Seagraves?"

Concepción shook her head. "Nothing. I saw her last week and she said nothing."

"It certainly surprised everyone in Boston."

"Grandpa, look at the compass Papa gave me," said Caleb, showing the Old Man the device. "He bartered it from a buccaneer."

"Trucking with pirates, again, is he?" said the Old Man.

"How far be Salem?" Concepción asked.

"Thirty miles, at least," Rebecca said sternly, "if you have a carriage and a day to spare, neither of which you have, Thankful Seagraves, so if you're thinking maybe you'll be paying your friend a visit, get that idle thought out of your head at once."

Thirty miles to Salem? It might as well be on the other side of the world. Concepción sighed, and a sharp pain sliced across her breast. Her throat closed and her hands shook as she cut wedges from the rye loaf Rebecca had brought for the meal.

"Look, Mama Becca," said Jerónima. "Thankful Seagraves is about to cry."

"You wait and see." The Old Man would not quit his tirade against Tituba's master. "That Samuel Parris will be stirring up some kind of trouble in Salem sooner or later. As the Book of James says, 'For where you have envy and selfish ambition, there you find disorder and every evil practice.'"

"You have no charity whatsoever, Father," Rebecca chided. "What did Samuel Parris ever do to you?"

"It doesn't bode well when a merchant becomes a minister, is all I'm saying, Becca. 'Because he is as greedy as the grave,' sayeth the prophet Habakkuk, 'and like death is never satisfied.'"

"I heard Scripture quoted all day today, Father. Can you just say grace, please, so that we can eat? I'm famished. I see you've made Caleb's favorite stew, Thankful Seagraves. It's the only time he'll eat squash. What are we calling it again?"

Albóndigas, Concepción wanted to say. "Meat dumpling stew, Mistress."

Concepción had lost her appetite. "Jerónima, go down and draw some cider," Concepción said, handing the girl the pewter pitcher.

"It'll be too heavy for her, Thankful Seagraves. Let Caleb do it."

"No, Rebecca. She can do it." The girl flashed an angry look at Concepción, but she held her ground. "Obey me, Jerónima."

"Do as you're told, Hanna," Rebecca said. "You stay here, Caleb."

After dinner, while Rebecca cleared the table and Concepción swept out the ashes in the hearth, Rebecca announced that it was time for Jerónima to start fostering.

"You'd like that, wouldn't you, Hanna? To come live with us in Boston?"

"Yes, oh yes, Mama Becca. Did you hear that, Caleb?" The girl started to squeal.

"Quit your yammering!" the Old Man bellowed over his pipe.

"What is fostering?" asked Concepción.

"It's a custom of the English," said Rebecca. "From the time our daughters are four years old until they're old enough to marry, they grow up in someone else's home to learn the skills of industry and society."

"What skills are those, Rebecca?"

"The skills of a worthy person. All you can teach Hanna is how to grow chickens, Thankful Seagraves. You don't expect your daughter to become a poultry peddler, do you? We should want better things for our children."

"I will bring down her copybook to show you her progress in writing and spelling. Do you not see her needlework? I taught her those things, how to write, how to stitch. Not you, Rebecca."

"You should want your child to have a civilized upbringing," Rebecca retorted.

"Look how you turned out at the Mathers', Becca," interjected the Old Man, puffing smoke all over the board. "Very civilized, indeed."

"Stop butting in, Father."

"Sounds to me like you're coveting another's child," said the Old Man.

"She's my child," said Concepción. "She can't go live with you in Boston."

Rebecca approached her angrily. "Don't forget your place, Thankful Seagraves. A slave's child belongs to the master."

"Why don't you have a daughter of your own, Rebecca?"

Concepción held the other woman's gaze, her fingers clenched tightly around the broom handle. She expected Rebecca to strike her, but she didn't. She walked off with Concepción's daughter instead. "Very well, then, Hanna will stay with us from Tuesday to Saturday, and you can have her back from Saturday to Tuesday. And since today's Thursday, Hanna is to come home with me. You can fetch her after the marketing on Saturday. Ready for an evening ride in the carriage, Hanna?"

Again, the girl squealed.

"I'll wager you don't know what direction we'll be going," said Caleb.

"Say good-bye to Grandpa, children."

After they had left, Concepción took the lamp outside to feed the chickens, allowing herself to sob out there in the dark, in the cloying smell of the chicken dung. *My mother, Sor Juana, Aléndula, Tituba, and now Jerónima, too. How many more pieces of my heart can I lose?*

"Marry me," the Old Man called out from the open door. "Marry me, and I'll make you a free woman."

BOOK III

Mistress Tobias Webb

(WINTER 1691/92)

CHAPTER 36

A t first she thought it must be the whippoorwills. She had stayed out too late. The blue light of dusk was starting to fall over the woods, and it was the time of day when the whippoorwills started their evening song. She loved the haunting song of the whippoorwills and the steady hooting of the owls and the tiny scurrying sounds of squirrels repairing to their shelters in the trees. After eight years of coming to this same spot by the creek to burn her letters to the dead, she had carved a rut through the woods. Even though she could not make out the outlines of the trees because of the gathering dark, she was not afraid. It had been a brisk October with no snow, but tonight the air had turned frosty and it chafed her face and her hands. Still, she felt warm under the new fustian cloak lined with thick flannel that she had made for herself last Christmas.

Her main worry was getting back to the cottage before Rebecca and Caleb showed up for their weekly supper with the Old Man. Today, Nathaniel was coming with them, and they always arrived famished after the last lecture. Concepción had made the pies already, chicken and carrots for the main meal and apple for dessert, and there was plenty of fresh cider in the cellar and a good new cheese for which she had traded the plumpest of her laying birds with Goody Thorn. All was ready except for the table setting and dressing the Old Man. If they found out she had gone out on Lecture Day again, Greenwood had promised her a lashing, and he never failed to make good on that promise. She knew they were going to scold her anyway, Greenwood for not having the account book balanced and Rebecca for leaving the Old Man in Jerónima's care. Jerónima would just sit there playing card games with Caleb, pretending Concepción was nothing more than a servant, a habit she had picked up under Rebecca's tutelage.

The dusk light was growing gray, and Concepción picked up her skirts and started to run. Even though this part of the woods was familiar to her, she did not want to meet the wolf out here in the dark. She heard the singing again and wasn't sure now if those were the whippoorwills or a human voice. Her flesh tingled at the small of her back, and she could almost feel arms reaching out for her in the dark that was closing in behind her.

When the woman appeared between a thicket of pines, Concepción was so startled she tripped on a stump and fell, hands scraping the mulchy ground, so shocked she could not stand up. The woman was dressed in a white robe with a red belt wrapped around her waist. Her long hair hung like a black veil all the way to the ground. In one hand she carried a clump of quills.

Was this an apparition? Concepción wondered. "Virgen Santa," she called out.

"Get up. What are you doing on the ground, Odey?" The woman spoke English, and Concepción realized that it was just the Indian woman named Makwa, whom she had not seen in years.

"You frightened me," Concepción said. "Where have you been, Makwa? Why have you taken no harvest this year? I ran out of firewood in the summer."

"We've been helping our people in the Eastward," said Makwa. "The war with the redcoats has taken many of my relations."

"I ground up all your corn for the chickens and traded your vegetables for wood," said Concepción, unaware until then of her own umbrage.

An owl hooted overhead. There was but the faintest trace of twilight left, and it surrounded them like a mist. The path had receded into darkness now, and Concepción had no idea what direction she should take.

"I don't know how to get back. I can't see the path," she said.

"Take my hand. I will guide you."

Concepción hesitated.

"Come, Odey; there's nothing to fear."

Makwa's hand felt like warm suede.

"Things are not good between the white man and the Dream People," Makwa explained. "I have come to tell you that we can help each other no more. It is not safe for us to come out of the woods. Just know that I will accept you as my sister if you are ever banished or if that child you love so much chooses another's bosom to call her home."

"How could you know—?"

Makwa squeezed something into her hand. "I made this for you. Hang it where your daughter sleeps. It will trap the bad dreams and send the good dreams to Sky Mother."

"What bad dreams, Makwa? My daughter doesn't have bad dreams."

"Not yet, but she will, and this will help. Good-bye, Odey. Keep the ice around your heart, for now. You will need it for what is to come."

Concepción's eyes turned moist. The owl hooted again, and for an instant they were enveloped in a wild flapping of wings as though several birds had converged over their heads. She heard hoofbeats and realized that Makwa had brought her to the edge of the woods already, the violet remains of the sunset streaking the sky. From here Concepción could see the blooming witch hazel tree at the end of the road and, across from it, the Old Man's cottage. She watched the Greenwoods' carriage pull up into the barnyard. A lanky Caleb tumbled out of the seat followed by Rebecca. Jerónima ran out to welcome them, throwing herself against Rebecca. Rebecca scooped Jerónima up into her arms and carried her indoors, though she was a strapping girl, nearly eight years old, now.

When Concepción turned to thank her, Makwa was gone. In her hand, Concepción found a small hoop laced with leather, webbed with sinew at the center, beaded feathers falling to each side. She hid the gift inside her pocket and hastened over the darkening road toward the cottage. Already Greenwood was yelling out for her from the yard, his voice echoing in the dusky air.

"Thankful Seagraves! Get home this instant! You'll be feeling the bite of my lash tonight, you blasted wench."

As she approached the gate, she took a deep breath. If she inhaled deeply enough, she could still smell the wild honeysuckle that she had planted around the perimeter of the house in the late summer. Each year she planted cuttings of different shrubs and vines she found in the woods and in the pastures along the Neck. Some were familiar to her. What the English called bindweed looked like morning glory, and there were wild roses that crept on the ground and violets with furry leaves. Others she had never seen. She would bring them to the Old Man and he told her their names: trillium, mandrake, foxglove, and tansy. Her favorite of all were the sweet-smelling night-willow herb and the wild bergamot, whose color and scent reminded her of blood oranges. The plants grew wildly, enclosing the gray stonework of the house with a rainbow of flowers all summer. Now in late October, after all the flowers had died, after all the vines had purpled and started to wither, and all but the pines and the witch hazel had dropped their leaves and stood bare against the bleak sky of winter, everything looked gray, the ground, the sky, the chickens, even the skin of the people. The only color to be found was on the spiky yellow bursts of the witch hazel flower.

"There you are, wench! I'll beat the insolence out of you yet."

CHAPTER 37

"V en acá, Jerónima. Come and help me with these pumpkins."

The girl didn't budge from the settle where she was stitching a sampler with a biblical verse that Rebecca had selected out of the New Testament:

Slaves must be respectful and obedient to their masters, not only when they are kind and gentle but also when they are unfair.

"Bebita. Did you hear me? I need you to help me seed these pumpkins." Concepción was making pumpkin pies for the morning's breakfast and she was busy rolling out the dough for the crust. The girl pretended not to hear her.

"Jerónima!" Concepción raised her voice.

"What?" the girl shouted, slamming down her needlework. "Why are you always pestering me, Thankful Seagraves?"

"Do not speak to me that way. Soy tu madre."

"I don't know Romish," the child said. After three years of fostering at Rebecca's, the girl refused to speak anything other than her stubborn English tongue. "It's evil. Mama Becca said so. She said you shouldn't make me write that evil language. She's going to tell Reverend Mather on you if you don't stop pestering me, Thankful Seagraves."

"Enough of this 'Mama Becca' nonsense!" Concepción wiped the sticky flour off her hands with a wet cloth. "You are my daughter, not hers. I'm the one who carried you in my belly, the one who brought you into this world, whether you like it or not. And enough of this *tontería* that Spanish is an evil tongue. That's just pure foolishness. Spanish is your mother tongue. I don't care where you were born."

"Everything about you is evil, Thankful Seagraves."

Concepción walked over to the girl and shook her shoulders. "Quiet! Why are you saying these foolish things? That's all Rebecca's doing with this foster-ing business; she's been teaching you to hate me."

Lately it had become more and more difficult to bring Jerónima back from Boston, as the child had become uncannily attached to Rebecca and at the same time less familiar with her own mother. Sometimes the child hid for hours when Concepción showed up at Rebecca's house on Saturday afternoons to bring her back to Roxbury and only Caleb could find her. Other times Jerónima would throw fits and refuse to go with Concepción, so that she had to be carried, with Sara Moor's help, screaming and squirming out of the house and strapped down to the cart with rope. For the last few weeks, Jerónima had taken to silence. She would just sit there, cross-legged in the cart, staring straight ahead of her, not speaking, not answering any questions, not moving in the least for the three-mile trek back across the Neck. The minute Concepción started speaking to her in Spanish, she would bawl, acting like the words themselves were damaging her ears. It used to be different when she was smaller and learning to write. The girl would sit on her side of the table and listen to Concepción's stories about Mex-ico, practicing her vocabulary exercises in Spanish while Concepción explained the meanings of the words. The girl had a good ear for Spanish and wrote with nearly perfect spelling. They would end each lesson by reading together one of the prayers that Concepción had written into the little copybook that Tituba had made so long ago with those handmade pages. Now the very sight of the prayer book gave the girl nightmares. "But it's just the Our Father, *bebita,*" Concepción would say, "and the Ave Maria, and the Credo. You used to say these prayers every night." But the girl refused to look at the book, much less say the prayers.

Indeed, the girl rebuffed all of her mother's gifts. The poppets Concepción continued to make her for each birthday, the scapular of the Virgin of Guadalupe, and especially the sampler. The sampler of Madre's verse that had taken Concepción over a year to finish, embroidered on that dear bird's-eye silk and embellished with gold thread, Jerónima hated most of all. Concepción had caught the girl with the sampler and a pair of scissors in the barn one day, ready to shred the cloth. It was evil, she said; it said the word "devil" in it and it made mockery of men while uplifting women of ill repute. At least the girl hasn't for-gotten how to read Spanish, Concepción thought, but it was a shallow comfort compared to the well of dread that the child's loathing of the sampler inspired in her. It was all Rebecca's doing; Concepción was sure of it. Perhaps to pay Re-becca back for teaching her child to hate her mother and her mother's language, Concepción had tacked the sampler to the wall above the feather bed where she slept and where the child slept with her when she stayed at the farm. "Dare you touch that sampler, Jerónima, and the Devil himself will drag you by the feet out of the bed at night," she had said. A stupid thing to say to an already-frightened child. She regretted it immediately, but it was too late to take back the words. It was then that Makwa's gift of the dream web became useful.

"Now stop arguing with me," said Concepción, "and get to seeding those pumpkins. I'm not your servant, that you should be sitting here enjoying yourself while I do all the work."

The child stared at her with hot amber eyes, so like the pirate's it made Concepción shudder, despite the heat rising out of the hearth pit.

"Obey me, Jerónima."

"My name is Hanna Jeremiah. I hate being your daughter. I wish Mama Becca were my mother!" The girl was so angry bits of spittle flew out of her little mouth. "I hate you, Thankful Seagraves!" she shrieked. "You're mean and ugly as a witch!"

Concepción raised her hand to slap the child, but the girl bolted out of the cottage, leaving the door wide open behind her. Snow swirled into the room, the cold wind sparking the coals in the hearth. Concepción pressed her hand to her eyes and shook her head to keep herself from sobbing.

"There's a damn icy draft in here!" the Old Man yelled from behind the drapes of his bed. "You're asking for it, Thankful Seagraves!"

"Shut your face, Old Man!" she muttered at him. "If you want your dinner today!" Gathering her waistcoat about her, she walked to the doorway, forcing herself to breathe deeply, letting her gaze linger on the yellow petals of the witch hazel tree while she whispered a quick prayer to the Virgin of Guadalupe.

"Le suplico, Madrecita. Please illuminate my daughter, divine Mother, let her stop hating me, and let me not take my anger at Rebecca out on the child." Prayer had helped Concepción overcome bitterness over the years, though still, at times, a hopelessness that tasted of bile welled up in her, and only by breathing deeply and looking at something beautiful could she dispel the anger.

But today even that didn't work. She could not stay the tide of fury that kept swirling up like a sour liquid from her stomach and poisoning her heart. Once, Rebecca had been kind to her. She'd cared for Concepción during her illness and given her a room in her own house when the time of her delivery came. As soon as Juana Jerónima was born, the trouble had started between them. Rebecca would try to wet-nurse the babe and wanted to hold her all day long. When they came back to Roxbury and Concepción took up the work of the chickens, Rebecca would visit all the time, not just on Lecture Days, and all she was interested in was seeing the baby, crooning to the baby, bouncing the baby on her knee, dressing and undressing the baby in the new clothes she brought her, teaching the baby to toddle around in Caleb's old go-cart, singing little rhymes and limericks to the baby, making sure the baby was brought up English and not learning the foul language of the Spanish.

With Concepción, Rebecca became short and cold. Often she did not speak to Concepción at all, unless there was something she needed to scold her for or there was some neighbor stopping by to visit. Then Rebecca turned all sweet and solicitous.

"Thankful Seagraves, would you mind going down to the cellar and bringing up another pitcher of the cider, please?" Or, "This stew is quite delicious, Thankful Seagraves; I really must take down the recipe. You should taste her corn-husk dumplings, Goody Thorn. Indeed, they're steamed right inside the corn husks, and they can be filled with just about anything, even raisins. We'll make you a batch next time. My father is quite pleased with Thankful Seagraves. And just look around, Goody Lowe; look at how spotless she keeps the place. One wouldn't even know there was a half-breed Indian living here. She's completely Christianized, you see, Reverend Lowe? Why, she even learned our language in less time than it took this child to take her first step."

When the visitors were gone, Rebecca would go back to her cold ways. "Don't think it's you I'm showing off," she'd warn. "I don't want any of our Roxbury neighbors to be talking about Father behind his back, or fearing for his life, either, worrying that you might lose your senses one day and take his scalp and his possessions."

"The only possession that I care about, and that you've already taken, Rebecca, is my daughter."

"I've taken nothing from you, Thankful Seagraves. That child was a wild Indian, the way you were letting her run loose. Frolicking in the woods, no less. She needed a proper fostering. All English girls get fostered, even the peasant girls. It's our custom. Why should your child be any different?"

"That's what I'm saying, Rebecca. She is my child, but she thinks she belongs to you. You have turned her against me."

"Stop prattling on with all your complaints. How ungrateful can you be?"

"Close the blasted door, woman! My legs be starting to cramp!"

"I hope you have your overcoat on, Jerónima!" Concepción called out into the wind. She knew the girl was hiding out in the barn and that she was as cold-blooded as the country into which she was born and never needed more than a couple of layers to keep warm. The girl was going to sulk the rest of the day and wouldn't change her demeanor until Concepción dropped her off at Rebecca's house the next day before the marketing, and then she would turn to butter, soft and sweet and pliant.

Concepción took another deep breath, but she could still hear the girl shouting, "You're mean and ugly as a witch. I hate you!" She slammed the door so hard the bottles rattled on the windowsill.

That night Jerónima woke terrified from a dream and pressed herself against Concepción in the feather bed. The girl's heart pounded hard between them.

"It was just a dream, *bebita.* Do you remember it?"

The girl shook her head against Concepción's breast.

"Perhaps you are feeling sorry for having been so rude to me earlier."

The girl sniffled and grunted but stayed close.

"Do you want to hear a story?" said Concepción, her mouth close to the girl's ear. She whispered, even though the Old Man was snoring and curtained off in his bed down below.

"In English?"

"You know I don't tell stories in English."

The girl shrugged.

"*Entonces,* I want you to listen closely, *bebita.* This is the only time you will hear this story."

"Why?"

"Because tomorrow is the twelfth of December, and it is a sacred day, and this is a sacred story, and can only be told once. It is the kind of story that, once told, remains in the heart forever."

"*Tengo susto;* I'm afraid," mumbled Jerónima.

"No, this story will not frighten you. Just listen and don't interrupt. A long time ago in the country of my birth, there was a very poor and humble man of the Aztec people whom the priests had baptized Juan Diego. One day, he was climbing a sacred hill near his home, and he was very downhearted because his uncle was dying of a strange affliction that none of his people had ever seen until the strange bearded men on horses arrived on their shores and infected them with the illness. The healer had told him that there was no cure for this disease, and suggested that he climb the hill of Tepeyac and take an offering to the goddess Tonantzín—"

"Tepa . . . what? Tona . . . who?" Jerónima interrupted.

"Tonantzín, the goddess of life and death."

The girl opened her mouth but didn't say anything.

Concepción continued her story. "But Tonantzín's temple had been defiled by the invaders, and then there was nothing left but rubble and ashes. This only increased Juan Diego's misery, and he knelt there at the top of the hill and cried for what had been taken and what had been lost, and for his uncle whose life nothing would be able to save. While he knelt there, weeping, the sun darkened, as if it had been covered by the moon, and a voice called out to him, a woman's voice, calling him 'dear one' and 'my little child.' Juan Diego was afraid of looking up. There was a radiance in the sudden darkness, and when he dared to raise his eyes, he saw the most beautiful woman hovering over the remains of the temple. She was standing on a dark crescent moon, dressed in a cloak of stars and encircled in rays of light. She asked what was troubling him and he told her about his uncle's strange disease. She instructed him to gather the roses growing on the side of the hill and take them to the priests who had destroyed her temple—"

"That was the goddess?" Jerónima interrupted again.

"—as a sign of her existence, for she lived not in temples, but in the land and in the hearts of the people they had conquered, and her cult would never be eclipsed. 'With all my respect, Mother,' the humble man said, 'it is the middle of winter; there are no roses on this hill; the ground is hard and cold.' 'Go, my son,' she said. 'The roses are there; gather them, and tell them that I live. And your uncle will live, as well.' "

Jerónima's breathing had deepened, and Concepción thought the girl had fallen asleep. She was about to kiss her forehead when the girl said, "Did he find the roses?"

Concepción sighed, moved by a deep love for this child that she could only express in the lightest of touches, a stroke of her hair or her cheek. "The Lady disappeared, and Juan Diego scuttled down the path and found tall rosebushes growing from the rocky hill of Tepeyac, heavy with pink and red roses the size of his outspread hand, just as the Lady had told him. He took his machete and cut them all down, wrapping them in his own homespun cloak to take to the priests. He delivered the Lady's message to the priests, but they did not believe him at first, until he unfurled his cloak and the bundle of roses rolled to the ground. The priests were in shock. Everyone knew that roses, especially huge, perfect roses like that, did not grow in mid-December. It was the Lady's first miracle."

Jerónima sat up. "A miracle?"

"But the real *milagro* was something else, for there, imprinted upon the

Indian man's cloak, was the image of the Lady, exactly as she had appeared to him on Tepeyac, wearing a cloak of stars, encircled in rays of light, and standing on the crescent of a dark moon."

Jerónima gasped. "How did it get there?"

"It was Our Lady's second miracle. There and then the priests had to acknowledge that Juan Diego had spoken the truth, and since then, we tell Juan Diego's story on December twelfth. The final miracle happened when Juan Diego returned home, and saw his uncle sitting up on his *petate*—"

"His what?"

"His sleeping mat, rubbing his eyes as though he had just come out of a long sleep and asking for something to eat."

"Who was that Lady, Thankful Seagraves?"

"Our holy Mother, la Virgen de Guadalupe. The one we pray to every night."

Unexpectedly, the girl's arms wrapped around Concepción's neck, and she started to cry, deep, mournful sobs that carried long into the night until at last, spent of whatever sorrow her little heart was carrying, her breathing slowed and she drifted into sleep.

Concepción held the girl and said an Ave María in thanks for this small miracle that meant the sun and the moon to Concepción. She changed the words of the prayer as Sor Juana had taught her long ago:

"Hail Mary, full of grace,
the Light is with thee.
Blessed art thou among women,
And blessed is the sacred fruit of thy womb.
Holy Mary, Queen of Heaven,
Pray for us, your children,
Now and at the hour of our death,
Amen."

"I think you're saying it wrong, Thankful Seagraves," Jerónima mumbled, halfway asleep already. "You're leaving out the part about the baby Jesus."

CHAPTER 38

The snowfall had made the children sleepy. Tired of playing at cards and working at their respective diligences, she at her needlework, he at his reading or his accounting, for he had now inherited the keeping of his father's ledgers, Caleb and Jerónima lay cuddled up under Rebecca's cloak on the trundle bed, the girl's small head on the youth's shoulder, the glint of their hair—his almost white, hers like honey—bright against the dark carmine of the cloak. They could be brother and sister, thought Concepción, sitting at the table balancing her account book while Rebecca worked on her needlepoint on the settle. The cottage smelled of green pine and baking bread and the Old Man's tobacco. The only sounds were the children's breathing, the scratch of Concepción's quill on the paper, and the slow burble of water boiling in the hearth.

All winter long the Old Man had been sick, coughing up chunks of blood and running high fevers at night that left him completely feeble and bedridden during the day. For weeks, Concepción sponged him down with melted snow, fed him chicken broths and light porridges that he was not able to keep down for more than a few minutes. His bowels were loose, though he had nothing in his stomach to digest, and she took to diapering him like a baby, for it was too cold out to wash the bed linens. She tried it once. The well water had iced over, so she scooped buckets of snow from the yard and set up the wash kettle inside the chimney, keeping the water at a low boil. The steam, she found, eased the Old Man's cough, especially if she steeped pine needles in the water. Taking the washed sheets out to the barn, she strung a rope between two posts and hung the sheets to dry, but found them hard as boards the next morning.

There was an easy silence between them after these eight years of living together, and the Old Man had stopped pawing at her as he used to do. Still, there were times when she bathed him or changed his swaddling that his member responded to her touch, and she caught him looking at her with the yearning of a young man.

Rebecca brought a physician from Boston to see to her father. After leeching his arms and cupping his back, the man pronounced that the Old Man was suffering from a severe case of the whooping cough and that he was on his deathbed and would not last through the season.

"It won't be long, now," the physician said to Rebecca. "Keep him warm and comfortable. That's the best you can hope for."

Now she visited every day. After Caleb had finished his shift at his father's warehouse in Boston, Rebecca and Jerónima would bundle into the carriage with him, braving snow and sleet and icy winds just to spend an hour or two with the Old Man before he died. That's what Rebecca would tell Caleb when he fussed about having to make the trip every day. Now that he was fourteen years old, he was the one who drove the reins. "I'll hear no more of your grumbling. Grandpa might pass on today. Don't you want to say good-bye?" They had been saying good-bye for weeks. For Jerónima and Caleb, it had become a yarn they enacted when they grew bored beyond all measure. Caleb would start to cough, pretend to be choking, and then, holding on to his heart, he'd swoon into a slump on the trundle bed. Jerónima acted as if she were Rebecca, kneeling beside him, pining away in sorrow for the poor dead Old Goat. When Caleb farted, they would both dissolve into frenzied giggles. "It's most unseemly for you to be acting like a child, Caleb," his mother would scold. "Your father would be very disappointed if he knew how much you lack a serious mind for a young man." Lately, though, they'd not been able to play their game, because the Old Man had been asking to eat his dinner at board and he remained in his chair afterward, reading most of the afternoon, unless a coughing fit overtook him.

"I think it's high time this wench and I were married," the Old Man said, looking up from his book, blue eyes bright and lucid.

Rebecca glanced over at him, scowling. "What are you saying, Father? Are you running a fever again?"

"I told you when you first brought her here, Becca, that I weren't going to have a woman servant in my house. I told you she was to be my wife or nothing at all. Her being a foreigner, I waited a seemly number of years. Now I'm dying, and I want to have a wife again before I go."

"I don't think I can allow that, Father."

"I don't need your permission, woman! I may be on my deathbed, but I'm still the father, here. Thankful Seagraves will be my wife, and that's all there is to it. Send word to the town clerk so as he can publish my intentions."

"I don't want to marry you, Old Man," Concepción interjected, appalled at the thought of lying with the Old Man. "I don't want to marry anyone."

"So you want to be a thornback forever, and a slave, to boot?"

"Thornback? What does that mean, Mistress? Thornback?"

Rebecca waved off her question. Her cheeks looked as though she'd been standing inside the chimney. "What nonsense are you prattling, Father?"

The Old Man had his bright gaze locked on Concepción. "I'll tell you what 'thornback' means. It means a wench that never marries, an unnatural wench that leaves her soul ripe for evil. You marry me, and your soul be saved, your slave days be finished. You'll be Mrs. Tobias Webb, my wife and heir."

"Father! Really! Have you lost your senses? Do you have any idea what you're saying? Nathaniel is going to pitch a fit."

The Old Man cackled, showing his purple gums.

"So that's why you're saying it. To get back at Nathaniel?"

"Bugger Nathaniel! I want a woman in my bed before I die. Look." He pulled down the blanket on his lap to show them his member erect under his bed gown. "I still have a few oats to sow."

Rebecca gasped. "Oh, my word, Father! What are you doing? Cover yourself this instant. There are children present."

Despite her own dismay, Concepción could not help laughing at Rebecca's distress.

"Don't encourage him, Thankful Seagraves. Does he behave like this often?"

"He hasn't done it in a while."

"Ah, there it goes," the Old Man lamented. The gown settled as his organ softened and lay flat again.

Rebecca jumped to her feet, her needlepoint frame falling to the floor. "Never in all my days would I have expected to witness such a gross display, and from a writing master and a church elder, too. Not even my own husband has ever exposed . . ." She was so mortified she couldn't finish her sentence. "I pity this poor woman who has to tolerate such coarse misconduct from you, Father. Children! It's time to go. Wake up! Wake up!"

The children rose dazed from their slumber.

"Did he die, then?" asked Caleb.

"Hurry up, Caleb. We're leaving. You, too, Hanna, what are you waiting for? Get your shoes on. It's late."

"What's the matter, Mama Becca?" said Jerónima.

Concepción still winced each time the girl called Rebecca by that name. She helped Jerónima tie the laces on her boots. Caleb shrugged on his coat and wrapped his knitted muffler three times around his neck. They were both still yawning and rubbing the sleep from their eyes.

"Don't forget to say your prayers to the Virgin," Concepción whispered to Jerónima in Spanish, buttoning up her little coat

"Mama, Thankful Seagraves is talking like a papist."

Rebecca trampled her needlepoint in her hurry to snatch up her cloak from the trundle bed.

"Good day, Father. I'm leaving before it turns into a blizzard out there."

"You just do as you're told, woman, and inform the town clerk. I may not even live the three Sabbaths we have to wait before the wedding."

"Is someone getting married, Mama?" said Jerónima.

Rebecca pulled the girl gruffly by the arm. "Come along. And stop asking so many questions."

"Don't be rough with her," Concepción protested, handing Rebecca the beaver hat she hung on the hook behind the door earlier. "It's not the child's fault your father is out of his mind."

When they were gone and she had swallowed the bile that never failed to rise in her throat when she saw her daughter going off with Rebecca without even offering her mother a kiss good-bye, Concepción turned on the Old Man.

"Crazy Old Goat," she called him. "I'm putting you to bed. I have had enough of you."

The Old Man grabbed the back of her neck and yanked her head down level with his. "My wife or a thornback," he uttered, showing her his gums, the stink of rank tobacco on his breath. "Now get me some more beer. I'll be the one letting you know when I want to go to bed."

She punched her fist into his testicles. The Old Man cried out and released her neck. "Do you see how close you are to the fire, Old Man?" she said through clenched teeth. "All I have to do is push back your chair. Pull on me like that again and your daughter will be picking your bones out of the ashes."

"Where's my beer?"

"In the cellar. Get it yourself." She climbed up the ladder and left him sitting there holding his groin.

"What?" he called out. "You going to marry me or not?"

"Not if Rebecca has her way."

"You ain't marrying Rebecca."

CHAPTER 39

The marriage caused row after row between the Old Man and Nathaniel and between the Old Man and Rebecca, but the Old Man had gotten his way. Three weeks later, on the last Saturday in January, the sky a pristine deep blue and the snow melted into slushy pools, the ceremony took place. Minister Jacob Lowe, as wizened and ornery as the Old Man, married them in the drafty little meetinghouse of Roxbury. The Old Man was carried in by his neighbor the blacksmith Goodman Thorn, who had given them a ride in his wagon and picked up the Old Man in his arms as though he were a sick child. Suited up in his Sabbath clothes, his hair and beard washed and combed for the first time in months, cheeks rosy with cranberry wine, the Old Man looked as if he'd lost a few years. He had given Concepción two guineas for a new dress, and she'd chosen one with a yellow satin bodice and a blue velvet skirt with a matching waistcoat. On credit, she had also bought two yards of sheer blue silk for a shawl to drape over her head and a new neck cloth for the Old Man, both of which she embroidered with a motif of witch hazel flowers. She trimmed the Old Man's neck cloth in yellow ribbon to match her dress.

The meetinghouse was filled. All of Roxbury had turned out for the "unseemly spectacle," as Rebecca had called the wedding. Many of those in attendance Concepción had never even seen, though she recognized Goody Thorn; Polly Griffin; the minister's wife, Goody Temperance; and the two young men who came to the cottage to trade their firewood for her poultry, one of whom had tried to fondle her in the barn one day until she kneed him.

When Rebecca arrived, showing up with Caleb and Jerónima but without Nathaniel, a lap desk was brought to the Old Man, upon which rested a goose quill, a bottle of ink, and Concepción's bill of sale. The Old Man inked the pen ceremoniously. In a tremulous but elegant penmanship that surprised Concepción he wrote *Manumitted this 30th day of January 1691/92 by Tobias Webb, her husband, of Roxbury, Massachusetts,* across the top of the bill of sale, signing it.

The reverend and Goodman Thorn signed their names as witnesses under his own, and it was done. She was free.

Tears bubbled up in her eyes, I'm free, she thought. To think that's all it took to change the condition of her life: a sheet of paper, dated and signed by men, one proclaiming her enslavement, the other her liberty. Sor Juana would contradict her, would remind her that now she belonged to the Old Man. "It is the logic of men to enslave women, Concepción. With chains, with vows, or with children—one way or another—we are all enslaved by the destiny that men have imposed on our bodies."

The minister pronounced their vows. Concepción wasn't really listening, though she nodded and said, "I will," when her turn came. She was remembering being sold by the pirate. It felt very much the same, except this time she would not be jumping to her death in the sea. She had more prudent plans than taking her own life.

"The mandrakes yield their fragrance,
the rarest fruits are at our doors;
the new as well as the old . . ."

"Rare fruits, indeed," Concepción heard Goody Thorn mutter behind them.

The minister finished his reading from the Song of Songs in the Bible. The Old Man slipped his dead wife's ring on Concepción's finger, and they were married. She was now Mrs. Tobias Webb, his wife and heir, emancipated by marriage and now, legally, Rebecca's stepmother. Rebecca wept through the whole ceremony.

"Call her Grandma Thankful or I'll box your fat ears," the Old Man scolded young Caleb as he was being carried out of the meetinghouse. "You Greenwoods are going to respect my wife or, by God, I'll be writing you out of my will."

It was not an empty threat for Rebecca and Ruffled Collar. Little as it seemed, the account books showed the value of the farm.

All Concepción had to do to pay the price of her freedom was sleep with the Old Man until he died. Mainly, he wanted to be held and suckled like a newborn. Some nights, when he'd had too much beer at supper, he wanted her to straddle him and move against him until his member stiffened enough to put inside her. Sometimes his withered penis did not respond, but the softness of it squeezed between her legs gave her pleasure, and she would rock her hips and grind against him until something rattled inside her and made her gasp. Other times he would make her strip off her shift and lie beside him so he could pet her from breasts to thighs with his spotted hands, then wiggle one of his fingers inside her, the nail grazing her flesh. He could fall asleep like that, but if she moved, he would scold her and curse at her and call her a half-breed daughter of a papist whore. If Jerónima were spending the night and Concepción tried to resist his advances, he would waken the child with his cursing, so it was best not to move, best to try to sleep with a gnarled white finger trespassing her body, the flaccid purple sac of his manhood grazing her thigh. It would end soon, she had thought, dying as he was.

But he didn't die. He quickened. He wanted to be taken outside, count his hens and roosters, help her with the candling of the eggs, scrutinize the account books, and make sure that his son-in-law wasn't cheating him out of yet another house and home. She took to bathing him once a fortnight in water boiled with bergamot and bayberry leaves to deodorize his skin, each time trimming his beard and cutting the claws of his toenails of his only foot. The physician said the baths were clearing his lungs but that it was the marriage keeping him alive, giving him something to look forward to in the final flickering of his days. So Concepción would lie there, allowing him to touch and squeeze and probe, all the while reminding herself that he could not last forever and that she was free. For the first time since she was pulled from the water nine years ago, dragged to the cold shore of this place called Massachusetts, she was a free person. She could do anything she pleased once he had passed, a thought that kept her going even in her most desolate moments.

She could stop the peddling. She could sell the farm and buy two passages back to New Spain. Take Jerónima with her. They could leave, finally. Go back to New Spain, where she belonged, and where her daughter, too, would belong once she forgot her English upbringing. If she sold it all, how much could she profit? It was a game she played with herself, a tiny bit of torture that kept her mind engaged while she willed her body into numbness under the dry calluses of the Old Man's hands. The board and bench at which they all sat down to eat in the charade of a godly family, the pots and pans and kettles in which she had learned to make and eat the strange food of the English, the lion-pawed armchair with its iron wheels where the Old Man liked to read his books and watch her cook, the settle where she spent untold evening hours embroidering things for Jerónima, the big blue cupboard filled with the linens and tableware that had once belonged to the Old Man's first wife, the bedstead and bed hangings, the trundle bed, the quilts, pillows, blankets, and counterpanes, the trunks and books, the cottage, and the barn and the chickens—all of it would yield a good sum, certainly enough to either buy or bribe her way into a ship's hold.

And yet, she knew it was impossible. She knew her daughter would never leave New England. Assuming there were any ships that sailed to New Spain these days, she would never be able to pull her daughter away from Rebecca, and without her daughter she wasn't going anywhere. She had already lost one Jerónima when the chess piece Madre had given her drifted away into the sea of her drowning. She would not willingly lose another. No matter who she had been at one time, where she had lived, she had to accept that Massachusetts was her destiny. She would never return to her Mexico. She just had to resign herself to the Old Man and the English.

Deep inside her, she also knew something else. Although he could be rough and cantankerous, the Old Man expected nothing more from her than some moments of kindness, and for this he offered her the protection of his name. She did not have to sleep with him every night or change her behavior in any way. He trusted that she would care for his chickens and his farm, he ate the food she made him, he tolerated the malicious pranks that Jerónima played on him when he slept, he came close to being excommunicated from his church for having married a papist, a threat he had welcomed with the words "a pox on religion," and he insisted that everyone respect her as Mrs. Tobias Webb. For all of this Concepción had grown fond of the Old Man. As a gift of her gratitude, she had given him the red ribbon she had found in the trunk when she had first arrived, the one embossed with the image of a she-wolf being suckled by two boys. It would make a nice bookmark, she thought, surprised that it had never occurred to her to use it herself for the same purpose. The Old Man had wept like a little boy when he saw it and inserted it in the page of his *Almanac* that marked the date of their wedding.

When they had traded her life for fifty pounds and changed her name, they had given her no say in the matter, and it had taken her all these years to figure out who Thankful Seagraves was: a foreigner; a pirate's wench; a half-breed mother of a half-breed child; a slave. What did it mean to be Mrs. Tobias Webb? She was still owned by someone and given yet another name not her own, but unlike Thankful Seagraves, Mrs. Tobias Webb had some say in things. She could make decisions on matters that pertained to her daily life, especially since the Old Man was in such a weakened state. She could make changes in the cottage if she wanted to; who was to stop her?

* * *

The first change she made was to buy a casement of real glass for the cottage window. The snow had melted and she could take her eggs and chickens into town again. On her return from the market she saw a sign posted to the big oak tree outside Samuel Sewall's house about the arrival of lights and leaded casements on a recent merchant ship from London, the sale of which was to take place behind the King's Head Tavern for one week only. Without telling anyone about it, she had taken the dimensions of the window using her broomstick, and when she next made her delivery of eggs at the King's Head she stopped to look for a window. Surrounded by chattering townsfolk in hats and walking sticks, she found a casement almost to the exact length, width, and depth of the cottage window. The one she most liked had clear colored glass running down either side of the main sash, but it was wider than she needed, so she had to settle for one with cloudy green glass and a latch that opened from the inside. Double-sashed, framed in iron, and divided up into diamond-shaped leaded panes, the casement was too heavy for her to lift.

"Put that down or you're likely to break it. Where's your master?"

It was the glass merchant, knitting his brows together as he chastised her.

"I want this one," she said, ignoring his assumptions. "What it cost?"

"Aren't you Greenwood's jade? The chicken peddler?"

"I am Mistress Tobias Webb of Roxbury." She flashed her wedding band at him.

Folks had grown quiet, and she could feel everyone's eyes watching her.

"Beg your pardon, Mistress." The glass merchant changed his tune. "Price includes delivery, and for a bit of an extra fee my son and I can set the casement in your window for you. A little wattle and daub around the edges and it will be a good, tight fit. Bring in some nice light, too."

The thought of having natural light inside the cottage nearly made her cry.

"How much extra?" she said, though she already knew she would pay whatever he charged. The total came to two pounds sixpence. It was more than she made in a month with her peddling.

"I pay you half now, and the other half I will pay when you deliver," she said.

She paid the man out of the money she made selling her needlework on consignment to the Widow Cole, whose goods catered to the refined tastes of the merchants' wives and other worthy ladies of Boston. Ruffled Collar had stormed into the farmhouse when he found out about Concepción's embroidery business and demanded a percentage of what she sold, arguing that she was taking time away from the farm to peddle her own interests.

"She be my wife now, Mr. Merchant! What she does is my business, not yours. You leave her be!" The Old Man's pewter mug flew across the room and landed square in Nathaniel's ruffled collar, staining the linen with what was left of his hot chocolate. Since then, Mr. Merchant didn't meddle in her personal business.

When Nathaniel and Rebecca heard about the casement, as Concepción knew they would from one or another of the busybodies watching her transaction with the glass merchant, they were on the doorstone of the cottage before the daub was dry.

"We heard, but we didn't believe it, Father. I told Nathaniel, I didn't think you even knew about it. Did you ask Father's permission to install a light in the window, Thankful Seagraves?"

"She were the wife here, Becca," said the Old Man. "Your mother never asked my permission. Just did what she pleased with the house. What business is it of mine if we have a casement or not? Or is it only merchants' wives who can have real glass in their windows?"

"Tobias, the neighbors are saying—"

"Shut your trap," said the Old Man. "What do I care what the neighbors say?"

"You should care, Tobias. People are saying you've been bewitched by this walleyed, papist wench."

The Old Man reached across the table and smashed his gnarled fist into Nathaniel's jaw.

"Father! Are you mad?" cried Rebecca, rising from her stool by the hearth to stand between the Old Man and her husband.

"If you weren't such a pitiful old geezer, I'd give you a piece of my own fist," said Nathaniel, holding his jaw.

"Nathaniel! Really! The two of you are impossible. See what you've done, Thankful Seagraves?"

But Concepción turned her back on them and climbed up to the loft. She had curtains to embroider for her new window. The Widow Cole had commissioned her to embroider a set of initials—two interlocked *S*s in Gothic script—on two dozen lace-edged handkerchiefs of fine Mantua silk for Samuel Sewall. In exchange, she had chosen two yards of heavy silk sarcenet in a sky blue, which she was decorating with a landscape of two snow-topped volcanoes.

There would be butterflies and dragonflies flitting over the volcanoes and spikes of agave cactus growing at their base. And a lizard lounging on a stone under the cactus.

She realized after they had left that with all the commotion about the window and her mind absorbed with the curtains she hadn't even noticed Jerónima had not come with Rebecca and Nathaniel. She hadn't even thought about the girl. It was the first time she could ever remember not having the child occupy the center of her attention. It scared her to think she might be forgetting her daughter, but how could that be possible? Perhaps, all it meant was that her daughter was becoming less of her reason for living.

CHAPTER 40

The body beside her kicked. For an instant Concepción thought it was the Old Man, and she was about to kick him back, but then she felt a small cold foot wedging under her leg and remembered that she was sleeping with Jerónima up in the loft. Still half-asleep, Concepción touched the girl's face. She'd lost her cap in the middle of the night, and her little ears had become stiff; her whole face felt stony cold. Concepción drew the counterpane over the child's head, stopping to kiss her on the cheek.

"You're poking me!" the girl whimpered into her pillow, and Concepción realized her elbow was digging into the child's side.

"Sshh. Go back to sleep," she whispered in the girl's ear. "Mama's going to get up and write a letter. You sleep, *bebita*." She tucked the covers tight around the girl's legs and shoulders. The girl winced and curled up into a ball.

Concepción took a brimstone-covered stick from the tinderbox, struck it until it sparked and a flame came to life at the tip, and then lit the tin lamp on the large trunk she used as a table. Her teeth chattered so hard it made her head ache. February was by far the coldest month, though her daughter always slept barefoot and with one of her little legs outside the covers. Concepción put on the thickest pair of woolen breeches under her three layers of petticoats, a shirt and waistcoat buttoned to the chin, a muffler for her neck, and a woolen cap pulled low over her frozen earlobes. She had been too tired to scrape the mud from her shoes the previous night, and the soles felt bumpy under the two pairs of stockings on her feet. Although her cheeks and nose were frigid, at least the trembling had stopped and the frozen feeling in her chest was beginning to thaw. She untied the strap around the writing box and removed one of her goose quills, two sheets of paper, and the smallest of the ink cakes she made in the fall and slipped them into the pocket of her apron.

She could hear a draft whistling down the chimney. No wonder it had gotten so cold inside the cottage. She had forgotten to close the flue when she banked the embers last night, and the coals had expired overnight. Now it would take longer to get the fire started. She climbed down the ladder to the keeping room, carrying the lamp in one hand, her stiff bones aching. Sometimes that action alone, climbing up or down the loft ladder, could send her back in her memory to the pirate's ship. She dispelled the memory immediately, before it unleashed a whole wave of dismal remembrances about her passage from New Spain to New England and Aléndula's bones at the bottom of the sea. It's my daughter's birthday; I have to be happy today, she reminded herself.

She made a tent of fresh logs in the chimney, lit the kindling with the burning wick of the lamp, and worked the bellows hard over the kindling until she got a good bed of flames going, then added a handful of dry corn husks to fuel the fire. Other than the crackling of the pine logs, the only sounds heard in the cottage were the Old Man's snoring and the wolves howling in the nearby woods.

Hearing the wolves, she worried about Pecas. Pecas slept in the root cellar when the weather turned, but she was an early riser, like Concepción, and was out hunting in the dark morning hours. If she weren't afraid of waking the Old Man and spoiling her only time for writing her letter, she'd open the door and let the cat in. She would check on the cat later and take her the slices of pudding she had saved from last night's supper when she went down to the cellar to collect the potatoes she was going to need for today's special breakfast.

She sat down on the bench, her back to the fire, and rubbed her palms together to get some heat into her fingers. The ink had become like a chunk of ice. She shaved a few slivers of the black cake into a porringer and mixed in some saliva to liquefy the ink. Almost immediately a thin film of ice started to form over the ink. The morning twilight had started to clear, and she noticed that there were icicles growing on the inside of the windowpane. Outside, the yard looked gray and abandoned.

Loneliness was her daily bread in New England, but today she felt desolate. She had not seen Tituba in four years, and ever since she had married the Old Man neither Sara Moor nor Mary Black would talk to her. It was the same thing that had happened to her in the convent. As a mestiza, she wasn't "clean" enough, racially, to be a novice, but because of her Spanish blood, she had a higher status than the black slaves or the Indian maids and so was accepted by none of them. Only Aléndula locked up in the shed could be her friend.

It must be Jerónima's birthday making me so melancholic, she thought. It brought back memories of the pirate's ship, of Aléndula's illness, of their escape from the convent, images of her life there as Madre's scribe and assistant, and, most painful of all, the memory of her own mother abandoning her in the convent and leaving Mexico without saying good-bye. All she had left was a note, written to Madre, not to Concepción, about the reason for her leaving. Something to do with marrying Concepción's father and going to make their fortune in the north.

Sometimes Concepción wondered what had become of her mother's life in the north. Did she have more children? Did she live or die? Sor Juana's life, she assumed, must have continued as before, with her commissions and her noble guests in the locutory and her troubles with the church. There was so much Concepción had forced herself to forget, that beyond the memory of copying Sor Juana's manuscripts and sneaking off to visit Aléndula imprisoned in the toolshed, beyond her last conversation with Madre the night that she and Aléndula escaped from the convent, and her memories of their long trek to Vera Cruz, there was little else that surfaced without having to be lodged out of her memory with the quill.

Her stomach gurgled with hunger, and hunger reminded her of Jane, Madre's slave in the convent, grinding cornmeal on the metate for tortillas and tamales and *champurrado,* roasting green chiles for stew and red chiles for sauces, crushing spices, pulping fruit, boiling chocolate. How she would love a cup of Jane's frothy hot chocolate to warm her this morning. A steaming bowl of the hominy and tripe soup that Madre said could burn the tongue of the dead with its spiciness. Concepción could almost smell the scent of saffron and garlic from Jane's kitchen. What had happened to Jane? she wondered. Had her pregnancy come to term? Had Madre really sent her away? Jane of the harsh tongue and the shifty eyes and the voice strident as a food monger's, hawking gossip like vegetables at the Thieves Market.

"Men's got one weakness," she used to say, "and it's always hanging in the same place."

And then Jane had gotten pregnant and Madre had become angry with her and said she was going to send Jane back to her childhood home in Panoayán.

"I can't have an infant living in my quarters. It would be too distracting."

"But why do I have to go away, too, Madre?"

"These are bad times in the convent, Concepción. The Archbishop hates me and the new Mother Superior is making my life miserable. I've heard rumors that she plans to take you away from me as soon as she takes office. I can do nothing about it since your indenture is to the convent and not to me. She could sell you to a workhouse and I wouldn't be able to stop her. When my sister comes to take Jane back to my mother's house in Panoayán, why don't you go with them, Concepción?"

"Aléndula wants me to go with her to a place called San Lorenzo de los Negros, a village of *cimarrones* near Vera Cruz. That's where her family is, what's left of it."

"Have you located this place in an atlas?"

"It isn't in the atlas, Madre. It's a village of refugee slaves."

"In Panoayán, your writing skills could be useful to my mother. For as brilliant as she is with numbers, my mother doesn't know how to write, and you could be in charge of her correspondence, or become a scribe in your own right. Hire yourself out as a calligraphist. You may even be able to teach in the Amigas School, if you take a letter from me. Wouldn't you like to choose what to do with your own life, Concepción?"

"I won't be choosing my own life if I go where you want me to go, Madre. I don't want to leave you. I don't want to serve anyone else but you. But if you're saying I have to leave the convent, I would rather go with Aléndula, to her village of *cimarrones* where everyone is free."

"And how is it that you plan to get your friend out of her chains, Concepción?"

"I can bribe the gatekeeper to give me the keys."

"So you need money."

"Yes, but not for the bribe. The only thing that will bribe the gatekeeper is a letter of yours, Madre, preferably one from the Vicereine."

"Dear God, have you been conspiring with the gatekeeper behind my back?"

"No, Madre, but I know that it would be the only way to free Aléndula."

"I see you've been planning this departure of yours already."

"I haven't planned anything, Madre. But it isn't fair that Aléndula is suffering so much. You should see how badly Sor Agustina treats her. Why does she have to beat her with that whip that leaves holes in her skin? And then she makes her wear this horrible lice-infested hair shirt over the wounds to work in the fields. It's so cruel, Madre. I have to do something to help her. Aléndula says that if I free her from her shackles, I, too, will become a *cimarrona* and I can go live with her in that village of *cimarrones*."

"I didn't realize things were so bad for your friend."

"You never want me to talk about her, Madre; you say she keeps me from concentrating on my work."

"Are you sure you can bribe the gatekeeper with a letter of mine?"

"Positive, Madre. She wants to get in the good graces of the new abbess."

"Let's give her what she wants, then, but we'll play a little trick on her. Make a new copy of my *hombres necios* poem, but write it in a plain penmanship, in the form of a letter from the Vicereine to me, and give that to the gatekeeper. It will actually absolve me of any blame once they discover that you and the prisoner have escaped. But first, I want to challenge you to a game of chess, Concepción."

"Chess, Madre? Right now?"

"I want you to reconsider going to Panoayán. I would hate to see your education go to waste in some godforsaken village leagues away from civilization. If I win, you will go to Panoayán. If you win, you can go wherever you desire."

"That's not fair, Madre. You always win."

"Then I shall let you have the white advantage so that you can make the first move."

Concepción played halfheartedly. She lost knight after bishop after castle, hardly noticing that Sor Juana, too, was losing more pieces than usual. They were both so immersed in their own thoughts, they stopped heeding the glass that timed their moves. And then something shifted. Madre's black queen took Concepción's remaining knight, foolishly placing her in a position to be captured by one of Concepción's pawns. With the powerful black queen out of the way, Concepción found her white queen disposing of Madre's battlement of bishops and quickly checkmating Madre's king. Concepción felt no sense of victory, knowing that Madre had yielded the game on purpose.

"Yes, I let you win, Concepción, but only because I was persuaded by your logic. No matter what I think is best, you should be the one to decide what path you want to take. Nobody would take a voyage if they considered the hazards of the sea. But heed me, Concepción, on this point. Just because you're escaping the convent, and following your friend to this village of refugee slaves, don't make the mistake of thinking that you're free. It is the logic of men to enslave women, Concepción. With chains, with vows, or with children—one way or another—we are all enslaved by the destiny that men have imposed on our bodies. As long as men rule the world, women will be destined to captivity. That is the cage every woman is born with. It doesn't matter if you're a *criolla* or a *mestiza*, a servant or a nun. You will never be free, Concepción."

"But didn't you free yourself by joining the convent, Madre?"

"Don't you see the band on my finger, Concepción? I married Christ. I'm not free. Vows are vows, whether we say them to living flesh or to an abstraction on the cross."

"Is there no escape, then, Madre?"

"What you can hope for is that flesh dies, while abstractions live forever."

But death doesn't work, Madre, she would say now. I tried that and it didn't work.

She realized the icy tracks running down her face were tears. Stop this foolishness, Concepción, she thought. These memories do nothing but weaken you. You have to be strong today. It's Jerónima's birthday.

She stirred the icy ink with her quill and started to write.

CHAPTER 41

22 February 1691/92

Querida Madre,

Today is my daughter's eighth birthday, and it is you on my mind more than Aléndula. The roosters are starting to crow, and I am reminded of the crazy roosters that would run around in the courtyard of the convent, waking everyone before the bells of San Jerónimo, the bells of all the churches in the city, announced the prayers of the first office. I remember how you loathed that ritual, how you were forced to awaken after only three or four hours of sleep, for you and I always worked late into the night and you had no choice but to dress and trudge to the choir with the other nuns to sing the prayers of the Prima. I remember how sluggish and bad humored you were, so that not even the hot chocolate that Jane prepared for you would sweeten your mood. If only you knew how much I miss being in Mexico, in the convent with you, at this very moment. I wonder who is making your morning chocolate? Who is staying up long past the curfew bells taking dictation and copying manuscripts for you? Does anyone rub the lumbago pains in your back now that I am gone? Do you miss me, too?

It is my daughter's birthday, and I must shake off all this melancholy. Can you imagine me as a mother? It has been difficult for me.

At first I wasn't even aware of wanting or loving the child that was growing inside me, for she was placed there by a pirate's violation. Everything changed when she was born, and I saw that she would be the only thing of mine in this strange world to which I was brought against my will. But I have lost everything here—my name, my language, my freedom, even my child, who desperately wants to belong to my golden-haired mistress and not the half-breed slave (for that is what I am considered here, even though I've been manumitted by marriage) that bore her. What is so eerie is that each year, my child resembles Rebecca more and more. All of her is golden. Her hair is gold, her eyes amber, like the pirate's, her skin the color of ripe wheat. Although you are her namesake and I am her mother, she rejects everything papist, as they call us Catholics, for they say we worship the Pope, who is nothing more than the Devil in human form and rich raiment.

Still, I love my bebita. She is my flesh and blood, even if they have turned her against me. Rebecca said she expected the child to be sickly or deformed because of the fever I had when I was first brought from the ship. But she emerged, my Jerónima, almost perfect, only a small part of her afflicted, her right foot thin and curved as a toy scythe. The midwife said she would be crippled the rest of her life, but I prayed to la Virgen to make her well, and she heard my prayers, even here. I bound Jerónima's piecito tight with bandages soaked in a heavy starch, and had special wooden shoes made for her with the shape of a healthy foot carved into the sole. Month by month I watched her tiny foot straighten out. By the end of her first year, she could stand on her own, and though her footprints showed that her feet were different, there was nothing else that could tell them apart, and she learned to walk and run and climb like any child. It's only now that she's entering her eighth year that the story of her foot embarrasses her. I have watched her playing tag in the Common with Caleb and his friends. The kids call her Squaw and Crooked Foot and make whooping noises while they chase her. Once, Caleb covered her in chicken feathers in the barnyard.

"I'm not a redskin," she screamed at him, and I wanted to run outside where he had her tied to a barrel, auctioning her off the way they see the grown-ups in town auctioning the Africans and the Indian women on the docks. But I don't go out there. She doesn't want me to be her mother. My own child, delivered of my own body, has been taught to fear and despise me.

When we're alone here, she practicing her lettering or the embroidery stitches I'm teaching her, I doing my piecework or my accounts, she's very quiet, almost doll-like in her stillness. She refuses to speak Spanish, though she understands it well enough. I only speak to her in Spanish when we're alone. It's a secret that she shares uncomfortably with me. Once in a while, she lets me read to her out of a storybook that Rebecca gave her, but only when she's sick, which is rare for that hale little body of hers. Though she in-sists on bathing herself and doesn't like me to touch her very much, she still lets me braid her hair and rub her bad foot with an ointment that eases the cramps she gets when it gets too cold or she's been running too much. She doesn't admit it, but she enjoys looking at the aprons and neck cloths that I embroider for her with birds and flowers that I never see in this country. She admires the needlework and the colors, but I think Rebecca doesn't want her to wear any of it.

It's my accent that Jerónima hates the most, and she won't let me so much as say her name when we go into town. She says she hates the way I pronounce her name, with that hissing sound that gives away my alien tongue. My poor Jerónima, how she hates being the child of a foreigner. She looks nothing like me, is not my double as I used to be my mother's double. I remember the matching clothes my mother and I used to wear, even the same color ribbon in our braids, the same necklaces and earrings, the same beauty mark on the same cheek. I imitated everything about her. Even now, in this foreign life, I find myself making her gestures, talking to Jerónima as my mother talked to me, calling her hija de mi alma, pedazo de mi corazón, niña de mis ojos, chiquita, linda, preciosa. I thought it would be the same with Jerónima, that she would want to be a miniature of me as I was a miniature of her grandmother. And perhaps it would have been that way if I had birthed her in Mexico, if she were not growing up in a place that teaches her to fear her own mother.

Jerónima calls me Mama sometimes, but only if we're alone and she's been frightened by a bad dream. It's Rebecca she wants to be her mother. I don't blame her. She calls me an Indian when she's angry with me for being so different. "You're so ugly," she says. "You're just an Indian. You're not my mother. You're a liar. I don't want you." She breaks my heart, because she's confused, this child of my soul, piece of my heart, apple of my eye, little precious one.

I can hear Jerónima stirring now, and I must quit this letter before she wakens. I think I shall wait till after breakfast to give her her present—her eighth corn-husk doll. After that incident with Mary Glover's trial four years ago, she has never recovered the joy she used to take in the poppets I'd make her every year, so I wanted to make this one very special, dressed in a red skirt, white blouse, green sash, the bright clothes of a china poblana. I have given it real trenzas, using a swatch of my daughter's own hair so that it will have golden braids woven with red ribbons. Then I wrapped the head in a piece of starched lace to make a starburst form of turban. Her apron is made of yellow silk, embroidered with eight tiny turtles in different shades of green and enveloped by a red heart. I was tempted to embroider a face on the doll, like the others, but decided against it. I left her name off the apron, too, as "Juana Jerónima" distresses her so much and I refuse to call her Hanna Jeremiah. On the back, in the most diminutive cross-stitch I know, I write Concepción Benavidez. I hope or imagine that one day these will become valuable to her; perhaps she may even pass them down to her own children, and she can remember the trouble I took to make them for her.

Rebecca and Caleb are coming for breakfast, and I must go and gather the eggs and collect the potatoes for the tortilla española I'm making. I would give anything for some good olive oil to fry the potatoes and some chorizo to spice up the egg. The sausages they use here, called black pudding, are too rich with the flavor of organic meats. Today, there will be no pudding, just eggs, potatoes, garlic, and onions fried in goose lard. At least I can make chocolate, and here they use milk instead of water, so it makes a better froth than in Mexico. I must wait for the milk lady, Goody Thorn, to pass by on her daily trek to Boston. On her return, she picks up the eggs I save for her in exchange for the milk. It is a system of trade that I fear would never work in Mexico, as there are too many hungry people there, and too many thieves waiting to abuse an advantage.

I don't know how different your life is right now, Madre, but as you see, I am in a different world altogether, and all that keeps me rooted to myself is my memories of Mexico, of the convent, and of you.

Do you remember me? I wonder.
Concepción

CHAPTER 42

The wolf was back. All summer long Concepción had found wolf tracks trampling the strawberry and vegetable bed in the garden. The wolf liked to skulk around the chicken coop, sniffing for a way to get inside and terrorize the poor birds. Once he had managed to dig a trench under the coop, and Concepción found it turned into a slaughterhouse the next morning, clumps of feathers smeared with blood and egg yolk and the mangled bodies of capons and cockerels strewn on the floor—a loss that cost her yet another debit in Greenwood's ledger and a swollen lip for good measure. Only the roosters had gone unharmed, both of them escaping through the trench and running loose in the yard while the wolf worked his mayhem. Goodwife Thorn had told her the only way to stave off wolves was to plant garlic around the coop, so she'd spent an entire Sabbath digging a shallow moat around the coop to seed with garlic cloves. Now the chicken house was barely visible behind its screen of dried garlic stalks and the eggs she sold at market were pervaded with the taste of garlic. The wolf had stopped coming at the beginning of the autumn rains, and now, in winter, he had returned, and there he was, shameless in the daylight. Wielding the broom like a scythe, Concepción charged outside, yelling at the wolf in Spanish.

"¡Me la vas a pagar, lobo maldito! You'll be sorry, you damn wolf!"

Cornered against the barn, the wolf watched her calmly, eyes like live coals in his thin gray face. Her knees shook, and her wrist ached with the weight of the broom. The wolf's red tongue hung out and she could see the white points of his eyeteeth. She held the broomstick with both hands and poked it at the wolf. The wolf lowered his head and flattened his ears, crouching low with his hackles raised as he prepared to pounce. Without thinking and not knowing what else to do, she threw the broom at the wolf, watched it fly across the short distance between them and crash into the side of the barn. The wolf had bounded away, leaping over the fence and heading for the woods, his bushy tail dragging in the slushy road.

She didn't realize she was being watched.

"A fine display that was, wouldn't you say, Polly? Broomsticks flying in broad daylight!"

The neighbor Goodwife Thorn and her maid Polly Griffin were standing in the middle of the road with their water buckets, their breath steaming around their faces in the frostbitten morning.

"Thankful Seagraves!" Polly Griffin called to her. "I didn't know you was so familiar with them wolves."

"You two gossips should mind your own business," she replied, not afraid to speak her mind now that they had to think of her as Mistress Webb. She turned her back on them and went to collect her broom. She had not noticed until then that Jerónima was standing barefoot on the doorstone, observing the exchange.

"You take care of yourself, little girl," Goody Thorn called out to Jerónima. "When broomsticks be flying, witches be dying. There be talk of witchcraft in Salem Village; haven't you heard, Thankful Seagraves?"

"What be wishcraft?" Concepción had asked.

"Did you hear that, Polly?" Goody Thorn scoffed. "What be witchcraft! Indeed!"

"Ask the wolf, Thankful Seagraves," Polly Griffin called out over her shoulder. "The wolf will tell you."

CHAPTER 43

Deposition of Goodwife Mehitable Thorn of Roxbury
Boston, Massachusetts Bay Colony
1 (3) 1691/92

Polly Griffin said it was a broomstick. Are you sure, Mehitable?

Reverend Mather, if you please, Sir, I been using a broom all my life. I know what a broomstick looks like.

And you say she made it fly across the barnyard?

That she did, Sir. Straight as an arrow. And she were yammering on and on to the wolf, Sir, like they was familiar with each other, only the wolf didn't look none too happy with her throwing the broomstick at him.

And what did the wolf do, then, Goody Thorn?

Is any of this going to be used against me, Sir?

Whatever gives you that idea, Mehitable? Your reputation is not at stake. The clerk is simply doing his duty and transcribing your statement for the court records.

Polly Griffin and I seen it with our own eyes. The wolf stood on his hind legs and walked away, Sir. Like a man.

Like a man, you say?

On two legs, Sir. That's when we knew 'twere no ordinary wolf.

What do you think it was then?

Please, Sir, this is not a jest. Both you and I know that only the Devil can hide in the skin of an animal and make the animal walk on two legs. 'Twere the Devil she be talking to in that familiar way, is my thought on it, Sir.

The Devil in the shape of a wolf, then? Is that what you saw, Goody Thorn?

No mistake about it, Sir. And Thankful Seagraves speaking to the Devil in her weird tongue.

You didn't say she'd been speaking in the popish way, Mehitable.

It must have slipped my mind, Sir. But popish it was, because she were yelling out to the wolf and neither Polly nor myself could make any sense of what she were saying, so we knew she weren't talking English to the devil-wolf.

Are there any other animals she is familiar with, that you know of, Goody Thorn?

Yes, Sir. There always be a white cat with big black spots beside her, and once we saw her faint right on the doorstone and the white cat were sucking on her mouth, like it were trying to pull the breath right out of her body.

When was that, Goody Thorn?

A long time ago, Sir.

It is of the utmost necessity for us to be precise in these depositions. Whether or not King James reinstates our charter, we do things by the book in New England, the *Holy Book,* that is. So can you please rake your memory, Mehitable, and tell us when it was you saw this cat suckling at the lips of Thankful Seagraves. She is, as you know, wedded to an elder of the church, and we must be very careful not to accuse her unjustly.

She were not Mrs. Tobias Webb then; I know that for sure.

So this incident with the cat happened before she was married?

Long before, Sir. Before that brat of hers were even born.

The child is . . . what? . . . ten years old, thereabouts, Goody Thorn? You've been carrying this information all this time without reporting it?

Didn't think it meant nothing, Sir, other than a cat were trying to steal her breath as cats do to infants. But now, after all these years, I can't help but pass in front of her house every day on my way to the Neck, and I been seeing what she does there, Sir, how she's wrapped that old Tobias around her little finger, how she works the earth with her black magic so she were the only one in Roxbury with corn in her garden nigh the whole year round, pumpkins the size of carriages, and squash half a rod long. Even the eggs and chickens she sells be cursed. Reeking of garlic, they are, and we all know garlic is the witch's herb.

Are you sure you're not accusing your neighbor's wife because you are envious of her gardening skills, Goody Thorn?

I take offense at that, Sir; 'tisn't envy I feel toward Thankful Seagraves. Plain old fear is more like it, for both myself and all her other neighbors, and most especially for Tobias Webb. The old fool's probably gotten himself bewitched and doesn't know it.

Are you accusing Thankful Seagraves of bewitching Tobias Webb, then?

It's the bindweed that made me think of it, Sir.

What bindweed?

The cottage be nearly overrun with hedge-bindweed, Sir. It's a wonder she can even open the door, or that fancy window of hers, with that weed creeping all over the house. Flowers pretty as a trumpet vine, but a very poisonous plant, Sir, for those of us that knows the difference. Of course, it could have other uses.

What uses would those be, Goody Thorn?

A pinch of bindweed added to a posset is said to cause heat in the loins, Sir. It were called bindweed for a reason. Not to mention the sweet nothings that spring from ingesting too much of a powder made with the evening primrose, also called night-willow herb. Indeed, I have seen her make a salad of it, Sir.

So she grows this night-willow herb as well as the bindweed?

I tell you, Sir, you can hardly see the cottage, it's so choked by weeds.

Are you proposing that this papist woman is giving Tobias Webb possets and powders to waken his loins, then, Mehitable?

It would explain the marriage, I think, Sir.

Yes, indeed, Mehitable, such a thing would certainly explain the marriage. It's good that you came to us with your concerns and observations, Goody Thorn. Was there anything else?

That be all for now, but I'm keeping an eye out for the troublemaker.

Now, then, about the fine.

What fine, Sir?

I regret to inform you, Goody Thorn, that the court must fine you for withholding information. Had you come to the court with this information sooner, Mehitable, you might at the very least have prevented the bewitchment of Tobias Webb with this bindweed potion.

I did not know it were a crime not to speak badly about your neighbors, Sir.

Which is it, Mehitable? Is this a bona fide deposition or are you just bearing false witness against your neighbor?

She were not my neighbor, Sir. She be an outsider and a witch.

Withholding information has a fine of, what? Two guineas, I believe.

I got no guineas, Sir, no money at all. And even if I did, that were cold-blooded highway robbery is what it were. Besides, who's ever heard of such a crime?

Of course there are other ways to pay your fine, Goodwife Thorn. You can sit in jail for a few days, or you can procure some evidence against Thankful Seagraves for the court. Whichever you like.

CHAPTER 44

A witch cart!" someone cried out in the square. "It's the witches of Salem Village!"

Through the window of Widow Coles's shop, Concepción watched as a flurry of townspeople started to gather in the middle of Dock Square. The constable's cart trundled into the muddy cobbles in front of the shop. Three women were chained back-to-back on the cart, a dark woman and two white ones, manacles around their necks and ankles. One of the white women seemed beggarly; the other looked like an old goodwife, almost as ancient as the Old Man. And the dark woman . . . Concepción squinted through the leaded green triangles of the windowpane and dropped the bolt of silk she was holding. It couldn't be! That emaciated figure chained with the others could not be Tituba!

Concepción ran out of the shop and up to the cart. "Tituba!" she shouted. "What's going on? What have they done to you?"

Tituba stared back at Concepción as though she didn't know her old friend.

"Don't you recognize me, Tituba? It's me, Concepción."

Tituba's haggard face looked bruised, and one of her eyes was swollen twice its normal size and veined in bright red.

"Get back, wench!" the constable yelled at Concepción, keeping her at bay with a short whip. "Talking to the prisoners is not allowed."

Now a crowd had formed around the constable's cart.

The constable stood up in his seat and addressed the onlookers. "Beware, good citizens of the Bay Colony. The Devil walks amongst us. These three wicked women of Salem Village have been accused of witchcraft. Their names be Sarah Good, Sarah Osborn, and the tawny one there goes by the name of Tituba Indian. They will wait for trial in the Boston jail. Look upon these wretched handmaidens of Satan, all of you, that you may learn how the Visible Saints punish those that dare to traffic with the Evil One."

"I do not understand," Concepción said. "Why have you got them in chains? What did they do?"

"The Devil's bidding, what else?"

Tituba stared straight at Concepción, but it was as though her friend had gone into a trance. There was no flicker of recognition in her eyes, no light in them at all. Tituba's expression was completely blank.

"Tituba! Can't you hear me? It's me. Concepción."

She tried to climb onto the cart, but the constable cracked his whip in the air. "Get back, wench, if you don't want me to flog your hide." He turned his attention back to the crowd. "The black one has confessed her crimes. If any of you in Boston has had dealings with any of the accused, you were required to make an appearance at the Court of Assistants to depose yourself."

"Where are you taking them?" Concepción interrupted him.

"Not to visit the Governor, I assure you. To Stone Prison, of course."

"Can they be visited?"

"For a fee of threepence and a deposition, the jail keep will let anyone see the witches of Salem."

"Will they be fed? Will they have blankets?"

"Now there's a brilliant way to punish Devil worshipers in New England." The constable guffawed. "Give them the royal treatment. Serve them tea and thank them for their trouble."

Some of the townspeople laughed.

Concepción would not relent. "When will they be released?"

"You have tried my patience enough, woman! What is your name? I'm having you pilloried for pestering an officer of the law."

"I am the wife of Tobias Webb, an elder of the church at Roxbury."

He scowled. "A foreigner married to an elder of the church. I don't believe it." He looked up. "Can anyone vouch for this wench?"

"I will vouch for her, sir," called the Widow Cole from the doorway of her shop. "It be unusual, but what she says is true."

That information made the man think twice about arresting her.

"You should know better than to question a constable, then, Mrs. Webb."

"Tituba is a Christian woman. She does not worship the Devil."

"Mind your tongue and your business, Mrs. Webb, if you don't want the magistrates to come knocking on your door as well. From what you see on this cart, this witchcraft business knows no boundaries of color or station. Out of my way!"

He spurred the horse, and the cart trundled down Cornhill Street in the direction of the Town House.

A bevy of goodwives closed in around Concepción, their voices rising to a din.

"That were a fine display of loyalty," muttered Goody Thorn behind her.

"Witches bond together, didn't you know?" said Polly Griffin.

Concepción turned to glare at them. "I suppose it takes a witch to know a witch," she said. She walked over to the Widow Cole to thank her for intervening and pushed her poultry cart away from the shop.

"But we're not finished, Thankful Seagraves," the Widow Cole called out. "There's still the matter of the neck cloths to discuss. I need them by next Saturday."

"I will pick up the fabric later, Goody Cole," Concepción called over her shoulder. But in her mind, all she was thinking was, I have to see Tituba. What does he mean, she's confessed?

For threepence and a deposition, the constable said. Concepción couldn't figure out what a deposition was, and she didn't have any cash to pay the fee, but maybe she could bribe the jail keeper with some tobacco. She still had a small hen in the cart. The nearest tavern was the Blue Cat. Maybe the innkeeper would trade her a pouch of tobacco for the hen. Or maybe Mary Black could lend her some cash, though she wasn't counting on that, since Mary Black didn't even speak to her these days. If all else failed, she knew of an infallible way to get what she wanted, but that would be her last resort.

The innkeeper was serving a round of pints to some men standing at the bar. He nodded at Concepción as she passed.

"Well, if it isn't Goodwife Webb gracing the premises, eh, Mr. Scoggins?" called Mary Black from the back of the tavern. She had a spread of fortune-telling cards laid out in front of a drunkard with a patched eye. "Thankful Seagraves in the flesh." Mary Black looked a little tippled herself.

"You have to stop what you're doing, Mary." Concepción had no time for idle chatter. "Tituba's being accused of witchcraft."

"Tituba's back?"

"She's in trouble, Mary. They arrested her for witchcraft in Salem Village and brought her to Boston on a witch's cart. They've put her in the jail."

"I'm not going to jail," the drunkard slurred. "I'm going to . . . where am I going?"

"To Hell if you don't pay me," Mary Black teased him, prying his hand open. "Hey!" She slapped him, finding his fist empty. "Where's my shilling?"

"Mary, there's a fee of threepence to see Tituba in jail. Can I borrow it?"

"I don't have threepence. This fool ain't even paid me."

"I bought you a nice toddy, didn't I?"

"That ain't payment!" Mary Black slapped the man harder.

"Tituba needs our help, Mary!" Concepción was getting impatient.

"I mean it, Thankful Seagraves, or should I say Goody Webb; I don't have any money. And even if I did, I'd use it to go see Tituba myself. Why don't you borrow it from your old man?" She dissolved into laughter and Concepción rolled her eyes. She would have to try to trade with the innkeeper after all.

The jail keeper's name was Horace Gibbons and Concepción found him leaning against the stone doorjamb of the jail, smoking a pipe, his nails long and crusted black, his greasy gray hair almost green with mold. He stank worse than a pirate.

"Welcome to the house of the damned, girlie," he said, grinning. What teeth he had left were completely black. "What might your business be?"

"I come to see my friend, Tituba."

"Is that the Indian woman? Your friend, is it?"

"Yes. She's not a witch."

"Not a witch? Well, the court says different. Court says she were the queen of the witches in Salem. Herself be the one that confessed."

"I don't believe it. Tituba would never confess to such a thing. It would be a lie."

"Be that as it may, girlie, nobody gets in to see the witches of Salem without a fee and a deposition."

"How much to see just one?"

"A penny for each witch."

"I just come to see Tituba. I don't care about the others."

"They all be locked up in the common cell. See one, see all. Pay for one, pay for all. Three pennies it be, or none shall you see."

He chortled, enjoying the powers of his own rhyme making. She took the pouch of tobacco she got from the innkeeper out of her pocket and offered it to the jail keeper.

"This costs more than threepence," she said.

The man grabbed the pouch with mangy fingers. "The fee is paid; now the words be said. Go around the front to the Court House. Judge Danforth be waiting to take your deposition." The man chortled again as he filled his pipe with the fresh tobacco. "You be his first victim."

CHAPTER 45

Deposition of Goodwife Tobias Webb, née
Thankful Seagraves (papist)
Boston, Massachusetts Bay Colony
7 (3) 1691/92

How is it you know this woman that goes by the name of Tituba Indian?

She is my friend. I knew her when she lived in Boston.

How long ago was that?

Four years ago her master moved her to Salem.

Are you aware that your friend stands accused of witchcraft? Indeed, that your friend has confessed to making a covenant with a man in black from Boston and nine wicked women who did sign his book and meet with him as if in congregation?

I do not know what wishcraft is, Sir.

We're not talking about *wish*craft, woman. *Witch*craft is the crime. Witchery. Traffic with the Devil.

I do not believe in such things, Sir.

What is your religion, please?

I believe in Jesus Christ, Sir, and the Holy Trinity, and the Virgin Mother.

You are, in other words, a papist.

It were called Catholic in my country, Sir. It be a Christian faith.

And do you still practice your papist religion?

One cannot be papist in New England, Sir. That were many years ago, in another life and another place.

But you do admit to having once pertained to the papist religion?

Everyone in New Spain is of the Catholic faith, Sir. I did not choose it.

Were you ever baptized in our faith? The faith of the Visible Saints?

No, Sir.

Then you remain a papist, whether you practice your wickedness or not, and we cannot expect you to know the difference between papacy and witchcraft, as they are one and the same thing.

I have lost your question, Sir.

Do you know the two who are locked up with your friend the Indian woman?

I have never seen them before.

Are you not one of the nine who signed their name in blood in the Devil's book?

I know not what you mean, Sir. I just came to see my friend. To make sure she is not cold or hungry.

Your Indian friend, Goodwife Webb, is evil incarnate. A baker of witch cakes, a necromancer, and a pagan. Had you but seen the torture she and her two cronies inflicted upon the innocent girls at Salem Village you would not be concerning yourself with her welfare. No Christian woman would.

Tituba is not evil, Sir; she would harm no one.

Do you own a black silk hood with a topknot and a white silk lining?

I have been a servant until my recent marriage, Sir. Servants do not wear silk.

Do you know someone who does?

There were many fine ladies in town that might own such a hood.

I repeat: Do you know someone who does?

I have seen something like it on Mistress Rebecca Greenwood, but I believe it is blue, not black.

With a white silk lining?

I believe so, Sir. May I see my friend now, please?

What are your intentions for this visit?

I told you, Sir, I only come to see how she fares. It looked like she were badly beaten. I want to make sure she has food and blankets.

Do you know how much it costs to board a prisoner each a week?

No, Sir.

Two shilling, sixpence, Goodwife Webb, for the base expenses; that means food and shelter. Even the rent of her chains costs extra. There are no provisions for blankets.

I can bring her these, if you will allow it, Sir.

So you know nothing about her covenant with the Devil?

I don't know this word, "covenant," Sir.

Pact, bargain, contract. Call it what you will, woman!

I do not believe Tituba has made a contract with the Devil, Sir.

It is by her own testimony that we know these things to be true, Goody Webb, whether you believe it or not. And by the witness of our own eyes, for we saw six girls of differing ages all become afflicted with strange contortions of their limbs and rolling of the eyes and foaming of the mouth, the minute that your witch friend walked in the room. The only time we've seen such torments in New England has been on the children bewitched by that Widow Glover.

May I speak with her? I would like to hear it from her own lips, Sir.

Have you ever seen a yellow bird in her presence?

There were times when we saw yellow birds in the woods. Finches, I think.

And what were you doing in the woods with an accused witch, pray tell?

She were not a witch, Sir, and we were just gathering nuts and berries. There are many birds of many hues in the woods.

She did not seem to speak to a yellow one?

No, Sir. She spoke only to me.

But you did see a yellow bird in her presence?

As I said, Sir, there be many birds in the woods. Finches, blue jays, cardinals, whippoorwills.

Answer yes or no, please, Goodwife Webb. We don't need a lesson in ornithology. Did you ever see a yellow bird in the presence of Tituba Indian?

Yes.

And what about a black cat?

No.

A red cat?

No.

Any cats at all?

The only cat I have seen in her presence is my own white one in Roxbury.

You keep a white cat?

A white cat lives at the farm, Sir.

Isn't it a chicken farm you're running? What purpose would a cat serve on a chicken farm if not to kill chickens?

She kills mice, Sir, not chickens.

Is this cat your familiar?

I do not understand this word, Sir.

What about a wolf? Have you ever seen a wolf in Tituba Indian's presence?

Sir, wolves run wild through the woods.

Does that mean yes, Mistress Webb?

I have seen wolves in my own kitchen garden while I were gathering eggs and picking apples. They want to hunt the chickens. Has nothing to do with Tituba's presence, Sir.

I submit, Good wife Webb, née Thankful Seagraves, that you and the accused Tituba Indian, whom you freely refer to as your friend, have a mutual conspiracy with the Devil, that you use cats and wolves and yellow birds as your familiars, and furthermore, that you must be one of the nine women that she saw convening round this man in black from Boston writing in the Devil's book.

I know nothing about the Devil. And if he be a man in black from Boston it is likely he were a minister or a teacher, as they are the ones that wear black.

Bite your wicked tongue, woman! Constable! Get in here, man! There you are! I want you to take this impudent woman and lock her up in the stocks for a full turn of the hourglass. I care not whose wife she is. She will not be maligning ministers or teachers in my presence.

But, Sir, may I please see my friend after the hour has passed?

Permission to visit the witches is denied. Constable, tell Horace Gibbons that if this papist ever shows her face near the jailhouse, she is to be locked up with the witches.

I am not a witch, Sir. And neither be Tituba.

Woman, you protest too much.

CHAPTER 46

Concepción finished her marketing earlier than usual that Saturday. Her plan was to go to the jailhouse and visit Tituba before she went to fetch Jerónima from Rebecca's house. The plan would have worked, had Concepción not had the bad luck of running into William Reed outside Greenwood's warehouse, and had they not had to wait for Greenwood to return from his midday meal and had Reed not pestered her again about not accepting any of his proposals and how it was clear she thought herself too good to be a fisherman's wife but how it didn't matter to him anymore since he'd found himself a better woman, now, happy to bear his children. Had William Reed not taken his sweet time unloading his sacks of salted cod onto the balance and had Nathaniel not been interrupted by first one, then two, then three customers needing something from his shop, so that he'd have to start in with the weighing and the figuring all over again each time. But then Rebecca herself came into the shop with Jerónima and Caleb in tow, talking about a sewing circle meeting, and before she knew it Caleb was helping his father with the fish, the girl was waiting for her in the cart, and Rebecca was riding away from the shop in the direction of the North End. All of this before Concepción had even cracked her ledger to show Greenwood the spoils of the day. She had no choice but to take Jerónima with her to the jailhouse, but she would leave the girl in the yard outside the prison, watching the cart.

"I'm just taking a few things to Tituba. Do you remember Tituba?" Concepción spoke English to her daughter when they were in public.

"Why can't I see her?"

"Because she's in trouble and I'm not sure what conditions they've got her living in and I don't want you to see any of it."

"I'm not a baby anymore, Thankful Seagraves."

"Wait for me out here. I will not be long. You are not to move from here." She shook the girl's shoulder. It was imperative that the girl not follow her inside. She wanted no witnesses to what she had to do. "¿Me entiendes?"

"Yes, I understand you, Thankful Seagraves."

"The Virgin help you if you disobey me, Jerónima."

"You're disobeying the magistrates, Thankful Seagraves. You're not supposed to go in there."

"How do you know that? I didn't tell you that."

"Everyone knows everything about you, Thankful Seagraves."

"Well, you just mind me and stay outside. No matter what happens, you don't go in there, or you'll be sorry." She showed the girl the palm of her hand to indicate a spanking. The girl rolled her eyes and turned her back to Concepción.

The magistrates had banished Concepción from the premises of the Court House, and Horace Gibbons was required to report her and lock her up if she showed her face at the prison. Her only recourse was to offer him something she knew he would not refuse, something Jane had taught her and that she, herself, had used with the pirate captain so long ago, to make sure she got on the same ship with Aléndula.

She had brought the jail keep a healthy portion of blood pudding and a half a loaf of bread and some of the cranberry wine that Temperance Lowe had given her last week in exchange for a tub of Concepción's soft soap. She had also thrown in some of the Old Man's tobacco. But she knew none of it would do the trick. The foodstuffs and the tobacco were just a way to get in the door without being reported.

Horace Gibbons sat behind a small, burn-marked table cleaning the locks on a pair of fetters with an awl. Although a fire blazed in the grate in the far corner of the room, the place was cold and dark and musty.

"I've come to see my friend, Tituba," Concepción said as soon as she set foot inside the door.

The man shook his crusty finger at her. "Now you know I ain't allowed to let you in, girlie."

"I paid my fee last time and didn't get to visit."

"Magistrate said I had to lock you up if you ever showed your face here again." Horace Gibbons eyed the bottle poking out of the basket she was carrying.

"Here's some nice cranberry wine," she said, setting the bottle on the table in front of him. His eyes opened wide. She unwrapped the rest of her bribe. ". . . and bread and pudding enough for a feast, and a bit of sweet tobacco for your pipe."

"What else you got in that basket, girlie?"

"Just some bread and a blanket for my friend."

The man's tongue waggled over the chancres on his lips, his eyes shifting back and forth between her face and the foodstuffs in front of him. "Ain't never tasted cranberry wine," he said. "But I know ye be trying to coax me, and ye won't be getting in, girlie, no matter what temptations ye lay before me." He wiggled his eyebrows.

"Very well." Concepción shrugged. "I suppose I shall have to drink the wine myself." She knew what was coming next and needed to guard herself against the nausea already roiling in her gut.

She uncorked the bottle and held it to his nose to give him a good whiff of the cranberry liquor. Seeing him hesitate, she put the bottle to her lips, tilted it back so that the wine splashed into her mouth, and took a deep swallow, letting a drop of the wine slip out the corner of her mouth. She grimaced at the tart sweetness.

"Good and strong," she said, licking her lips. "Are you sure you won't have any?"

He jumped to his feet and came around to her side of the table.

She left her mouth open as he approached, holding her breath to keep from inhaling the stink of his body. As if mesmerized, he bent his head forward and was about to lick the drop of wine sliding down her chin, but she slipped her hand down his breeches and disarmed him.

"Do you sleep here?" she whispered. There was no resistance from him after that. He practically yanked her into the little room adjoining the jail hall, icy cold and lit only by an oil lamp. She could make out a pile of tossed-up bedding on a pallet on the floor. The place reeked of damp stone, urine, and old tallow.

"Here," she said, reaching out to untie his codpiece, as she had been forced to do more than once on the pirate's ship. "Let me ease you."

The man grunted, already wetting the front of his breeches.

"But you must promise to let me see my friend, or I walk away right now," she said, digging her nails into the hairy sac under his member. "And you'll be sorry if you ever tell anyone about this. . . ." He grunted again, nodding. She had no intention of using other than her hand to accomplish the deed. The man's grunting and humping turned her stomach, but she forced herself to finish what she started. It was the only way to see Tituba.

"Touch . . . let me touch . . . your tits," he panted, humping her hand. She unbuttoned her waistcoat, unlaced the stays of her gown, and bared her breasts to hasten his culmination. The moment his hand felt her nipple he released, the stream of it hitting the wall with a splat.

"Do it again," he ordered, "do it again, or you don't see the Indian woman."

She squeezed his still-erect member as hard as she could. He squeezed her breast with the same strength and released again, groaning and trembling.

"Hello? Is anyone here? Thankful Seagraves?"

Concepción yanked her hand away from him, laced up her gown again, and quickly buttoned up her waistcoat. Her breast felt bruised, but she ignored it.

"What did I tell you, Jerónima?" Concepción fumed, coming out into the hall, her face burning with anger and shame.

"There's boys out there yelling mean things at me, Thankful Seagraves. I'm afraid of being out there by myself. Besides, I want to see Tituba, too."

Concepción hurried outside to vomit near the doorstone.

"I can't see!" Jerónima whined, her hand clenched in Concepción's fist as they picked their way through a dark stone corridor littered with dead rats. The light of the oil lamp that Horace Gibbons had given her was weak in the midst of that icy blackness. It felt colder here than outside. The smell rankled Concepción's nostrils and made her nose drip.

"Stop whining, *bebita*. I told you I wanted you to wait outside. This is no place for a child. Now pick up your skirts."

"I can't with one hand."

"Well, use both hands. Let go of me and pick up your skirts. I don't want you getting near those rats."

The girl gathered up the front of her petticoats with her free hand, but she did not loosen her grip of Concepción. "Why is Tituba in here, Thankful Seagraves? She must have done something bad."

"Hush. You don't want to offend Tituba, do you?"

"If she weren't bad, she wouldn't be here."

"Hush, I said, or I shall leave you here in the dark while I go the rest of the way, Jerónima."

The girl's shadow jerked. "I'm Hanna!" she said petulantly, pulling her hand out of Concepción's grasp.

They continued down the corridor in silence, their shadows wavering on the moss-covered walls. The corridor separated into two at the end. To the right, the lamp illuminated a hallway of four wooden doors with grated openings at the top and big tarnished locks hanging from the rusty hasps. Down the left hallway she could see a large cell enclosed by iron bars that reached all the way up to the rafters. A sconce on the far wall cast a flickering light into the cell. She heard Jerónima's teeth chattering and brought the girl close against her, keeping her arm around her shivering shoulders. The girl did not pull away.

"Vamos," said Concepción, moving in the direction of the sconce.

Jerónima whimpered. "Our Father, who art in Heaven . . ."

They approached the cell, and the reek of excrement and burnt pitch surpassed the dankness. Save for the sconce and a barred little window high in the wall that let in a slit of light, everything was dark. The three prisoners were chained to a great iron ring in the middle of the cell.

"Tituba, where are you? It's me, Concepción." She spoke in Spanish.

Jerónima twitched.

"Tituba, why don't you speak to me? Why do you pretend not to know me?"

"Who are you?" one of the others spoke. "What are you saying?"

"It's better for you if I don't know you, Concepción," Tituba spoke at last.

"Is that the Romish tongue you're speaking, Tituba Indian?"

"The Romish, the Romish," a child's voice shrieked, and suddenly there was a little girl staring up at them through the bars, her face sooty under the soiled flaps of her lappet. She couldn't be more than five years old.

"Come here, Dorcas. Get away from them."

"Who is she?" Jerónima asked. "Why did they lock up a child, Thankful Seagraves?"

"I'm Dorcas Good," said the little girl. "They say I'm the apple that don't fall far from the tree, but I don't know what that means; do you?"

"It means they think you're a witch like your mother," Tituba explained.

"A rotten apple!" The girl grinned, showing blackened little teeth.

What a nightmare. This was worse than the pirate's ship. Why had she allowed Jerónima to come with her? She should have disciplined the girl for her disobedience and made her stay outside with the cart. No matter what epithets were being yelled to her outside, nothing could be worse than this.

"Let's go." Concepción tugged on the girl's arm. "I'll be back another time, Tituba."

Someone moaned, and Jerónima twitched again, shivering harder than before.

"I'm ill," said an old woman's voice. "Please help me. Do you have anything to drink? I'm so thirsty."

"That's Sarah Osborn," said the girl. "She's dying."

The woman moaned again.

Concepción had brought cider and salt pork for Tituba.

"If you have any food or drink, Concepción," Tituba said, "give it to Dorcas and she will divide it among us."

"Take it, Dorcas, and bring it here to your ma."

"Let the girl divide it, Sarah Good," said Tituba.

Concepción poured the cider into a wooden mug. The girl's filthy little hands flew out and yanked the mug out of Concepción's grasp.

"Careful, don't spill it," said Concepción. "Take it to the lady who is ill first."

The girl held the mug in both hands and drained it.

"More," she said, giving the mug back to Concepción.

"This is for the rest; it's not for you," Concepción said, refilling the mug. "Take it to the sick lady. Go on."

"Bring it here, Dorcas; don't give it to that one that's dying. Give it to your ma."

"If you dare to drink from that, Sarah Good, it will scald your tongue and set your belly on fire," said Tituba.

"Go on, then, Dorcas. Give it to the old bitch. I don't need to be cursed by that black thing."

The girl retreated into the dark maw of the cell. Concepción heard the woman's thirsty slurps.

"Leave some for the rest of us, Sarah Osborn," said Tituba.

"I have more," said Concepción. "Bring me the mug, Dorcas."

"Did you bring any food?" said Sarah Good.

"Salt pork. There's enough for all of you."

The girl reappeared at the bars with the empty mug.

Concepción unwrapped the burlap and canvas in which she had brought the meat. "Take the cup, Jerónima."

Jerónima shook her head and buried her face into Concepción's apron.

"Food. We want food now," cried Dorcas Good, throwing the mug down. It clattered to the side of the cell, landing near a decomposed carcass of a rat.

Concepción sighed but didn't scold the child. She took her knife out and cut a chunk of the salt pork and gave it to little Dorcas.

"Take this to your mother," she said.

Dorcas retreated again and Concepción heard snarling. Jerónima started mumbling the Lord's Prayer again. The girl's shivers had given way to quaking.

"Ya mero, bebita. We're almost done."

The next piece was for Sarah Osborn. The last and biggest piece for Tituba.

"What about me?" said the girl.

"Did your mother eat it all? That was meant for both of you."

"I ain't got no more meat," grumbled Sarah Good. "You hardly gave me none."

"Come here, child. Have some of mine," said Tituba.

"Where's the cider?" snapped Sarah Good. "You better not have drunk it all, or I'll punch you in the gut, Sarah Osborn."

"Dorcas, come," called Concepción. "Take the jug to Tituba, and then to your mother. Don't drop it. And bring it back to me when it's empty."

"I ain't drinking after no Romish black thing put her lips on the jug," said Sarah Good.

"Suit yourself," said Concepción. She could hear Tituba swallowing from the jug in deep gulps.

"Give me some of that, you greedy bitch!" said Sarah Good.

"Thank you," said the Osborn woman, "whoever you are. God bless you."

"Don't be blessing that Romish thing; she be just as evil as this black thing that got us both locked up. That Romish one be in here with us soon enough."

"Bring me the jug, Dorcas," said Concepción.

"You! Romish one!" said Sarah Good. "What's that next to you? Looks like a monkey clinging to your skirt. You better watch yourself, little missy, or you'll end up like Dorcas here in jail with her mother. Witch's daughter be a witch, too. The apple don't fall far from the tree, remember?" The woman cackled.

Jerónima started to cry, her little fists clenched in Concepción's petticoats.

"Don't pay attention to her, Concepción," Tituba said in Spanish. "She's a mean old hag and everyone despises her in Salem Village. But get away from here as quickly as you can and don't come back. It's dangerous here. For both of you."

"Mama, take me home!" Jerónima was yanking at Concepción's arm. The girl hadn't called her Mama in a long time.

"But what did you do, Tituba?" Concepción couldn't help herself. She needed to hear Tituba's side of the story. "Why are they saying you're a witch? They say you confessed. Did you really hurt those girls in Salem?"

"I hurt nobody. Abigail and Mercy wanted me to look in the water and foretell their future, see who they were going to marry. They went crazy after that. Scared little Betty to death with their stories, and made her crazy, too."

"I knew that thing you did with the water was going to get you in trouble someday, Tituba."

"Just giving the Devil his due. Ain't no different than what Mary Black does at the Blue Cat Inn."

"Mary Black!" called Dorcas. "Mary Black! Mary Black!"

"Take me home!" Jerónima started to shriek, pulling Concepción's apron so hard she tore the seam. "Take me home, Thankful Seagraves!"

"The monkey's having a fit right here," said Sarah Good. "Look, Dorcas, her own mother be bewitching her."

Jerónima started to yelp and stomp her feet.

"Get away from here, Concepción! Don't ever come back. You'll die here."

Jerónima cried the whole three miles back to Roxbury, huddled at the far end of the cart behind the chicken cages, holding her knees.

"*Bebita,* I told you to stay outside. Why did you follow me? I knew it were an evil place, and I did not want you to see that."

"You're the one that's evil," the girl muttered, glaring at her under the blond ledge of her eyebrows. "Why did I have to be your daughter? I don't want to be your daughter anymore. You're mean and ugly as a witch."

CHAPTER 47

Deposition of William Reed of Marblehead
Boston, Massachusetts Bay Colony
14 (4) 1692

It's a sad lot we're in, William, the Evil One has again betrayed New England, and we find ourselves plagued once more with frontier wars, savage raids, and now even bewitched children in Essex County. There are those among us, ministers and magistrates alike, who believe New England has become like the whore of Babylon, opening her harbor to any who would find purchase there, and leaving her soul ripe for the dissipations of other worlds and other faiths. Are you following me, William? You know what this means, don't you? That, as a loyal subject of the King and Queen of England, it is your duty to depose yourself of any dealings, associations, or tribulations you may currently have or ever have had with any foreigners. The magistrates' clerk here will record what you have to say.

>I know no foreigners, Sir, other'n the wench in Roxbury that goes by the name of Thankful Seagraves.

What dealings have you had with Thankful Seagraves, then, Mr. Reed?

>None at all, Sir. Just a small grievance of no account now.

And what grievance is that, William?

>Only that she refused to marry me, Sir, and when I asked her why, she always laughed in me face and said she not be the marrying kind, so to leave her be or I'd be sorry.

When did all this transpire, Mr. Reed?

>Last spring, Sir, and every spring 'fore that for five years.

You asked Thankful Seagraves to marry you six times, then, Mr. Reed?

>I reckon so, Sir. Once a year I got me hopes up, and then she'd dash them to pieces.

Pray tell, William, why did you persist in proposing marriage with that foreigner?

I couldna help it, Sir. She musta put a spell on me; that be what Mammy thinks. She were forever appearing in me dreams, luring me on to sinful acts, Sir.

Can you be more exact, Mr. Reed? How does she appear?

Very tempting, Sir. She would come to me naked in her spirit form and sit atop me chest, Sir, and do all manner of lewd things. 'Fore I know it, Sir, I'd be doing something sinful with myself, and with Mammy snoring away right next to me in the bed.

You know that self-gratification is punishable by law, don't you, William?

Aye, Sir. But I couldna help it. Like it were herself moving my hand, Sir.

Do you think she sent her spirit out to torment you, then, William?

Torment me she did, Sir, till just a few weeks ago, when me and Martha tied the knot. Every night 'fore that, since I first laid eyes on her when she were bedridden in Roxbury, Thankful Seagraves were a wicked torment.

Can you describe the first time you saw the foreigner Thankful Seagraves, Mr. Reed? I need to write it all down in my book here. What were the circumstances? Proceed, William. The clerk wants every detail you can remember.

It was when she were first brought to Old Tobias Webb's house. She were sick and feverish, near to dying, and yammering on and on in the popish tongue. Master Greenwood asked me to come along to Roxbury with him and see if I could make some sense out of what the girl were saying. My pappy, as some folks know, Sir, sailed the Spanish Main with Sir Francis Drake in his youth, and learned a word or two of the Spanish tongue that he spoke to me brothers and me when he were angry and flogged us for misbehaving. I had told Master Greenwood that story, and he asked me to have a listen to Thankful Seagraves and see if I might could understand what the wench were muttering. When I first saw them two-colored eyes of hers, I admit I felt afraid, Sir. I couldna make out hide nor hair of what she were trying to say. But even then, she bewitched me.

How did she do that, Mr. Reed?

Sat straight up in the bed and raised her shift, Sir, and showed me her naked tits.

And what did you do, William?

I felt me arms reach out to her, like I had no say over me own body. Like she were pulling me to her nakedness with them weird eyes of hers, and

'fore I knew it, me hands were all over her and she were writhing in the
bed, laughing, and opening her legs and wanting more, Sir.

Did you give her more, William?

No, Sir. I snapped out of whatever spell she'd cast on me and ran out of there.

Did you tell Mr. Greenwood about it, William?

No, Sir. Ashamed of meself is how I felt. Scared, too. I knew Goody
Greenwood would box me ears for me and send word to Mammy that I
were trespassing against her sick servant. If you ever seen me mammy, Sir,
you'd understand how much you wouldna want to get on her bad side.
'Twoudn't make her no difference that I be a grown man, now, Reverend.
She'd a whipped me with her cat-o'-nine-tails in an instant.

**And since then, Mr. Reed, Thankful Seagraves has been appearing to you in
the night and performing all manner of lecherous deeds with you in your bed?**

Till just a few weeks ago, Sir, that be absolutely true.

**And yet, still, you persisted in asking her to marry you, William? Did you not
fear that you might be marrying a witch?**

Didn't think on that notion, Sir. I don't know much about witches. Just
thought it were because I wanted her so much that she stayed lodged in me
brain and me loins.

**But your desire was fueled by her unseemly act of showing you her nakedness,
William. She's been wielding her power over you since that day. You shouldn't be
surprised that she refuses to marry you, any more than we should wonder at
your persistence in asking for her hand every year for the last six years. If she
were to have married you, William, she'd have lost her influence over you. Don't
you see? The wench kept you tithed to the hope that one day she'd accept your
offer of marriage, and meanwhile she continued to torment your manhood.**

Cunning witch she is, then, Sir.

**Aye, William. That Thankful Seagraves is a cunning witch, indeed. Of course,
you know that she has most recently become the wife of Elder Tobias Webb?**

I heard the news, Sir. I couldna believe it, him being so late into life and all,
and her so steadfast that she were never to marry at all.

**And why do you think she chose to marry an old man like Tobias and not
yourself in the peak of life, William?**

I couldna say, Sir. 'Tis a mystery to me.

**Would you say, William, that perhaps old Tobias has more to offer the wench
than you do, and she, being a papist and greedy to the core, would rather give**

herself to one whose widow and heir she'll become soon, than to one with little more than a fishing boat and a long stretch of life ahead of him?

Not to mention, Mr. Reed, that this marriage liberates Thankful Seagraves from her indenture, and that, as a Visible Saint himself, Tobias Webb gives his new wife the same status in the church as he.

    She be worldly wise, then, Sirs.

Consider yourself a fortunate man, William, that you are not wedded to this foreigner. Would you truly want a wise witch in your bed wreaking havoc on your immortal soul?

    I were spared, it looks like, Sir.

Light dawns over Marblehead.

CHAPTER 48

" 'Some hide themselves in Caves and Delves,
in places under ground:
Some rashly leap into the Deep,
to scape by being drown'd . . . ' "

Balanced on the stool, Caleb was reciting a poem called "Day of Doom" for Jerónima and the Old Man, his adolescent voice vacillating between octaves.

"Isn't that what you did, Thankful Seagraves? Didn't you leap into the deep, too? That's what Mama Becca said."

"Pipe down and let me listen," the Old Man scolded the girl.

" 'Some to the Rocks (O senseless blocks!)
and woody Mountains run,
That there they might this fearful sight,
and dreaded Presence shun.' "

"You senseless block!" Jerónima laughed at Caleb.

"Girl, you interrupt one more time, and I'll be boxing your ears till they're blue."

Concepción had no stomach for supper this evening. Rebecca had brought smelts and expected her to cook them in the pie she was making for the Old Man.

"He never likes these fish, Rebecca. It will spoil his supper."

"Nonsense. Do you think you know more about my father's eating habits than I do? You may have married him, but you don't know everything there is to know about my father. He used to love fresh smelts, didn't you, Papa?"

"What?"

"Smelts! Remember how much you used to love fresh smelts?"

"Pelts? I don't have any pelts. What do I look like? A redskin?"

"Never mind. Just do as I say, Thankful Seagraves. They'll make a nice filling in that pie."

"He's been having a hard time with his stools, Rebecca. For the last three days he's been sitting on the chamber pot straining and cursing. I was just going to make a vegetable pie with turnips and peas."

Rebecca's face colored, but she kept her voice low. "I may not be your mistress anymore since you've finagled your way into my poor old father's bed, but I will not be crossed today, Thankful Seagraves."

Their battle of wills was interrupted by a sharp knocking.

"Go see who's at the door, Caleb," said Rebecca, but Jerónima had already run to open it.

There stood Goody Thorn, wringing her apron on the doorstone. "Just stopping by to collect my eggs this evening and give you the bad news, in case you didn't hear of it," she said.

Concepción asked Jerónima to go to the barn to fetch the basket of eggs she'd laid aside for Goody Thorn, then went back to rolling out the piecrusts on the sideboard. The girl bolted outside, nearly toppling Goody Thorn in her haste.

"Hanna, be careful," said Rebecca. "Pray come in, Mehitable. Please take some refreshment with us. I can offer you some hot cider, freshly mulled."

Goody Thorn shook her head, and the flaps on her bonnet jiggled over her face. "Thank you kindly, but I have to get my own supper started at home," she said, though she stepped into the keeping room just the same.

"What news, then, Mehitable?"

"Sarah Osborn of Salem Village died in prison, I heard. The wicked crone never confessed. Took her sins with her."

"Who died?" yelled the Old Man.

"Sarah Osborn, Grandpa," shouted Caleb. "From Salem Village. Died in prison."

"Is that the old one who called for a minister?" the Old Man asked, puffing on his pipe.

"How do you know anything about Sarah Osborn, Father?"

"Jacob Lowe were here yesterday. Said none of them Boston worthies could be bothered to minister to a so-called witch, so he did it, himself. Said the only bewitchment he could find was Goody Osborn being old and sickly. Damn nonsense, calling women witches just for getting on in years."

"Not just women anymore, Tobias," said Goody Thorn loudly. "Giles Corey's been put in jail. And George Jacobs and George Burroughs both been accused."

"Burroughs? As in Minister Burroughs?" asked Rebecca.

"It be a true shame, a man as good-looking as that," answered the goodwife.

"That Burroughs fellow were sweet on you once, weren't he, Becca? Before that thief of a merchant of yours stole your fancy."

"Father!"

"I wouldn't be saying that too loud, Tobias," warned Goody Thorn, "seeing as how they be calling him a witch now, too."

"Whole damn colony's lost its mind."

"You don't believe it, then, Tobias? That they be witches?"

"Pack of nonsense," guffawed the Old Man. "Them magistrates be in cahoots with the merchants, is how I see it. They'll do anything to take people's property."

"Oh, there he goes. Pay no attention to him, Mehitable. He's just being a cantankerous old goat right now. Are you sure you won't have some cider with us?"

Jerónima bolted into the cottage, red-cheeked from the cold and empty-handed. "The cat was eating a mouse, Thankful Seagraves," she said excitedly.

"Where are the eggs, Hanna?" Rebecca asked.

"I gave the basket to Polly. She says she were freezing her bum out there."

"Wasn't it just spring a few days ago?" said Rebecca. "Who understands the climate in New England? All my bulbs froze over yesterday."

"I told you the *Almanac* were predicting a late storm this spring," the Old Man intervened.

"Hot cider'd be nice," said Goody Thorn, "but I best be taking my leave now."

"Caleb, walk Goody Thorn home, please. It's nearly dark out."

"Ma, I have to learn this whole section by tomorrow."

"It's Wigglesworth," Rebecca explained to the goodwife. "His teacher wants him to learn it by rote."

"'Tis a good poem to know in these times," said the Old Man. "Days of doom, indeed."

"Leave the boy be," said Goody Thorn. "Polly and me walk this path to and fro every day. I don't expect we'll run into any wolves or Indians tonight. We'll manage just fine without an escort."

"Godspeed, then, Mehitable," said Rebecca. "And thank you for taking the trouble to stop by and give us the news."

At the doorstone, Goody Thorn said, "I'm surprised that one didn't tell you about Osborn already. . . ." She pointed her chin at Concepción. "I hear she's been keeping company with Horace Gibbons since they brought that Indian friend of hers to the dungeon."

Rebecca turned to glower at Concepción. "You have?"

Concepción was chopping turnips now. "You heard wrong, Gossip Thorn," she rejoined. "I went one time, back in March, when they first brought Tituba. I took her some food and haven't been back since." She stared at Jerónima and warned her with a look not to speak.

"Everyone tells it different," said Goody Thorn. "Days of doom, days of doom," she murmured, walking away from the door.

Jerónima closed the door and skipped jauntily over to the Old Man's chair. Without asking for permission, she sat in his lap and turned his face toward her, holding his stubbly chin in her hand. "You know what, Grandpa? Thankful Seagraves took the jail keeper some of your wine and tobacco so he'd let her see Tituba Indian. She made me go in there with her, and it was full of dead rats."

"What?" Rebecca gasped.

Concepción stared aghast at Jerónima.

The Old Man pushed the girl off his leg. "Are you a tattletale or a tart?"

Caleb laughed and Jerónima ran to smack him on the face.

Rebecca took deliberate steps toward Concepción. "Have you forgotten the Widow Glover's trial and the effect it had on this child? You dared take her into the dungeon to see a witch? You should be put in the stocks for torturing your own child."

Concepción forced herself to ignore Rebecca. She knew Rebecca was eager for a confrontation. Concepción scooped out the dried peas she'd been soaking in hot water, wicked the water from them with a towel, and added them to the chopped turnips and sage inside the bottom crust. She covered everything with salt and pepper, slices of garlic, and thick pats of butter and threw the top crust over the pie.

"Answer me. How could you do something like that, Thankful Seagraves? No wonder Hanna's scared to death at night. You don't deserve to have a child."

"Where's my supper?" grumbled the Old Man. "We eat later and later these days. A man could starve to death waiting on you two gossips."

"Stop griping, Old Man," Concepción told him.

Rebecca flipped back the top crust of the pie and picked up the earlier argument where they had left off. "I don't see the smelts in here. I told you I bought them special for my father, so you will obey me and put them in the pie, Thankful Seagraves."

Concepción rinsed her hands in the wash bucket and squared her shoulders. "No, Rebecca, I am not required to obey you ever again. If you want to muck up a good pie with these smelts, please yourself." She dried her hands on her apron and headed for the ladder.

"Where do you think you're going?"

"To finish the cushion covers I'm making for Widow Cole."

"You're going to do needlework while I cook supper?"

"This is your night for supper with your father, Rebecca. Make whatever meal you want."

Rebecca turned her ire on Caleb. "Don't you have some memorization to do, young man? We'd better not receive another complaint from your teacher."

Concepción called Jerónima over with a finger. "I asked you to fetch the cider as soon as you arrived. What are you waiting for?"

"Mama?" Jerónima turned to Rebecca.

"Do as your mother says, and fetch the cider, Hanna," Rebecca said, removing her waistcoat, her blue gaze level on Concepción.

The girl stared at Rebecca as though she'd just been slapped. She wasn't used to having Rebecca take Concepción's side or, worse, to Rebecca calling Concepción her mother. The girl ran outside, slamming the door behind her. The panes in the casement rattled.

"Why should the child obey you, Thankful Seagraves?" said Rebecca, pinning up the front of her petticoats to keep them from catching on the hearth fire. "She's got your example of impudence to follow. Do you see, Caleb, why young girls have to be fostered outside their homes? Someone's got to teach that child Christian manners."

"After four years, you don't seem to be doing a very good job of it, Rebecca," Concepción said, climbing the ladder.

The Old Man chuckled in the background. "This is better than cricket," he said.

"It's all your fault, Father. You've given that papist license to rule our lives."

"She just be a bigger bully than you, Becca."

Up in the loft Concepción lit the tin lamp, aware of a throb in her temples. She changed her mind about the needlework. The pattern she was working on was a tricky one, using a complex combination of feathered and knotted stitches. The central image was the fiery oval and crescent moon of the Virgen de Guadalupe's image, which the Widow Cole called "sun rising over a boat," with a border of fish and triangles. Concepción needed daylight for that work, not these yellow spots that the lamp threw out and that barely broke the darkness of the loft. She heard Jerónima come back inside and the Old Man scolding her to close the door behind her. Caleb went back to practicing his poem and Rebecca to complaining to her father about the impertinence of Thankful Seagraves. To drown Rebecca out, Concepción settled down on her feather bed to read Anne Bradstreet's poetry in a voice louder than Caleb's.

"The Tenth Muse Lately Sprung Up in America," she read,

"'To sing of Wars, of Captains, and of Kings,
Of Cities founded, Common-wealths begun,
For my mean Pen are too superior things . . .'"

"Give it back, Hanna!"

"It's not 'in vain do they to Judges say'; it's 'in vain do they to Mountains say.' You got it all wrong, Caleb."

"Mama, look! Hanna's taken my book."

"Both of you, come here right now," said Rebecca. "Each of you will write one full page of the commandments here in this ledger before supper."

"Who first, Mama Becca? There's only one pen."

"Caleb first."

Concepción proceeded with her recital, running her finger down the text of "The Prologue" until her eye found the lines she was looking for:

"'I am obnoxious to each carping tongue
Who says my hand a needle better fits;
A Poet's Pen all scorn I should thus wrong,
For such despite they cast on female wits.
If what I do prove well, it won't advance;
They'll say it's stol'n, or else it was by chance.'"

"Ma, I can't hear myself thinking with Thankful Seagraves up there reading at the top of her lungs," moaned Caleb.

"Pipe down, woman!" the Old Man yelled. And then, rebuking Caleb, he said, "And you, Sir, are you wearing knickers or skirts?"

Concepción stopped reading and decided to write a letter, instead. That verse of Anne Bradstreet's had reminded her of Sor Juana. Concepcion put the book down and opened her writing desk, taking out her quill and inkpot and a sheet of deckle-edged parchment. She would have to wait until next Thursday to burn it, but it would keep, and there was something oddly thrilling about writing a letter in Spanish out in the open with Rebecca and the others below. I'm the wife here, Concepción thought. I'm the wife of this house and I shall do whatever I please.

12 May 1692
Dearest Madre,

There is a woman poet in New England named Anne Bradstreet who is called the Tenth Muse. Her poetry is simple enough for me to understand in English, and her style is plain compared with yours, but it seems she, too, was persecuted by men for writing and using her wits, and was told she'd be better off wielding a needle than a pen. I wonder what the chosen children of God would say if they could read your words, Madre. I wish I remembered more than that poem about stubborn men that continues to haunt me, whose verses I have embroidered on a sampler that I have tacked to the wall over my bed, as it gives me great comfort to sleep beneath your wisdom. Perhaps I should translate these verses into English and use stanzas in some of the needlework I sell to the Widow Cole. I can just imagine it: a pillow cover embroidered with "Whose is the greater fault in an errant passion? She who falls for pleading, or he who, fallen, pleads?" Or, perhaps, an apron stitched with a condensed version of one of your observations, Madre: "How is virtue spoiled, if not by the spoiler?"

Down below she could hear Rebecca chastising the Old Man about the smell of his wind, and Caleb about oversleeping that morning and the fine his father had had to pay for his lateness at the morning Lecture, and Jerónima about the chicken droppings she'd gotten on her apron when she went out to the barn.

"All three of you are just insufferable," said Rebecca.

"Good Christ," the Old Man cursed. "You're worse than your mother."

Your words about stubborn men accusing women for no reason are eerily appropriate right now, Madre, as New England is plagued by talk of witches, and women in every town are being accused by children, by their neighbors, even by their own kin, of committing evil acts against them. My best friend, Tituba, is among them. She was one of the first to be accused, though they say that, unlike the others, she's the only one that's confessed. She says she's just giving the Devil his due, but I don't understand what that means. It's one of those English expressions she uses sometimes that make her sound like one of them.

"Did you sift the flour, Thankful Seagraves?" Rebecca called up the ladder. "The crust keeps falling apart. Have you still not learned to make a piecrust correctly?"

Concepción ignored her and continued to write. Rebecca went back to banging lids and pots.

It's been a strange spring this year, Madre, with the snow not melting until the middle of April, followed by a blaze of heat that made the green beans blossom and the corn tops show, and now it's winter again. The only thing that's flourished so far in 1692 is the witchcraft. The seed of it was sown in Salem Village at the end of February. By

March the stalks were full-grown, and the April winds pollinated the curse all over the colony. Now every town in New England is sprouting witches, a royal crop of witches. Already they have accused more than a hundred people, most of them women. The dungeon where my friend Tituba has lived in chains since March is overflowing with bodies, and they say hundreds more are in the gleaning. None have been hung, yet, though one of them died of illness inside the prison, all because there are foolish men in the disguise of magistrates and ministers who, as you so wisely said so many years ago, incarnate the sins of the world and the flesh of the Devil.

"Thankful Seagraves, are you listening to me? I need your help."

"Quit picking on my wife, woman!" growled the Old Man.

"She's up there reading Robin's books, Mama," Jerónima gossiped. "She even writes in them in popish."

"How would you know that, Hanna? Do you read popish?"

"She tried to teach me when I was little, but I never learned. I knew it was bad."

Concepción shook her head at her daughter's lies but said nothing. What the girl revealed next froze her hand.

"And you know what else, Mama Becca? Thankful Seagraves writes popish letters to her friend who died in the sea and she burns these letters in the woods on Lecture Day, and she has this thing hanging in the garret that looks like a little web that catches dreams. She said her Indian friend in the woods gave it to her."

"Can I see it?" said Caleb.

"Enough of all this racket!" the Old Man roared. "I am near to giving all of you a good, sound whipping. Woman, get thee down to supper! There'll be no more tattling or tomfoolery in my house."

There was a taut silence at the board. Concepción saw that Rebecca had given up on the pie and made a pottage, instead. A smelt pottage with irregular-looking dumplings and overboiled peas and turnips floating in garlic and butter and salt.

Jerónima was pouting about something and Caleb was reading his Wigglesworth and the Old Man was picking the smelts out of his food with the long nail of his index finger.

"I hate these damn fish," the Old Man complained, gnashing his gums.

"They're smelts, Father. You used to love smelts."

"Never liked smelts. Them damn little bones get caught in my gullet."

"They're not going to kill you, Father."

"Much you care." He turned to Concepción. "If you let her cook here again, I'll be taking the rod to you," he said, pushing away his trencher. "Get me some cheese."

"You can't eat cheese, Old Man," Concepción told him. "You need something to loosen your stools, not something that's going to make them stick together."

"That is not conversation for the table," Rebecca said, crinkling her nose.

"I'll eat what I please, woman! Now get me some cheese."

Concepción went to the cupboard and cut a wedge of Goody Thorn's sharp cheese and dropped it on the table in front of the Old Man. "Eat your cheese, then. And don't be cursing me when you can't shit in the morning."

The children giggled, but Rebecca stopped them with an icy blue glare.

"Well, I see how much I'm appreciated here," said Rebecca. "I don't even know why I keep coming every Thursday."

"Me, either," muttered Caleb through a mouthful of dumpling.

"I hope you're not getting smart with me, young man," snapped Rebecca. "I don't care how tall or how old you get, you will honor and respect me at all times. And you, young lady . . ." She turned to Jerónima. "I can't tell you how disappointed I am in the behavior you've shown tonight. What kind of manners are those, slamming doors and pitching fits? You will stay here for the next week and think about how to atone for it."

"I'm not coming home with you?" said Jerónima, her chin already trembling.

"Not for a week. In the meantime, you'll work on a sampler with this verse from Scripture: 'An insolent daughter puts father and mother to shame, and will be disowned by both.' I want it finished by next Lecture Day. Do you understand?"

"What about school?"

"Your classes at Mrs. Foster's will have to wait until you learn how to behave like a proper young lady."

As soon as he'd finished with his cheese, the Old Man relit his pipe and blew the smoke over the board. Rebecca and Caleb left immediately after supper.

Jerónima followed them outside and begged not to be left behind, but Rebecca climbed into the carriage and ignored the girl completely. Jerónima stayed outside by the fence, crying for Rebecca at the top of her lungs. Concepción left the door open as she washed the dishes, looking out every five minutes to make sure the girl hadn't taken off in pursuit of Rebecca. But the night was black and moonless, and Concepción knew how afraid the girl was of the dark. The Old Man shivered violently on the chamber pot but didn't object to the open door. Concepción waited for him to make his water before changing him into a clean sleeping gown and putting him to bed.

"She's a mean woman, that daughter of mine," said the Old Man as Concepción tucked the covers tightly around his frail bones.

"Put your cap on, Old Man," said Concepción, handing him the clean cap. "It's going to be another cold night."

The Old Man puckered his lips at her and she bent over so he could kiss her on the cheek. He turned her face toward him and she expected him to kiss her on the lips, but he didn't. Just stared at her with his silver-blue eyes.

"You're Mistress Tobias Webb. Don't forget that."

"Sleep well, Old Man."

She closed the curtains around the bed and went to fill the warming pan with hot coals. When the curfew bells on the steeple of the meetinghouse started to clang, she dragged Jerónima back into the cottage with her arms wrapped tight around the girl's chest. The girl kicked her in the shins. Jerónima's little body was shaking with cold and her lips had gone blue.

"No matter how much you cry, she can't hear you all the way to Boston," Concepción tried to reason with the girl.

"It's your fault, Thankful Seagraves. If you hadn't made her angry, she wouldn't be sore at me."

"It's not going to kill you to live with your own mother for a week."

"You're not my mother. She's my mother. She's my Mama Becca!"

"She's not your mother. Don't forget it was me who brought you into your life. You're just Rebecca's poppet, because she can't bear any more children."

"I am not her poppet," Jerónima shrieked so loud the Old Man yelled at them from behind his curtains.

"Cut out that caterwauling, you two!"

"Mama Becca loves me," Jerónima said, lowering her voice to a hiss. "She loves me more than Caleb, more than her own son."

Concepción shook her head. "Poor Jerónima," she said.

"Don't call me that!" the girl screamed again. "I told you! That's not my name!"

"By God, I'm going to flog someone," the Old Man yelled out.

"Calm down, *hija*."

Concepción reached out for her, but the girl pulled away.

"I am not your *hija*. Mama Becca says you're a foreigner and a pirate's wench, and I hate being your *hija*. I wish I could be Mama Becca's daughter, not yours! Not yours, Thankful Seagraves!"

Jerónima refused to sleep with her up in the loft. The girl wrapped herself in a woolen coverlet she pulled from the cupboard and curled up on the settle, crying herself to sleep in front of the fire. Concepción sat at the board and tried to work on balancing her account book, but her own tears were streaking down her face and staining the paper.

She stared at the bill that she still owed to Greenwood. With the interest he charged on the balance, the debt just got larger and larger each year. She was still paying off the new cooking pots she got after her wedding to the Old Man, the repair of the iron wheels on the Old Man's armchair, and the foodstuffs that came in on the buccaneer ships that Nathaniel did business with and that Concepción could not do without—olive oil, oranges, coffee, cocoa, saffron, cinnamon, and coriander seed. She kept the spices displayed on the lintel in the tiny green jars she bought at the apothecary's for a penny apiece. Jerónima had outgrown all of her clothes that year, and each year the girl needed a new pair of boots as well, the left one specially made for her bad foot, with a deeper heel bed. And now Rebecca had made arrangements for Jerónima to receive instruction in arithmetic, music and Latin at the home of one Mrs. Foster, and the year's tuition of six dollars had also been added to Concepción's account. And for what? She wiped the tears from her face with the back of her hand. So that the girl could hate her and spite her and refuse to speak her native tongue, the only request Concepción had ever made of the child.

"Stop pitying yourself, Concepción Benavídez," she said aloud in Spanish. "Better to think about how you're going to pay off this bill."

She raked her eyes over the numbers again to make sure Greenwood hadn't added incorrectly, as he was wont to do, but noticed some writing on the next page of the ledger. She turned the page and saw that it was just the Ten Commandments that Rebecca had made the children write in the ledger. On one side, Caleb's pinched, nearly illegible writing, on the other, Jerónima's wide cursive. She was about to close the book, but she saw that, behind the commandments the children had written something else, something that chilled Concepción's heart, a silent dialogue in writing:

I want to see that dream-catching thing. Go get it.

I can't touch it. It's evil.

What does it do?

I don't know.

How do you know it's evil?

Thankful Seagraves has a graven image of a cloaked woman standing on a black moon with flames all around her. She lights candles and prays to this image every day. Do you think that's evil?

Maybe she's a witch.

Should we tell Mama Becca?

Concepción pulled out the page and tore it to pieces over the fire. The girl twitched under her blanket on the settle.

BOOK IV

Days of Doom

⬦

(JUNE–OCTOBER 1692)

CHAPTER 49

It was near to summer solstice, and a decent rain had not fallen all year. The gardens stood bare, the fields fallow. In the Common, the cows and goats languished, lanky and bad humored. All spring, Concepción had had trouble with the chickens. They'd grown scrawny from lack of water, their eggs dappled with blood, chicks too weak to hatch from their shells. Corn and grain were scarce, so she'd been forced to feed them crushed acorns and mashed turnips mixed with salt and sage and dried garlic. What little water remained in the well had turned to vapor. Even the forest looked slaked, smelling of straw rather than pine. But today Concepción could sense rain. A storm was brewing. She could feel it in her bones, that deep ache right down to the marrow.

She was cleaning up the cottage after breakfast, while Jerónima chased down the few biddies and cockerels she was taking to market later, when a red-wheeled rig rolled into the barnyard with Rebecca at the reins. Concepción stepped outside, wiping her hands on her apron.

"Mama Becca! What are you doing here today?" Jerónima squealed.

"We're off to Dorchester!" said Caleb, puffing out his chest. "How do you like our new rig?"

"I've come to get Hanna," Rebecca said to Concepción.

"She's mine until the end of the day, Rebecca. I'll drop her off when we finish the marketing. There's no need for you to come get her."

"Yes, I know, but I have to pay a visit to Nathaniel's sister in Dorchester; she's got a new baby that I haven't met, yet, and I thought Hanna might want to join Caleb and me for the ride in our smart, new carriage."

"She can't go. There's a storm coming."

"What nonsense are you inventing, Thankful Seagraves? Are you a weather vane, now? I don't see a single cloud on the horizon. What say you, Hanna? It's not a long ride, and I've got you a copy of the new translation of *Aesop's Fables* to read on the way."

"I want to go with you, Mama Becca," Jerónima whined.

"Fine, I'm glad that's settled. Jump on up here, then. That's right. Tuck in right here between me and Caleb." She clucked her tongue to get the horse moving. "Till Saturday then, Thankful Seagraves."

"Good riddance, Thankful Seagraves," called Caleb.

"Hush, Caleb," Rebecca said.

"Good-bye, *bebita*," Concepción called, but the girl buried her nose in her book.

Concepción stood in the barnyard, watching them leave, wondering why they were going back in the direction of Boston when Dorchester lay south of Roxbury, but the Old Man was yelling for her to take him out of the blasted outhouse and she still had to finish Jerónima's job of chasing down the chickens. At least the eggs had been gathered into their shallow baskets in the cart, though Concepción doubted the girl had taken the time to wipe them clean, as she'd asked her to do.

Each year the three-mile trek to Boston along the Neck got longer and longer, much worse in a summer of relentless heat like this one, the wheels of the cart cracking and crunching over the rocks in the hard earth. Even at this early hour of the morning, the leaves on the trees hung limp and pale with thirst. A charwoman was scrubbing the doorstone at George's Tavern, where Tituba used to work. Concepción waved, but the woman ignored her. She noticed the clouds beginning to gather at the river's edge, the stark outline of the windmill etched against the gathering storm.

She pushed the heavy cart past the town gate where the Neck became Orange Street all the way up to the giant oak tree on Essex Street. Sometimes, if she were early enough, she liked to take Frog Lane to the left and walk along Tremont Street where she could watch the cows grazing in the green grass of the Common for a few minutes. But there was no time to take the long way around today, and besides, the grass was more hay than green. Past Essex, Orange changed to Newbury Street up to Samuel Sewall's house. Up until last May, she had used to deliver six eggs a week at the Sewall place, but then one of the eggs turned out bloody and Judge Sewall's maid refused to buy from her anymore. From Sewall's place, Newbury turned into Marlborough Street and two blocks later, at the South Church, Cornhill Street, where she could at last see the turrets of the Town House at the corner of King Street. Four blocks down King Street was Merchants Row, where Greenwood's warehouse backed up to the Town Dock.

She had to report to Greenwood first. "No marketing until I see the inventory and tally up how much you're going to owe me at the end of the day" was his rule.

It was always the same inventory, unless there was a drought, as there was this summer. "In that case, we raise the prices," he'd say. "That's the way of business. The more we have of whatever it is people want, the less it costs; the less we have, the higher it costs." Today, there were only enough eggs for the three inns she delivered to, and she worried some of them wouldn't be healthy. Although Jerónima said she had candled the eggs when she gathered them up earlier, the child wasn't always trustworthy. The nine chickens Concepción had managed to catch were rangy and belligerent, and they pecked and ruffled one another's feathers through their cages.

"That's a meager cart," said Greenwood when he saw the inventory. "Not worth the trip, really."

"The best I could do, given the drought."

"It'll have to be a shilling and a half on the chickens," Greenwood told her. "And a penny for each egg. Ready money. We'll take no credit, today. Folks have fallen behind on their accounts. Cash or barter, only." He gripped her arm and dropped his face so close to hers she could see the hairs inside his nostrils. "But don't be too generous with the barter, either. It's the coin we need."

The inns that were her regular customers all lay half a mile north of the Town Dock in the North End: a dozen eggs and two roasting hens at the Red Lion Inn on Wood Lane, a dozen eggs and two cockerels at the King's Head Tavern on Fleet Street, and another dozen eggs at the Noah's Ark on Foster Street. Today the Noah's Ark only wanted six eggs, so she had six left to sell to the goodwives waiting for her in the North Square.

In front of the North Church on Moon Street, the four of them stood close together with their baskets, ready to pounce on her cart. They got first dibs over the people farther south at the Market Place in Dock Square. Today Greenwood had told her no more credit, except for the inns. She hated haggling with the maids and goodwives, and with no option for credit she steeled herself against their ill will.

"You missed it, Thankful Seagraves," said Mistress Dempsey, one of her few cash-paying customers, helping herself to four of the largest speckled eggs from the cart.

"A penny for each egg, today."

"Have you got change for a shilling?"

Concepción showed her the empty money box. The woman gave her a four-pence coin.

"Missed what, Mistress?"

"The hanging in Salem Village, what else? Bridget Bishop were the first witch to get hung. Looked like a May Fair with all those people."

"And Goody Bishop standing there like a ghost already," added Goodwife Earle, "pale as a cow's bone."

"Poor woman pissed herself before they even drew the noose."

"Reminded me of the Glover hanging here in Boston a few years back."

"But that one were a Catholic, weren't she?"

"And this Bishop woman be a trollop, is what I heard," said Cotton Mather's kitchen maid, Mary Penfield.

"Well, that be the end of her sultriness. How much is that one?" Goody Earle pointed to the hen she wanted so that Concepción could crack her neck for her.

"A shilling and a half, Mistress."

"Are you completely daft? Do you really think I'm going to pay a whole shilling and a half for a skin-and-bones chicken?"

"Merchant Greenwood's price, Mistress. You can take it up with him, if you like."

"I guess I'll just have to buy my bird from someone else." She started to leave.

"A shilling, then, Mistress."

Goody Earle rummaged through the coins in her gloved palm, muttering something about highway robbery under her breath, and handed her a shilling.

Concepción grabbed one of the chickens out of a cage, quickly wrung her neck, and handed the bird to the goodwife.

"You tell Nathaniel Greenwood I'll be buying my poultry elsewhere after today," she said, swinging her basket angrily as she stalked off.

"Reverend wants capon for supper, Thankful Seagraves," said Mary Penfield. "No one seems to have any capons."

"Running low on cocks," Concepción said, "so there's no chance for capons, Mary. All I have left are four hens and that little cockerel there. He's small, but he's got a good chest on him."

"He looks like a quail, Thankful Seagraves. And those hens look ancient."

"They've laid a few eggs in their lifetime, that's true, but they're all I can spare, the way things are with this drought."

"Give me the cockerel, then. Just add it to our account."

"Afraid I can't do that today, Mary. Merchant Greenwood says no more credit until all the accounts get paid."

"Your master's gonna refuse credit to Cotton Mather?" Mary Penfield's blue eyes gaped at her.

"I have no say in it, Mary. Merchant Greenwood says everyone's got to pay up first. Cash or barter. You got something to barter, I'll take it."

"It's no wonder folks have stopped buying from you, Thankful Seagraves," said Mary, giving her a shilling for the cockerel. "It's the last time I bring my basket to you."

"Well said, Mary Penfield. I'm with you," said Goody Hibble, who had not purchased anything. "You can forget about coming up this street in the future, Thankful Seagraves. Don't come anywhere near North Square, again."

"Price is a shilling and a half for the cockerel," Concepción said to Mary Penfield, but the girl pretended not to hear. Instead of three shillings for two birds, she'd only collected two. That was one shilling Concepción was going to have to make up for somehow. She watched the four women scurry across to the church, their heads bent together like outraged biddies.

"You still have to pay your accounts, ladies," she called after them. "Merchant Greenwood will be calling on you."

Concepción turned the cart around and headed for Dock Square, seven long blocks down North Street that ran parallel to the wharves, the smell of her sweat mingling with the stench of horse dung and spoiled fish. The clouds looked like burlap sacks piled on the horizon. She paid no mind to the men who whistled and called out to her from the wharves, though she still liked to gaze out over the bay and imagine herself stowing away on one of those merchant ships heading to the West Indies. The cackling in the cart reminded her that she still had four more chickens and two eggs to get rid of before she could return to the warehouse and then trek the three miles back to Roxbury.

In Dock Square, she parked her cart in her usual spot, in front of Widow Cole's shop, and broke the news about the credit situation to all her regulars.

"That's ungodly, Thankful Seagraves." Goodwife Hale frowned. "Nathaniel Greenwood can't expect us to pay cash with the way things are right now."

"I heard Judge Sewall had to lend the Governor two hundred pounds," said Widow Wescott. "If the Governor doesn't have money, where are we supposed to get it?"

"It's downright beastly, Thankful Seagraves," added Eunice Fry. "Aren't we cursed enough with all these witches and Indian raids?"

"It ain't my rule, ladies. Cash or barter, that's what Merchant Greenwood said."

"But none of us has cash," said Goody March.

"And what are we supposed to barter with?" asked Widow Wescott. "This drought's thinned out my cow and dried out her milk. I can't make cheese. I can't make butter. My garden's nothing but weeds. I have no corn to feed the pigs. Am I supposed to trade my last sack of flour for one of these bony chickens?"

"I got twelve children at home so bloated on leek soup it's coming out their ears," said Goody March. "They ain't tasted solid food in a week."

"I guess we're supposed to starve to death while the merchants line their pockets," said Goody Hale.

"It's the same thing as what's happening all over Essex Couny," said Eunice Fry.

Goody March touched her lightly on the shoulder. "I got a farthing from the Old Country," she said, digging to the bottom of her pocket. "It's been my amulet for years, but I venture it be worse luck to let twelve children starve." She placed the flimsy coin in Concepción's palm.

It felt lighter than a ladybug and probably had less value than that. Still, a coin was a coin. She didn't feel like carrying the crosses of Goody March's twelve starving children on her back, and it was too hot to be arguing with goodwives over scrawny hens.

"Does anybody else have coin? I'll take anything."

Widow Wescott showed her a penny. "That's the last of it," she said, puckering her wrinkled lips.

"A lucky bunch of gossips you are," Concepción told them, raising the gates on the cages. "Today, one penny and a farthing buys the rest of these chickens. One for each of you."

White arms arrowed into the cart. She couldn't tell if all the ruckus came from the startled chickens or the goodwives. "One apiece, ladies. Don't get greedy."

"Those of us that paid cash should get first dibs," said Goody March.

"I'm the one who gave her real money," said Widow Wescott. "I should pick first."

"How about if I give you these last two eggs, Goody Wescott? Is that fair?"

The widow shrugged and puckered her mouth again, but she tucked the eggs into her basket before anyone else could take them.

When they were gone, Concepción stared at the empty chicken cages and egg baskets. Greenwood was going to pitch one of his fits. The burlap-colored clouds had started to move across the sky, and a sudden wind fluttered the loose feathers on the boards of the cart. So far, feathers and a farthing were the only profits of the day. She held the farthing up close to her eyes. An amulet, Goody March called it. She dropped the farthing into her pocket and the penny into the money box along with the two shillings and four pence she'd collected in North Square and headed back to Greenwood's. She was dreading the confrontation with him, knowing he would never condone her generosity with the goodwives. No doubt he would add the difference in the price of the chickens to her own account.

"Ni modo," she said out loud. "What's done is done."

"Are ye talking to yerself, Thankful Seagraves?" said a man's voice behind her.

She jumped and turned so quickly her neck twisted. "Oh, it's just you," she said, recognizing William Reed. She should have recognized him by the smell of fish guts that always followed the man. She tried to push the cart forward, but he stepped up and leaned against the side, letting the fishing net he always carried sag on the ground.

"Just coming from Master Greenwood's," he said, crossing his arms and eyeing her breasts.

Despite the heat, she buttoned up her waistcoat. "I'm heading there myself."

"Looks like ye overshot it. Merchants Row is a block behind us. What brings ye here, anyway? Only trollops gather in the dockyard."

"It's none of your business, William Reed."

He shrugged and spit a stream of black tobacco juice into the cobbles. "Did ye hear the good news, then? Master Greenwood be getting ready to buy himself his own wharf. The one closest to the Battery, Union Wharf, be called Greenwood Wharf and Ship Yard soon enough. He's giving me twelve months with no docking fees."

"Very generous of him," she said. "But you'll have to walk near to a mile to get from the far side of the North End down to his warehouse, just to save yourself the halfpence of docking in the Town Dock here."

He frowned. Clearly he hadn't thought of that. "A ha'pence is a ha'pence," he said. "I'll be saving meself . . ." He counted on his fingers. ". . . twopence a month. In one year, that'll be twenty-four . . . two shillings . . . in me own pocket 'stead of the dockmaster's."

Or in Greenwood's pocket after he underpays you, she wanted to say, but decided to curb her tongue. She pointed to his empty net. "Looks like Greenwood did well by you today."

"Actually, it were Judge Sewall that took my best catch today. He and Judge Winthrop be hosting the magistrates of the high court for dinner at the sign of the King's Head. Twelve men and a king crab for each of them. Claws as big as mutton shanks."

"That's a lot of magistrates," she said.

"There be a lot of witches in Essex County," he said.

"A lot of women being called witches," she retorted. "The Old Man says it all be a ploy to take their property."

"Mammy doesn't set much store by all this talk of witchcraft, either," he said.

She was weary of speaking to him. "Your mammy's a smart woman, William. Please tell her I said so. And I best be on my way. A storm is coming, and I want to be back in Roxbury before it hits."

He glanced up at the sky, covered now with gray-bellied clouds "Mammy said the same thing this morning. Said she could smell rain. You smell rain, too?"

"I feel it in my bones. My joints start to ache. Excuse me, William." She gave a little push to her cart to get him to move, but he didn't budge.

"I wanted to tell ye something more," he said, eyes darting back and forth as though he were trying to make up his mind about something. "Something about yer friend from Salem Village I heard from Horace Gibbons, but it slipped me mind, now."

"Something about Tituba? What is it, William?"

"Give us a kiss, first," he said.

"And be tied to the whipping post for lewd behavior and deceiving my husband with the likes of you? Do you think I'm an idiot?"

"I were just teasing you, Thankful Seagraves," he said, his face as red as the crabs he caught. He moved away from the cart. "I got me own wife, now, my lovely Martha, and she gives me plenty of kisses."

"Aren't you the lucky one?"

"You're a cruel one, Thankful Seagraves. After you spurned poor William Reed all those years, the least you could be is happy for me I finally found a wife."

"I am happier than you know, William. At least it got you to stop pestering me with your proposals."

"I know the truth about you, you pirate's wench," he said, pointing his finger in her face. "You married the Old Man to inherit his property, you corrupt whore."

"Damn you to hell, William Reed," she said in Spanish.

Raising his voice so that the men in the dockyard could hear what he said, he called out, "Take care, Thankful Seagraves. You could be swinging from the hanging tree if you don't watch your papist tongue."

CHAPTER 50

Nathaniel stared at the money box as though a snake had just jumped out of it.

"Two shillings, five pence? Where's the rest of it?"

"That's all I got, Nathaniel. Nobody could pay."

"What d'you mean, they couldn't pay?" Nathaniel shouted. "I told you no more credit till all the accounts cleared. Are you trying to steal from me, woman?"

"I did not give credit, Nathaniel. I gave the chickens to them."

"Gave? You mean you *gave* away my chickens?"

"The Old Man's chickens. Poor Goody March said her twelve starving children been eating nothing but leek soup for a week."

Nathaniel's face had mottled to different shades of purple. She expected him to strike her at any moment. "How dare you be so impudent?" The expected blow fell across her face. She felt her bottom lip start to bleed and dabbed at it with her tongue. She held his gaze. She would not look down or appear frightened.

"They were hungry. They had no cash, nothing to barter, and they said they would never buy from me again. I did not think you wanted to lose all our customers. As it is, Reverend Mather's maid were so angry I would not put her meat bird on the account, she and the others from North Square said I were not welcome there again."

"Now you've put me in a tight spot with Cotton Mather. Damn you, you slipshod, good-for-nothing wench," he said, but she could tell that the part about losing customers had made an impression.

"It were not my doing. You did not say make an exception for Mary Penfield."

"And the eggs? D'you pass them out, too?"

"I were lucky to have just enough eggs for the inns, Nathaniel. There weren't none left for market. And the chickens be old and tough. Withered biddies, the lot of them."

"You had four cockerels in the cart today, Thankful Seagraves; don't think I didn't see them."

"I couldn't catch but three cockerels. The King's Head took two, and Mary Penfield the skinny one that was left. The rest be all withered hens, no good at laying, either."

"You can't make those decisions by yourself, don't you understand? You should've come to me, first."

"They were not going to wait for me to come all the way down here and ask your permission, Nathaniel. And some of them started to say this was one more curse, like the witchcraft and the Indian raids. I did not think you wanted to be accused of cursing them to starve. Better to show charity, I thought. I will take in more needlework to pay for the loss, if you wish."

"Yes, I do wish, you thieving jade. It's as good as stealing, what you and those cheap gossips have pulled."

She wanted to remind him that this was exactly what the Old Man accused him of, stealing his poultry business in the name of saving the farm. But a slap and more needlework had been the only consequences of her generosity, and she thought it best to leave it at that.

"If that be all, then, I best return to the farm, now. I want to make it back before the storm. I hope Rebecca and the children will get back from Dorchester safely."

"Dorchester? What is she doing in Dorchester?"

"To visit your sister, she said. The new babe. She picked up Jeró . . . my daughter this morning—"

"Oh, that," he interrupted, his brow furrowing. "Yes, yes. I'm sure they'll be fine. Begone, then," he ordered, dismissing her with a wave. "But remember this: the next time you get charitable on me, I'll have you put in the stocks. I'm not running an almshouse."

He gave her one of his weird looks, nostrils flaring, eyes narrowing, teeth showing over his lower lip. She turned her back on him, but of a sudden he was standing so close to her in the back hall of the warehouse that she could smell his arousal. Other times he had surprised her this way, standing close enough for her to feel the hairs on his arms, but he never went further than that, and she did not expect him to do anything else now. She was wrong.

Before she could turn around to face him, he punched her so hard on the back she doubled over, and then he was yanking up her petticoats, his fingers groping between her thighs, thumbs burrowed into her naked buttocks. She tried to elbow him, but he punched her again, harder, taking her breath away. She realized he was opening the flap on his breeches, and suddenly his member plunged inside her.

"No!" she cried out, straining to pull away from him, but he had an arm wrapped tight around her belly and the weight of the rest of him on her back. "No! Stop it!" Staring at a coil of rope on the floor, she wriggled and kicked at his shins, but it was too late. He groaned and she felt his seed gush inside her. He released her, and she fell, hitting the floorboards hard on all fours.

"Think of it as country pay," he said, wiping himself off with a kerchief. "First installment. Now get out of my sight, you half-breed harlot."

For an instant, crouched on the floorboards with a man's seed spilling down her thighs, she was transported to the pirate's ship, to the memory of constant violation and Aléndula's beating and drowning in the sea. Concepción felt herself shrinking, her mind separating from her body, her body filling with a rage that seemed to rise from deep inside her navel, like the time on the ship that she had set fire to the Captain's cabin. A bizarre strength propelled her to her feet, to the coil of rope and the stubborn man pissing into a bucket with his back to her. She watched her hands throw the rope around his neck, pull it tight under the ruffled collar. His hands clawed her hair and face, but he tripped on the piss bucket and she pushed the man facedown on the floor, straddling his back for purchase.

"Flesh, world, and devil!" she hissed at him in English. "Flesh, world, and devil!" Entwined in the rope, her fingers had turned to metal. Her arms were cabled with fury. Her knees were a vice on either side of him.

Nothing existed in the world but that rope. She tightened the noose, crossing her arms until they shook from the strain. The man tried to raise his head and she dropped her knee into the back of his neck and pulled the rope even harder, twisting it with both hands until it formed a thick spiral that burned her palms. Twisting harder, she pulled the man's face sideways, and harder, till the veins in his neck bulged blue and his tongue lolled out of his sputtering mouth, and harder, still, until finally the man ceased straining and his hands dropped and his eyes closed.

Afterward, she realized that her skirts were soaked in piss.

CHAPTER 51

W as it twilight already, or was it just a trick of the clouds? She couldn't remember where she'd been since she left Greenwood's warehouse, but when the storm hit she was at the town gate, near the bridge. The rain felt good at first, and she welcomed the breeze lifting the flaps on her coif and cooling her hot face. And then the lightning started and the rainwater pelted down in gray, cold torrents. The pastures began to flood on either side of the Neck. The boughs of the willows along the river's edge whipped as furiously as the windmill in the gusting wind, and water streamed off her face, soaked through her skirts and shift and shoes. Her apron was plastered with mud as though she'd been rooting in the ground. Where had all this mud come from? The wind answered her, whipping up the wet earth and sending it flying into her face. Up ahead on the Neck she could see the salt-works, and beyond that lay George's Tavern. But the cart refused to budge more than an inch out of the muddy road. She had no choice than to push the cart down the embankment and take shelter under the bridge, watching the wind carry her egg baskets off into the river. She climbed into the cart to wait out the storm, watching the water in the riverbed rise nearly to the top of the cartwheel. Arms wrapped around her knees for warmth, head buried in her sopping skirt, she was engulfed by a deep and sudden fatigue. It was all she could do to keep her eyes open.

She awakened to the sound of drums. The rain had stopped, but the wind was still blustering, and thunder continued to peal over the bay. She crawled out of the cart and climbed up the embankment, watching a procession of people with lanterns and sconces coming down Orange Street, led by a young boy beating his drum as if for meeting. Where were they going? she wondered. For a fleeting moment, she thought someone had seen her get caught in the storm and maybe they had come to rescue her.

"There she is!" cried the boy. "Over there, by the bridge."

People gathered all around her. The boy pounded relentlessly on the drum, cutting his eyes at her under his straw-colored brows. She recognized him. He was older, now, but he was the same towheaded boy who had hit Jerónima at the trial of the Widow Glover, the son of Hoped For Ruggles. Goody Ruggles was standing in the crowd behind him. The wind was blowing right into Concepción's eyes and she had to blink to clear her vision. Why was Cotton Mather here? And Mary Black and Mr. Scoggins from the Blue Cat, William Reed, Goody Thorn and Polly Griffin, Mary Penfield, and a number of the good-wives Concepción had argued with earlier. Goody Hale. Goody Earle. Goody Dempsey. Even the Widow Cole was there, touching a lace hankie to her eyes. Concepción saw the rest of them, then. Rebecca and Caleb. Didn't they go to Dorchester? Where's Jerónima? she wanted to ask, but suddenly there stood Greenwood beside Rebecca, a bandage around his neck and his eyes simmering, lips snarled back over yellowing teeth. She hadn't killed him, after all. It gave her no relief.

She figured it out, then. They had not come to guide her home. Two young men with swords walked up to her and stood on either side, guarding her like sentinels.

A square-faced man in a pointy neck cloth stepped out from the crowd, and she recognized him as William Stoughton, the lieutenant governor.

The man shouted over the wind at Nathaniel. "Is this the woman that tried to murder you, Merchant Greenwood?"

"That's the one, Sir. She is known as Thankful Seagraves."

Stoughton turned to look at Concepción and yelled in her face. "Thankful Seagraves, on behalf of Their Majesties, William and Mary, King and Queen of England, you stand charged of having attempted murder upon the person of Nathaniel Greenwood, your former lord and master. You are also charged by your neighbors of committing sundry acts of witchcraft in the Massachusetts Bay Colony. We are come to remove you to Stone Prison, where you will be kept secure until you shall be delivered by due order of law to be examined by the Court of Oyer and Terminer."

The sentinels clutched her elbows.

"I am no witch, Sir." She turned to face Rebecca. "Who accuses me of such? Were it a crime to defend oneself against a violation?"

"It were with demonic strength that she tried to choke the life out of me," said Nathaniel to the crowd, touching his bandaged neck. "After everything my wife and I have done for the wench!"

"Not only does this papist woman attempt to strangle her former master,"

Cotton Mather's voice boomed out louder than the thunder, "a crime that by itself is punishable by death; now, she slanders him, as well. A murderer, a maligner, and a practitioner of the malefic arts all in one. Do you see what is happening to New England, why we are plagued by witches and Devil worshipers? It is because we allow women of her kind to find purchase on our soil, to breed on our soil, to marry our men, and, yes, even to peddle our chickens. Need we wonder that the Devil is back in Boston?"

"Save it for the meetinghouse," a voice called out. "Pillory the witch!"

"Pillory the witch! Pillory the witch!"

Concepción glared at Cotton Mather, nostrils flaring, breathing heavily.

Mather held her gaze, a vein twitching in the middle of his ashen forehead. "Are you attempting to bewitch me with your evil eye, you Devil's jade?" he clamored. "Know you not that your eye poison cannot penetrate a true man of God?"

"Take her to the Town House!" Stoughton ordered.

The sentinels wrenched her around and pushed her forward. Their shoes churned in the mud. She twisted her neck back to look at Rebecca, but Rebecca lowered her eyes.

"He violated me, Rebecca," Concepción cried. "Country pay, he called it." She noticed a little hand clutching to Rebecca's apron and realized that Jerónima was there, too, hiding behind Rebecca.

"Jerónima, *hija*. Don't pay attention to them. I'm not a witch. It's not true."

"There she goes again, speaking the Devil's tongue," someone said. It sounded like William Reed.

"Rebecca, please." Concepción continued to crane her neck. "Why did you bring my daughter here? Take her away from here. Please."

"Stop all your thrashing about or I'll truss you up," said Stoughton behind her.

They marched her into town, and a pebble struck her on the ear.

"¡Ayúdame, Virgencita!" she entreated the Virgin's help, but her voice was drowned out by a peal of thunder. A sudden torrent of rain sent all but the drummer boy and the sentinels and Cotton Mather under the cover of trees and gables.

She faced forward, weeping, the sobs rising from her belly, trapping in her throat until she could barely breathe. Another stone hit her on the back of the head.

Mistress Dempsey, one of her best customers until that morning, came up to her and smashed an egg on her wet hair.

"Take your poisoned eggs, you witch!" she cursed.

Another egg hit Concepción on the jaw. A third broke against the Ruggles boy's drum, streaking the wood with yolk and blood. When a gust of wind broke a branch from the tree in front of Samuel Sewall's house, someone cried out, "It's the witch's doing!" And all of them jumped back away from her, even the sentinels. When a company of footmen marching down Frog Lane from the direction of the Common crossed her path, the horses at their flanks reared, toppling one of their riders.

"She'll curse the lot of us!" someone else cried.

They dragged and pushed her down Newbury and Marlborough Streets, which were lined on both sides with gawkers standing in the doorways of the shops or sitting in their carriages, yelling and pointing their fingers at her. A pair of young bootblacks threw cow turds into their path, and in his zeal to chastise the boys Cotton Mather stumbled into the dung. They locked her in the pillory in front of the Town House, with her backside rising behind her like a horse's rump and her neck and wrists pinched by the swollen wood. The Ruggles boy and the men had come to the front of the group—Greenwood, Mather, William Reed, Mr. Scoggins of the Blue Cat, Lieutenant Governor Stoughton—and their faces were contorted with anger and fear. Concepción started to laugh, then, uncontrollably, at the sheer dread in the men's faces, all of them terrified of a poultry peddler. She realized that fear could make men evil. They were afraid of her and wanted to hurt her to take away their fear. Her only protection was the verse.

"Stubborn men!" she yelled with all her strength, the blood rising to her face, filling the pinched veins in her throat. "You accuse women for no reason. You don't see yourselves as the occasion for the very wrongs you accuse."

"It's the Devil's verse," a young voice shouted. "She's speaking the Devil's verse." It sounded like Jerónima's voice.

"The child has a forked tongue!"

"Depose the child."

"What is she saying?"

"Jerónima!" she cried out. "Por favor, cállate. Don't say anything."

Lieutenant Governor Stoughton came up to her and the rain tumbled over the brim of his black hat. "Shut your Romish mouth this instant!" he barked, backhanding Concepción, but the verse came as relentlessly as the rain.

"Hombres necios que acusaís
A la mujer sin razón."

She repeated the opening verse like a litany, abandoning fear and hope of succor.

"Sin ver que soís la ocasión
De lo mismo que culpaís—"

The last thing she saw was the man's fist between her eyes.

CHAPTER 52

Deposition of Hanna Jeremiah of Boston and Roxbury
Massachusetts Bay Colony
14 (6) 1692

Other than the putrid ink she makes from toadstools and the papist letters she
writes on Lecture Days, why else say you that Thankful Seagraves is a witch,
child?

    I am afraid to speak of it.

Speak freely, child. You are safe amongst God's chosen.

    She bewitches me with her two-color eyes, Sir, and she forces me to write
    and speak the Devil's tongue.

Do you mean the Spanish tongue? Do you speak Spanish?

    I refuse to speak it, Sir, but she speaks it to me. She thinks I understand.

So you have no idea what she's saying?

    No, Sir.

None at all?

    Just what she tells me, Sir.

What more evidence have you that Thankful Seagraves is a witch?

    She has a thing like a spiderweb that catches dreams hanging in the garret
    where we sleep. Her Indian friend in the woods gave it to her.

What Indian friend? Does she consort with Indians in the woods?

    She goes to the woods to burn her letters for the dead. This Indian woman
    were her friend once, but I think she disappeared.

And this spiderweb thing, where is it now?

    Still hanging in the garret, Sir.

You must bring it to the court, do you understand?

    Yes, Sir. But I be afraid to touch it if it's full of the evil dreams of Thankful
    Seagraves.

We'll ask Rebecca Greenwood to bring it hither. What more do you know?

> She prays to a graven image of a cloaked woman standing on a black moon. She calls it by a foreign name.

Speak this name, child, if you know it.

> Virgin of Cataloop, I think, Sir.

Have you seen this image?

> She has an embroidery of it that she wears over her neck. A scapular, she calls it. She won't take it off for anything. She tried to make one for me, but I burned it, Sir.

What more can you tell us about these "letters to the dead," as you called them?

> Yes, Sir. She writes to a dead friend of hers who was pushed into the sea by the pirates.

Have you seen these letters with your own eyes?

> I have, Sir.

But you cannot read them, because you don't read the Romish tongue?

> I don't read or speak it, Sir.

What do you know about this Devil's verse?

> She has embroidered it on a sampler and pinned it to the wall, Sir, and she makes me sleep under it when I stay at the farm.

What makes you believe it is the Devil's verse?

> Because it says so, Sir, on the last line. 'Flesh, world, and devil.'

So you do read Spanish, then, child?

> No, Sir. You're torturing me. Please stop.

Calm down, child. We mean you no harm. But we do need your assistance. We need you to tell us what it says, this Devil's verse. We need you to translate it for us.

> I know not how to translate, Sir.

We will bring Thankful Seagraves to a private cell where you can ask her what it means.

> No, Sir, please, don't make me go back to the dungeon. They'll put me in the cell like that little Dorcas girl.

You'll be safe, child. We'll have a constable and Rebecca Greenwood there to escort you. You won't be left alone with Thankful Seagraves, I promise.

> I don't understand what you want me to do, Sir. Why can't you make Thankful Seagraves tell you the meaning of the verse? Why must I do it?

It's a simple task. Ask her to explain what the verse means. Remember what she says and report it back to us. Can you do that for benefit of your own soul, Hanna Jeremiah? It would be a boon for the court and for the Greenwood family, as well. Your name would be cleared of any suspicion of witchcraft.

    I will try, Sir.

One last question for the record. What is your relationship to Thankful Seagraves?

    You know that already, Sir.

Yes but the record has to show what you have said in your own words. Answer the question, child.

    She is the one that gave birth to me.

She is your mother?

    No, Sir. Rebecca Greenwood is my mother. Thankful Seagraves just brought me into the world.

So you disown your own mother, is that it?

    Mama Becca is my mother. Thankful Seagraves is just a mean and ugly old witch.

And if this witch is the one who brought you into the world, and you fed at her witch's teat, then that must make you a witch as well, is that right?

    I disown her, Sir.

What did you say, child? Speak up so the clerk can hear you.

    I DISOWN THANKFUL SEAGRAVES.

What do you disown?

    Everything.

Do you reject her evil influence over your life?

    Yes, Sir. I reject her.

Do you renounce any evil words or actions that she may have taught you?

    Yes, Sir. I renounce her.

Do you forsake your kinship ties to the witch who bore you?

    Very much, Sir. I forsake her.

Whose child are you?

    I am the child of Rebecca Greenwood.

And will you help the court to decipher this needlecraft that you say is the Devil's verse?

    I will do my best, Sir.

Let it be written, then, that of her own accord the deponent has disowned all kinship ties with the accused witch, Thankful Seagraves, and has declared herself to be the child of Rebecca Greenwood. It is the court's decision, to wit, that, upon providing the court with the evidence she has spoken of in this deposition, including a written interpretation of the Devil's verse which Thankful Seagraves has stitched upon a sampler, the deponent, named Hanna Jeremiah, be removed from Thankful Seagraves, and given to the care and keeping of Rebecca and Nathaniel Greenwood.

Upon threat of excommunication for any perjury you may have committed in front of this court, Hanna Jeremiah, do you swear you are telling the truth and nothing but the truth?

I swear it, Sir. If you don't believe me, ask Mama Becca.

CHAPTER 53

She knew she was in some delirium, some alienation of the mind, a madness of stubborn men. Vaguely she remembered being punched in the face.

The sharp tang of night soil brought her back to her five senses. A child's face mottled with dirt and shadows was leaning over her.

"She ain't dead no more," the child announced.

"Get over here, Dorcas," a woman's voice said.

Her mouth tasted of blood. She moved her tongue and found one of her back teeth loose. Her nose felt clogged and she was breathing through her mouth. Every bone in her body felt broken. She was lying in a pile of rank hay on the stone floor of the prison. The only light in the place was the glow of the sconce outside the cell. She lifted herself on an elbow. The pain in her head sliced down the back of her neck, making her dizzy, and she lost her stomach. Nothing but a tart liquid came up.

"Concepción? Wake yourself. Get out of it."

"Aléndula?"

"Who's 'Lendula?" the child said.

"Name of the popish Devil she consorts with, I warrant."

"She consorts with no Devils. Her only crime is being a foreigner. Just like me."

It was Tituba speaking to her, not Aléndula.

"Did she confess like you did, Tituba Indian?"

"You be in the witch's hole, Concepción. I told you it were dangerous for you to have come here. You've been out of your mind for days."

Concepción sat up and let her eyes adjust to the wan flicker of the sconce. She blinked and felt something crusty around her eyes. She saw that both of her ankles were chained to the iron ring in the middle of the floor. She had not heard the chains until now. All of them shifting around, moving their legs, trying to stretch. She was not able to draw up her knees.

"What's your name?"

"Say your name."

"My name is Concepción Benavídez."

"Damn foreigners," someone said.

"She is called Thankful Seagraves," Tituba interjected.

"She's the pirate's wench."

"They say she's part Indian."

"No wonder."

"Thankful Seagraves. Thankful Seagraves," Dorcas sang out.

"Shut up, brat!"

"Your face is all bloody, Thankful Seagraves."

Concepción raised her arms to her face, realizing her wrists were shackled, too, and felt the bloody crust around her nose. She picked dried blood off her eyelashes from the oozing gash in her forehead.

"I think my nose is broken," she said.

She remembered the stoning at the pillory, the Ruggles boy on the drum, the lieutenant governor's fist in her face. When her eyes fully adjusted to the darkness, she saw that there were many others in the cell, legs chained to the same iron ring. The child, Dorcas, sat huddled in the lap of one of the women like a cat. There were two figures silhouetted against the back wall, separate from the others.

"How many are you?" Concepción asked.

"There be thirty-five now, with you," a man answered. "But there be twice that in the other jails, I've heard."

"Thirty-two. Did you forget the three that died?"

"Roger croaked yesterday," Dorcas said. "Rat bites."

"Sarah Good, is that brat of yours ever going to shut up?" the same man kept complaining.

"Stop your bellyaching, man," said a woman. "Sarah Good were taken back to Salem days ago, and you know it."

"Why didn't they take the damn brat, too?"

From the back of the cell, a voice Concepción knew well, with an accent as heavy as her own, said, "If you confess, they won't hang you, Thankful Seagraves. Will they, Tituba?"

"Shut your face, Mary Black. They're going to hang the whole stinking lot of us."

"You shut your face, Arthur Abbott, or I'll ask the Devil to prick your tongue."

"Mary? From the Blue Cat?" said Concepción. "But you were there, with everyone else when they arrested me."

"They brought me in the next day," said Mary Black. "Someone reported my fortune-telling to the lieutenant governor. I told him it was just playacting to make ends meet, but they took me before the court and them girls started to scream about how I pricked them with needles."

"I suppose they were playacting, too," said the one named Arthur Abbott. "I suppose I'm the only one who heard you just now threaten to send the Devil after me to prick my tongue."

"Listen, they tell me to say something and I won't hang, so I say it. I won't be no martyr to no truth if I can help it. Ain't my truth, anyway. I ain't got no powers."

"Much good all our evangelizing has done," said another man quietly.

"What do you know about evangelism, John Proctor?" said a man with a voice sonorous as a minister's. "You're nothing but a fornicator, begging your pardon, Elizabeth."

"Our Father, who art in Heaven . . ."

"All your praying isn't going to take away your husband's stain, Elizabeth."

". . . hallowed be thy name, thy kingdom come . . ."

"Ma said Goody Proctor be in a family way," said little Dorcas.

"I pity you, Elizabeth. Giving birth in this hole."

"I can see Roger and Lydia and old lady Osborn," said the girl. "They're right here laughing at us."

"I swear I'm going to wring that kid's dirty little neck if she steps within arm's reach of me. I've had it with that brat."

"She thinks she can see the ones who died," offered another older voice.

"I can see 'em. They're right there." The girl pointed at nothing in the middle of the cell. "See? Roger's sucking on Goody Reed's tit."

"Enough now, Dorcas."

"Everyone's gone crazy," said Tituba in Spanish. "We will all lose our wits as well as our teeth in here."

Concepción turned her head. "Tituba, ¿dónde estas?" It was difficult to discern Tituba's shape in the thick shadows at the back of the cell.

"None of that popish talk! Please! Aren't we afflicted enough?"

"It's better if we speak what they know, Concepción. That way they can't say we're cursing them or accuse us of speaking in tongues."

"I'd like to spit in your face, Tituba Indian," said another woman. "And yours, too, Mary Black. Your confessions got everybody locked up."

"Your soul be damned, Alice Parker," said Tituba. "You start this every time they bring a new one."

"Every new one they bring is thanks to you and your fortune-telling and your witch cakes and your damn confession."

"Witch cakes weren't my idea." Tituba defended herself. "Mary Sibley said—"

"Mary Sibley!" Dorcas called out in a high-pitched voice.

"Not so loud, Dorcas."

"Mammy, can't you kill that brat?"

Concepción thought she recognized the man's voice. "William? William Reed, are you in here, too?"

"Don't speak to me, Thankful Seagraves. It be your fault I were even here."

"They arrested his hag of a mother two days after the other black thing," the one named Alice Parker said. "She and her herbals and such, cursing people's animals from Marblehead to Billerica."

"I never curse anything," a gravelly voice said.

"Well, you cursed me, Ma," said William Reed. "You told them I danced in the barn with the specter of Thankful Seagraves. How do you think my Martha felt about that?"

"It wasn't me put a hex on your marriage, Son. It was that pirate's wench that did it. Herself didn't want you and didn't want nobody else to have you, either."

"You're a vile thing, Wilmot Reed. I hope to God they hang you."

"My William and me will hang, yes, but so will you, Goody Parker. So will you."

"What did you confess, Tituba?" Concepción asked in English.

"I were beaten to confess, Concepción. First by the magistrate, and then, more vigorously, by Samuel Parris. That day you saw me on the cart, he had beat me in the jail in Salem Village. He said no slave of his was going to make him look a fool in front of his congregation, so he kicked and punched me until I agreed to do what he wanted. He promised it would go better with me if I made up these stories about the Devil trying to tempt me and the yellow bird and a hairy man in Boston who had nine evil handmaidens signing his book. They be his ideas, not mine. He made me put my mark to the paper he wrote. Said it was me and mine's salvation."

"What about the scryin', Tituba Indian? Did your master beat you into scryin' in water and reading the cards, too?"

"That's rich, Mary Black, coming from you."

"What I did were bogus," Mary Black protested, "just a little amusement for sailors and soldiers hopin' to hear a bit of good luck comin' their way. You be seein' things for real, Tituba Indian. I seen the way you conjure up—"

"Everyone's got their due," Tituba interrupted. "Even the Devil. Those girls in Salem Village grew wicked just to spite their godly parents. Betty Parris were the first. Why did the Devil choose the minister's daughter to afflict first?"

The man with the sonorous voice started to quote from Scripture. "Isaiah says: 'Woe to those who call evil good and good evil, who substitute darkness for light and light for darkness.' You're the only Devil amongst us, Tituba Indian."

"Why don't you stuff your Scripture, George Burroughs? The only Devil I know is Samuel Parris! Anyone in Salem Village will tell you that. He told me the only way to save my life was to put my mark in the book, and I did."

"I won't be puttin' my mark to anything," the older voice said. "I'd as soon hang from the gallows as damn myself with lies."

"You're already damned, Martha Corey," said Arthur Abbott. "You and that black child you bore with your own slave."

"I were raped," said Martha Corey.

"That's not what I heard," added Goody Reed.

"Poor Giles, the old fool," said Arthur Abbott. "Cuckolded by his own slave."

"Why is there such enmity here? Surely all of you aren't horrible people. Is it just being in prison that makes everyone's basest nature present itself?"

"Don't bother with them, Elizabeth. We'll be moving to a private cell soon."

"Looky there!" cried Dorcas. "There's a white cat in here. It's sucking on you, Thankful Seagraves. It's got big black spots on its face and brown ones, too."

"Pecas?" Concepción gasped. "You couldn't know—"

"No digas nada, Concepción." Tituba warned her quickly not to speak.

"Will somebody shut that little mongrel up?"

"Stop whining, William; you're worse than a woman," retorted another man. "It's not enough to be locked up here, is it, Lord? I have to be surrounded by lunatics twenty-four-hours a day, smelling their shit and their piss and their wind. God, why don't they kill me now and get me out of my misery."

"Maybe you'll get the apoplexy and die, George Jacobs."

"I pray that were so, Goody Reed. Truly, I do."

"Have they examined you yet, Concepción?" Tituba asked.

"They put me in the pillory. They said there were accusations of witchcraft against me, but I don't know from whom. Probably Greenwood and the good-wives that were angry at me for denying them credit."

"Did you really put a noose around your master and try to kill him, Thankful Seagraves?" Mary Black's voice betrayed a trace of awe.

"He were not my master, anymore, not since I were freed by my marriage."

"She's the one that wedded Tobias Webb."

"No wonder they be calling you a witch."

"Witch or not, the pirate's wench be dangling from the hanging tree along with the rest of us."

"Will all of you stop calling me a pirate's wench? Call me a merchant's wench, an old man's wench, even a papist wench. All these years and people still can't forget the blasted pirate."

"Horace Gibbons says one of your accusers is your own daughter."

"That's a lie, William."

"There's depositions against you."

"There's depositions against all of us," Tituba said.

"Not from our own children."

"That's a lie," Concepción said again, as though the repetition could erase the memory of her own daughter calling her a mean and ugly witch. I hate you, Thankful Seagraves; I wish I weren't your daughter. What have they done to you, *hija mía*?

"Don't listen to their drivel, Concepción."

"I think I've lost her, Tituba," she said, speaking Spanish again "I think Rebecca has taken my daughter away for good."

She sobbed for hours, and the downpour of tears washed the dried blood off her face. Her head ached like nails were being driven into her skull.

Their bickering continued until Horace Gibbons showed up with an oil lamp and a bucket of slimy gruel that he slopped into dented tin bowls and passed around to everyone. On purpose, he stood in front of Concepción, with the crotch of his breeches near to touching her face.

"How about some cranberry wine?" he cackled.

In the yellow light of the oil lamp, she saw that the gruel was riddled with weevils. She picked up the bowl with both hands and turned it over into the hay.

"No!" the woman next to her screamed. "Don't waste it."

"What? You didn't like your porridge?" Horace Gibbons feigned dismay. "Maybe your decrepit husband brought you a nice cup of tea. Too bad you won't be allowed to see him."

"The Old Man is here?"

"Giving his testimony to the magistrate. No doubt he's got some good stories to tell, but I got a better one, don't I, Mistress Webb? Now where's that naughty hussy? Get over here, Dorcas Good!"

Concepción heard the clanking of chains. He was scuffling with someone.

"Let her go, or I'll beat your brains out, you black bitch!"

"¡Cerdo!" hissed Tituba. "I hope your prick falls off. She's just a child."

Concepción clung to her scapular. Sacred virgin, give me strength, she prayed. Give me strength to wring the jail keeper's neck.

CHAPTER 54

Deposition of Tobias Webb, Elder of the Church of Roxbury
Boston, Massachusetts Bay Colony
22 (6) 1692

I demand the release of my wife, Constable. If she says Greenwood violated her, then by God, that's what happened. She's no witch and she's no harlot.

We need your deposition, Tobias. It's the last thing we need to condemn her.

Why would I want to condemn my own helpmeet? 'Twould be like condemning myself. May as well hang me from the tree in front of Nathaniel Greenwood's house.

You make blasphemous references in your speech, Tobias.

I'll make whatever bloody references I please. I've got only one thing to say to you, Mr. High-and-Mighty Cotton Mather. Do not forget that I be the one who taught you your cursive. That I be the one that helped you remove that god-awful stutter of yours that made you sound like the town idiot. That woman you be calling every heinous name in the book, Sir, that I chose to grace with marriage and my name, that's been seeing to it that my bum is clean and my belly fed and my chickens cared for for the last nine years, she be an industrious, God-fearing woman. The worst thing she's ever done, as far as I can tell, is be better than the rest of us. Better at lettering, better at stitching, better at cooking, better at peddling, and much, much better at mothering than any woman in the Bay Colony, including my own daughter. That, Mr. Mather, and the fact of my grievous disappointment at what you've become, a posturing, postulating pompous ass, is all I have to say to you. All of you magistrates, save perhaps your father and Jacob Lowe of Roxbury, are in cahoots with the merchants to take people's property and steal the good credit of their name. That is what all of you are plotting with this so-called witchcraft. I see you, Sir. And all I see is the stammering lad who embarrassed his father. You'll never be a John Cotton or an Increase Mather. Now, show me my wife.

Tobias, out of respect for your elderly status and your ill health, I shall offer no rebuttal to your argument, no matter how flawed your logic. You may live out the rest of your meager days believing whatever you like about me. But you have not studied on these matters of witchcraft as I have. Nor have you witnessed the possessions that I have witnessed, the tortures and agonies that witches like your wife perpetrate on innocent children. I have set myself the task of cleansing the Bay Colony of such torments, and if that means losing fellowship with you, Tobias, then let that be the penance of my mission. What I see before me is a bitter and demented old man who has fallen under the spell of the foreigner who shares his bed. I pity the condition of your soul, Tobias. You can rest assured of one thing: that woman will be dangling from a noose before the year comes to a close. You may see her, then, Sir. Constable! Elder Tobias is ready to be carried out to his daughter's carriage now.

CHAPTER 55

The only reason that I've dared to set foot in this lion's den, Thankful Seagraves, is for you to remove the bewitchment you've placed upon Hanna with that papist verse of yours."

"I don't know what you mean, Rebecca. I would never harm my daughter."

"Then why does she keep repeating that vile verse?"

"Does she say it in Spanish?"

"That is how you taught it to her, isn't it? She says you used to dictate the words and make her write them down in her copybook. Of all the devious things . . ."

"She never said it to me, Rebecca. I have never heard her say the verse, in Spanish or English."

"Well, she says it in her sleep, over and over. What does it mean? At least tell me that much."

"Will you let me see her if I tell you?"

"She's terrified of seeing you, Thankful Seagraves."

"I have to see her, Rebecca. She has to know I've committed no evil against her."

"She knows you tried to strangle Nathaniel. All of Essex County knows by now. Nothing could be more evil than that."

"He forced himself upon me, Rebecca . . ."

"That's a malicious lie!" Rebecca interrupted. "Nathaniel is a moral man. He would never stoop to such criminal behavior. The very fact that I'm standing here before you begging for your help instead of taking a knife to your breast for daring to harm my husband should prove to you how much I love that child and how much I am willing to set aside for the sake of her well-being."

"You're the one who lied to me that morning, didn't you, Rebecca? You weren't going to Dorchester. You just wanted my daughter out of the way. You knew I was going to be arrested that day. And you brought the girl to watch it happen. You, who always rebuked me for letting her see things she shouldn't."

"How could I have known you were going to be arrested, for goodness' sake? It wasn't me who put a noose around Nathaniel. That's what got you arrested. Of course I didn't let Hanna come with me. I forbade her leaving the house, but you raised her to be defiant and she followed us. Now, you must tell me what that verse she keeps repeating means, or else it shall be your fault if they drag her into the dungeon with you. Is that what you want, Thankful Seagraves? Would you see your own child strung up from the gallows?"

"I'll put the verse in English for you if you give me something to write with, but please let me see her, Rebecca."

"Mr. Gibbons! Quick! Please! I need pen and ink and paper. Hurry!"

"How much paper, Mistress?"

"Several sheets, man. Whatever you have."

"Jerónima, is that you? Is that her I see just outside the door, Rebecca?"

"Tell her not to call me by that name, Mama."

"Don't confuse her any more than she is, Thankful Seagraves. Come in, Hanna. Don't fret. I'm right here."

"Don't leave me, Mama Becca."

"I'm not going anywhere, Hanna."

"Come closer, *bebita.* My eyes have gotten bad living in the dark."

"I don't want her to touch me, Mama."

"*Bebita,* please don't be afraid of me."

"I am not a baby, and I am not your baby, Thankful Seagraves."

"You are my heart, my reason for living. I would never harm you. Only your fear of me can harm you. But how can I make you believe what I say is true when everyone around you is telling you the opposite?"

"Don't torture her with conundrums, Thankful Seagraves."

"Can I go now, Mama Becca?"

"Please, Jerónima, let me hold you. I will not hurt you."

"Thankful Seagraves smells bad, Mama."

"Ah, there you are, Mr. Gibbons. Thank you so much. Here's the pen and paper, then, Thankful Seagraves. Get to it. Hanna, dear, to help purge you of your fear of this Devil's verse—"

"Please don't call it that, Rebecca. It were not related to the Devil at all."

"Thankful Seagraves is going to write out the meaning of the verse in English, so that you don't have to be bewitched by the papist words anymore. You can go, now. Caleb! Come in here, Son. Take Hanna outside and wait for me in the carriage."

"I love you, Jéronima. You're my flesh and blood. No me olvides. Soy tu madre. Don't forget that I'm your mother."

"Even a cat is a better mother than you've been, Thankful Seagraves."

"You have made the child hate me more than ever, Rebecca."

"Am I to be blamed for feeding and clothing and sheltering her, as well? You should blame your own perniciousness, Thankful Seagraves. I warned you not to speak that foul language to the child. Now look at all the trouble you've gone and caused. Go on, then. Write down the verse in English. It's getting late."

"It's a long verse. I don't remember every word of it, Rebecca."

"Then write the ones you do remember. Even a partial purging is better than none."

"It will take me days to change it all to English."

"We don't have days, Thankful Seagraves. Don't tax my patience."

"I shall have to say the Spanish aloud. It might offend you, Rebecca."

"Nothing could offend me more than what you've done to that child. Proceed. I'll leave the room if it becomes unbearable."

" 'Stubborn men who accuse
Women for no reason,
Not seeing yourselves as the occasion
For the very wrongs you accuse,
If with unequaled fervor
You solicit their disdain,
Why do you expect them to behave
When you incite them to sin?' "

"What does that mean, Thankful Seagraves? Are you saying men are to blame for women's transgressions? That's even more inflammatory than Anne Hutchinson's preachings."

"Who is Anne Hutchinson? I know only Anne Bradstreet."

"Another blasphemer. Another woman who thought herself above the laws of God and Scripture. Because of her wickedness, she gave birth to a monster, horribly deformed. Thank God it was stillborn."

"Anne Bradstreet were like my mistress in New Spain, persecuted by men for writing verses."

"Never compare a good Christian woman like Anne Bradstreet to a papist. She may have exceeded herself with her writings, but she was never insubordinate, and she never wrote anything profane like this Devil's verse. Continue. We have no time for idle chatter. The children are waiting."

" 'What humor could be rarer
than the one who, lacking counsel,
complains that the glass is foggy
when he himself has fogged the mirror?
With either favor or disdain
Men have equal displeasure,
If a woman mistreats they complain
But if she loves too well they censure.' "

"I was under the impression that papist nuns were chaste, Thankful Seagraves. What would your old mistress have known about the ways of men, unless she were a counterfeit nun?"

" 'Of such obstinacy are you men made
That with unequal measure,
The one who spurns you is called cruel,
But the one who surrenders is corrupt.
How is she to be tempered,
The one who seeks your affections,
For the difficult one offends
Yet you weary of her if she be too easy.' "

"Really! What cheek! Maybe nunneries really are houses of ill repute. Only a trollop would know or utter such things."

" 'Whose is the greater fault
In an errant passion?
She who falls for pleading,
Or he who, fallen, pleads?
Who is more to blame,

Although both be guilty of transgression.
She who sins for a commission,
Or he who for sin will pay?' "

"Have you no shame? How could you be teaching this to a child? Christ's wounds, Thankful Seagraves, you might as well have painted a beauty mark on her face and passed her around the docks. What need does a child have for such ideas?"

"I told you that you would find this offensive, Rebecca."

"Is the thing finished?"

"There's one last verse that I remember."

"Well, what are you waiting for? I don't want the children out there in the dark."

" 'Hence with much logic do I unravel
That men's arrogance wins the battle
For in ways direct or subtle
Men are the sum of world and flesh and devil.' "

"See? There it is. The reference to the Devil."

"That's all I can remember. I know I have left out verses and have done no justice to the original in my bad English, but at least it can be read to the magistrates. If they hang me, Rebecca, please don't let my daughter go to the execution."

"I'm not you, Thankful Seagraves. I know how to protect a child from seeing what she shouldn't. I won't even allow Caleb to attend. Nathaniel and I will be there, as must needs be, but it would be too much for any child to witness such a travesty."

"What if she follows you again?"

"I'll lock her up in Caleb's room if I have to."

"Will you bring the Old Man . . . will you bring Tobias to the examination? I would like to see him one last time."

"He's made his peace with losing you, Thankful Seagraves. No need to disturb him any further. Just as you must now make your own peace with God. Is it finished then? The translation?"

"Take it. I know it will condemn me. My daughter was my entire reason for living, but she's yours now. What do I care if they hang me?"

"Don't you worry about Hanna Jeremiah. She'll forget about all this in due time. I'll make sure of it. She's got her classes and a young ladies sewing circle, and of course she impresses everyone with both her penmanship and her needlework. At least we can say you taught her these good skills, Thankful Seagraves. That should give you much peace while you wait for your judgment day."

CHAPTER 56

Sarah Good and Elizabeth How along with three others from Salem Village—old Rebecca Nurse, Sarah Wilds, and Susannah Martin—were found guilty of witchcraft at their trials, and the court remanded Good and How back to the Boston jail to await their hanging. Dorcas would not be budged from her mother's arms. When Horace Gibbons tried to have his way with the child, Sarah Good cursed him: "If I be condemned for a witch, then I shall be a witch, and I call on Satan himself to curse your rotten bowels, Horace Gibbons, for the damage you have done to my little girl." They watched the jail keep stagger out of the cell, grabbing at his belly, and the man was not seen again for days.

It was difficult to know how much time was passing. Concepción had not yet been examined by the magistrates. Her stomach had grown concave from lack of eating, and her skin shriveled from lack of water. Her menses came once, spilling down her legs in dark rivulets.

"The Romish is bleeding! The white cat is sucking the blood!" Dorcas cried out.

Concepción had only one more visit after Rebecca's. Temperance Lowe came to see her, bringing her some fresh cider and a basket of biscuits soggy with butter and heavy with raspberry jam. Because of Temperance Lowe's position as a minister's wife, she was allowed a private audience with the prisoner in one of the private cells.

"Came to tell you your husband died in his sleep, Goody Webb."

Concepción heaved a sigh. "I had not heard."

"I figured that daughter of his wouldn't be telling you. It were quite sad. He wanted very much to come visit you. He came once, you know, and wasn't allowed to see you, and Jacob and I were set to bring him back, but there was a terrible quarrel with his daughter and it caused him a fit of apoplexy from which he did not recover. Poor man died with a twisted mouth."

Concepción started to weep. "When?"

"A week, now. I were the one caring for Tobias after they arrested you, Goody Webb. I'm the one that found him the morning after his row with his daughter. And a dreadful row it was. I witnessed it all. Rebecca wanted to take the sampler you'd embroidered with that verse and have it burned in front of the Town House, said it were the thing bewitching little Hanna. Tobias ordered me to stop her, called her a thief like her husband. But how could I have stopped her, Goody Webb? Was I supposed to tear the sampler out of her hands or wrestle her for it? The fury was twisting up Tobias's face something awful, and I couldn't take it anymore, Goody Webb. I'm sorry to say I ran out of there. He must have collapsed in his bed from so much ire to the spleen. God forgive me, but I think Rebecca left her father to die."

Concepción swallowed hard.

"And the chickens? What of the poor chickens, and the farm?"

"Mr. Greenwood came and put it all up for sale. All save the cottage and the land it's on. Good thing I'm the one who found him first, else they'd have sold the things he specifically wanted me to give you. Things I took with me for safekeeping, and will return unto you when you're set free."

"What things?"

"His *Almanac,* for one. He left you some important documents in that *Almanac,* the deed to the cottage and some of your own papers, I believe. And a trunk that used to belong to his son, and his wife's sewing basket, too. Tobias were very insistent about you getting these things. He said all of it was to be your property and should never be opened by anyone except yourself."

"And the writing desk? I think I left the writing desk in the trunk."

"I'll make a clean breast of it, Goody Webb, I did try to open the trunk, but it be locked tight and Tobias didn't give me the key. God forgive me for prying."

They sat in silence for a few moments, Concepción worrying at her thumbnail with her teeth. She'd gotten into the habit of chewing her nails until they bled.

"Do you have any news of my daughter?"

"All I know is that the court has given her to the Greenwoods. I am sure she fares well. It's you that Jacob and I worry about. As Tobias's wife and heir, Goody Webb, that homestead should be yours. They had no right to take your property. It were in the will Tobias dictated to me."

"What does it matter, now, Mistress Lowe? They've already taken the thing I love best in the entire world. Why should I care about the farm?"

"Well you should. It'll be your only livelihood once they release you. Surely they plan to release you, I would hope, once this is madness is over."

"This madness is just beginning, I think, Mistress."

"Tobias wanted you to know he was always grateful for your service. You gave him something to live for, and he wanted to make sure you were provided for after his death. Of course, he knew he couldn't trust Nathaniel Greenwood to honor his wishes, so he dictated his last will and testament to me, leaving the farm entirely to you, Goody Webb. We had the will witnessed by the Roxbury clerk to make it binding. So you'll have something when they release you from this wormhole in the heart of God's chosen."

"There are some letters in the writing desk that I wrote to my daughter when I were carrying the babe in my womb. If they don't release me, Mistress Lowe, will you make sure my daughter gets these letters? I beg you."

"Should anything happen to you, Goody Webb, I'll be sure to get your letters to little Hanna." Temperance Lowe squeezed Concepción's hand. "But don't lose heart. My husband and I pray for you every night. One day this, too, shall pass. Tobias had much faith in the strength of your spirit."

The cider and biscuits were sitting heavy inside her belly, and Concepción swallowed hard the bile that was forming at the back of her throat. "Who would think that the Old Man would end up being my only friend in this alien land, Goody Lowe?"

Temperance Lowe handed her a canvas sack. "Not your only friend, Goody Webb. You can count Jacob and me in the lot. I've brought you a change of clothes. Try not to wear them until the day of your examination so you don't make such a foul impression upon the magistrates. Perhaps they would even let you wash."

Concepción had been wearing the same clothing since the day of her arrest, and it was stiff with mud and infested with lice. No doubt it stank of the smoke and sewage of the jail cell. Temperance Lowe had brought her Concepción's own winter clothing, the worsted cotton shift, a pair of woolen petticoats, the serge waistcoat, the wool stockings, and one of her embroidered coifs. Seeing the poinsettias stitched on the band of the coif, she remembered Christmas in the convent, and she wept.

"When you get released, Jacob is prepared to present a petition to the court on your behalf to defend Tobias's will. I'll keep an eye on the place, don't you worry. Your things will be safe with me until you're freed. Keep the faith, Goody Webb. This, too, shall pass."

When she returned to the cell, Horace Gibbons was unlocking the leg irons of Sarah Good and Goody How.

"Where are you taking us now, you swine?" asked Sarah Good.

"It be ye two hags' day of doom," Horace Gibbons announced cheerily. He looped a chain through their manacles to keep them bound together. "Ye'll be riding back to Salem in the witch's cart, and dancing the Devil's jig off the gibbet today, along with three more of your wicked sisters."

Goody How started to wail, and little Dorcas had to be held down to keep from doing violence to herself as she watched her mother being dragged out of the cell.

"Say your prayers, Dorcas," Sarah Good instructed her daughter. The little girl bawled and struggled until she'd pulled out of Elizabeth Proctor's grasp and run to the bars of the cell.

"Mama!" Dorcas kept wailing. "Come back, Mama!"

"They ain't killed no one since Bridget Bishop," said Mary Black.

"I told you they mean to hang the lot of us. Not a one of us is going to escape the noose."

"Escape the noose!" shrieked Dorcas. "Mama's going to escape the noose!"

"Why didn't they take the goddamned brat?"

"I told that mealymouthed Goody How that she was going to get it, didn't I?"

"I'm sure it will be your turn soon enough, Goody Reed."

"And yours, too, Martha Corey."

"And yours, Mary Bradbury."

Horace Gibbons told them later how Sarah Good, belligerent to the bitter end, had cursed Reverend Noyse of Salem Town instead of confessing her crimes on the gallows. "Cursed the man to drink the Devil's blood, the evil witch."

"He'll be choking on his own blood, mark my words," said Mammy Reed.

"And God sayeth, 'Suffer not a witch to live.'"

"You're next, Burroughs."

"You'll be hanging right beside me, Abigail Hobbs!"

"Day of doom, day of doom, day of doom."

"Swallow your fucking tongue, you Devil's whelp!"

"For the love of God!" Concepción cried out in Spanish. "Can't they shut up?"

"Don't let them torture you, Concepción," Tituba said. "It's just fear turned to venom. It's a miracle we don't kill each other."

CHAPTER 57

Days, maybe weeks later—it was difficult to know how much time passed in that dark hole—Horace Gibbons unlocked Concepción from the ring.

"Hang the Romish! Hang the Romish!" shouted Dorcas.

"Shut up, ye barmy little witch!" hissed Horace Gibbons, slapping the girl so hard he knocked her cold. "The papist be put on trial 'fore they can hang her."

"Did they ever examine you, Concepción?" asked Tituba.

"They asked me questions the day I came to visit you. That's all."

"You mean you gave them a deposition?" said the man with the minister's voice.

"Yes, that was the word for it. Without it I could not see Tituba."

"But they did not examine you physically? The procedure is to look for witch marks."

"They just asked me questions about my friendship with Tituba."

"A deposition is not the same thing as an examination. They are going contrary to the law. They owe you an examination before your trial."

"Move your arse." Horace Gibbons kicked her backside. "The court is waiting."

She picked up the bundle of clean clothing that she'd been using for a pillow and asked to change her clothes.

"Mayhap ye'd like a bit of powder for your wig, me lady. Get on, wench! Move the shank's mare! The rest of you nosy Nellies won't be getting any breakfast today."

He yanked Concepción out of the cell and dragged her by the hair through the dark corridor, her feet tripping on the carcasses of the rats that seemed to have multiplied since the last time she had walked that passage. She clutched the bundle of garments tight to her chest. No doubt they smelled as bad as the rest of her, but at least they were unworn.

"Tell them what they want to hear, Concepción." Tituba's voice echoed in the jail hall. "It's the only way to escape the gallows."

But she didn't want to escape the gallows. She wanted the ordeal of what her life had become in New England to be over. If the only way to end her suffering was to dangle from the end of the rope, then she prayed for that providence.

"You want to change your putrid rags, girlie?" Horace Gibbons laughed, pulling her into his sleeping chamber. He ripped the dirty clothing from her until she stood stripped naked in front of him, and then he pushed her to her knees and forced his member into her mouth.

"Take it or I'll throw all your pretty little clean things into the privy."

She gagged and tried to pull away, but he kept her head pinioned between his hands until he'd finished. She heaved and the clot he'd discharged into her mouth came back up in her throat.

"If you lose it, I'll make you lick it up," he snarled. She forced herself to swallow and kept the stuff down.

"I need to wash myself before I go out there."

He scooped a handful of water out of a bucket near the door and threw it in her face. "There, all cleaned up," he said. "Now get dressed. You got yourself some spectators. Everyone in Essex County has come to behold the papist witch. Got more people here than came to see the Glover trial. Courthouse ain't big enough to fit everyone in, so they moved your examination to the Town House."

Like one perambulating in her sleep, she pulled on the stockings and shift, slipped the petticoats over her head, buttoned up the waistcoat, adjusted the coif, stepped into her old shoes, and tied the frayed laces. She could feel the cold, damp stone through the holes in her soles.

She covered her eyes as they stepped out into a hot morning, the air dry and blazing with light. She had expected it to be fall or winter, as cold as it was inside the jail, but the trees were still green and the branches drooped with thirst. The pungent smell of the sea hung like a vapor over her woolen clothes. She breathed it in deeply and started to cough, unused to breathing clean air. Two ministers were waiting for her outside the jail hall, the two Mathers, father and son, standing there in their black robes and white wigs. Increase led the way; the son, Cotton, followed behind her.

A horde of gawkers had crammed into Prison Lane, but the crowd extended far beyond that. A multitude poured west to east from Queen Street past the Town House and down to the docks on King Street, and north to south folks swarmed from Dock Square to South Church. She didn't realize there were that many people who lived in Boston.

"It's the pirate's wench. Here she comes."

"Death to the papist!"

"Hang the Romish!"

She felt a rain of stones on her head. One struck her between the eyes, another on her chin, a heavy rock hit her on the chest, and something sharp nicked her earlobe. Her fists clenched and she dug her nails hard into her palms. The ministers had left her standing in front of the Town House and taken refuge under the balustrade allowing the crowd to stone her before hauling her inside. Posted on one of the pillars of the Town House was a bulletin announcing "The Tryal of Thankful Seagraves, foreigner, half-breed papist, pirate's wench." The image showed a black-hooded woman hanging from a noose under a pirate flag.

CHAPTER 58

The second floor of the Town House had been transformed into a trial chamber. No women or children were allowed to go beyond the open space of the ground floor, though they surged at Concepción's entrance and attempted to follow her up the stairs. At the front of the chamber, behind a long black table, sat eight white-wigged men in high-backed chairs, among them the magistrate named Danforth, who had deposed her when she'd come to visit Tituba the first time, Judge Samuel Sewall, and, serving as Chief Justice, Lieutenant Governor Stoughton, whose fist had plunged Concepción into oblivion the day of her arrest. Across from them sat the men of the jury. The Mathers took their seats at either end of the judges' table. A clerk sat at a small desk beside the bench, quill in hand.

"The stink on her!" Concepción heard one of the men in the jury say as she was led to the bench by the constables.

Samuel Sewall quieted the room. He was wearing a lace neck cloth that Concepción recognized as one of her own, one of the Holland linen pieces commissioned by the Widow Cole, with long lace peaks and a Gothic double-*S* motif embroidered in a cardinal red.

"Reverend." Judge Sewall directed his gaze at Increase Mather. "Will you please select an appropriate Scripture to open today's examination?"

Increase Mather was about to stand, but Cotton Mather beat him to it, opening his Bible to a marked page. His resonant voice exploded over the room.

"Jeremiah Fourteen: One. 'God speaks to Jeremiah on the occasion of the great drought: Judah is in mourning, her towns are disconsolate, they sink to the ground; a cry goes up from Jerusalem. The nobles send the lesser men for water, they come to the cisterns, and find no water, and return with their pitchers empty. The ground refuses its yield, for the country has had no rain; in dismay the plowmen cover their heads. Even the doe abandons her newborn fawn in open country, for there is no grass; the wild donkeys standing on the bare heights gasp for air like jackals: their eyes grow dim for lack of pasture.' "

Mather raised his eyes from the page, throwing the blue darts of his gaze out to the lot of white faces staring at him in absolute stillness. He had not yet finished.

"And Jeremiah said . . ." Mather lowered his eyes and continued to read. " 'Lord . . . why are you like a stranger in this land, like a traveler who stays only for a night? . . . Have you rejected Judah altogether? Does your very soul revolt at Zion? Why have you struck us down without hope of cure?' "

Mather snapped his Bible shut and paced to one end of the table, in front of the judges.

"Drought!" The word boomed out of his mouth. ". . . and famine. Anarchy and ruin." He paced end to end. "The French attacking our ships. Indians raiding our homes. Witches throttling our children." He approached Concepción and pointed the Bible at her, shouting his next words: "And do you know *why* God is punishing his chosen in New England? Why he has consigned us to doom and disaster?" He faced the crowd again. "Ask yourselves, goodmen and gentlemen," his voice just above a whisper now, "how long this Devil's jade has lived amongst us. How many times has she quarreled with authority and questioned our godly ways? Ask yourselves why it is another redskin, another foreigner with a forked tongue and a papist faith, who brings grievous trouble to the colony?"

He set the Bible on the magistrates' table but did not take his eyes from the jury. "And once you have asked yourselves all of these questions, my brothers, and once you have seen the architecture of her heathen bewitchments over our lives for nigh a decade, you will know why God revolts against Zion, and why we must, I repeat, we must obey the Lord's decree: thou shalt not suffer a witch to live!"

Mather speared one more look at Concepción, picked up his Bible, and resumed his place on the bench beside Judge Sewall. The courtroom was choked with silence. Concepción could hear the seagulls circling the wharves a hundred yards away.

"The trial will begin," announced William Stoughton, pounding the gavel. "The court clerk will now read the charges."

The clerk held up a large piece of parchment and read aloud, " 'Thankful Seagraves, a foreign woman from New Spain, bought from a buccaneer ship in

1683 by Nathaniel Greenwood, merchant of Boston in the Massachusetts Bay Colony, and the servant of Tobias Webb, farmer and elder of the town of Roxbury: contrary to the peace of our Sovereign Lord and Lady, William and Mary of England, and King and Queen, you stand accused of having feloniously committed forty-eight counts of witchcraft, the ten most graven of which include the following: (one) speaking the Romish tongue, (two) stitching the Devil's verse on a sampler, (three) conducting heathen rituals and consorting with Indians in the woods on Lecture Days, (four) keeping a cat for a familiar and speaking to the Devil in the form of a wolf, (five) bewitching Tobias Webb into marriage and scheming to rob him of his possessions, (six) performing lewd acts in your spectral form, (seven) cooking dark concoctions and odd foods, (eight) selling tainted poultry and spoiled eggs, (nine) forcing your own child to partake of papist customs, and (ten) writing letters to the dead.'"

Concepción clenched her fists and willed herself not to weep. Some of those things could only have been revealed by Jerónima.

The clerk continued. "'In addition to these crimes, Thankful Seagraves stands accused of attempting to murder her former master, for which crime, alone, she stands to be executed. The court has collected depositions from all her accusers, among them such Boston worthies as her former owners, Merchant and Mistress Greenwood, Reverend Cotton Mather, Merchant Samuel Shrimpton, tavern keepers John Vial and Matthew Scoggins, midwife Jane Hawkins, Goodwives Dempsey, Earle, Hale, and March. We also have depositions from her neighbors Goodwife Mehitable Thorn and Polly Griffin of Roxbury. Reverend Samuel Parris, of Salem Village (formerly Merchant Parris of Boston), Martha Reed of Marblehead on behalf of her husband, the fisherman, William Reed. Mary Penfield of Andover and Hanna Jeremiah, also of Boston.'"

She raised her hands over her face at the sound of Jerónima's name.

"The accused will uncover her face."

"You heard the Chief Justice."

She obeyed. It was true, then. Her daughter had given a statement against her.

"The Court of Oyer and Terminer will now begin the examination of Thankful Seagraves."

"Point of clarification, Your Honors," interjected the clerk. "Will she be listed in the record under her maiden name, Seagraves, or her married name, Webb?"

"My good man, since one of the crimes she is charged with is feloniously ensnaring Tobias Webb into marriage, which has caused the marriage to be annulled by order of the General Court, it will be necessary to list her in the records under her unmarried name, Seagraves."

They were speaking so fast and in such convoluted ways that it was difficult for Concepción to follow what they were saying, but the words "marriage annulled" echoed loudly in her head. Neither Rebecca nor Temperance Lowe had said a word about the annulment.

Magistrate 1:	You will recite the Lord's Prayer for the court, Thankful Seagraves.
Accused:	I do not know it in English, Sir.
Magistrate 2:	How long have you lived in New England?
Accused:	Nine years, Sir.
Magistrate 2:	And in nine years you have not seen fit to learn the Lord's Prayer?
Accused:	I know it, Sir, but not in English. I can recite it in my own tongue, if you wish.

A hubbub went up in the courtroom. Cotton Mather sprang to his feet.

"Do you see how wily she is, gentlemen, that even now under the judgment of God and magistrate, the wench persists in wanting to speak her heathen tongue? Very much like one that hung from the scaffold not too long ago."

"Thank you, Minister, but the court needs no advocates at this time," said Samuel Sewall.

Cotton Mather resumed his seat, his neck flaming red under his flouncy collar.

Magistrate 3:	We shall tolerate no popish talk in the court. Since you cannot say the Lord's Prayer in English, we must deduce that you cannot say it at all, Thankful Seagraves. Can you at the least tell us how many persons there are in the Godhead?
Accused:	I cannot make sense of your question, Sir.
Magistrate 1:	Perhaps if you had shown your face at a meetinghouse in the nine years that you have lived among

God's chosen, Thankful Seagraves, you could make sense of it. I will ask you again: how many persons compose the holy trinity of the Godhead?

Accused: Two, Sir.

A collective gasp was followed by a clamor of whispering from the spectators.

Accused: The Holy Spirit is not a person, Sir. Only the Father and Son are persons. The third is the spirit of the Holy Mother.

"Will a witch be preaching us a sermon, then, and a sacrilegious one at that?" Cotton Mather said, getting halfway up from his seat. Judge Sewall stayed him with a look and a lifted hand.

"We shall add one tithe to the jail fees of the accused each time she makes an impious remark," Judge Sewall said.

Magistrate 4:   Is it true, Thankful Seagraves, that when you first arrived in New England and were purchased by Merchant Greenwood, you attempted to drown yourself in the sea?

Accused: I come from a land where people of my caste are not slaves, Sir. I could not conceive of living the rest of my life in bondage.

Magistrate 4:   What mean you by "caste"?

Accused: A quality of race, Sir. Only the black race and the mixture between black and Indian and black and Spanish were enslaved in my country. Not the Indian race or the mixture of Spanish and Indian or any Spanish and black mixtures that were not born to slave mothers, such as my caste, Sir, and for that reason I cannot be a slave.

Magistrate 4:   Stop confounding the court with this talk of racial mixtures, woman. Are you admitting to being part blackamoor as well as Indian?

Acccused: And half-white, Sir, from my Spanish father.

"Not even Sodom and Gomorrah were so tainted as that heathen country from which this handmaiden of the Antichrist issued," Cotton Mather called out.

Magistrate 5:	And yet, for all your trouble you did not drown that day, did you?
Accused:	Unfortunately not, Sir.
Magistrate 3:	Do you know why you did not drown?
Accused:	I have heard it called a witch test. There are some among you who believe that if one does not sink in water one must be a witch.
Magistrate 4:	And what do you believe, Thankful Seagraves?
Accused:	I believe it was my daughter already growing inside me that kept me afloat.
Magistrate 4:	And what is your daughter's name?
Accused:	She is called Hanna Jeremiah.
Magistrate 5:	Has she no other names she goes by? Do you not use a different name for her and for yourself as well?
Accused:	Some call me by my married name, Sir. Mistress Tobias Webb.
Magistrate 6:	Mistress Tobias Webb. A worthy name. How came you by this worthy marriage, pray tell?
Accused:	I do not understand the question, Sir.
Magistrate 6:	It is not a common practice for a slave to end up in a sanctified union of husband and wife with her master.
Accused:	It was the Old Man's will to marry me. I had no say in it.
Magistrate 7:	And who would the Old Man be, pray tell?
Accused:	My husband, Elder Tobias Webb of Roxbury, rest in peace.
Magistrate 7:	Do you always refer to your husband with such disdain and lack of respect?
Accused:	It is an endearment, Sir.
Magistrate 6:	What caused dear Tobias Webb's desire to wed you, his own slave, though he be decrepit and infirm, and you not even baptized in the faith?

Accused: You would need to ask that of him, Sir.

Magistrate 7:   There are those who say you bewitched him,
                     Thankful Seagraves, that you spiced his food with
                     herbs and powders meant to waken his old loins
                     and make him desire to wed you and liberate
                     you from your enslavement. Do you not grow
                     such flowers and spices, Thankful Seagraves, for
                     your neighbors have seen these things growing
                     prolific in your garden? Did you not cast a spell on
                     Tobias Webb to force him to marry you and make
                     you his legal heir and thus rob him of his posses-
                     sions?

Accused: I know nothing about herbs and powders, Sir, other
                     than what enhances the flavor of food. The Old Man
                     were always much of a gander with me, since I ar-
                     rived. He wanted to fornicate before he died, is what
                     he said. Ask Rebecca Greenwood. They had an argu-
                     ment about it. If I had been allowed to choose for
                     myself, Sir, I would not have married him. I had no
                     desire to be wed.

Magistrate 8:   And you did not find it ungodly to have a child and
                     no husband?

Accused: I had no choice in that, either. I was much dishon-
                     ored on the pirate's ship and had a child planted
                     inside me.

Magistrate 8:   And yet, once the child was born and was in need of
                     a father, you rejected all the marriage proposals
                     made to you by a seaman from Marblehead. Not
                     only did you shame this suitor with your flagrant re-
                     calcitrance, but your spectral form has appeared to
                     him in his bed and tormented him with lewd dis-
                     plays and actions, compromising his own godliness
                     to such a degree that he now stands accused of
                     witchcraft, as well.

Accused: If you mean William Reed, marriage weren't the
                     only thing he were proposing. He wanted me to lay
                     with him in his boat. I reported it to Merchant

	Greenwood. But the more I refused him, the more he persisted in his lechery.
Magistrate 3:	Because he was under your influence! Why else would a sound man persist in being spurned by a slave?
Magistrate 4:	I submit to the jury evidence from midwife Jane Hawkins who attended the accused at her birthing. Hawkins has testified that there were grossly enlarged flaps in the privates of the accused that near to suffocated the child when it were born. I submit that the Devil suckles on these flaps, causing her to bewitch the opposite sex, which would explain why a man advanced in age would want to fornicate with her.
Magistrate 6:	What manner of temptress are you that makes a rejected man pine for your specter and an elder of the church forget his crippled bones and believe he can sow fresh oats? Why do you beguile these good men?
Accused:	I do not beguile anybody. I would rather not have a man in my bed.
Magistrate 2:	What would you rather have in your bed, then, Thankful Seagraves, the Devil?
Accused:	My daughter, sir.
Magistrate 3:	Your daughter? You mean the child currently being fostered by Rebecca Greenwood, wife of the man who took you from the pirate's ship, the very same man you practically choked to death inside his warehouse after attempting to seduce him and him refusing your advances? The child who fears you as though you were the Devil's own nursemaid? Are you speaking, Thankful Seagraves, of the very same child who deposed against you, and told the court of all the iniquitous acts you perform in front of her and that you enjoin her to perform with you?
Accused:	Rebecca Greenwood has turned my own daughter against me. Since the day the child were born, Rebecca has been trying to take her away from me. The girl will say anything to please Rebecca.

Magistrate 5:	But it were not Rebecca Greenwood who saw you gathering toadstools in the woods. Your dear daughter told us all about it, how you and the confessed witch, Tituba Indian, would go out to the woods together—on Lecture Day, I might add—and collect the toadstools and make foul concoctions with them.
Accused:	They were mushrooms, Sir, and we were making ink.
Magistrate 4:	Ink?
Accused:	Ink, Sir.
Magistrate 6:	And what, pray tell, did you use this foul ink for, Thankful Seagraves?
Accused:	For writing, Sir.
Magistrate 1:	Yes, woman, that is the usual purpose for ink. But what did you write exactly? Did you not use this accursed liquid to manufacture your witch's calligraphy in the Devil's book?
Accused:	I write in my account book, Sir. I am a peddler and Merchant Greenwood makes me keep an accurate accounting. Perhaps for some a merchant's account book be the equivalent to the Devil's book.

A few of the men in the jury laughed.

Magistrate 8:	Pray refrain from making levity of these proceedings, Thankful Seagraves. Is that all you write, then? Your accounts?
Accused:	I write in my diary, Sir.
Magistrate 3:	Do you not also write letters to the dead that you burn in the woods?

Oh, Jerónima, she thought, is there nothing you didn't reveal? "The accused will answer the question," said Judge Sewall.

Accused:	Was it my daughter who told you thus, Sir?
Magistrate 3:	Never mind who told us. Answer the question.
Accused:	Sometimes, Sir.

Magistrate 7:	Sometimes what? Speak up, woman!
Accused:	Sometimes I write letters to my mistress in New Spain. As far as I know she were not actually dead, Sir. She is just dead in my memory.
Magistrate 2:	And who is this mistress? Were she not one of those papist women who are known as nuns, who live unnatural lives in the cloister and pray to the Antichrist, the Pope?
Accused:	She were a nun, yes, but she were not religious, Sir. She were a scholar and a poet. I used to be her scribe and would copy all of her writings.
Magistrate 1:	And why do you write letters to this woman that you burn instead of post? Those of us who wish to communicate with our friends or relatives across the sea post our letters on a ship; we do not send them up in smoke.
Accused:	I do not know, Sir. I just know that I burn them.
Magistrate 4:	What language do you use in these letters, Thankful Seagraves?
Accused:	The correct language, Sir.
Magistrate 4:	Which is what, pray tell?
Accused:	The language understood by the intended audience.
Magistrate 7:	And who is the intended audience if the missive is received in smoke, woman? Only a heathen or one who is surrounded by flames reads the language of smoke.
Accused:	It were simply a way to remember someone. Not a wicked ritual.
Magistrate 5:	And what of the Devil's verse, then, Thankful Seagraves?
Accused:	I know of no such verse, Sir.
Magistrate 6:	The one with which you have besmirched the virtue of a sampler, the one you have embroidered in the heathen tongue of the Spaniards, the verse that you flagrantly displayed on the wall and required your daughter to sleep under, that you compelled her to learn by rote. The one that you were using against

	the lieutenant governor and the rest of your accusers while locked to the stocks on the day of your arrest.
Accused:	It is not a Devil's verse. It is a poem written by my former mistress.
Magistrate 5:	Your mistress, the nun? The wife of the Antichrist?
Accused:	Her name is Sor Juana Inés de la Cruz of the convent of San Jerónimo.

Chief Justice Stoughton cracked his gavel. "There shall be no papist talk in this court! One more instance of it, and we shall have a noose wrapped round your neck immediately."

Suddenly a shrieking began on the first floor.

"It be the Romish. The Romish is torturing them," she heard a woman cry out.

One of the constables ran to the balustrade and looked down.

"What is the nature of the disturbance, Constable?" asked Judge Sewall.

"It be some of the Salem girls, Sir. They seem afflicted. They're pitching a fit."

"Bring the girls hither," declared Cotton Mather. "Let them look on the papist."

A chorus of foot-stamping agreement rose up in the courtroom.

"Bring the Salem girls."

"The Salem girls! The Salem girls!"

All of the magistrates pounded their gavels in unison.

"There shall be order in this court," bellowed the Chief Justice.

"Constable, bring up the Salem girls," ordered Judge Danforth.

"None but the Salem girls," clarified Judge Sewall.

Cotton Mather riveted his icy gaze on Concepción. There was a triumphant gleam in his eyes that terrified her more than the mayhem that was breaking out as the Salem girls cleared the landing to the second floor. There were four of them, one who looked to be the same age as Jerónima, two others no older than twelve or thirteen, and the last perhaps sixteen or seventeen.

"She pricks me!" howled the oldest one.

"Who pricks you, Mercy Lewis?"

"That one. The Romish woman. She pricks me with a quill. She wants me to write the Devil's verse!"

The others started to squirm and cry and red blotches appeared on their arms and faces.

"I see a woman in black standing next to her," cried the youngest.

Magistrate 8:	Thankful Seagraves, why do you torment these girls?
Accused:	I do naught but stand here, Sir.
Magistrate 8:	Do you not see how you torment them?
Accused:	It is not me, Sir. If they are bewitched it is by some-one else.
Magistrate 6:	Who bewitches these girls, then?
Accused:	How should I know?

"Have her recite the Devil's verse!" called Cotton Mather.
At the mere mention of it, the girls started to tremble and moan.

Magistrate 4:	You will recite the Devil's verse, Thankful Seagraves.
Magistrate 6:	Did you not hear him, woman? You will obey the court.
Accused:	"Stubborn men who accuse Women for no reason, Not seeing yourselves as the occasion For the very wrongs you accuse."
Magistrate 6:	What do you think you're doing, woman? You were ordered to recite the Devil's verse.
Accused:	That be the verse I am reciting, Sir, in English so that the court may hear the meaning of the words and not the distraction of the language.
Magistrate 1:	So you admit that it is the Devil's verse.
Accused:	That is what you are calling it, Sir.
Magistrate 5:	Do not play verbal games with us, Thankful Sea-graves. You are to recite your demonic ravings in the papist tongue.
Accused:	"Hombres necios que acusaís A la mujer sin razón . . ."

The girls went dumb. One by one they started to crane their necks as though someone were trying to twist off their heads. The oldest one's eyes fol-lowed something only she could see moving above their heads

Accused: "Sin ver que soís la ocasión
                     De lo mismo que culpaís . . ."

And then the oldest girl began clawing at her neck cloth, her face turning blue, her tongue poking out of her mouth as if invisible hands were choking her. Suddenly all four of them burst into shrieking.

Magistrate 2:   Continue your recitation!
Accused: "¿Porqué queréis que obren bien,
                     Si las incitaís al mal?"

The youngest girl fainted. The middle girls fell to the floor and started convulsing, foam dribbling out of the sides of their mouths. Two goodwives waiting on the landing rushed forward to attend to the fallen girls.

"She's poisoned them with her eyes!" cried one of the goodwives.

"The touch test! Use the touch test!" cried the other.

Judge Sewall pounded his gavel. "Enough! We have seen and heard enough. Take these womenfolk back down, Constable."

"I see no harm in trying the touch test," offered one of the magistrates.

"I agree with Judge Noyse," called Judge Danforth. "Let us try the touch test."

"Lead the prisoner over to the girls, Constable," William Stoughton ordered. "Thankful Seagraves, you will place your hands upon each of these girls and stop their torments at once."

Concepción bent down but couldn't bring herself to touch the writhing girls.

"Touch them!" ordered the Chief Justice.

Lightly, she grazed a shoulder, a chin, a hand, a foot. The fits stopped immediately, and the girls lay perfectly still, eyes closed, breathing calmly as if asleep.

"Remove the girls," said Judge Sewall. "And take the prisoner back to the bar."

"Need we have more proof for the jury to make its determination?" asked Chief Justice Stoughton.

Magistrate 1:   Do you confess yourself to being a witch, Thankful
                Seagraves?

Accused: I know not what a witch is. I know only that I am different from you, Sir. That I came on a pirate's ship speaking a different tongue and practicing different customs. None of it be evil, just different. But for difference alone will people be condemned to hang in New England.

Magistrate 3:   Was it difference that caused you not to drown when you jumped into the sea upon being sold to Nathaniel Greenwood? Know you not that witches float, carried aloft by the breath of Satan?

Accused: It was a pirate that saved me from drowning, Sir.

Magistrate 2:   Did you or did you not attempt to strangle your master, Nathaniel Greenwood?

Accused: He were violating me, Sir, and I did but protect myself against him.

Magistrate 2:   Plead you guilty or not guilty of seducing Elder Tobias Webb into marriage with your witchly potions and powders?

Accused: I had no say in the marriage. I gave him no potions or powders.

Magistrate 2:   Guilty or not guilty of selling tainted poultry to your neighbors, and performing sundry other deeds of the crime of witchcraft?

Accused: I am not a witch.

Magistrate 1:   If you do not know what a witch is, then you cannot know whether or not you are one, Thankful Seagraves.

Accused: I have done no evil, Sir.

Magistrate 2:   And what of the damage you have just inflicted on those Salem girls with your wicked papist verse?

Accused: The Spanish language is not wicked.

Magistrate 1:   We submit to the court that the accused is as obstinate and unrepentant as Lucifer himself. We have heard the testimony and witnessed the effects of her maleficence with our own eyes in this very courtroom. Is the jury satisfied with the examination? Are you ready to deliberate upon the verdict for this case, gentlemen?

The men in the jury looked at one another and nodded. One of them stood up. Concepción saw that it was Mr. Scoggins, innkeeper of the Blue Cat.

"The jury is satisfied, sir."

"Go, then, into the jury room and deliberate."

Mr. Scoggins ran his eyes over the jury and they all nodded in unison. "We can state the verdict now, Sir. The jury finds the foreigner, Thankful Seagraves, guilty on all counts of papacy, attempted murder, and witchcraft."

Concepción gripped the sides of the stall to keep herself from keeling over.

The courtroom erupted into cheers.

"Hang the witch!"

"Damn the Romish!"

On the floor below, the women were praising God for his mercy and clamoring for the papist's death sentence as well.

"Silence!" demanded Chief Justice Stoughton. "Constable, go down to the blacksmith's shop and tell him that we are ready for the instrument. The rest of you will remain silent or I shall have everyone clear the Town House!"

The judges put their heads together and muttered among themselves while the clerk recorded what they were saying, until the constable returned with a cauldron full of live red coals and an iron sticking out of it.

The clerk handed the page he had written to the Chief Justice, who cleared his throat to pronounce the sentence. "The magistrates of our Sovereign Lord and Lady, the King and Queen of England, do present that the foreign woman known as Thankful Seagraves, having been arraigned on several counts of papacy and witchcraft, has maliciously and feloniously practiced and exercised certain detestable arts and sorceries against her kin and neighbors in the towns of Roxbury and Boston in the county of Essex, in the province of the Massachusetts Bay in New England. Added to these crimes is her attempted murder of her master, Nathaniel Greenwood. Let it be written that on the twenty-ninth day of July in the year of our Lord 1692, the aforesaid foreign woman named Thankful Seagraves has been found guilty of committing sundry acts of witchcraft against the peace of Our Majesties, the King and Queen, their crown and dignity, and the form of the statute in that case made and provided. She will be branded with a papist cross and hung from the neck until dead at the next execution."

The constables approached her.

"You will hold out your right arm, Thankful Seagraves, and receive the mark of the papist on your hand," called the Chief Justice.

She did not understand what they were talking about. One of the constables had wrapped a piece of hide around the hot iron, and the other jerked her right arm up and gripped it between wrist and elbow with a numbing strength. She tried to tug her arm away from him, but he dug his thumb into the crook of her elbow and she was paralyzed with pain.

"The papist witch is ready for her brand," called the other constable, raising the hot iron.

Concepción realized, then, what they intended to do. "Please!" she cried, her voice catching. "Is it not enough that you condemn me to hang? Why must you mark my flesh as well?"

She watched the iron hovering over her hand and felt her knees buckle. Her hand shook as the man lowered the iron to her flesh. The other constable's grip was cutting the flow of blood in her arm, and there was no pain, at first, as the iron lifted and she saw that the brand had the shape of a cross, the blackened skin already oozing. Inanely, she thought it resembled a Gothic *t*. Suddenly the smell of burning flesh made her dizzy and she heaved a yellow tartness over the floor of the courtroom. A rash of heat rose in her face. The tears that had been lurking in the corners of her eyes throughout the trial turned to dust. She blinked to get the dust out of her vision. The rage in her burned hotter than her charred skin.

"'Because of your great wickedness your skirts have been pulled up, and you have been manhandled,'" Cotton Mather's voice reading from the Bible resounded in the chamber, his spittle landing on her face. "'Can the Ethiopian change his skin, or the leopard his spots? . . . I will scatter you like chaff driven by the desert wind. This is your share, the wage of your apostasy.'"

Just as suddenly as it had risen, the heat drained from Concepción's face, her hands grew clammy, and she collapsed.

CHAPTER 59

Weeks passed and more were convicted and condemned, and still Concepción's sentence had not been carried out. Some of the accused were moved back to the Salem jail to hasten their trials, others dispersed to Andover, Gloucester, Ipswich. Horace Gibbons kept them informed of all the latest hangings. Six more—four men and two women—were executed in August, followed a month later by William Reed, Alice Parker, Martha Corey, and five others. In Salem, Martha Corey's husband had been excommunicated and then pressed to death with stones, his last words being "more weight" in defiance of the magistrates who were trying to make him confess. With Bridget Bishop's death in June and the eight new ones in September, the death toll reached to twenty. Twenty more, no longer just beggars and widows and foreigners but men and women from the worthy class, were accused and brought into the prison.

Concepción waited impatiently for it to be her turn in the witch's cart. Picking off the scabs that formed on her branded hand, she prayed a daily rosary of fifteen Padres Nuestros and fifteen decades of Ave Marias, mumbling the words under her voice and keeping count by making a nail scratch on her arm for each prayer. Tituba thought she was praying for deliverance and intercession.

"Why do you keep praying, Concepción? The saints aren't going to change your sentence. The saints don't hear us in New England."

"Who said I wanted them to change anything, Tituba? I want them to take me to the gallows straightaway. What's taking them so long? Can't they see I'm ready? I'm losing my wits with all this waiting."

"Do you want your child to see you hanging from a noose, then?"

"My child has always wished I were dead, Tituba."

Tituba grew cold and taciturn with her and then refused to speak to her altogether. With nothing to do but compound the agony of waiting with the torture of thinking about Jerónima, Concepción allowed herself to remember small details of her life in Mexico: playing chess with Sor Juana, sneaking fruit from the convent orchard to Aléndula in the tool shed, helping her mother in the *pulquería*. Other memories were more complex, more troubling. Her mother abandoning her without a warning, meeting her father for the first time, the fight between them about placing Concepción in a convent. "Mestizas do not embroider in convents. . . . Mestizas scrub floors and slop chamber pots," Concepción's father had said. "She's your bastard, Federico, and if you won't place her in that convent, Señor, then I won't run your tavern anymore. . . . Bring your lady wife to run the tavern. . . . Better still, run it yourself. . . . Concepción? We're leaving!"

One morning, everyone was in an uproar in the cell. Two more of the better-off prisoners, Edward Bishop and his wife, had escaped from their private cell. All it took was a rope and an ox in the middle of the night to pull off the bars on the window of that cell, and the prisoners were long gone. Some said Horace Gibbons had been paid off.

"They were wealthy. No wonder they got away."

"It had nothing to do with wealth," the jail keep said, slopping their night soil pail. "For repairs the court don't pay, the wily prisoners won't stay. I told the magistrates we needed to fix them bars in that cell. But they ain't even paid my salary in a year, and all because you bitches won't pay your damn fees."

"What are we supposed to pay with, our hides?" Mary Black asked.

"Aye, you'd like that, wouldn't you, blackie? It'd take a lot more than your ugly hide to clear your charges.

"The magistrates got bigger fish to fry than bother with two escapees." He looked over his shoulder as if expecting someone to be lurking in the corridor and lowered his voice. "There's talk of the witchcraft court being disbanded and the governor putting an end to the witch hunt. Some fool cried out on Lady Phips, the Governor's wife, and now all hell is breaking loose. You bunch of rogues might even get pardoned."

"Lady Phips!" shrieked Dorcas. "I see your specter on Horace Gibbons's head, Lady Phips!"

"Will they be setting us free, then?" said Mary Black.

"What about those of us that were condemned?" said Concepción.

"No one leaves until you pays your fees. A shilling, sixpence a week plus the cost of your chains for all these months."

"But the court's taken everything and we ain't got nothing to pay our fees with," said one of the other women.

"My children be scattered all over New England," another woman spoke. "My husband be doing odd jobs wherever he can just to get by. We ain't got any extra."

"At least you have a husband," said the first woman.

Cackling, Horace Gibbons locked the cell behind him and walked away muttering, "Even if you do get pardoned, you be mine till you pay your fine."

"Come back here, Lady Phips!" Dorcas called after the jail keep. Nobody paid any attention to the child's outbursts any longer; it was clear she'd lost her wits being in jail so long.

"Mr. Scoggins might pay my fees," said Mary Black.

"Don't hold your breath on that one, Mary Black," said Tituba.

"Mr. Scoggins were on the jury at my trial," said Concepción in a low voice. "I thought he would say something to help me, but he didn't. He won't help you, either, Mary Black."

"You're just a blackamoor to him; don't you see that, Mary?" added Tituba.

"Better a blackamoor than a real witch."

Tituba didn't answer.

"They may as well hang us all," said Concepción. "That's the only deliverance."

"Speak for yourself, Thankful Seagraves," said Mary Black. "It be bad luck to wish for death."

"Do you call this good luck, Mary?" said Concepción. "I'd rather hang than have any more good luck in this hellhole, waiting for someone to take pity and pay my fees."

"Didn't you hear him, Concepción? We could all get pardoned."

"So what, Tituba? What good is a pardon now? Do you think Rebecca and Greenwood are going to pay my fines? Do you think my daughter might change her mind and stop wishing she were born to someone else? At least my marriage to the Old Man liberated me from that bill of sale, but now the Old Man's passed, and the marriage has been annulled. I don't have anything, Tituba. And I don't want to go back to being someone's slave. The gallows is the only escape. Give me the gallows!"

"I'll give you a pop in the face," said Mary Black. "You're the one got me locked up here in the first place. You and Tituba Indian coming to the Blue Cat all the time, bothering me while I were trying to make a living. Pair of Indian witches."

"The Devil's an Indian!" shrieked Dorcas Good. "He's coming to scalp us!"

With the long nail of her index finger Concepción peeled the fresh scab that had formed over the branded cross, a part of her daily ritual, like praying the rosary. The pain gave her hope that her day on the gallows was coming.

CHAPTER 60

B ut how can you support the touch test, Reverend Noyse? A mind as
learned and reasonable as yours? Surely you cannot believe that a witch
touching a victim can actually reabsorb her evil influence like a
sponge."

"Sir, you were not at the last trial. You did not witness the transformation
of those children when the papist witch but grazed her fingers over their flesh."

"That is not scientifically possible, Sir. Who could believe such superstitious nonsense?"

"These cases are not about science, Merchant Brattle. The Devil is not a sci-
entist, and his influence over his minions can take many forms, as we've seen
day in and day out in court. Surely you are not suggesting that those girls have
twisted their own bodies into those exaggerated contortions, or that they have
scratched and burned themselves just to deceive the magistrates. We have seen
with our own eyes how their fits and torments stop when the witch they are accusing places her hands upon them. What could be more scientific than the
proof of our own eyes, gentlemen?"

" 'Tis nothing but a mockery of Christ, Reverend Noyse. Only Christ can
heal with touch, not the Devil."

"Your observation is noted, Reverend Lowe. But, please, gentlemen, it's the
spectral evidence that is at issue here," said Increase Mather, trying to steer the
conversation back to the original point of the gathering. On Governor Phips's
request, he had assembled a group of ministers and magistrates and some of the
more influential merchants, such as Samuel Shrimpton and Nathaniel Greenwood, to join him at Harvard College for a discussion of the trials. Increase had
purposely not invited his son, Cotton, as Cotton's view of the witchcraft had
grown exceedingly fanatical and Increase wanted to partake of a cogent discussion, not be sermonized by his son. Nonetheless, some who shared Cotton's
views must needs be present, such as Nicholas Noyse, who'd been cursed by

Sarah Good on the day of her execution, Michael Wigglesworth, author of *Day of Doom,* and the lieutenant governor William Stoughton. Increase had made sure to include those on the other end of the spectrum as well, levelheaded men such as the astronomy scholar Thomas Brattle, the rational Samuel Sewall of Boston, old Simon Bradstreet, who had once governed the Massachusetts Bay Colony with a firm but humane hand, and the shrewd Jacob Lowe, minister of Roxbury.

"But spectral evidence has been a keystone part of the testimonies we've taken, Reverend Mather," said Stoughton. "We can't suspend it from the proceedings. Many of the accused are sitting in jails across Essex County on the charge of spectral evidence."

"Weren't it your own argument, Reverend Mather," added Michael Wigglesworth, "in that early book of yours, your *Remarkable Providences,* I believe it were titled, that, indeed, evidence of this spectral nature was not only to be trusted but to be viewed as proof positive of the existence of the supernatural? When did you part ways with your own argument, Increase?"

"When the number of creditable people such as the likes of Rebecca Nurse and George Burroughs started to multiply in our jails and swing from the hanging tree, Minister Wigglesworth, and it became sorely obvious that spectral evidence were being used by the greedy and the envious to plague New England with imaginary offenses and delusions of Satan."

"Accept the key role you've played in these so-called delusions, Increase. My *Day of Doom* may have presaged the winds of tragedy that were to knock down our city on a hill, Sir, but in matters of the witchcraft in New England, you sounded the first clarion nigh ten years ago."

"Are you recanting your original views on the matter, Reverend Mather, or are you doubting the existence of the Devil in Massachusetts altogether?"

"The Devil cannot be doubted, William. But the Devil, as we saw with the Witch of Endor, can make himself appear in the form of an innocent individual. The prophet Samuel were no devil, and yet his form were conjured by the Devil's minion. If he'd been in New England, the prophet Samuel would be rotting away in a dungeon because of the Devil's subterfuge."

"Surely you are not comparing a prophet with the hags and wizards we've routed out of Essex County, Reverend Mather."

"Wasn't Christ himself accused of wizardry, William?"

"Or Martin Luther, needless to say," added Samuel Sewall. "The way these trials have proceeded, the court gives more weight to the possessed while they are under the spell of the Devil, in which case it is the Devil we are using to prove that the accused is a consort of the Devil's. I fear the Devil has become our most trustworthy witness, gentlemen."

Some of the men around the table chuckled.

"It appears to some of us in this room, Reverend Mather, and even to some who are not in this room and who count themselves among your own family, that your new book is trying to deny the existence of witchcraft, altogether."

"I severely beg to differ, Minister Wigglesworth. And if you are referring to my son, Sir, Cotton and I may not stand on the same side of the scale, but he knows that I am not a disbeliever of witchcraft. All bona fide witches should be exterminated forthwith, in my opinion. Witchcraft is a crime, no doubt about it, but how we determine the authenticity of a witch is my point, Sir. We accept no magical proof for other crimes. A man cannot petition that he dreamt he saw his neighbor stealing his cow and expect the court to apprehend the neighbor for the crime of theft. Similarly, gentlemen, and because we are a civilization of upright Christians that abide by the laws of mercy and truth, we cannot condemn people for witchcraft on the basis of apparitions or superstitious tests. We must judge witchcraft as we would judge any other capital crime. With reliable testimony, not flights of fancy or gossip. And that, gentlemen, is the sole purpose of *Cases of Conscience*. Not to cast doubt on the existence of witchcraft, but to remove spectral evidence or any other form of folk magic from these proceedings. It were better that ten suspected witches should escape than that one more innocent person—a Rebecca Nurse or a Lady Phips—should be condemned."

"Where does confession fit in your view, then, Reverend Mather?"

"Ah, Merchant Greenwood, so good of you to join the discussion. Of all of us here this evening, you are the only one who knows what it feels like to have harbored a condemned witch."

"Not to mention a murderess," added Reverend Noyse.

"Attempted murder, Sir," interjected Thomas Brattle, "or else we would be in the presence of Merchant Greenwood's specter and could be accused of trafficking with the supernatural ourselves."

Even Lieutenant Governor Stoughton chuckled at that.

"You were saying, Nathaniel," prompted Increase Mather.

"If a woman admits that she has signed the Devil's book, that she has baked witch cakes and pricked poppets and performed demonic rituals in the woods, all of which this Tituba Indian woman confessed to Magistrate Danforth when she was brought before the bar in Salem, does this not count as reliable testimony, Reverend?"

"Perhaps. If she has not been tortured into confessing. It was not the Devil that administered the beating she were given when she were brought to Boston in the witch's cart. It was Thomas Danforth, himself, who enjoyed that privilege."

"Or, indeed, if such testimony can even be trusted," added Thomas Brattle. "A confessor, after all, is one who admits to having renounced God and sworn allegiance to the Devil. Can we believe that person to say the truth when she has covenanted with the Great Deceiver? It is the paradox of the liar all over again, gentlemen."

"Then what would you deem reliable testimony, Merchant Brattle? You would have us suspend spectral evidence, eliminate the touch tests, distrust confessions, and no doubt you would be contrary to using witch marks as evidence, as well."

"Witch marks?" rejoined Jacob Lowe. "Who among us is not blemished in some way?" He rolled up his sleeve and bared his arm. "I have had this hairy mole on my elbow all of my life; would this count as a witch mark, Reverend Noyse? Poor Giles Corey were pressed to death in Salem because of warts, gentlemen. The man was more ancient than I am and had warts upon his face that did not bleed when pricked. Hence, they were called witch teats, not warts."

"As ridiculous as the dog of Andover," added Thomas Brattle. "The poor animal was deranged, no doubt, but it was not the Devil's specter, as that foolish girl was claiming. What kind of specter succumbs to gunpowder? It was just a dog afflicted with some sort of canine fever."

"Things do seem to be getting out of hand, Sirs, and I for one am set to heed the advice of our good reverend, here, and eliminate anything that might be deemed superstition from the trials," said Samuel Sewall. "After all, one is not appointed president and then rector of Harvard College if one does not have the utmost competency in logic, judgment, and prudence."

"What are you trying to say, Judge Sewall?" interrupted the lieutenant governor.

"Simply that it would seem likely, the way these proceedings are being handled, that anyone with enemies can be a witch these days. My wife tells me that poor Lady Phips has still not recovered from the accusation on her person. What would happen, gentlemen, if your own worthy wives were to be accused? Would you tolerate such iniquity? Would you be so apt to believe confessions and touch tests if it were your own helpmeets being denounced and imprisoned?"

"It seems we have made little progress in the way of consensus, gentlemen," said Samuel Shrimpton, looking at his timepiece. "It gets late, and we wouldn't want to be stranded here in Cambridge if the rain floods the Neck and prevents our passage back to Boston."

"Before we adjourn, I would like to request a point of clarification from Merchant Greenwood," spoke Simon Bradstreet in a quiet voice. "If I may?"

"It would be my pleasure, Sir," said Greenwood, his cheeks coloring worse than a schoolboy's.

"Please correct me if I am mistaken, but were it not so that at one time you and Samuel Parris, now the minister of Salem Village, where these troubles began, were partners in the mercantile business?"

"That be a long time ago, Sir. Samuel had just returned to Boston from Barbados and he were trying to make a go of it with his father's inheritance, to no avail, Sir."

"To no avail, was it? Poor man must have been sorely tried to wager an inheritance on bad commerce."

"Indeed he was vexed, Sir. Drove him into the pulpit, I say."

Again, some chuckling around the table, though not from either Jacob Lowe or the lieutenant governor.

"Forgive me, gentlemen, for my digression," Simon Bradstreet continued, "but I was struck by a coincidence that perchance means nothing or perchance could provide an interesting footnote to our conversation here, if those in the present company would indulge me with a few more moments of their attention."

"By all means, Simon, you have the floor," Increase encouraged him gladly. This was exactly the kind of thing he had hoped for by inviting Bradstreet to the convocation.

"Thank you, Rector Mather. We were beginning to talk about confession, if I recall, and your comment about Merchant Greenwood being the only one among us to have harbored a condemned witch made me wonder about Samuel Parris, and how he, too, harbored not just a condemned witch, but a confessed one, as well. Seeing the partnership between Samuel Parris and Nathaniel Greenwood, and noting the remarkable coincidence of each of their cohabitation with a condemned witch, who themselves also share the happenstance of being both tawny and foreign, it occurred to me, gentlemen, that perchance it is not spectral evidence that Providence is warning us against, but the possibility of a preternatural coalition between merchants and witches."

CHAPTER 61

"Y ou're mov'n' up in the world," Horace Gibbons mocked as he unlocked their leg irons. "Move your bony arses!"

Including Tituba and Concepción, there were ten of them left in the Boston jail. Three named Sarah, Eunice Fry, Mary Black, Dorcas Good, and two others who never spoke. Eunice Fry started to wail. "They're going to hang us!"

"Hang from the neck till you're dead!" cried Dorcas.

"Shut your traps! Only thing getting hung now is the asses of the magistrates. Governor Phips has dissolved the Court of Oyer and Terminer."

"What are you talking about, Horace Gibbons?"

"After his lady wife were accused of being the witchy sort, our spineless Governor Phips is saying the witchcraft thing be getting out of hand. They say Phips has writ to the King, himself, asking permission to stop the trials."

"Have they pardoned us, then?"

"Don't you wish, you slimy hag. Charges ain't been removed, yet. You're all still witches, as far as the court's concerned. Besides, you be mine till you pay your fine."

"What about those of us that's been sentenced?" asked Concepción.

"If you want, I'll wring your neck for you. I'm sure the court won't mind."

"You're a fiend, Horace Gibbons," gasped Eunice Fry.

"Such a fiend I be, none today shall have their tea."

"Keep your swill," said Tituba. "You're poisoning us anyway with that slop."

Horace Gibbons punched Tituba in the face. Concepción heard something crunch.

"He broke another tooth," Tituba muttered.

"I'll break your ugly skull next time."

"You'll be paying for all this cruelty one day, Horace Gibbons," said Tituba.

"Not as much as you're gonna be paying me to get your Indian pelt out of here! It's October already. Close to five pounds you owe me, counting your chains." He laughed.

"Indian pelt! Indian pelt!" shrieked Dorcas.

Horace Gibbons smacked the child with the back of his hand.

"For God's sake, man! Can't you see the girl's gone crazed ever since they took her mother?"

"Shut your face, Eunice Fry, or you'll be getting my fist next. Go on, all of yous; line up over there by the door."

"Where are you taking us, then?"

"If 'twere up to me, I'd leave you here to freeze your bums off and stop burdening the court with the price of coal these days, but the Governor's ordered me to take you wenches to one of the smaller cells. Seems Lady Phips be the one that wears the breeches in that family. She wants you moved afore the winter sets in. Bring your crap bowls with you, and your blankets, too. You ain't gettin' another blanket no matter how cold it gets."

Gibbons left their manacles on and herded them to the other end of the corridor. In the dim light of the jail keep's oil lamp, their shadows loomed against the walls. Concepción hadn't walked since her trial, back in the summer, and her legs started to cramp immediately. Tituba and Mary Black were stumbling and crying out from the pain.

"My legs!" cried Tituba. "I got hundreds of needles stabbing my legs!"

"Pull me, please," begged Mary Black. "My legs won't move."

"Bleedin' crybabies. I'll take you back where you came from if you don't shut it."

"No, please, no," pleaded Eunice Fry. "It's just that we haven't moved in so long. It hurts to walk."

Dorcas pressed herself against Concepción.

"Don't lean on me, Dorcas," she told the child. "You're going to make me fall."

The new cell was smaller but cleaner and had a barred window in it and a hearth pit in the middle of the floor, where Horace Gibbons lit a small fire. A bar ran along each of the four walls, but he didn't chain them to it. And he didn't put the leg irons back on them, either.

"One fire a night, that's all you get. Not enough fuel to last the winter otherwise," he told them as he bellowed the kindling.

"Where's our supper, Horace Gibbons?"

"No tea today, lassies," the jail keep snickered. "Governor's called for another day of fasting to protect us against the likes of you."

"Didn't you say he'd stopped the witch hunt?"

"That don't mean he wants to invite the Evil One to supper."

When Gibbons left, they sat in a circle around the fire, huddling inside their threadbare blankets and holding their feet up close to the flames to take in as much of the heat as they could.

"Even the warmth hurts," said Mary Black.

"Look at your hair, Concepción! It's all white."

Concepción stared at the white strands hanging over her shoulder. After months of living in darkness and seeing only in silhouette, they could finally gaze on one another face-to-face. Purple sacks had formed under Mary Black's eyes, and her hair stood out from her head, stiff as rope. Tituba looked more haggard than a pauper in the street, her eyes drooping from their sockets. We look worse than the *zaramullos,* Concepción thought, remembering the drunks and beggars who used to clutter up the Thieves Market in Mexico. Same filthy faces and tattered rags on frail bones. Same dead eyes and straggly hair.

For a long time, Tituba stared up at the square patch of gray light coming in from the window. Concepción watched Tituba, wanting to say something but too tired to speak. She noticed that her friend was weeping.

"What's the matter, Tituba?"

"That's the most daylight I've seen in seven months. Dorcas and me been in here since March. The longest of anyone."

"Sarah Good were here, too," said Dorcas, "but she be in Hell now."

Dorcas curled up in Concepción's lap and fell asleep. The gesture reminded Concepción of Pecas, the white cat, and she started to cry, too. To think the cat had been closer to her than her own daughter. If only Jerónima had ever curled up in my lap, she thought, stroking the greasy strands of Dorcas's hair off her pale forehead. Despite the proximity of the fire, the girl's face felt ice-cold. "Thankful Seagraves smells bad, Mama," she could still hear Jerónima saying the last time they saw each other, when she had not allowed herself to be touched or held by Concepción. What irony, she thought, cleaning some pitch off Dorcas's cheek with her thumb. Here's a daughter with a dead mother, and a mother whose daughter wishes she were dead.

"I think they're gonna let us go," whispered Mary Black. "I got a feeling about it. That's why they moved us; don't you think so, Tituba? Maybe

Mr. Scoggins will pay my fees. I know he misses me; I know he does. He were in love with me, I think."

Tituba continued to stare up at the window, as if listening to something.

"I wish Tituba would speak to me," said Concepción. "Does she speak to you, Mary?"

"Tituba be the only real witch here," said Mary Black. "I seen it with my own eyes. She can see things in the water."

"I wish she would speak to me. I miss her."

Suddenly Dorcas Good sat up in Concepción's lap. The girl was asleep with her eyes open. "Dorcas be the only real witch here," she said, and fell backward, nearly toppling into the hearth pit. Concepción caught her before the girl's hair went up in the flames.

"Church bells." Tituba finally said something. "It must be Lecture Day."

"Why don't you send your specter through those bars up there, Tituba, and get yourself to meeting?" said Mary Black, tucking in under her blanket.

Concepción took her scapular out and kissed it. Please, Virgencita, she prayed, please, let this nightmare of waiting be over. There was nothing else she could do but pray. She started another rosary, using strands of her own hair to keep count of the fifteen Our Fathers and the 150 Hail Marys.

BOOK V

Riddle Wolf

(MAY 1693)

CHAPTER 62

The only way of telling how much time had passed was by the length of her hair. When she had first been locked up, her hair fell to the middle of her back, and now, after three seasons, it had grown down past her waist, though she could feel patches of scalp showing where the hair had fallen out or never grown back. Her clothes hung like an oily sack on her bones. The wound had healed into a thick, cross-shaped scar, a relief of pink, tender skin against her brown hand. Even her desire to die had waned after all these months of torturous waiting. It was just Concepción and Tituba and the three Sarahs now, one of whom had almost died over the winter, her lungs racking with a flux that gurgled green phlegm.

When the snow started to fall through the barred window and the cell turned into an icy crypt, Tituba turned mean. She would snap at Concepción to leave her alone, to stop asking her questions. Dorcas was released in December, bonded by a relative of Sarah Good's. Tituba cried for days. "The little one, I miss the little one," was all she would say. On a petition and a hundred-pound bond by her husband Eunice Fry was allowed to return home for the winter, though she was still condemned and beholden to return to the Salem jail in spring. And in January Mary Black's case was cleared by proclamation, her fees paid by her owner. It was Concepción's turn to cry. She missed Mary's loquacious nature, their arguments and conversations. Instead of being happy for the women's release, Tituba got angry. Each time Horace Gibbons brought news of another one who'd been reprieved and released, Tituba ground her teeth and clenched her fists, looking like she wanted to hit something but not saying a word. Concepción grew weary of her silence.

The winter passed, and the spring rain started to fall into the cell, and the smell of sickness in the room grew sharper with the heat, and still Tituba would not speak. She didn't eat, didn't sleep. Just sat in the corner and rocked back and forth. Finally, Concepción could take no more of Tituba's sullenness.

"What's the matter with you, Tituba? It's spring, now, and you're still not talking to me. Why are you so angry? Did I do something to you?"

"Why do you insist on vexing me with so many questions, Concepción?"

"I don't understand what's happened to you, Tituba. You look deranged."

"Now you know how I felt when you kept praying to be dragged off to the gallows."

"They condemned me to hang, Tituba. I was meant to die a witch's death. I wasn't punishing you. I just wanted them to get it over with."

Finally, the stone mask slipped off Tituba's face. Her eyes spilled over with tears, and she wept into her hands. Concepción went over to her and held her as best she could with the manacles on her wrists.

"I were the first one to confess because they said it would save me, but it didn't," Tituba said. "It just kept me from being condemned to the hanging tree. I been locked up longer than all the rest; I seen more deaths and illnesses than anyone; I suffered countless jibing and cursing from the other prisoners. How do you think it makes me feel, Concepción, when the others be released before me? When that stinking Horace Gibbons keeps reminding me of the bill I owe him that I know Master Parris ain't never going to pay? Don't you see what my fate is, Concepción? They mean to let me die in here."

"Are you so eager to get back to your master?"

"I were not so keen on dying, as you, Concepción. I rather be going home."

"Home, Tituba? Is your master's house home to you? What is home for me, now? The Old Man's cottage without the Old Man, without the chickens, without my daughter? If we do get out of here, and they don't hang me, after all, who knows where I'll end up. Probably scrubbing chamber pots in some workhouse. What do you have to go back to, Tituba? Eternal enslavement to the Parrises?"

Tituba turned her back on Concepción and curled up to sleep near the fire.

"She has probably forgotten me by now," Tituba whispered.

"Who? That little Betty Parris that accused you?"

"I thought you of anyone would understand, Concepción. But I see it's no use telling you things. Let me sleep."

The next morning was clear of clouds, and sunlight slanted into the cell through the bars, illuminating the crusty pitch of the fire pit and the swarm of flies that gathered inside their shit pail. Horace Gibbons was whistling a tune when he came into the cell to slop the porridge into their bowls.

"What are you so cheerful about?" asked Tituba.

"One less shit bag to clean up after."

"Who is it? Is it me?" asked Tituba.

"Is it me?" chorused each of the Sarahs.

"Shut your faces. Yes, it's you, Tituba Indian. You been sold for the price of your jail fees."

"Sold?" Tituba looked perturbed. "What about—"

"Your new master's paying your bill, eight pounds on the money," said the jail keep, rattling through his nest of keys until he found the one that unlocked Tituba's manacles. "The rest of you hags is still mine till you pay your fine. Here, witch." He threw a bundle at her. "Strip them rags off and put on these clean garments. Your new master's a weaver; he brung you these, you lucky scumbag." He walked out of the cell, locking the gate behind him.

Tituba held up her bruised-black wrists and let her tears run.

"Be happy, woman, you're leaving this hellhole," said the oldest of the Sarahs.

"It's my arms. They hurt so much without the irons."

Slowly, Tituba peeled off the tatters she'd been wearing for over a year. They've become like a second skin, thought Concepción.

"Where will you go, Tituba?"

"You heard him. Master Parris has sold me to a weaver. How do I know where I'm going? I don't even know who I belong to now."

"We could escape like those other two did," Concepción whispered in Spanish. "I know a way of convincing Horace Gibbons to let us go. We could escape into the woods and live among the Indians. They would take us in. There is a woman I met in the woods once who told me I could live among them if I chose. I'm sure they will take you, too."

"Estas loca, Concepción. You're crazed. I can't live in the woods among the Indians."

"Why not, Tituba? Do you prefer to be a slave all your life?"

"That is all I know, don't you see? I have been a slave since I were taken from my people at thirteen. What kind of life would I have among the Indians?"

"You would be free, Tituba." She realized they had switched to English.

"What does it mean to be free when you are not among your own people? The Indians would be more foreign to me than the English, and I would have to start all over again learning a new language and new ways. What for? And what of your child, Concepción? Do you really think she will go with you into the woods? She's a proper English girl now. Were you planning to take her captive or just leave her behind?"

"My daughter goes where I go. If I have to take her captive, I will."

"I cannot do that with my own child."

Concepción gawked. "You have a child, Tituba? We've lived together in this jail all these months, and you only now tell me you have a child?"

"I rather not talk about her. She is Master Parris's slave. She were not mine. I just pray John Indian is still with her."

"How old is she? When did you have this child, Tituba?"

"I gave birth to her the year after we got to Salem. Master Parris made me marry John Indian, remember? She be four years old now."

"Tituba, I can't believe you never told me. What's her name?"

"The name of my favorite flower. You know I were always crazy about violets."

"Violet. Oh, Tituba! How you must suffer not having her close to you."

"Not any more than you suffered watching your child be ripped from your bosom by your mistress. You were the one that kept me going in here, Concepción. I'd remember you with your own child, how no matter what they taught her or how she treated you, you never stopped loving her. You never quit hoping she'd love you one day. And so I never quit hoping that I'd get out of this prison and see my Violet again. I couldn't tell you or anyone about her. It were the one little thing I kept for myself."

"I love you, Tituba."

"Love your gods, Concepción. They're the only ones that'll never leave you."

"Tituba Indian!" Horace Gibbons yelled out from the far end of the hall.

"I guess I'm going now," said Tituba. "Adiós, Concepción. May your Virgin protect you."

Concepción clung to Tituba's arms. "Say you'll go with me; please, if I get out of here, say you'll go with me. We can escape and go to Makwa's people in the woods."

"That better not be Romish I'm hearing, or by God, I'll be flaying some hide!"

Tituba took her in her arms and held her tight. "You have been closer to me than a sister, Concepción, and we have gone through much travail together. But I cannot go where you are going. The Indians might take you in, but you'll not be able to take your daughter, and even if you do, she'll just run away from you and return to your mistress. Leave her be. She is not a slave. She will grow to be an Englishwoman and have her own life and her own home and her own family. She has no need of you, or you of her. Let her go. And let yourself be free of the loss of her. That has been your true bondage, Concepción. You can be free of it now."

"Quit your sniveling and hurry up!" yelled Horace Gibbons, turning the key in the grate. "Your new master's a deacon."

Tituba wiped her face with her sleeve, matted down her hair with saliva, and walked out of the cell with a firm chin and a straight back.

"I'll look for you if they release me," Concepción cried out after her.

Tituba did not look back. "Forget about me. See to your own life, Concepción."

Concepción tried to say something more, but there were thorns suddenly growing in her throat.

CHAPTER 63

The only thing that consoled her in the long days of waiting for her own reprieve was imagining her new life as a free woman with Jerónima at her side. A part of her knew she was fooling herself, knew it was dangerous to have such hopes. No doubt the child would hate her more than ever. But you can't believe that she hates you, she told herself. The girl's confused, yes, but it's not her fault. Rebecca has made her hate you. Maybe the girl has missed you all these months in jail. Maybe she'll want to see you, at least. That's when she noticed that she'd opened the wound on her hand again, fretting at the scar with her dirty nails until it bled again, the cross of the papist they branded on her skin. Your mind is playing tricks on you, Concepción.

Six days after Tituba's release, Nathaniel and Rebecca came to pay Concepción's jail fees. The Grand Jury had dismissed all of the remaining cases, even those of the ones who'd confessed and the ones who'd been found guilty of making a covenant with the Devil, like Thankful Seagraves. Nathaniel had even dropped the murder charges against her. It was the middle of May, they said, but the air when she stepped out of the shadows of Stone Prison felt frigid as February. She realized she'd missed Jerónima's ninth birthday.

"Where is Jerónima? Why isn't she with you?"

They had allowed her to sit in the red-wheeled carriage with them on the way back to Roxbury, Rebecca pressing her muff to her nose, Greenwood his kerchief, to protect themselves from the stench that permeated Concepción's body after eleven months in jail.

"Hanna's our child, now, Thankful Seagraves. The magistrates have signed her over to us for us to raise her."

"But why, Rebecca? She is my child, and I'm free now. I can take care of her."

"Actually, you are not free, Thankful Seagraves," said Greenwood. "You were manumitted by virtue of an annulled marriage. And, in the eyes of the law, you're a dead woman. A death sentence, whether it's executed or not, still causes you to be dead. You forfeit your motherly rights if you're dead. And you can't inherit the Old Goat's property, no matter what his will says."

"I may be dead in the eyes of the law, Nathaniel, but I will not be a slave again," Concepción said, pronouncing her words deliberately. "My bill of sale says I were manumitted, and I will stay manumitted until the day I die."

"We thought you would be hanged like the others," said Rebecca. "Were we supposed to let the child run loose through the woods like a savage?"

"I am not the same woman that I was when they dragged me into that prison, Rebecca. You cannot convince me that you are not trying to steal my child."

"She's doing so well, now." Rebecca changed her tone. "She's got a real family now, a mother and father, and a brother who loves her dearly. I even moved her to a new school, Mrs. Cook's, right around the corner from the Latin School, so that Caleb can walk her to and fro every day. The nightmares have finally stopped. You wouldn't want to hurt her again, would you, Thankful Seagraves?"

"What nightmares does she have?" Concepción asked.

"It's the same dream she's been having since they took you away. She says she sees a woman in a black veil in her dreams, with you standing beside her, Thankful Seagraves, and you are both talking to the child in your heathen tongue, forcing her to play with a wooden doll that you call the black queen. She wakes up terrified, I tell you. I have to make her a posset of mandrake root to ease her back to sleep."

"My poor Jerónima. I guess she's forgotten that the black queen was a chess piece I told her about, given to me by my mistress the night I ran away from the convent."

"I told you not to call her by that foul name, not to tell the child any stories about your past, didn't I?" Rebecca remonstrated. "I knew these stories would come back to haunt you, and now look what you've done. You've frightened the child so much one of the judges pronounced her 'crazed in her intellectuals,' and we had a difficult time of it convincing him that she were normal, just afflicted with fear like the Salem girls."

"Be honest with yourself, woman!" said Greenwood when Concepción started to sob. "What can you offer the child, especially now after all this disturbance? The Old Man's dead. There's nothing left of the peddling business since the chickens starved to death with no one to care for them. We had to sell the furniture to pay your prison fees. What can you give the child other than hardship and bad memories?"

"But we can offer you something, Thankful Seagraves," said Rebecca, very quietly, as if afraid that someone was eavesdropping on them in the carriage. "Since it won't be possible for you to live here all alone and with your livelihood gone—"

"For pity's sake, Rebecca, just get it over with."

"What are you saying?" Concepción asked, feeling, in spite of the pain in her chest, a fluttery sensation in her belly.

"We know how isolated you've been here all these years, how homesick you've been. Perhaps what you really need is to return to your own people, be yourself again, speak your own language. Isn't that what you've always wanted, Thankful Seagraves?"

"There's a merchantman sailing to the West Indies as soon as the repairs are finished," Greenwood interjected. "The *Conception,* it's called—"

"The what?"

"The *Conception.* It were engaged in the troubles with the French in Canada when the *Nonesuch* was in trouble, but now it's been discharged for business again. Repairs are almost finished. Should be less than a week for it to sail, if the weather doesn't turn cold and cause another blizzard in the bay. From Barbados it won't be difficult for you to book a passage to New Spain, and it can all be arranged from here. My wife has persuaded me to pay for everything out of my own pocket."

"Cabin fare, Thankful Seagraves," added Rebecca, "with your own berth. We'll send you off with full provisions for the journey, and perhaps, perhaps even a small dowry, in Spanish coin, if Nathaniel can manage it."

"Don't make foolish promises, Rebecca. I most certainly cannot manage a dowry of any sort. Think you twenty pounds for the passage and ten for provisions be not enough after everything this wench has cost us?"

"In any case, Thankful Seagraves, you'll cross the ocean like a lady, this time, rather than a prisoner. We even saved your wedding dress so you would have something nice to wear on the voyage."

"Jerónima couldn't mean that much to you, Rebecca," Concepción said. "And why would you spend so much if she's already yours? You're trying to bribe me, aren't you? Nathaniel paid the pirate fifty pounds for me, and now he'll pay my passage to New Spain to keep my daughter."

"How wrong you are, Thankful Seagraves," said Rebecca, wiping tears from her eyes. "For a woman with a fallow womb and a child without a mother this means everything."

"She is not a child without a mother, save you have led her to believe she is, Rebecca. For ten years you have been the only person who was ever kind to me, who took the time to teach me your language and your ways, but now you wrench my heart out. You want me to sell my child to you, knowing she is all I have!"

"Don't be idiotic!" snapped Greenwood. "We've no need to buy your daughter. The girl renounced you as her mother. She begged us not to bring you back into her life. She's scared stiff of you and your alien ways."

"We're simply giving you something to take in her place," said Rebecca.

"Make no mistake about it, woman. I do this only at my wife's behest. If it were up to me I'd have let you die in that jail, you and your murderous ways. Or I'd throw you like the mongrel you are on the first ship out of New England and bid you good riddance. Plenty of ships carrying cargo back to the Spanish Main, and it wouldn't cost me a bloody shilling. I'd make a profit in the bargain off of you, if it weren't for the charity of your mistress."

"Please, Nathaniel, you promised to curb your tongue. Take the offer, Thankful Seagraves. You'll have no friends here, and we can't allow you to see the child, not even from a distance. It'll be easier on you if you're far away. In your own world. Tell me you agree, Thankful Seagraves. Tell me you know that this is the best thing for your daughter. It may not feel like the best thing for you. What mother wants to be separated from her child, after all? But think of her, Thankful Seagraves. Think of your child's happiness."

"Think of how much you've already hurt her, for God's sake," said Greenwood.

"I did not hurt her! That was a lie! All of it was lies!"

"What's done is done, woman! Now you can either sail on that ship or die in the woods for all I care, for you'll not have the farm at your disposal after it's sold. You'll save me thirty pounds if you stay; I can tell you that. But if I ever catch you lurking around my property I'll have you whipped in public and returned to the dungeon. Is that clear enough for you?"

They had just passed George's Tavern and were almost to the Roxbury line. Concepción realized she had never seen this view from inside a carriage. On either side of the Neck, river to the right, flats and grazing land to the left, water and grass were furrowed by the cold wind. Concepción turned to look at Rebecca, fixing her with her stare. "I will accept what you propose under one condition."

"You're not entitled to place conditions on us, woman!"

"Let her finish, Nathaniel."

"Rebecca, I will always hate you for stealing my child, but I know that you love Jerónima and always have, and I know she will be well and happy at your side. I will accept your proposal and leave Massachusetts without cursing you for coveting my child if you promise me that you will tell my daughter the truth of what happened: that I were not a witch, that I did not harm her, and that you took her from me against my will, filling her heart with hatred for me so that she could love only you as her mother. Do you promise to tell her that truth, Rebecca, and to give her the letters and things I will leave for her in the Old Man's cottage before I go? Do you promise?"

"God forgive me," Rebecca muttered through her tears.

"If you do not I will curse you and yours—"

"How dare you!" Greenwood backhanded her face.

Concepción tasted blood on her lip, but she had grown inured to physical pain by now.

"I give my word on it," whispered Rebecca.

"You have no backbone, Rebecca. No wonder this jade has run roughshod over our lives." To Concepción, Greenwood said, "You can use the cottage until the ship sails, but you'll have to fend for yourself. We owe you nothing more."

"We had to sell the furniture, Thankful Seagraves, but I left you Father's old bed rug and one of his pillows and some blankets and linen. There's plenty of hay in the barn you can use to soften your bed, if you like, and some pieces of firewood in the cellar. There might be some apples or tubers down there, too, if you stored any, if they haven't spoiled in a year. You won't have any more fresh apples, I'm afraid. The poor tree was struck by lightning the very day you were arrested. Some were even blaming you for it, saying your ghostly powers had caused the lightning to strike."

"This is far enough," said Greenwood, stopping the carriage outside the fence of the Old Man's farm. "No need to be giving you door-to-door service."

Concepción fixed her gaze on Rebecca one last time, shook her head, and said nothing as she climbed out of the carriage.

"Godspeed on your journey," Rebecca said. "Good-bye, Thankful Seagraves."

Yes, good-bye to Thankful Seagraves.

"Don't forget, the ship is called the *Conception*," Greenwood called out behind her. "I'll send word to you when it's ready to sail. I'll make all the arrangements with Captain Quelch. Remember that. Captain Quelch. Your name will be on the manifest."

Ten years ago, she had come to New England on the *Neptune,* god of the sea, god of fish and of silence. She would be returning on the *Conception.* There could be no clearer sign that she was meant to return to New Spain.

"You work in mysterious ways, Mother," she said to the Virgin, walking across the road to touch the bare limbs of the witch hazel tree by the well. She had missed its hardy soul and bright yellow blooms. It occurred to her that she was like the witch hazel tree: awakening in a cold season. Though her limbs and heart felt numb right now, there were buds on the dry bark, and soon there would be fresh leaves and a journey full of hope and light.

She turned to face the cottage, and a small cry caught in her throat. She ignored the little stone house grown over with vines, the lightning-blackened limbs of the apple tree, the barn with its sunken roof. She remembered her kitchen garden, the chickens clucking loudly in the yard, the corn patch thick with corn, and little Pecas curled up on the doorstone. I raised a daughter here, she thought. I was married and learned to tend to a home here. I learned to speak the English, to make ink, to run a poultry business. Difficult as her life had been in this country, it had not been in vain, she realized. None of it had been in vain.

She turned her gaze to the dirt road that led into the woods and was struck by the beauty of the trees, their emerald branches, the fog weaving its net between the trunks, filling the undergrowth with a damp, green light. What would happen if instead of getting on that ship she really did go into the woods and join Makwa's people? She would have a different life, a different name, a friend in Makwa, and she would still be close enough to watch Jerónima from a distance. How difficult could it be, now that she had learned a second tongue, to learn a third? To go by yet another name and forge another life?

CHAPTER 64

As soon as she stepped across the doorstone, Concepción knew her life as Thankful Seagraves was finished. The cottage was empty, except for a tin lamp on the mantel, some bedding rolled up in the corner where the Old Man's bed had stood, and the cooking utensils Rebecca had left her inside the chimney, a kettle caked with black grease, a salt cellar, a tinderbox, a paddle for stirring, a pair of spoons, a knife and fork, a mug, and a trencher—all coated with soot. No cupboard, no table and bench, no settle, no poster bed, no curtains, no cushions, no stools. Even the ladder that led to the loft was gone. There was nothing left but the shell of the cottage, the dirt floor littered with old chicken droppings, and the hearth heaped with ashes. Outside, the chicken coop and the barn were in disrepair, the fence sagged, the corn patch was barren, but at least the rosemary, an herb consecrated to the Virgin Mary, and the night-willow herb were was growing strong in the garden, as were the bindweed vines that covered the house.

Concepción walked around the room, much smaller now with nothing in it, and noticed the blue and yellow dress she had bought for her wedding to the Old Man hanging from the hook behind the door. In front of it hung her sewing basket. Had Temperance Lowe left it for her there? she wondered, remembering the goodwife's visit to her in jail. Temperance had kept the sewing basket, she said, and Robin's trunk, but the trunk was nowhere in sight.

Concepción took down the basket and held it against her belly, afraid to open it. What had she been working on when they took her prisoner? She couldn't remember. She lifted the lid and took the items out one by one, setting them on the ledge of the casement in a patch of weak light. Her thimble and scissors, the heart-shaped pincushion pierced with needles of different sizes, her embroidery hoops, spools of silk thread in black, green, and red, half a spool of gold metallic thread, patches of old fabric, stray pieces of ribbon. She unfolded a piece of light blue sarcenet tucked at the bottom of the basket, a remnant from the curtain she had made for her new casement, and let out a cry. On it she had started to embroider an image of the Virgen de Guadalupe, the red robe, the brown face and hands, and the little angel at her feet finished, the rest of the image already outlined—green cloak, black moon, black hair, gold rays—in a tight running stitch. All she needed was to fill in the colors, add the gold stars to the Virgin's cloak, and make a border of roses around the image.

"Hail Mary, full of grace," she spoke the Spanish prayer aloud,

"The Light is with thee.
Blessed art thou among women,
And blessed is the sacred fruit of thy womb."

Perhaps she would embroider those words as a border instead, punctuated at beginning and end with a red rose. Yes, she decided, this embroidery of the Virgin, along with her old letters, was what she wanted to leave Jerónima before she left. Greenwood had said the ship would sail in less than a week. She had no time to lose.

She took a needle, threaded it with black, and went to sit on the doorstone to work on the dark crescent that served as the Virgin's pedestal. It was all she could do before an immense fatigue overtook her and she barely had time to go inside and unroll the bedding. She was asleep before her ear touched the pillow.

It was night when she awoke to the howling of wolves and hooting of an owl. At first she felt completely disoriented, like she'd just woken up from a very long dream after having thrown herself into the sea, a dream where she'd been a slave and given birth to a daughter and lost her daughter and been imprisoned for witchcraft. But no, it had been no dream. All of it had happened, and she had lost more than her daughter: her mother, Sor Juana, Aléndula, Tituba, all of the people she loved. A glimmer of moonlight broke through the dark and streamed in through the tangle of vines that covered the casement, illuminating a small square of the dirt floor. At least she was not in prison anymore. She was free and sleeping in the Old Man's empty cottage, waiting for a ship to take her away from New England and back to Mexico.

Ten years ago, she had gone in the opposite direction.

She sat up and hugged her knees to her chest, staring at the patch of moonlight on the floor, and a strange memory surfaced in the hazy lake of her mind. Of all things, she remembered the triumphal entrance of the new Spanish Viceroy and his wife, the Vicereine, into Mexico City. Such a meaningless memory, but it came to her as if in full regalia.

It was the fall of 1680 and she was nearly eighteen years old. She remembered the buglers standing on the central balcony of the royal palace in bright magenta cloaks. They sounded their clarion, and the huge restive crowd that filled the Plaza Mayor in front of the palace swelled like a human wave to the west side of the square. From here they watched the imperial pageant coming down the causeway that branched off from the aqueduct and passed in front of the alameda, in the deep green shade of the ancient elm trees. First came a company of cavaliers on caparisoned white steeds, followed by a procession of floats representing each of the churches of the city: Regina Coeli, San Pedro y San Pablo, San Juan, San Agustín, San Jerónimo, and the Virgen de Guadalupe. On flower-festooned pallets, huge statues of saints in velvet cloaks and Virgins in mantillas and pearls were carried on the shoulders of slaves and Indians. Behind the floats walked schools of priests in brown and black—Jesuits, Franciscans, Dominicans—hidalgos in feathered hats and jeweled swords, and city officials in ruffled collars. Riding alone in an open carriage decorated simply with white velvet ribbons and red roses sat Fray Payo, the Archbishop and current Viceroy of New Spain, in a golden mitre and white vestments embroidered with red and gold thread.

The procession advanced toward the Plaza Mayor and the cathedral bells started to toll the Te Deum. Behind Fray Payo's carriage, in a closed gilded coach drawn by eight raven-colored Arabian horses and garlanded with enormous poinsettias and sunflowers, came the monarchs, whom Concepción would know later simply as the Viceroy, Don Tomás, and *la Condesa,* Doña María Luisa. The throng cheered, and flowers of all kinds rained over the plaza and collected on the street, dropping on the green velvet caps of the liveried footmen who rode at the back and at either door of the monarchs' coach.

"¡Que vivan los nuevos monarcas de la Nueva España! Long live the new monarchs of New Spain!"

Concepción could not have known, standing there agape at the pageantry of that triumphal entrance, that the new monarchs would become avid champions of the writings of Sor Juana Inés de la Cruz and royal patrons of the convent of San Jerónimo, nor that *la Condesa* and Sor Juana would develop an intimate friendship, which would waken the monster of jealousy in Concepción. It was the real reason, she realized now after all these years, that Sor Juana had wanted Concepción to leave the convent.

CHAPTER 65

Come, Odey. We are waiting in the woods.

"Makwa?"

The drumbeats awakened her with a jolt. Where was she? She looked up and saw nothing but blue flowers in front of her. Had she gone into the woods, after all? She closed her eyes and listened to the drumbeats and realized it was nothing but her own heart thrumming in her chest. The blue flowers of the bindweed were pressing against the glass of the casement, telling her it was morning. She untangled herself from the bedding and got her bearings. Jerónima came to mind, briefly, and in that instant Concepción was consumed with yearning; she needed so much to see the girl, to hold her and hear her voice. Stop it, Concepción, she told herself. You can't have any distractions now. Finish the embroidery, first. Find the writing desk. Get yourself ready for the journey. Then you can see her. She allowed herself to imagine going into Boston, waiting for the girl outside her school, just around the corner from the Latin School, Rebecca had said. The thought of it overpowered her and she doubled over with a sharp pain in her womb. Enough. Stop torturing yourself. Get up and do your work.

She went, first, to the outhouse to relieve her bladder. There were basic things she needed to do. For the first time in months she felt hungry, no, famished, and the first thing was to find something to eat. She would have to build a fire and draw water from the well. She lit the tin lamp and took it down to the root cellar to look for firewood and see if maybe she had left the writing desk hidden down there under the little hay mattress she had made for the cat. Where was the cat? No doubt she had found someone else to care for her in Concepción's long absence. The cellar smelled of damp earth and mold. She found some pieces of cordwood stacked against the pilings. A cask of rank cider. A barrel of black moldy corn and a bushel of the green apples she had picked last summer, before her arrest, most of it wormed through and rotten.

Still, it was no worse than the jail food she had been forced to eat for eleven months. She was inured to the sour taste on her tongue and the queasiness and the running bowels.

After the sour breakfast, she went to look at the condition of the barn. The roof had fallen in and months of rain had rotted the timbers from the inside. The ground was a mulch of mud and dung and chicken feathers. The cart was gone. Only one cage remained, turned on its side and wedged under the nest box. She went to right it and found the little skeleton of an animal curled inside.

"¡Ay, no!" she cried. "What did they do to you?" Someone had put the cat in there on purpose. Concepción opened the cage and scooped the bones out on her apron, dried tufts of white fur still stuck to a piece of the spine, and her tears fell over the remains of sweet little Pecas. She buried the bones in the garden, under the rosemary bush.

"Descansa en paz, gatita," she said, making a sign of the cross over the bones and kissing her thumb to seal the blessing. Her voice sounded loud in the silence that surrounded her.

She stood in the middle of the yard and listened to the silence. She'd been living in a squalid cell for nearly a year, but at least she had been with Tituba and Mary Black and there had been many other bodies in and out of the cell, voices to argue with, anger and pain and desperation to keep her company. This silence was terrifying, the solitude so immense it took her breath away. She had to go somewhere. But not to town. She couldn't risk being seen in town and thrown back in the dungeon. No, she would go to the woods and look for Makwa. Maybe she could find Makwa, and if not, there would be birdsong, hares and squirrels making their noises in the trees, maybe a deer drinking from the creek. She could almost hear the rippling and the splashing of the water over the stones. Already she could taste the clear, cold water, the sweet blueberries and blackberries growing wild on their bushes, just waiting to be picked.

She hurried out of the yard, paying no mind to the shooting pains in her legs, and ran down the rutted road past the tree line and into the woods. Being engulfed by the green light of the woods and the trilling of warblers and red-winged blackbirds filled her with a chest-pinching joy. She had forgotten what happiness felt like and how much she had grown to love this stretch of forest. Kneeling on the bank of the creek, she drank her fill of the pristine water. She stripped and left her clothes in the giant hollowed-out trunk of a dead juniper to keep them dry and walked into the icy, burbling water. She scrubbed her skin with clumps of cattails growing wild along the bank and pounded the dirty rag of her white hair on the rocks to loosen the clumps of soot and hay clinging to the strands. When she was clean again, she felt lighter. She played like an otter in the creek, dipping and splashing. She lay out naked and wet on the stones, enjoying the breeze on her skin until she saw the condition of her toes. It was the first time she had seen her bare feet in months. The nails were long and black with fungus. They looked worse than the Old Man's. She would trim the nails with her sewing scissors when she got back . . . her high spirits sunk abruptly . . . when she got back to the cottage. To the silence and the memories of the daughter she was leaving behind when she boarded that ship and left New England forever. The thought sobered her immediately. She dressed herself, and felt the heavy weight of her dirty clothes again, and forgot about picking berries.

When she returned to the cottage, another pang of hunger hit her hard. She rummaged around the chicken coop until she found what she was looking for, dried heads of garlic that she would boil into a soup. There were rangy stalks of night-willow herb growing wild in one of the vegetable beds, and she dug up the bulbous roots and some old tubers still buried in the earth, spongy carrots and parsnips. She carried the kettle to the well and filled it, but she had lost much of her strength in jail and had to drag the kettle back to the cottage, spilling half the water. She boiled the tubers and the night-willow roots and stalks and some of the garlic with plenty of salt and a sprig of rosemary, and it was almost like the old days with a soup going in the kettle.

While the soup cooked, she dragged the better hay bales from the barn to use for sitting and sleeping. She made a broom with dried boughs from the witch hazel tree tied with a strip of canvas from the sewing basket, and swept the smelly straw from the dirt floor of the cottage. She scrubbed the kitchen utensils with cider and hay. Used moldy corn husks to clean the panes in the casement and went outside to cut the bindweed vines that were covering the window. She had nothing but her sewing scissors and the dull blade of the kitchen knife and the job was arduous and long, but finally she got some sunlight into the cottage. She took cuttings from the rosemary bush and placed them on the mantel to add some scent to the blue shadows of the cottage.

The sun was long past its zenith when at last she was able to eat. The broth was salty, and the scent of garlic permeated the cottage and cleared her head.

She ate without chewing, swallowing the soft pieces of vegetable whole, savoring the taste of garlic and salt on her tongue. The whole time she ate, she stared at the loft, trying to figure out a way to get up there. Maybe Robin's trunk was up there, and her writing desk with the letters she had written to Jerónima before her birth. She had left a hunk of ink in the writing desk, and at least one good quill, and some sheets of paper. It occurred to her that she had to write a new letter, a final letter, to explain to Jerónima why she had left. She couldn't do to her daughter what her own mother had done to her, leaving Mexico City without a warning or an explanation. Besides, she was beginning to worry that Rebecca wouldn't honor her end of the bargain, or that her version of the truth wouldn't match what had really happened.

After dinner, Concepción spent the rest of the afternoon sitting cross-legged on the doorstone, working on the embroidery. She'd just finished stitching the last star on the Virgin's cloak when Goody Thorn stopped in on her way back from peddling her goods in Boston. Concepción hid the embroidery in her apron pocket.

"I heard you been released, Thankful Seagraves," said Goody Thorn, glancing behind her at the empty cottage. Concepción did not invite the woman inside.

"Almost didn't recognize you with all that white hair, Thankful Seagraves. When I saw you outside earlier today, I thought it were some ancient gossip that had taken over old Tobias's farm. Other than that, you don't look the worse for wear. Must be the Indian in you that can tolerate such abusive conditions. I heard there were several that died down there. Of course, there is quite a smell coming off you."

"Is there? I can't smell myself, so I don't notice it."

"A nice bath in lye is what you need."

Concepción did not respond.

Out of charity, Goody Thorn gave Concepción a small wedge of cheese. Concepción gulped it down without ceremony while the goodwife confided that the Old Man had refused to testify on her behalf because he was too embarrassed to show his face in the courtroom, and, out of neighborly honesty, she added that he had died of shame at having a witch for a wife. Concepción knew that was a lie. Temperance Lowe had told her the truth of the Old Man's feelings, and she knew how the Old Man had felt about the witchcraft business. The old cheese monger was just trying to bait her.

"Always so generous with your gossip, Goody Thorn," was all she said, anxious for the woman to leave so she could get back to her needlework.

"Heard you'll be heading back where you came from," Goody Thorn said. "Got yourself a passage on Captain Quelch's merchantman. I ain't never heard of a condemned witch sailing off into the sunset. The Greenwoods have treated you like royalty, I daresay. When will you be sailing?"

"As soon as possible, I hope."

"That'll be a good day, won't it, when you get to leave the Bay Colony and bid us all a good riddance?"

"Good riddance, then, Goody Thorn." She practically pushed the old gossip off the doorstone.

"Count your blessings, Thankful Seagraves," Goody Thorn called out from the gate. "While you get to return to kith and kin, some of our own are burying their young. Cotton Mather's son, rest in peace, were born deformed, you know, and had to be set in the ground just last month. Some say it was one of the witches that cursed him, just like Sarah Good cursed Judge Danforth to die a bloody death."

Perhaps it was God that punished Cotton Mather, Concepción wanted to say, for his zealous persecution of innocent women. But she just stood there, watching her old neighbor push her cart toward Roxbury.

Later, close to sunset, when Concepción had finished the soup and had started filling in the letters to the prayer that she was stitching as a border around the Virgin's image, she had another visit. She heard voices outside and saw Temperance Lowe and her husband, Jacob, the Roxbury minister who had performed Concepción marriage ceremony to the Old Man, standing out on the doorstone, their cheeks bright pink and their breath misting all around their faces. The goodwife was clutching her Bible.

"Just stopping by after the last Lecture, as we got into the habit of doing with Tobias," said the minister. "Once his daughter stopped seeing to him."

Concepción invited them inside.

"Goodness, it's as cold in here as it is outside," said Goody Lowe.

"Is it?" said Concepción. "I have not paid much attention to the fire. Please sit down." She motioned them to the hay bales. "I wish I had saved some of the soup I made earlier," she added.

"Nonsense," said Jacob Lowe. "It is we who should be bringing you food, Mistress Webb. We just wanted to see how you were getting along. Tobias would have wanted us to do that for his widow."

"I think there be a blizzard on its way," said Goody Lowe. "Are you sure you have enough fuel, Goody Webb?"

"A blizzard? I don't think so. I would feel it in my bones."

"But you should have enough wood, just the same."

"In the root cellar. Plenty of wood." She didn't care about warmth or wood right now. And besides, compared to the cold crypt of the jail cell, the cottage felt cozy.

They told her again the story of the Old Man's death. His ugly row with Rebecca, the apoplexy, the permanent twist to his mouth.

"And all over a poem stitched on a sampler," said Concepción.

"Tobias's quarrel with his daughter had nothing to do with that sampler, Mistress Webb," the reverend said, frowning. He turned to his wife. "Is that what you told her?"

"Well, it didn't help matters, did it? Tobias did want me to stop Rebecca from removing it."

"No, Mistress Webb, it wasn't the sampler. It was the shares he owned of the Latin School that Tobias sold to Merchant Brattle. Rebecca was counting on Caleb inheriting those shares."

"But at least he died in his sleep," said Temperance Lowe, "and we laid him out in his master's robe and his son Robin's shoes."

"Thank God the good man had the foresight to dictate his will to my wife before the quarrel took place."

The goodwife removed something from inside her Bible and handed it to Concepción, the Old Man's dog-eared *Almanac*.

"It's in here," said Temperance Lowe. "Tobias's last will and testament. And some other documents he wanted you to have."

Concepción opened the *Almanac* and the red ribbon she had given to the Old Man for a wedding present fluttered to the floor. She picked it up and stared at the image of the she-wolf nursing the two boys. *"Schola Latina Bostoniensis,"* she read aloud.

"It's the legend of Romulus and Remus," said the reverend, "though for Tobias it was Robin and Robert he was meaning to suckle at the bosom of the Latin School."

"It's the saddest thing to bury a child," said Temperance Lowe. "The poor man buried two sons. Who can blame him for selling those shares?"

"Tobias wanted to leave you provided for," added the minister. "He knew he couldn't trust Nathaniel Greenwood to do it."

"In his own way he came to care for you, Goody Webb," said Temperance

Lowe, dabbing at her eyes. "Poor Tobias. You gave him something to live for in his last days. He was always grateful for that."

"But the judges said the marriage had been annulled," Concepción said. "So the court had to refer to me as Thankful Seagraves rather than Mistress Tobias Webb."

Jacob Lowe shook his head. "Who knows what that Greenwood may have done?" he said. "Tobias always said he was capable of all manner of deception. The annulment, if there was an annulment, must have happened after Tobias's death, for it could not have taken place without his consent . . ."

". . . unless he were already dead," Goody Lowe finished his statement for him, "in which case the annulment were false."

"Of course, a charitable way of seeing it," added the minister, "would be that the merchant acted thus to prevent the court from confiscating your property, Mistress Webb, and leaving your daughter both motherless and penniless."

"Tobias convinced me that the whole thing was but a gainful ploy for the merchants and the magistrates," said Temperance Lowe. "In all the towns that had witches, people's property was taken willy-nilly, whether you had a farm or a field or nothing but a cow. It all got seized by the court."

"Are you saying, then, that they didn't take away the Old Man's farm because our marriage were annulled?"

"You were his heir," said the minister, "according to the wishes he dictated to Goodwife Lowe here. They would have taken all of it, otherwise."

"You should see how many folks has been left penurious," said Goody Lowe. "All over the colony. The whole thing was a sham, if you ask me. A way to build up the stores for the Governors."

"You mustn't speak such, Goodwife," the minister chided her. "Who are we to second-guess Their Majesties' laws?"

"Their Majesties' laws are only meant to protect those with property, Husband. That's why Governor Phips put a stop to it, because in having his own wife accused, along with the wives of those other worthies, untold amounts of property were at stake."

"Exercise the counsel of your own name, Goodwife." The minister got to his feet. "Temperance above all things. We will take our leave now, Mistress Webb, as Goody Lowe is stepping outside of herself and speaking on subjects that do not concern her."

Temperance Lowe jutted out her chin. "Forgive me, Husband. I have no kindness in my heart for those ungodly proceedings. Look at what they've done." She raised her arms and looked around the empty cottage. "How is a body supposed to live like this, with one old kettle to cook in and a hay bale to sleep on? What charitable Christian would allow it? They would treat an animal better than they are treating you, Goody Webb. Look at those bruises on her wrists, Husband. Those scars on her arms. And what is that, pray tell? Do not tell me they put a brand on you."

Goody Lowe picked up Concepción's right hand and held it up to the light. "Christ's wounds! What inhumanity!"

"It matters not, Goody Lowe; I will be leaving on a ship, soon, and it is just a matter of staying alive until it sails."

The minister put his arm around his wife to comfort her. "Perhaps you could bring Mistress Webb any items that you feel are necessary to help those days pass in better comfort, Goodwife. Now, we really must take our leave."

"Is there anything in particular that you need?" Goody Lowe asked her.

"A ladder," said Concepción.

"A ladder?" they said in unison.

"I need to see if Robin's trunk is up in the garret, and I can't reach it without a ladder. I would like to leave Jerónima—I mean Hanna, my daughter—a final letter to read when I'm gone."

"But you can't eat a ladder, Goody Webb, and besides, Robin's trunk isn't up there. I've got the trunk at home. I shall bring it to you on the morrow, first thing."

"Please, Goody Lowe, if I can borrow your ladder, just the same."

"Tobias always said you were a stubborn one, Goody Webb. Very well, then, I shall bring our ladder tomorrow as well, and some decent food, fresh eggs, a new loaf of bread, a nice ale, some good strong tea. We'll sort you out; you'll see."

Concepción wanted to weep. "You are very kind," was all she managed to say.

"Be sure to look at those documents in the *Almanac*," said Goody Lowe.

When they were gone Concepción allowed the tears she had not shed since her release to flow out of her, a weeping that lasted as long as it took for her to finish embroidering the Hail Mary border in Spanish. She would not let herself rest until the piece was done.

That night she dreamt that she was sitting by the creek with Makwa, both of them soaking their feet in the cold water, and Makwa was making a doll out of cattails that looked like the corn-husk dolls Concepción made for Jerónima. Makwa threw the doll into the river and it floated downstream. Concepción realized in the dream that Makwa was giving her a sign, telling her to leave New England by water rather than go into the woods. In another dream, Tituba was sitting across the board from her in the cottage, both of them patching a sail with fortune-telling cards.

CHAPTER 66

"Weather's turned for the better, Goody Webb," said apple-cheeked Temperance Lowe, riding up in her ox-pulled wagon early the next morning.

Concepción was coming up the stairs from the root cellar with an armful of kindling. She dropped the wood inside the cottage and helped Goody Lowe unload the wagon—a basket of the food she had promised, some candles, two bars of hard soap made with oatmeal, a water pail, and a large wooden tub for bathing. But it was the ladder and the trunk that made Concepción happy.

In the food basket she found a small tin box and a dried piece of sponge. "What's this, Goody Lowe?" Concepción peered into the box and saw that it was filled with what looked like a coarse white meal.

"Ground eggshells. For your teeth. Wet the sponge and dab a bit of the shell powder on it and scrape your teeth. It'll take the black right off; you'll see."

Concepción covered her mouth with her hand, embarrassed at what her teeth must look like. She ran her tongue over them and they felt slimy and sore.

"Your footwear were looking mighty poorly, Goody Webb, so I took the liberty of bringing you a pair of my son's old school shoes," said Temperance Lowe, handing her the scuffed brown shoes. "Hard to tell what size your foot might be, but let's give it a try, shall we?"

Concepción took the shoes from her but did not try them on, uncomfortable now about showing her long, blackened toenails to her neighbor.

"My feet." Concepción shrugged. "They look bad."

"If it's the smell you're worried about, Goody Webb, you got plenty of rosemary growing wild in the garden. Rosemary makes an excellent purifier in the bath," said Goody Lowe on her way out. "You might want to air out your clothes, too. You've got this other nice dress hanging here behind the door that you can wear once you're clean."

But Concepción was not interested in a bath; she wanted only to open the trunk and look for the writing desk. She tried to lift the lid, but the trunk was locked.

"Tobias didn't give me the key, Goody Webb, so I couldn't help you there."

"Up in the garret," she said, "I hid it in the knothole."

"The knothole, is it? Well, no wonder you wanted the ladder, then. Let me help you carry it in."

Together they hefted the wooden tub and rolled it in front of the hearth. They leaned the heavy ladder against the platform of the loft. Although Concepción wanted nothing more than to climb up there to get the key to the writing desk, Goody Lowe was laying out the foodstuffs on one of the hay bales and it looked like she was intending on staying to breakfast with Concepción.

"You go on," said Goody Lowe over her shoulder. "Get you what you need from up there. I'll be needing to take my ladder back when I go. I'll just set these things out for you and get some water started for tea."

Concepción climbed up slowly, enjoying the pull of her limbs up each of the rungs. From this vantage point, she felt like a cat, perched in a tree. Goody Lowe was still chattering away down there, but Concepción had stopped paying attention to her. She closed her eyes and saw her feather bed, piled deep with blankets, Jerónima's dolls lined up against the cushions, the two trunks that served as table and stool. She saw the sampler she had embroidered with Sor Juana's verse tacked to the wall over the bed. This tiny loft above the rafters had been her only sanctuary in the Old Man's house. Now it was just a bare platform of dusty boards. She took three steps to the back wall and found the knothole covered over with a spider's web, a large brown spider guarding her lair. For an instant, Concepción remembered the dream web that Makwa had given her to ward off Jerónima's nightmares. What had happened to it? she wondered. The judges had used it as evidence of her traffic with Indian devils in the woods, and only Jerónima could have told them about it.

"I just want the key," Concepción said to the spider, not wanting to disturb the intricate web but seeing no other way to pull the key from the knothole.

"Are you talking to me?" Temperance Lowe called from below.

"No, Goody Lowe, just to this spider that won't let me get my key."

"Be careful, Goody Webb; some might say talking to spiders be a sign of demonic familiarity, especially for one named Webb."

Concepción laughed at the joke, and Goody Lowe joined her. It had been a long time since she'd heard laughter, her own or anybody else's.

"Poor Elizabeth Proctor over in Salem Village," Goody Lowe was saying as Concepción climbed down the ladder. "To be released from jail with a newborn only to find everything stolen from her farm and no provision for her in her late husband's will. She didn't even get her dowry back. She's penniless, the poor woman. You're fortunate, Goody Webb, that Tobias were the grateful sort and had the foresight to make arrangements."

"Found it," Concepción said, dangling the rusty key in front of Goody Lowe. Concepción smelled her own stench rising from her armpits and knew she needed to give herself another bath, a good, scalding bath this time. Yesterday's dip in the creek had only skimmed off the surface grime that accumulated in prison.

"Tea's almost ready, Goody Webb, and I've taken the liberty of slicing the loaf for you. Brought you a pot of my currant jam and plenty of butter."

"Won't you stay for breakfast, Goody Lowe?"

"Goodness, no. I've already broken my fast. If you can just help me get the ladder back in the cart, I'll be on my way and leave you to your preparations. I'll collect the rest of my things after you've gone. Have you had a chance to look at the documents Tobias left for you, Goody Webb?"

Concepción had forgotten completely about the *Almanac*.

"Your husband were very, very insistent that you see those documents, Goody Webb. Even if you won't be staying on in New England, and won't be needing Jacob and me to stand up for you in court to defend your husband's will, at least you should take your marriage certificate with you, proving your manumission, and those other papers he left for you as well. I'll stop in on you on Lecture Day, and bring you some more provisions. This should last you a couple of days. Jacob and me will be happy to take you into Boston and see you off at the wharf. Just let us know when you sail. Good day, Goody Webb. Enjoy your tea and your bath."

Still dazed by the rich breakfast, Concepción took a long time drawing the pails of water she needed from the well, and it took even longer for the water to boil, but at last she had gotten the tub half-full of steaming water and the rosemary scent was so strong it stung her nostrils. She stripped naked and stepped into the tub. The water felt so hot it sent shivers up her spine. She folded herself down slowly, exhaling with each inch of her body that went into the hot water. With one of Goody Lowe's oatmeal soaps Concepcións scraped nearly a year of filth from her skin and scalp. She examined the dark marks on her wrists and ankles, thick bands of purple and black mottled with yellow. The bruises hurt only if she pressed them, and the pain made her feel, somehow, more alive.

When she stepped out of the tub, a film of scum floated over the water, pocked through with drowned lice. It wouldn't do her any good to wash her shift and petticoats in the same water, and she would have to leave them out for days to air out the stench of the jail from the thick wool and cotton. Because of Makwa's sign in the dream, the cattail doll floating down the creek, Concepción knew her destiny lay across the water. She wouldn't wear the blue and yellow dress until the day she sailed. Her only hope of fresh clothing until then was in Robin's trunk. Taking the soiled garments she'd been wearing since her trial, she started tearing them to shreds, throwing the shreds into the fire one by one to keep from smothering the flames. The stink and smoke of the burning clothes nearly choked her. Using the pail, she scooped the dirty water out of the tub and splashed it over the doorstone, making a little mud pit on either side of the door. Tomorrow she would wash out the tub and give herself another bath, this time in water boiled with garlic to kill the vermin on her body. But for now she needed to get dressed. Sensations were coming back to her body and she was starting to feel a chill.

Naked, she unlocked Robin's trunk. Inside she found Robin's books and clothes. Three of Jerónima's dolls, the two she had rejected as a little girl and the special *china poblana* doll Concepción had made for Jerónima's eighth birthday . . . a sob bubbled up from Concepción's belly and she pressed her face into the three dolls for a moment, then continued. She sorted out all of the different pieces she had embroidered for herself and her daughter: neck cloths and aprons and coifs. She closed her eyes and willed herself not to linger on the memory of her daughter. And, underneath it all, the writing desk.

She shivered and realized her naked body was completely cold, her skin like chicken flesh. She unfurled the articles of Robin's clothing, picking off the moth eggs that had formed on the cloth, and shook them out, piece by piece. The wide-sleeved brown Holland shirt, the dark green camlet breeches with wooden buttons, the leather doublet lined in a mustard-yellow frieze, and the red stockings with black garters. An olive serge jacket with brocaded cuffs and lapels, three cotton handkerchiefs edged in lace, a black woolen cap with a leather brim, two blue drawers, another pair of stockings, three woolen gloves (two rights and a left), and a blue woolen cloak, lined in black silk, with a deep hood, embroidered to the right of the clasp with the letters *RW* in gold silk thread.

She remembered the day she came down from the loft wearing Robin's clothes and the anger and indignity it produced in the Old Man. These were the first clothes she had worn in this country; now they would be her last. She took the scissors from her sewing basket, cut her brittle toenails as short as possible, then slipped her feet into the thickest pair of stockings, the ragged skin of her calluses catching on the wool. Even with the padding of the stockings, the shoes that Goody Lowe brought her were too loose, but if she pulled the buckles tight, her feet would not slip out of them, though the high backs started to chafe against the bones of her ankles. She paid no mind to the pain. She was enjoying the warmth of the clothes, the scent of the soap on her skin. Without reflecting on it, she took the scissors in hand again and cut her hair off at the ears. She felt as though years and years of weight had been lifted from her shoulders. Even her neck felt longer.

"Now, Concepción," she said out loud, "it's time for the letter."

Inside the writing desk she found a dried-out cake of ink, her inkpot and sand caster, the goose quill with a brittle, crusty point. She would never have left it in that condition and suspected it was the Old Man or Temperance Lowe who had used the quill last and neglected to clean it. Concepción found the old letters she had written front and back when Jerónima was but a hope growing inside her and later a babe learning to walk on her crooked foot. Concepción felt her chin trembling but willed herself not to cry. She found the water-damaged page from the pirate's book where she had scribbled the name *Jerónima* over and over, on both sides. But no blank paper. How was she going to write her letter to Jerónima without paper?

You will just have to go to the Widow Cole's shop and trade one of these embroidered aprons or neck cloths for some sheets of paper, she told herself. Better still, you can trade them all for a blank book, and then you can take the book with you and have something to write in during your journey. Jerónima's garments were as good as new, for the girl never wore anything Concepción embroidered for her. She was certain the Widow Cole would take all the pieces in exchange for a blank book.

But Nathaniel had warned her to stay away from Boston if she didn't want to be dragged back to jail. He had threatened to have her pilloried if she was ever seen anywhere near his property, and the Widow Cole's shop was in Dock Square, but two blocks away from Merchants Row where Greenwood had his warehouse. She couldn't risk it. There was no certainty that the girl would even read the letter or that Rebecca would keep her side of the agreement and tell Jerónima the truth. Better stay put, she thought. Although the witches had been reprieved and no more trials or executions were being held, the English still hated Indians and Catholics. She had more enemies than Nathaniel Greenwood. And one of them was her own daughter.

Her throat ached from stifling the memory of her daughter and all the other memories it brought in its wake. Worse than childbirth, this torture, this pain of a vital organ being removed, of her heart being pulled out by the roots.

"She will grow to be an Englishwoman," she heard Tituba telling her. "She has no need of you. . . . Let her go. And let yourself be free of the loss of her. That has been your true bondage, Concepción. You can be free of it now." But nothing could erase the memory of the child's birth from her body. "That doesn't matter anymore," Tituba would say. "She doesn't want you. Let her go."

The letter. She had to get that letter written. Only the letter would release the sharp pain in her throat. She spotted the Old Man's *Almanac* on the mantel. Maybe she could use the backs of the documents that the Old Man left her, which she had no interest in looking at, no matter what Goody Lowe had said. She ate the last of the bread and butter that Goody Lowe had brought and kept the rest of the food in the basket for the next day. Fortified, she took the Old Man's *Almanac* to the doorstone and pulled everything out of it.

The marriage certificate. Her bill of sale with its spidery manumission. The Old Man's last testament, sealed with his initials in red wax, making Thankful Seagraves Webb his sole heir. A document reassigning ownership of the cottage to Thankful Seagraves Webb and her heirs. And a packet of something wrapped in a familiar remnant of threadbare cloth, a piece of the embroidered *huipil* she had been wearing when she arrived on the pirate's ship.

She unfurled the packet and dropped the contents on the doorstone, covering her mouth at what she saw. Ten bills of paper money, each indented for five pounds and dated January 6 1691/1692.

For her sturdy health and her knowledge of letters, her price is 50 sterling pounds,

the bill of sale read, and here the Old Man had given her the price of her freedom. There was no note. She glanced up at the road, afraid that Goody Thorn would be lurking about the well somewhere, watching what she was doing. She picked up the bills and counted them again. Fifty pounds. Was this a final act of kindness or just a credit against her indenture to the Old Man? It didn't matter. All she knew was that the money was hers.

She took the *Almanac* inside and bolted the door, feeling thirsty and light-headed. She would laugh if she weren't so stunned. She drank the pint of Goody Lowe's ale, swigging it hard from the jug, and a good, strong ale it was, which made her immediately giddy and brave and reckless. What if, she asked herself, she were to wear Robin's cloak over these clothes of his, and throw the hood over her head to hide her face and her two-colored eyes, and go to the Widow Cole's shop dressed as a man? She had no need to take anything to trade. She could take one of these notes and *buy* the blank book. Would she be recognized in Robin's clothing? Or would she be taken to be a man in a cloak and hood and square-toed shoes?

You'll never know if you don't go, she goaded herself.

CHAPTER 67

She watched her hand folding the wad of five-pound notes into the inside pocket of her doublet. Now she was wriggling her fingers into the gloves and pulling the woolen cap over her hair, donning the cloak with a flourish. She watched her breech-clad legs walking out of the yard at a fast clip, heading toward the Neck. She smelled the sea air and the cold earth. The road was hung with a fine mist. Many of the trees along the Neck had bloomed overnight as though it were a second spring, and there was a riot of pink and yellow on either side of her, green river to the left, slate-gray sea to the right. She clenched the hood tight against her chin to keep the breeze from blowing it back. Over and over she told herself she wasn't Thankful Seagraves anymore. Concepción had drowned when she jumped into the sea, and Thankful Seagraves had died in the prison with her death sentence. She was a man, now, with short white hair and a good cloak, whose initials were *R.W.* She didn't worry about the thinness of her body or the timbre of her voice. She knew they would see only what she wanted them to see: a man of breeding with a five-pound note in his hand. She had to remember to keep her right glove on at all times, or else the scar of the cross on her hand would announce her true identity.

It amazed her how quickly she covered the three miles into Boston without a heavy chicken cart to push through the mud. There were few people in the streets, and the smell of boiled food and baked pies emanating out of the houses and taverns she passed told her it was dinnertime. Bold as she felt, she dared not walk near Greenwood's shop, so she avoided Merchants Row and Shrimpton's Lane and Pierce's Alley, where all the warehouses stood, and instead entered Dock Square from the other end, the side of Brattle Square rather than the Town House. Goody Cole's shop was on the corner of Devonshire Street, two blocks away from Merchants Row. Concepción drew a deep breath, pushed the door open, and walked inside. By then, the brave effects of Goody Lowe's ale had worn off.

Nothing had changed inside the shop. Still the same goods arranged in the same fashion on the same tables and shelves, the same Widow Cole in her perpetual black lace neck cloth hovering politely next to her customers. The ladies in the shop turned to look at Concepción as she walked in. For a moment, even though her face was covered by the hood, she lost heart and felt utterly exposed and in peril, but then the Widow Cole greeted her with a "Good day, Sir," and the ladies went back to gossiping and trying on hats.

"Named after his grandfather, too," one of the ladies was saying.

"What I heard was that the child were born with no bowels," said the other. "It weren't passing any waste, the poor soul."

"It must have suffered so. Poor Abigail."

"Poor Cotton. His first son."

"The baby were bewitched, I hear. Cotton's father received a note from one of the reprieved witches, something about the sins of the father. Baby took sick right after."

"How have you come by this information, Deliverance?"

"Increase Mather's kitchen maid is the mother of my washerwoman, that's how."

"No wonder Cotton's sermons have been so unbearably sad lately."

"Ladies, please. There are others present in the shop who may not be interested in hearing about our domestic troubles."

Concepción knew exactly where the Widow Cole kept the blank books and the writing instruments, but she had to pretend not to know the shop and wandered around looking aimless. A blue-gray wolf skin on the table of furs caught her attention. Perfectly tanned and supple, it reminded her of the wolf in her garden that used to trample the strawberry beds and terrorize the chickens.

"May I help you find something, Sir?" The widow's voice startled her.

"A blank book," said Concepción, making her voice gruff. If there was one thing she had learned about gentlemen of breeding it was that unless they were with their own kind, nobody expected them to have much conversation.

Goody Cole led her to the side of the shop where she stocked the writing materials.

"Will you be needing an account book, Sir, or just a plain blank book?"

"Blank," said Concepción. She selected a thick one with deckle-edged pages and a red leather cover.

"Excellent taste, Sir. Those are our finest ones."

"How much?"

"They come all the way from Italy by way of London, you see."

"How much?"

"A pound, sixpence, Sir."

Concepción nodded. She spotted a writing set, with a new quill, a horn inkpot, a brown ink cake, a stick of sealing wax, and a small pouch filled with sand, all of which could be rolled and tied into a leather sleeve.

"That would be ten shillings for the writing set, Sir."

"That, too," Concepción said.

"Very good, Sir."

Concepción removed her left glove and tucked it into a pocket. She noticed her calloused, nail-bitten fingers, decided they worked well with her disguise, and took the wad of notes from inside her doublet. She handed one of them to the Widow Cole.

"Oh my." The woman blinked. "Five pounds. And it's dated last year."

Concepción swallowed hard but didn't say anything.

"Of course, that's not the problem. We're taking any notes in the Bay Colony these days. But I'm afraid I don't have that much change in coin, Sir. Perhaps the gentleman would like to take something else that would make his bill closer to the amount on the note."

Concepción spotted some swords on a shelf. "That sword," she said, pointing to a short one with an ivory handle. "How much?"

"The cutlass goes for a guinea, Sir, and for six shillings more you can get a good leather scabbard for it with its own belt. Tooled right here by our very own tanner."

"Yes, fine," said Concepción.

"Would you like to try it on, Sir?"

"No. Thank you."

The Widow Cole set the cutlass and scabbard next to the blank book and the writing set. "If you don't mind my asking, Sir. Where might you be from? Your clothes is English, but your speech is not."

For a second, Concepción panicked. She forced herself to remember what Nathaniel had said about the *Conception*. "Canada," she mumbled.

"Of course. You must have arrived on Captain Quelch's ship. Repairs are going slowly, I hear, after the battering she received from the French."

Concepción grunted in assent.

"Will you be staying on in New England, Sir, or sailing on to the Indies?"

Concepción didn't know what to say. Her pulse was growing loud inside her skull. "The Indies, yes. Leaving soon."

"I see. What about provisions for the journey, then, Sir? I'm sure you're well aware that rations aren't too generous on board, and often not even palatable. The latest thing in travel stores is this amazing dried venison that the savages make, called pemmican. They pound the meat with dried fruit, and it's quite tasty. We'll put in a month's worth of pemmican, a tin of dry biscuits, a pot of the best mustard you can imagine, Sir, to clear your nasal passages when the smell gets overbearing, and a nice conserve of wormwood for the seasickness. I assume you have your own tableware, Sir, your own fork and spoon and mug and such? Your own blankets? Yes, I thought so. That would bring up your bill to almost exactly five pounds."

"Fine. Good," said Concepción, starting to feel queasy about remaining in the shop too long. She could tell from the bustle outside that the dinner hour was over.

The Widow Cole tallied her bill, placed all but the cutlass and scabbard inside a burlap sack, and gave her five shillings for change. Concepción knew she was owed at least a piece of eight more, but maybe the woman was testing her. She didn't want to incur suspicion by being too clued-up about the bill.

"For those five shillings there, Sir, I can let you have a noggin of my own cherry cordial. A swallow or two and you'll sleep like a babe in a rocking cradle."

She nodded and the woman took a small wooden flask out of a drawer in the chest behind her and slipped it into the bag. Concepción handed her back the five coins.

"I hope you have fine winds on your journey, Mr. R.W. . . . ." The Widow Cole batted her eyelashes at Concepción, fishing for the "gentleman's" name.

Concepción's eyes were glued to the wolf's hide on the table. Makwa, she remembered, had worn a wolf pelt, and her mother's father had been a *lobo,* and it was a she-wolf suckling the Old Man's dead sons. "Wolf," said Concepción. "Mr. Wolf."

The Widow Cole chuckled. "Ah, of course. It would make a nice bed rug on the journey. Five pounds even."

"This is all. Many thanks." She turned to leave, but the woman called her back.

"Surely you didn't mean to leave your sword, Mr. Wolf."

Concepción stopped in her tracks, wincing under the hood. She turned around, standing with her feet wide apart as she buckled on the scabbard and jammed the cutlass into it. On a whim, Concepción took the woman's hand, kissed her knuckles, and bid her farewell. When Concepción looked back, the Widow Cole was fanning herself quickly and the other ladies in the shop were clucking at her and shaking their heads.

Concepción's heart was pummeling her ears as she left the shop lugging the heavy sack over her shoulder.

She cut behind the Market Place to reach the Town Dock and asked a young man lolling on the pier where the *Conception* was.

"That one there," the boy said, pointing to the first big ship in the harbor. "Fourteen guns. Sailing off to the Spanish Main."

"Are you on her crew?"

"I wish. My older brother be over at the Blue Cat, trying to sign on. They say Cap'n Quelch runs a tight ship. Tight, but fair."

Rebecca had told her not to fear, that the ship was a reputable merchant-man this time, not a slaver, not the vessel of a privateer, that she would be unharmed, a lady passenger rather than a prisoner, that she would arrive safely back in New Spain. But she had already decided that she would not be a lady passenger at all. Haggard as she'd gotten in prison, there was nothing to reveal her true sex. Even the monthly rule of her bleeding had stopped completely.

She walked to the end of the Long Wharf, trying to decide if that visit to the Widow Cole's had been a foolish thing or a wise thing, but at least now there was no doubt that she could pass for a man, one with the clothes and the manners and the money of a gentleman named Wolf.

She wound her way over to the sign of the Blue Cat, tempted to stop in and get herself a pie and a pint of ale, in honor of Tituba. Maybe she could overhear some conversation about when the *Conception* would be ready to sail. But the paper money would draw attention to her in the tavern, and no doubt Mary Black was at her usual table, keeping watch on everyone who stepped inside. She knew she could not fool Mary Black. Besides, they would expect her to talk in a tavern, and she was tired of talking.

The dinner hour had passed and people were roaming the streets again. It was a good time to disappear into the crowd. She headed toward the Neck carrying her bag full of supplies, checking behind her once in a while to make sure she was not being followed. She shifted the sack to her other arm, though her shoulders ached from dragging the weight of it on her back, and kept her free hand on the handle of her cutlass, just in case anyone recognized her and she had to make good on her escape. She walked with her eyes down, not wanting to recognize any of the goodwives she used to do business with in town or risk any of them noticing her eyes and crying out to her.

It's the Romish one! It's Thankful Seagraves dressed as a man! She could almost hear it. If they discovered her disguise she would be pilloried for sure and certainly thrown back into the dungeon for fraud. She knew there was much danger in what she was doing, but it was also the first time in ten years that she had felt anything akin to exhilaration.

CHAPTER 68

She was drowning. The sea was cold and black and she was sinking quickly to the bottom, heavy as a stone. Something white slithered past her face. She saw fangs and white gaping eyes. It was the corpse of Pecas, the cat, floating toward her. She kicked at it and its bones scattered around her like a web.

Startled, she sat up in the dark, her body surrounded by draft and the sound of dripping water. She got up to fan the embers in the hearth until the flames blazed, then added hay and another log. A hard rain had been falling for three days, and the air was a halo of misty gray. Her breath frosted over her face inside the cottage.

How long ago was it that Greenwood had sent Sara Moor's brother to tell her the *Conception* would set sail at the end of the week? "Master says be at Long Wharf at high noon this Friday. Today's Tuesday," the boy reported. "Bring your bedroll." She checked the Old Man's *Almanac* to make sure she hadn't missed the day. The boy had come on Tuesday, May 23, and the ship would sail on Friday and today was—she saw that both Tuesday and Wednesday on the *Almanac* were crossed out—Thursday, the twenty-fifth. She would be sailing tomorrow, and she still hadn't finished that final letter to Jerónima or packed her clothes and her bedding. *What have I been doing for two days?*

She remembered going into the woods again, taking Goody Lowe's basket with her to collect hemlock needles and pinecones. They would keep moths from nesting in the trunk and ruining the embroidered pieces she would be leaving for her daughter. She gathered cattails, too, for another doll, Jerónima's ninth birthday poppet, made with cattails, like the one that Makwa had been making in Concepción's dream. So much simpler than a corn-husk doll. She tore another piece of the canvas lining of her sewing basket to make an apron for the doll, made her braids using her own shorn hair, and embroidered a *9* on the doll's apron. This time, instead of stitching the name *Jerónima* on the apron, she stitched a family tree, with three names: her mother's in green, her own in black, and the girl's in blue. When it was done, she placed the nine-year-old doll next to the number-two and number-three dolls, on top of the aprons and the neck cloths inside the trunk. The *china poblana* poppet Concepción would take with her, the single vestige of her daughter.

"Keep these things safe, Madre," she said to the embroidery of the Virgin—more beautiful now that she had added the English words *blessed art thou among women, and blessed is the sacred fruit of thy womb* in a decorative script under the crescent moon. She laid the Virgin's image over the dolls, like a blanket.

Next to the dolls, she was going to leave the writing desk, its small compartment already holding the Old Man's *Almanac* with its papers—the Old Man's will, their marriage certificate, her bill of sale and manumission, the deed to the cottage, even the pages she had written aboard the *Neptune,* everything pertaining to "Thankful Seagraves"—and all of Concepción's old letters. She had one last letter to finish. What was she waiting for?

Here was the blank book on the writing desk, the fine goose quill that came in the writing set she had bought at the Widow Cole's resting beside it, inkpot full of ink. The first few pages were inscribed front and back in a simple cursive with no flourishes, but she didn't remember having written those words. Unlike the other letters, this one was not written in Concepción's native tongue. Its audience would not be the girl she had brought up in two languages but a young Englishwoman who had probably forgotten her real mother.

Roxbury, 21 May 1693 (Sunday)
My dearest daughter, heart of my life,
If you remember me at all, you will remember me as Thankful Seagraves, the half-breed mother of yours that you were taught to fear and reject. I don't blame you for being confused, for in your child's eye, in that madness of the witch trials and the persecutions of stubborn men, it must have seemed as if I, in all my difference, were hurting you, though perhaps now you see that your own fear was worse than any bewitchment. What I am guilty of, and I will confess it to you, now, is that when I was first brought to

these shores and sold at a fixed price by the pirate, I wanted to die. I wanted to drown myself in the sea. I was so alone. So terrified that I was being sold into slavery, that I had become chattel to be traded between men.

Even now, after ten years, I can see myself jumping off the ship.

The rebozo slides off my shoulders. I hear gunshots and shouting behind me. Feel the hard thump of my knees hitting the side of the ship. My hands grip the rigging. The muscles wrench in my shoulders and my body swings out past the rail, suspended for an instant, and then I'm sinking, sinking fast and heavy to join Aléndula at the bottom of the sea. You'll be free in the water, I hear Aléndula telling me. There's always an escape for a cimarrona. . . .

She read the rest of her attempted escape through a blur of tears. No wonder she had stopped writing. The words had plunged her back into that dark water of despair, and it was as if she had stabbed the quill into her heart and used her own blood for ink.

But my body refused to drown, and I failed to escape the destiny of Thankful Seagraves. Later I understood that it was you, who were already growing inside me, who forced me to live, though apparently even this was used as evidence of my covenant with the Devil, how I did not sink but rather floated to the surface like a witch, how I was carried, the magistrate said, on the breath of Satan. What foolishness. It was the pirate that pulled me out of the water.

In prison I had so much time to think about you, Jerónima, and I realized that, different as we perceived each other to be, you and I had something very significant in common. For different reasons, we were both removed from our mothers.

Odd, how the history of the blood repeats itself. I was three years older than you are now when my mother insisted to the man who was my sire (another commonality, this absence of fathers) that I be indentured to a convent to protect me from the bestias humanas, human beasts, as she called them, that patronized the tavern she kept for him.

My father was an hidalgo, of the same quality as Nathaniel Greenwood, to give you a better idea of his standing, and his mother was the prioress of one of the convents in the city. I don't think my mother understood what she was asking him to do, what it meant for me to be indentured. Neither of us did. All we heard was that it was possible for me to live in the safety of a convent, and so my father indentured me to the house of San Jerónimo for the minimum period of fifteen years. It was only after I arrived that we found out I would not be able to leave the convent until the term of my contract had been completed. Seven years later, my mother left Mexico with Don Federico. She never warned me that she was leaving, and she never said goodbye, just left a letter with my mistress explaining her sudden departure. I couldn't believe that she had left me, but when I got to the vivienda where we used to live above the tavern, it was as if the whole place had been pillaged. Everything was gone, including the furniture. The only thing of my mother's that remained was her memory, and that I could carry with me no matter where I went or what I did. This was the reasoning that allowed me to be convinced by Aléndula's insistence that we escape from the convent. If I had not escaped, if I had not pretended to be a cimarrona, I would have stayed *in the convent, in my own country, and you would never have been born, my darling daughter of a mestiza and a pirate. No matter how much I've suffered in this country, I would do it all again to bring you into the world, hija mía.*

She heard a scratching sound on the door the way that Pecas used to scratch when she was hungry or wanted to be let in. Looking up at the window, Concepción thought she saw someone standing outside in the morning twilight. Odey, she heard, come with us, Odey. She hurried to open the door, praying it wasn't Goody Thorn or Temperance Lowe but Makwa coming to offer her another alternative. There was no one outside, nothing but a wild turkey scurrying across the mud of the barnyard. Disappointed, she felt her eyes turn moist. Why was she thinking about Makwa? She was alone. She and the rain and the howling wolves in the distance. Once the howling had disturbed her, for it meant the wolf would be terrorizing the chickens and trampling her vegetable beds. Now she welcomed the sound. Any sound that broke the heavy silence was a blessing. She stroked the embossed image of the she-wolf on the red ribbon, a keepsake of the Old Man who had released her from servitude and misery, and imagined that it was the howl of her own Wolf heart that she heard, the howl of a mother separated from her young.

It was time to finish the letter. She had no choice than to finish it now.

She sat down on one of the hay bales closest to the fireplace. With the writing desk balanced on her legs, she stirred the shiny ink in the inkpot with her sharp quill and continued the letter, allowing the wounds of memory to bleed through the brown calligraphy of her words.

Ten years ago I was sold as a slave aboard a pirate's ship. How was I to know that I would live a lifetime in ten years, or that I would give birth to a beautiful daughter, who I would have to entrust to another's care? . . .

CHAPTER 69

When she finished, it was twilight. The whole day had passed. She rolled up and sealed the letter and slipped it into the writing desk. "Good-bye," she said to the desk. "You served me well." The last thing she folded into the trunk was her wedding dress. She would have no need of a dress on the journey, but the blue velvet waistcoat would be useful for the cold; she could wear it underneath Robin's doublet for added girth. She covered the dress with pine needles and closed the lid of the trunk.

The rain had stopped, but water still dripped from the eaves. She opened the door of the cottage. The yard was soaked, and a chilly wind was blowing in from the sea, and she stood there, letting the wind buffet her face. She knew it would not bode well to be sick on that long journey, but for now she needed to feel the bite of the cold air on her skin. From the doorstone she looked out at the garden, noticing the clumps of bergamot growing near the cottage door, the asparagus plants and sweet peas that had suddenly sprouted in the crooked vegetable boxes she had made so long ago, once the fever had lifted and she had found Jerónima like a thin, blue-white fish wriggling in her arms.

The moon looked the size of a schooner rising out of a turbulent sky, clouds moving over its gibbous face like dark sails. To the west lay the dark mouth of the forest where the wolves and the Indians lived, where Makwa once called her Odey and invited her to join them. To the east waited the ocean and the ship that would carry her away from New England, at last, a free person, the *Conception*.

It was then that she realized the true meaning of her name. An idea. A beginning.

At first light the next morning, Concepción set out for Boston in her male disguise, hood covering her face, cutlass strapped low across her hips. She carried everything she was taking with her inside her bedroll, The *china poblana* doll, the blank book and supplies she had bought at the Widow Cole's, her favorite of the Old Man's books—Mary Rowlandson's *Captivity Narrative* and Anne Bradstreet's *The Tenth Muse*—and all of Robin's clothing. The *Conception* would sail at high noon, but there was one last thing she needed to do before she left New England. She had to see her daughter one last time, no matter what the risk.

"I moved her to a new school," Rebecca had said, "Mrs. Cook's, right around the corner from the Latin School so that Caleb can walk her to and fro."

Her plan was simple. Across the street from the Latin School was the King's Chapel cemetery, and she intended to walk among the graves, looking at headstones until the girl arrived for school. She had not reckoned that her gait would be slowed by the weight of the bedroll. By the time Concepción crossed the Neck, passed Orange Street and Marlborough Street and Newbury Street, and finally reached School Street, half a block past South Church, the school bells were ringing. Please, Virgencita, Concepción prayed, don't let me be late. A momentary panic seized her when she realized she had no idea where the girl's school was located. She noticed an alley called Cook's Court half a block from the Latin School. Mrs. Cook's school had to be on that street. Let her be there. Let her not be absent. Let me not have missed her. She saw a group of children lining up in front of a red brick house, but her daughter was not among them.

Concepción crossed School Street to the King's Chapel burying ground, still praying. Please, Madre, let me see her one last time. That's all I will ever ask of you. The heavy bedroll was wrenching at her back and she set it down next to a tombstone, her eyes scanning for her daughter in every direction. Concepción felt her heart leap inside her rib cage. Was that her coming down Beacon Street next to that young man? Yes, that was her! Gracias, Madre! The girl was wearing a damask dress covered by a plain pink smock, her golden hair loose under a pink bonnet. Jerónima, she wanted to cry out. Concepción swallowed back her sobs. The girl was walking hand in hand with Caleb, each one carrying a book satchel, looking very much like duplicates of Rebecca and Nathaniel. Just across the street from King's Chapel, the girl paused, turned in the direction of the graveyard where Concepción stood like a hooded statue, and stared as though sensing her mother's presence.

Soy yo, tu madre, she said to the girl in silence.

The girl continued to stare. Concepción held her breath. Every limb and finger had turned to wood. The only things moving were the tears pooling in her eyes, spilling down her face and neck. Jerónima tilted her little head slightly, shrugged her shoulders, and turned to say something to Caleb as they walked the rest of the way to Mrs. Cook's schoolhouse. It took every ounce of Concepción's willpower not to follow them and pull the girl to her bosom.

"Adiós, hija de mi vida. No me olvides," she whispered. Don't forget me.

Concepción walked away from the churchyard with a throat full of needles. Her heart was a pincushion riddled with holes. She wept under the hood all the way to the wharf. For a long time she stared at the sea, the bustle of boats in the harbor, the frantic loading of cargo on the *Conception*. She was thinking about the journey, five or six weeks just to get to the island of Cuba, maybe longer if the ship made deliveries at different ports. She would have to find a way of getting herself to Vera Cruz. What would she do, then? She couldn't fathom staying in the hot jungle of Vera Cruz, but returning to the convent in Mexico meant making the long trip from the coast across the mountains. On foot or by mule, it would take longer than the voyage. Would Sor Juana even remember her or still want her as an amanuensis? Did she want to be an amanuensis and live locked up in the cloister with her mistress for the rest of her life? Would the nuns make her pay off the last eight years of her indenture? So many questions and unknowns. What she did know was that she never wanted to be a slave again. Or a prisoner. Or a mother.

For as homesick as she had been all these years, she realized that Mexico did not call to her anymore. Her life in Mexico was as distant as her own daughter. She had shed the skin of Concepción Benavídez, Thankful Seagraves, Mistress Tobias Webb, and now she was a Riddle in Wolf's clothing, free to choose whatever destiny she wanted. She had a past in Mexico, a child in Boston, and an imminent horizon on the Atlantic Ocean. Perhaps that was her true destiny. Not a convent, not any enclosure, but the open sea, where she could live in between New Spain and New England. She could see herself approaching Captain Quelch, offering her services as a cook or a bookkeeper, a scribe, or a translator—she had many skills. "What lucky winds be blowing in my direction today," the Captain would say. "Welcome aboard, Mr. Wolf." Yes that would be her new destination: the in-between, with no anchor but her own heart, no home but the one she carried in her memory.

The Pyre

Hanna Jeremiah

(ROXBURY, 1704)

Grandpa Tobias's cottage has stood empty for eleven years. Bindweed vines enshroud the stone walls; ivy covers the thatch and the chimney. Even the window is hidden under the weight of all those vines. An arched lintel of purple ivy shadows the door, and the hasp is so rusty, I have no need of the key, as the padlock comes apart in my hand. From the doorstone all I smell is damp earth and old chicken droppings. Although it is a clear October morning with the witch hazel in bloom by the old well and sunshine glinting off the snow that still clings to the perimeter of the house, the light filtering through the window is a violet blue. It takes a few moments for my eyes to adjust to the blue penumbra.

The walls look strange, alive somehow, as though there were live things moving up and down the stones. The room is freezing cold, and a draft that comes not from the chimney assails my face. I turn to the window and see what it is. Someone has removed the casement, and behind the decayed timber of the shutters hangs a curtain of icicles clinging to the bindweed vines. It is bindweed, I realize, that is growing on the walls. Everything is covered with blooming bindweed, a carpet of trumpet-shaped blue flowers hanging off every wall save the hearth wall, giving the room that eerie blue glow. It's been a warm autumn, with Indian summer coming late into October, but the bindweed should be dead by now, especially after the first snowfall.

A shuddering overtakes me. Very distinctly I remember my dream of a hooded figure standing in a graveyard, staring at me, and I feel the specter of Thankful Seagraves walking over my tomb. Oh, Mama Becca, why have you made me do this? I run outside, tempted to climb into my rig and run the horse at a gallop the three miles back to Boston, back to the sunny hearth of my own brick home, where I am safe from the memory of Thankful Seagraves. Such histrionics, Hanna, I can almost hear Mama Becca talking to me. Be sensible. Go back in there and get it over with.

The sky is a cerulean color; the witch hazel flowers spurt yolk-yellow light from their tangle of gray branches, and the air is sharp with the smell of wood smoke. That's what I need, a fire. Perhaps a fire will help to dispel the trembling, though I doubt it will have any effect on the quivery feeling in my throat. Behind the barn, the little plot that Thankful Seagraves used to plant with corn and beans and pumpkins has become a hay field. I find no woodpile back there, but the barn itself, with its collapsed roof and fallen timbers, provides plenty of wood.

Back inside the cottage, I avoid looking at the flowers. The room is bare except for some bales of hay sitting about like furniture, an old hand broom propped against the mantelpiece covered with cobwebs, a bucket filled with pinecones, and a dense bed of ashes in the hearth. Gone is the long oak board where on Thursdays we would gather round for family supper with Grandpa Tobias at the head, Mama Becca on the settle, and Caleb and me squeezed together on the bench while Thankful Seagraves served our food. Gone is the four-poster bed where Grandpa Tobias used to while away his days when he wasn't reading in his armchair by the fire. The blue lacquer cabinet filled with linens, the sideboard stacked with dishes and cooking utensils, even the ladder that led up to the loft where Thankful Seagraves used to sleep—all of it gone. Just this shell of stone walls, dirt floor, and a filthy hearth.

I take the hand broom and sweep the ashes from the grate, finding two rusty andirons underneath and a hook to open the flue. The flue refuses to budge, at first, and I push and pull with all my strength, wrenching a shoulder in the process, until at last it creaks open and something falls through the chimney in a shaft of light. A handful of icicles break over the ashy stones of the hearth pit. I bring in a load of lumber from the barn, picking up each piece carefully, for it is splintered and ridden with rot, and drop the wood on the irons, raising a cloud of ash. Thankful Seagraves used to keep the tinderbox in the oven, and I fumble around in the sooty alcove until I find it. There's naught in it but a key, a piece of flint, and a striking stone. The key doesn't belong there so I know Thankful Seagraves left it there for a reason. I strike the flint and the spark is good and strong over the handfuls of hay I have laid down for tinder. The smoke from the burning hay makes me cough. Once the flames take, I add pinecones and more hay to the pile of lumber and then bellow with my own breath until finally the old wood is alight with flames, and the smoke swirls upward through the flue.

When the firelight lifts the darkness out of the corners of the room, I see it. Under a stack of hay bales against the wall where Grandpa Tobias's four-poster bed used to be. I pull the bales off, and the copper hinges of the trunk catch in the firelight. Fear starts hammering in my chest, and the memories I have tried to keep at bay all these years pass in front of me like the colored squares of a kaleidoscope. A movement on the walls catches my eye. The flowers have closed. All around the room, the bindweed flowers have puckered into blue flutes that hang languidly from their vines. I feel myself swooning and take a seat on a hay bale, fighting off again the desire to run. But a promise is a promise.

What am I so afraid of, anyway?

I jiggle the key into the corroded latch until the lock clicks. The scent of pine is overpowering. I scoop out handfuls of yellowing pine needles and brittle pinecones and the first thing I see is a blue and yellow dress, the satin still shiny though stained and worm-eaten along the seams. The dress seems familiar, but I can't place it. I know a memory is trying to wedge its way out of the dark nest of remembrances I wanted to bury in oblivion. I remove the dress and place it against me, surprised that it is smaller than I am. Why do I remember Thankful Seagraves as being so large, even larger than Mama Becca? Perhaps it was my dread of her that made her seem so. I fold the dress up to take with me. I can certainly use the fabric for the girls. What I see next stops me cold. Not wanting to believe my eyes, I squeeze them shut, but there it is: an embroidery of that craven image, that cloaked Indian woman standing on a black crescent moon surrounded by flames, made even more sacrilegious by a verse of the papist prayer called the *Ave María* stitched around it in Spanish and English. How dare she? How dare she leave such depravity for me to find? I cast the thing down as though the flames around the image were already burning my fingers, only to find three poppets lying underneath. I place them on top of the dress; I cannot look at the poppets. I have to keep going.

Next, I pull up an embroidered pocket. More memories that make me feel faint. I find aprons, neck cloths, bonnets—all embellished with Thankful Seagraves's expert needlework in patterns of leaves and birds and flowers—in two sizes, for she would want to make us twins and stitch the same things for me as for herself. How I hated to wear what she wore, which is why I left it all here when I finally got to go live with Mama Becca for good. Only now at this distance of years and far from the effect of Thankful Seagraves's presence can I admit how unusual this embroidery is, ornate and meticulous. And yet I will not take it. For it is all worked by the hand of the witch that bore me and I want none of her influence in my life or my children's lives.

Perhaps Mama Becca thought I would want to keep the things in this trunk and that is why she sent me on this wretched errand into the past, but no. These things are the opposite of dear to me, and I would rather burn them than risk bringing Thankful Seagraves back from the dead, for I assume she must be dead after all these years.

At least, she is dead to me.

I roll up the embroidered things and set them on the dirt floor, fighting in myself the impulse to select this pair of aprons for my little girls, one decorated with butterflies, the other with violets. I have almost persuaded myself that it is sinful to waste this good cloth, but then I see it, my papist name—

Jerónima—stitched in black thread along each hemline. I add the aprons to the other things I am going to burn.

What am I to do with these three poppets, pray tell? There used to be eight of them that Thankful Seagraves made me, one for each birthday before she vanished. All made of corn husks stuffed with hay and dressed in outlandish colorful petticoats and crocheted blouses, bright bonnets and beaded necklaces. Each one had a tiny apron embroidered with a motif that corresponded in number to the age I was turning each year and, in the middle, the same doomed name—*Jerónima*—in loopy flourishes. The two-year-old doll's apron has the name in red set between two green hummingbirds. The three-year-old doll's apron has the name in pale blue floating over three fish. I wonder what happened to the other dolls? I know I did not take them with me. Did I throw them into the river as I used to threaten to do? Did Mama Becca hide them or burn them or give them away? It doesn't matter. I hated those poppets for the ugly brand they bore of that papist version of my name, and for the memory they brought back of the old woman who hexed children with poppets. Even now, I shudder at the memory of that trial.

I was still a child, perhaps four or five. It was before I started fostering with Mama Becca, and Thankful Seagraves had taken me to the trial of a woman who was being accused of witchcraft, a papist woman who didn't speak English. Tituba was there, too, and Sara Moor, and the daughter of the woman who was being accused of using poppets to bewitch children. I remember the sudden dread I felt when I realized that a poppet could be evil, and I had so many poppets, all of them worked by the hand of the papist woman with two-colored eyes and a forked tongue who was my mother. It was at that moment that I knew I didn't want to be the daughter of Thankful Seagraves.

I pick up the poppets again, but I can't bring myself to burn them, at least not these two. These two were my dolls and I used to play with them, before Mama Becca made me see how ugly they were. They don't seem ugly anymore, just lonely. I'm sure the twins will enjoy them. They have such few toys as it is. All I have to do is take off those aprons embroidered with those unwanted names and make them fresh little aprons of my own.

The nine-year-old doll scares me. I never saw it until now. Unlike the others, this one is made with cattails instead of corn husks, and all she wears is a piece of canvas for an apron embroidered with the number *9* and a pattern in black that I can't make out. Instead of a bonnet this doll has braids made of real hair and wound with green and red ribbons, but the braids are white and make her look like an old woman. Could this be Thankful Seagraves's hair? Maybe her witch-black hair turned white after all those months in the dungeon. She must have made it before she disappeared, fully expecting me to see it one day, no doubt, so that even from whatever distance of life or death she may occupy all these years later, she continues to haunt my life.

I take the cattail doll outside to see the pattern on the apron more clearly. It's a kind of chart, I think, a little genealogy chart with three names embroidered in tiny stitches. The second name says *Concepción Benavídez* and the third *Juana Jerónima Benavídez,* but it's the first one I can't make out. I turn the doll to and fro, move it around until the sun falls just right on the cloth. I make a tight funnel with my fist and peer at the name through the little hole at the bottom of my fist and I see, finally, what it says: *María Clara Benavídez.*

María Clara Benavídez, mother of Concepción Benavídez, mother of Juana Jerónima Benavídez. It's my own papist genealogy.

Dear God, what have I done? I named my daughter Clara after the mother of Thankful Seagraves. And my other daughter's name, Joanna, it sickens me to realize, is the English version of my own papist first name, Juana. No wonder Mama Becca was so disappointed. "It must be in the blood," Mama Becca had said, and now I know what she meant. The memory that lives in the blood, so that even for all my rebellion against the papist influence of Thankful Seagraves in my life, I have furthered rather than distanced myself from her legacy.

I need air. I need water. I see the well across the road and walk over to it, but all I find inside is a pile of rocks. The well has dried up. Dolls clenched in my fist, I sit out there under the witch hazel until my breathing returns to normal. A part of me is filled with rage, and another wants to weep like an abandoned child. Why are they both doing this to me, first Thankful Seagraves and now Mama Becca? Why are they making me go through this torment? I don't feel the strength to continue, and yet I know I must finish what I started. The sun is starting to tilt toward the river, and I know that in a few hours it will be too dark to remain. Caleb and the girls will start to worry if I don't get back before dark.

I go back inside the cottage and drop the three poppets into the flames, the corn husks and cattails curling quickly into black sheaves, the room stinking of singed hair. The embroidered coifs and aprons and neck cloths come next, the pieces fed one by one so as not to stifle the flames. Even with the door wide open, the smoke in the cottage is so thick I have to step outside to clear my lungs. When the smoke clears, I come back inside and look in the trunk again.

At the bottom, I see a writing desk and I know this is what Mama Becca sent me here to find. Therein lies the so-called truth.

The writing surface of the desk is a rich, smooth teakwood, but the hinges are almost fully rusted and break apart as I lift the lid. I remember how I used to watch Thankful Seagraves hunched over this desk in the dark hours of the morning scratching out her letters to the dead in the heathen tongue that she required me to learn. When I asked her, once, who she was writing to and why she had to burn those letters in the woods, she told me the story of her slave friend who'd been pushed overboard from the pirate's ship. There were more stories after that, about her slave friend and her life in the convent and her mistress who wrote the Devil's verse and her mother who loved her so much she left her in the care of nuns so that she would get a good education. "Why did you leave, then?" I asked, and she started to cry.

I lift the lid slowly, expecting some vile thing to crawl out and sting me, but all I find is her writing instruments—two old crow quills, a glass inkpot, a desiccated chunk of black ink—and a 1692 *Almanac* stuffed with documents and pages of writing. Is this the secret of Thankful Seagraves? This old sheet of parchment torn out of a diary with nothing but the name *Jerónima* on it, line after line, front and back, in my mother's curlicued hand, all but faded now. Or is it this bill of sale dated 21 June 1683, signed by one Laurens-Cornille de Graaf. Could that have been the pirate, my father?

> . . . captured in war on the coast of New Spain and subject to servitude. Her name is ~~Jerónima~~ Thankful Seagraves. . . . For her sturdy health and her knowledge of letters, her price is 50 sterling pounds.

I used to think it was *my* name she was calling in her sleep. But if my mother was Jerónima and it was *her* name that was changed to Thankful Seagraves, who was Concepción Benavídez? Tituba, I remember, used to call her Concepción. Was she both Concepción and Jerónima? Even now, this quandary of names continues. Across the top of the bill of sale, in fresher ink and spidery handwriting, it says:

> Manumitted this 30th day of January 1691/92, by Tobias Webb, her husband, of Roxbury, Massachusetts.

That's it. The memory of that blue and yellow dress, Thankful Seagraves's wedding dress when she married Grandpa Tobias. This is something else I had put out of my mind, that ungodly wedding that shamed Mama Becca so much she refused to attend the meetinghouse for a month. But now I remember being present at the ceremony, and what a scandal it all seemed to Mama Becca, who was very disgusted with her own father for marrying a foreigner and a slave. I think she expected him to be excommunicated. Papa would not attend the ceremony, certain as he was that the Romish woman, as he sometimes called Thankful Seagraves, had bewitched the old man.

Under these two pages, I find five letters addressed to me; four are in Spanish, the last one in English. The first one is undated and addressed to *you, the creature growing inside me.* The second one is addressed to *Little Heart,* also undated. The third one is addressed to *Little chick*, dated the sixth of January, and the fourth one is addressed to *Mi niña,* one of the epithets she used to call me, dated 24 March 1684, a month and two days after I were born. Only the fifth letter is sealed, and addressed, in English, to *My dearest daughter, heart of my life.* I will not break the seal on it, nor will I read the other four, for I have no wish to poison my soul with the lies of that papist witch. Still, what good does it do to Mama Becca's soul if I refuse to read the truth that Thankful Seagraves has left for me in these letters? What is truth, anyway, but one person's version of the story? This is my truth:

I was eight the last time I saw Thankful Seagraves, the age of an innocent child, except there were no innocent children in 1692. In 1692 the children were in charge and the grown-ups listened to what we said. If Abigail Addams in Salem Village said Tituba had made her sign the Devil's book, Tituba stood accused of witchcraft. If Constance Bower said Mary Black had pricked her with thorns in her dreams, Mary Black was paraded down King Street in a witch's cart. If I said Thankful Seagraves was bewitching me, forcing me to speak the Devil's tongue and pray to an Indian woman standing on a black moon, Thankful Seagraves joined Tituba and Mary Black in the dungeon. Her own daughter got her convicted to the scaffold. What kind of innocence is that?

It was not until all the bedlam started in Salem Village that I began to worry that Thankful Seagraves was a witch, and not until I went with her to the jail one day and saw five-year-old Dorcas Good with my own eyes did I realize a witch's daughter could be a witch, too, or at least she could be condemned as such and sentenced to hang from a rope beside her mother. That's when I knew I had to make Thankful Seagraves go away.

Some say Thankful Seagraves dangled from the giant oak tree in the Common when they hung the last batch of witches that September in 1692, but I know that isn't true. She was pardoned eight months later, like her friend Tituba and so many others, and walked out of the jailhouse a free woman. Not even a slave anymore, for she had been manumitted by marriage. Papa says he bought her a passage on a merchantman that was sailing back to the West Indies. No one knows why on the day the ship set sail Thankful Seagraves was not on board. Her name was the only one on the manifest not checked off. I wonder if they thought to look for her other name, the Spanish one that she preferred. I was afraid she would come looking for me, wanting to take me back with her, but I guess all those months of prison made her forget she had a daughter. Good thing, too, for I would not have gone. I was already home.

Papa says the last time he laid eyes on Thankful Seagraves she was dragging her raggedy bones onto Grandpa Tobias's farm and did not even bother to turn around and thank him for getting her out of that cold and filthy dungeon where she'd been imprisoned for almost a year, first condemned as a witch, then pardoned and waiting for her jail fees to be paid. Nobody saw her after that. Not even nosy Goodwife Thorn who was her nearest neighbor. There was a freak flooding in Roxbury that spring, followed by a blizzard, and the weight of the snow rended what was left of the roof of the barn. Mama Becca believed Thankful Seagraves had probably gotten trapped underneath and then was picked over by wolves. No sign of blood, though. No stink of death anywhere in the cottage or the barn. Fact is, other than this letter she left for me, dated 21 May 1693, and this chest of mementos, there is no evidence that she lived here at all. I think she went into the woods and disappeared. Probably went off to burn one of those ungodly letters she would write to her papist ghosts and never came back. Probably scalped by savages.

But sometimes, I still hear her calling me in my dreams. Hija, she cries in that hellish tongue of hers, hija, ¿que te han hecho? Eres mía; eres mi sangre. What have they done to you, my daughter, my own flesh and blood? The words are branded in my memory as clearly as the papist cross Mama Becca says they burned into the back of Thankful Seagraves's right hand, to mark her forever as a heathen, a foreigner, and an enemy of the Visible Saints.

Mama Becca wanted me to present a petition to the Great and General Court, like the kin of so many of the accused have been doing, requesting that Thankful Seagraves's name be cleared of the crime of witchcraft. For my sake, Mama Becca said, so that I would not carry the taint of witchcraft the rest of my life, but I will do no such thing. The taint is not on me. There are few that remember Thankful Seagraves was my mother.

It gets late. I hear owls hooting outside. I forgot how early dusk comes to Roxbury, even more so now that the farm's all grown over with vines and nearly swallowed up by the bindweed. In the smoky gloom of the cottage, the living walls seem to tremble.

What do I do with these letters? All but one are written in the Romish tongue, which I have, thankfully, forgotten. Only this one, sealed with wax and written in a plain hand, is in English. Will it be enough if I read just this one, Mama Becca? Will the truth you want me to find be in this one? Or would it be best to cast all of these letters into the pyre and make my peace with the only truth that concerns me and my children: that I am a Greenwood and have no other mother than Rebecca.

You shall have your truth or my soul will not rest for all the wrongs I committed against your mother, I hear Mama Becca's last words.

There is naught else I can do but read the letter. I take it outside and sit by the well again, catching the last light of the sunset under the witch hazel tree.

" 'My dearest daughter, heart of my life,' " I read the greeting aloud, feeling a funny catch in my throat as my fingers underscore the words. " 'If you remember me at all, you will remember me as Thankful Seagraves, the half-breed mother of yours that you were taught to fear and reject.' "

"Even a cat is a better mother than yours," I remember Mama Becca telling me. "She should not be teaching you papist things. She should protect you. She will be the death of you one day. Thankful Seagraves doesn't deserve you, Hanna."

I take a deep breath and carry on with my reading, surprised that I am engrossed by Thankful Seagraves's story. The attempted drowning when she realized she was to be sold into slavery. The story of her mother and father—María Clara and Federico—and how her mother had abandoned her to her indenture in the convent without so much as a farewell. If she hadn't escaped with her friend Aléndula, she tells me, I might never have been born.

" '. . . No matter how much I've suffered in this country, I would do it all again to bring you into the world, hija mía.' "

She would do it all again, the slavery, all the losses she incurred, the witch-craft, and the banishment, just for my sake. Was that love or folly?

" 'Ten years ago I was being sold as a slave aboard a pirate's ship. How was I to know that I would live a lifetime in ten years, or that I would give birth to a beautiful daughter, who I would have to entrust to another's care? Today it is the eve of my departure from New England, and I sit here in the Old Man's little stone cottage preparing myself to leave you, to climb aboard another ship and return to New Spain without my reason for living.

" 'If you have read the earlier letters that Rebecca promised to give you, you will know how much I love you and how much I always wanted to be with you. I did not abandon you; I left to protect you from your own fear. When Rebecca and Nathaniel paid my jail fees and removed me from the prison after the Governor's reprieve, they said that you feared me and had renounced me as your mother and that I would only hurt you if I insisted on seeing you. They threatened to have me whipped in public if I so much as came near their house, the very same house where I suckled you the first month of your life. I don't know if it's true that the court has given them the right to raise you as their child because I were condemned to hang as a witch and one so condemned is as good as dead in the eyes of the law. But I do know that you always preferred Rebecca as a mother. This much I learned to accept over the eleven months that I spent in jail.' "

I look up at the coral-colored sky and feel an immense sadness falling over me. "She loved me," I say aloud. "Thankful Seagraves loved me. I didn't want her and yet she loved me."

" 'The most important thing I want to say to you in this letter is that I was no witch. I committed no evil against you or anybody else. I was a woman caught between two worlds, between Mexico and Massachusetts, between Spanish and English, between the Catholics and the Visible Saints. I could not help where I came from any more than I could help the two colors of my eyes or the way that my tongue tripped over this language. All these years in this country, I have lived in between, and this, I think, is my true crime, this life in between everything that New England represents and everything that I learned in New Spain. And because you were born and bred on this soil, because you are not in between anything except perhaps two women, you can only see me the way the Greenwoods and the Mathers and the Thorns and all of my other enemies see me: as a foreigner, as a madwoman who would attempt to do harm to her own child, as one who deserved to dangle from the gallows.

"'They say it was you who damned me with your accusation and the evidence you presented in court of my bewitchment through the so-called "Devil's verse." How can I explain that this poem, which I regarded highly and wanted you to learn by heart, the same way Caleb's teacher wanted him to learn "Day of Doom," had nothing to do with devil worship or witchcraft? It was simply a satire written by a wise woman named Sor Juana Inés de la Cruz, my mistress in Mexico City, about the way in which men incarnate the sins of the world and yet stubbornly blame women for inciting them to sin. I can see how the Puritans would find this idea sacrilegious; indeed, I think even the Catholic Church would be in agreement, for I have learned that in the world of both the papists and the Puritans the closest thing to God is the masculine gender.

" 'I'll tell you something else I've learned. As a mestiza in Mexico I took my freedom for granted. And then I lost my freedom on these English shores and gave birth to a daughter; now, I must lose my daughter to reclaim my freedom. In other words, freedom itself is not free. It has a price. How much is it worth to you? Fifty pounds? The price of one of your own children, for I imagine you will have children one day and will be better able to understand the decision I had to make.' "

I think of the twins and know that I would die if they were taken away from me, or worse, if they rejected me for another. I swallow hard, but the pain rooted in my throat makes it hard for me to breathe.

" 'Aléndula once told me that there are always four choices to every decision: the wise choice, the foolish choice, the safe choice, and the choice that someone else makes for you. Tituba—do you remember her?—accepted the cage of her destiny, and so continued to allow others to make her choices for her. Aléndula called on one of her gods to release her from the fate of slavery, and so took the safe way out, through the water. The foolish choice for me would be to remain in New England. The wise choice is to leave on that ship and never look back, but you see, that, too, is someone else's choice. That is what Nathaniel and Rebecca want me to do. The way I will make it my own choice is by losing Thankful Seagraves altogether, as indeed I have already done. I have burned her clothes. I have shorn her hair. I have given away her daughter. When I walk onto the ship tomorrow, I will not be Thankful Seagraves anymore. Indeed, I will not be a woman at all. I will be a Riddle *dressed in Wolf's clothing, able to purchase my own transport to the West Indies with the same money that cost me my old life.'"*

"A Riddle dressed in Wolf's clothing?" "Not a woman at all." What does that mean? That she boarded the ship in disguise? That she didn't die? And if she didn't die, that she's still out there in the West Indies, and perhaps one day she'll come back?

" 'Just remember that, no matter who I become on the voyage, today and always, for all of the years of your life, I am the woman who carried you, who bore and fed you from her body, and who now leaves you to your chosen fate among the English.

" 'I wish you a long and happy life, bebita, daughter of my soul, light of my heart, niña de mis ojos. I forgive you for having revealed the secrets that we shared. Forgive me for the pain and the confusion and the sadness that being of my flesh caused you. I offer you two last gifts: this embroidery of the Virgen de Guadalupe, the Mother of God, whose miraculous apparition in Mexico I told you about many times, and your ninth-year poppet, for the birthday I had to miss while I was in prison. Know that every year on your birthday I will light a candle to the Virgin and ask her to bless and protect my Juana Jerónima.

She loved me. And she was not a witch. Her only crime was being of Spanish and Indian blood. That is the truth she wanted me to find. "The commandments, Hanna," I hear Mama Becca's frantic plea. "I am taking two broken commandments to my grave. Please don't let me die a liar as well." I refused to believe her, but I know now what she meant. Thou shalt not bear false witness against thy neighbor. Thou shalt not covet thy neighbor's possessions. I, too, must live with my own broken commandment: Thou shalt honor thy mother and thy father. Thankful Seagraves was my mother and I dishonored her.

"'With my heart in my hands, I leave you. Tu madre para siempre, Concepción Benavídez.'"

I remember the genealogy she embroidered on the poppet's apron, and in my mind I add the names of the twins under my own name: *Clara and Joanna Greenwood.* The legacy of Thankful Seagraves continues. By now I am weeping openly, sobbing into my hands as I think about the poppets and the embroideries that are still smoldering in the hearth. They were gifts, just gifts that she worked diligently with her brown hands, with those uncanny skills she had with both needle and quill. Year by year, she made me beautiful things, no matter if I spurned them.

Above me the yellow tendrils of the witch hazel blooms cast spidery shadows on the page. I blink the tears away and remember Jeremiah: woe is me, my mothers, for the two of you have made me a woman filled with strife and dissension.

For a moment I see their eyes, the crystal blue of Mama Becca's and those two-colored eyes of Thankful Seagraves. You're mine, says Mama Becca. You're a Greenwood now. Hija, ¿que te han hecho? I hear Thankful Seagraves's voice rising in the smoke coming out of the chimney. Eres mía; eres mi sangre. You're my flesh and blood.

Did I burn everything? Even the embroidery of the Virgin? I don't remember tossing the Virgin into the flames. I run back to the blue dusk of the cottage, and see it on the dirt floor, trampled and dirty but intact, the gold stars on her cloak glinting in the remains of the firelight. I pick it up and shake off the dirt.

"I'm sorry," I whisper to the embroidery, but it is really Thankful Seagraves I am seeing in the Indian face of *la Virgen.* Forgive me, Thankful Seagraves, née Concepción Benavídez. I stare at the image and realize the crescent moon could be a boat, a black canoe, carrying my mother back to Mexico with the rays of the sun at her back, eclipsing New England behind her. This is how I will remember you, *mi madre para siempre.*

I take the embroidery and all of the letters and a cutting of bindweed to plant outside my own kitchen window, and leave the cottage to its demise, feeling the end of my own rebellion against that part of myself that is rooted in a pirate and a papist.

Author's Postscript

The original version of this book was drafted between 1987 and 1989 in Boston and the final draft completed sixteen years later, on March 6, 2005, in San Antonio, with its revised incarnation finished on January 4, 2007, in Los Angeles, a few hours before my thyroid surgery. Between the story's conception and its fruition nearly twenty years later I have traversed not only locations but also lifetimes, careers, and relationships. There are three women, in particular, whom I must thank for their pains and enchantments: Liliana Jurewiez, my partner during the first five years of the novel's development in Boston, with whom I visited the Salem Witch Museum and the Plimouth Plantation Living History Museum, who took many a walk with me from the Back Bay to the Common, from Hay Market to the Longfellow Bridge; Deena González, my partner of eleven years, with whom I finished a dissertation, bought real estate, started a family of animals, wrote the prequel to Concepción's story, and found my vocation as an academic; and Gloria Ramírez, for witnessing my three-year transition into sobriety and offering me a room of my own in her hundred-year-old casita in San Antonio, where every day for the year of my sabbatical I rose in the dark morning hours to watch the South Texas sunrise as I worked to finish the final draft of the book.

There are others whose energy helped me to alchemize the story: Anne Wells, former assistant at Serendipity Literary Agency, for her keen eye for detail and character motivation; Regina Brooks, my agent, for her faith in the story and all those green candles; Diane Reverand, my first editor at St. Martin's Press, for her original enthusiasm for the book, her wild love of everything from calligraphy to witch hazel. And thanks to the Universe, for putting Daniela Rapp in my path, with her background on witchcraft studies, to save the day.

Between 1989 and 2006, several new studies were published on the Essex County witchcraft trials that helped me tremendously. I am especially indebted to the following texts: *The Devil in the Shape of a Woman: Witchcraft in Colonial New England* (1987), by Carol F. Karlsen; *A Delusion of Satan: The Full Story of the Salem Witch Trials* (1995), by Frances Hill; *Tituba, Reluctant Witch of Salem: Devilish Indians and Puritan Fantasies* (1996), by Elaine G. Breslaw; *Papists, Protestants and Puritans: 1559–1714* (1998), by Diana Newton; *In the Devil's Snare: The Salem Witchcraft Crisis* (2002), by Mary Beth Norton; and *The Salem Witch Trials: A Day-by-Day Chronicle of a Community Under Siege* (2002), by Marilynne K. Roach. Two crucial texts for anybody studying the witchcraft trials are *Salem-Village Witchcraft: A Documentary Record of Local Conflict in Colonial New England* (1972, 1993), edited by Paul Boyer and Stephen Nissenbaum, and *Witch-Hunting in Seventeenth-Century New England: A Documentary History, 1638–1692* (1991), by David D. Hall.

Tituba's story, as told by Maryse Condé in the novel, *I, Tituba: Black Witch of Salem* (1986), was particularly constructive for my own revision of the story of the witchcraft madness.

For detailed information on seventeenth-century life, lore, and custom in colonial New England, I drew heavily upon the following: *Boston, 1689–1776* (1970), by G. B. Warden; *Good Wives: Image and Reality in the Lives of Women in Northern New England, 1650–1750* (1980, 1982), by Laurel Thatcher Ulrich; *Divine Rebel: The Life of Anne Marbury Hutchinson* (1981), by Selma R. Williams; *Customs and Fashions in Old New England* (1893) and *Child Life in Colonial Days* (1899, 1993), both by Alice Morse Earle; *Everyday Life in the Massachusetts Bay Colony* (1935, 1988), by George Francis Dow; and *The Writer's Guide to Everyday Life in Colonial America: From 1607–1783* (1997), by Dale Taylor. Also tremendously useful, and with amazing illustrations, were the out-of-print, public domain books, *Boston Illustrated* (1891) and *Rambles Around Old Boston* (1921), both by Edwin M. Bacon, digitized online at the Kellscraft Studios Home Page: http://www.kellscraft.com/textcontentssubjectlist.html#Boston

The transcripts of the witch trial proceedings themselves became digitized as "The Salem Witchcraft Papers" and are now available online at http://etext.virginia.edu/salem/witchcraft/texts). All text quoted verbatim from Cotton Mather's essays "Memorable Providences, Relating to Witchcrafts and Possessions" (1689) and "The Wonders of the Invisible World" (1692) was taken from

"The Writings of Cotton Mather," also available online at the Cotton Mather Home Page, http://www.spurgeon.org/~phil//mather.htm.

The translation provided here of the "Philosophical Satire" by Sor Juana Inés de la Cruz is my own. The original poem and its more familiar translation by Margaret Sayers Peden can be found in *Poems, Protest, and a Dream: Selected Writings,* by Sor Juana Inés de la Cruz (Penguin Classics, 1997).

The names of some of the characters in the story will be familiar to readers who know the history of the Salem witch trials. Although these characters, and in a few cases also their texts, are taken from real life to help anchor the narrative in an infamous episode of American history, their representations are fictional. Furthermore, any omissions or additions to the documented chronology of the trials and of the people involved should be attributed to my own poetic license.

Concepción Benavídez was born in Boston, Massachusetts, in 1989, when I wrote the original draft of this book, but she makes her first published appearance in an earlier novel of mine, *Sor Juana's Second Dream* (University of New Mexico Press, 1999), forthcoming in paperback, where we see her life as amanuensis to Sor Juana Inés de la Cruz in Mexico City.

Finally, I would like to acknowledge the UCLA Committee on Research for partially funding my research on this novel. And a special acknowledgment to my cats, Rubi Tuesday and Luna Azul, for the magic of their presence. And to Pecaninis, whose calico spirit lives on in this book.